The Useful Stranger

A NOVEL

Peter Drejer Sundt

ISBN 979 8 9897223 0 3

This is a work of fiction. Unless otherwise indicated, all names, characters, places, businesses, organizations, events and incident are either the product of the author's imagination or used in a fictitious manner.

PART 1

1

Nairobi, East Africa, July 1992

Max Dubec was in the seventh year of wandering when he came to Africa. His father, Dmitri, called it wanderlust, a process akin to seeds blown on the wind. His mother, Alison, said it was a quest. '*Oh, what did you see, my blue-eyed son?*' So, on this new morning, Earth turned again and the sun found their Max deep in the Angelina Convent's walled gardens. The convent was one of those little discoveries in his notebook of names, addresses, maps and places to stay—at six dollars a night he could stay for months if needed. This morning he took the long path to the dining hall, through the gardens that led to the Madonna tucked among the waxy yellow blossoms and licentious vines. He watched as the bees hovered, and the iridescent bee-eaters hunted around her sublime face. Outside these walls and hedges, through the gates at the end of the drive, he listened to Nairobi going to work with a pulsing, mechanical energy. Every day for the past week he'd joined the rush down into the city.

His first stop was the US embassy, where he'd held his passport over his head, waving it until the guard noticed him at the back of the crowd. But the cool marble and glass interior lacked the connection he'd hoped to find. The Information Officer, Ms. Combs, tapped her long fingernails on each word of his hand printed card. Her nest of long black braids was sewn with shiny black, green and yellow beads and small brass bells swinging from each tip—the sparkle didn't reach her eyes.

"Do you have a CV?" she said.

"I do not."

She slid the card to the side of her desk and handed him a list of aid agencies with proposals for Somali relief. While this list was a good start, it revealed the difficulty of landing a spot without experience or degrees. As he turned to leave, he thought he heard her say, "Good luck."

By contrast the people (mostly women) at the convent were eager to hear about his search—his lack of religious affiliation notwithstanding. He knew the difference between the Sisters of Angelina and the visiting missionaries and aid workers, but to him, they were all the *Sisters of Mercy*. Leonard Cohen's hope for the weary traveler, played in his head a lot lately. Over common meals the sisters suggested mission fields, development projects, hospitals, clinics, schools, and orphanages from Sudan to Mozambique, even trying to recruit him for their projects. But, his plan to work in Somalia frustrated their efforts. They treated his goal as a vow, not questioning its source—this was something they understood and treasured. A Finnish Nurse joined their table this morning. Lilja worked in a clinic on the Tanzanian side of Mt. Kilimanjaro, and had worked in Somalia a decade ago. Her thin white hair framed the pink weathered skin around eyes the color of a gray winter sky. She turned to him and said, "I have a friend in Somalia, Rana. I believe she still works for Global Aid in Kismayo. You could see if they have a position."

Sister Neva, the official Sister of Angelina that sat at the head of their table, recognized the name. "Rana! Oh yes, she stays here when she comes out. I don't think she'll ever go back to Holland." Then she added, "It's part of her now." This comment started a few heads nodding in agreement, showing Rana respect. "Are they on your list?" He'd stopped bringing his notebook to the table a few days earlier. The pace of conversation, and their desire to include everyone, made it seem rude—he remembered Global Aid.

Max called for an appointment from the convent's office. The woman who answered introduced herself as Josie, and invited him to come in before noon. Sister Neva suggested the bus to Yaya Center as she pointed to the address on his city map, assuring him that their office could be seen from the back side of the shopping center. She patted the back of his hand and said, "Good luck." When Sister Neva said it, it was a prayer. Good luck is a lottery that depended on where you were born, the fullness of the breasts that fed you, and which of your ancestor's traits were passed along. Good luck was being two minutes late and avoiding the explosion, or bending down to tie your shoe as a stray bullet hits the wall behind you. The longer his walk-about went on, the more he owed—good luck was a debt, and a fortune to be given away.

He walked down the convent's drive and felt his new short bristles as he put on his blue cap. Living in a convent with his radically shorn hair made his plan indeed *feel* like a vow. The short walk to the bus stop wound through an old neighborhood above Uhuru Park, where large colonial houses and gardens were shaded by giant trees from a mythical forest. The lane passed below the grand Settlers Rest Hotel and ended at a small collection of shops—fishmonger, butcher, and florist, where he waited for his bus. The florist shop spilled its brightness out onto the sidewalk. If he lived here, he'd fill his apartment with these exploding colors, choosing new varieties on every trip to the corner market. Everything looked better framed by such organic beauty. He thought his mother, Alison, would be at home here.

When he stepped off the bus at Yaya he saw several houses across an open field, with one thin path snaking through it. Crossing the field, he walked with women carrying bundles of greens, small children with water jugs, and an old man with a scythe. The schoolchildren wore robin's egg blue uniforms, complete with red bandanas. Everyone had a place to go. In the neighborhood he looked for signs. One house had a Land Cruiser in the drive, and a white mini bus next to that. A gardener was dragging brush to a smoldering burn pile—the same smoke he'd been walking through since Yaya. He raised his eyes when the gardener looked his way and asked, "Global Aid?" The old gardener straightened up and smiled, nodding his head and pointed to the front door. Being that this was a house in design, the front door presented a little pause. The gardener, who had not taken his eyes off of him, motioned him to enter—go ahead, it's okay, go, go. His hand swept him in, brushed him through the entry, and dismissed him all with one smooth motion. The cool interior was like the convent—solid furniture, deep wood tones and steel framed divided windows looking through to the gardens out back. A bit further in he found Josie. She rose up and welcomed him, taking both of his hands in hers. Her eyes were wide open, surrounding him with a comforting acceptance as he stood before her. She breathed in and out, satisfied, it seemed. He saw two children, boy and girl, in the pictures on her desk. She was solid, ordering the world joyfully around her.

"Yes, it is certain, I know Rana." Still holding his hands, she seemed to be picturing Rana in her mind's eye. He could almost see her too, in the image of the Angelina's.

He started to explain, "I'm looking for a position in Somalia. The agencies I contacted from the States didn't have anything—they just wanted a donation. I know money is needed, but I want to be here, doing something useful."

She listened like someone who remembered everything, and who also knew what was coming next. The office was cool and clean. "You know that it is still very unsettled there. Yes?

"I understand, I do."

“And how is your family, Max? It is very difficult to worry about your loved ones in danger, very difficult.”

The question caught him off guard. “My mother died recently, so it’s just my sister and my father now.” He wanted to tell her so much more.

She nodded slowly. After another breath she asked, “How old are you?”

“Twenty-four.”

“So, you are not married? She asked this with a smile, and he saw her children smiling back from their picture windows on her desk.

“Single.”

“Well, that will make Somalia easier. We are grateful that you’ve come. Sit here and I’ll let Mr. French know you’re here.”

“Max? Don French. Come on in.”

They shook hands, and as Don closed the door, he thought he saw Josie wrinkle her nose. Don French had a face that Max couldn’t read. He didn’t have Josie’s welcoming eyes, only looking at him for a moment then turning away. He was middle age, medium height, and in the middle of something other than this meeting. The walls were lined with dark empty bookshelves. The large windows looked out on the coarse Kikuyu grass, red earth, and the haze.

"Good, well..." He swiveled all the way around in his chair, then refocused on Max. "How's Rana?"

“I don’t know her. I’ve never met her. A Finnish nurse named Lilja told me she’d worked with her in Somalia. You see, I’m wondering if you need anyone in Somalia.”

"Oh, I see…well, Rana is in Kismayo, but until I can get our project staffed in Mogadishu…" Don turned in his chair again. "You don't know her?" he asked the field outside.

"Rana? No, but I am looking for a job in Somalia. Do you plan to have anyone go in soon?"

"Josie said you might be who we're looking for. Who did you say you've worked with before?"

Josie walked by outside, standing just out of his sight talking to the gardener. Don was looking through his top drawer.

"I haven't worked in relief before, but I have worked as a merchant seaman…and I would be able to start right away." This was his CV. He'd thought about calling himself a logistician—having seen it on job postings, but Josie inspired truth. Usually, he'd had to fill in the information on the Employment section of an application, *merchant seaman, four years, on and off,* (He didn't list the two years spent working at Daisy's Bar in Venezuela.) The Education section would lack degrees, and the Willingness section was never a part of the process. He believed he'd get hired if he could talk long enough to the right person—Don was not his idea of the right person, but he felt that he might be slipping through.

"Oh, I see…so you have worked overseas before, yes?"

"In Asia and South America."

"We do need to staff our food security program in Mogadishu…an American nurse might be joining you in a few weeks."

Josie closed the door from the patio and walked back inside.

Not wanting to doubt what sounded like a yes, he asked, "When would I start?"

"Josie will arrange all of that. Are you free for dinner?" Without waiting for an answer Don went to the door and told Josie,

"Do the paperwork for Max here. He'll be going to Mogadishu to work with Sharif. You can send Annie's mail with him too."

"Ah that is very good Mr. French."

Don turned back to Max, "I'll pick you up at…where? Where are you staying?"

"I'm at the Angelina Convent on Ngong."

"Good, fine…six, ok?" Don turned away.

Josie motioned for him to take the seat across from her—a little closer, that's right, and she put a smile on him that quieted this spinning sequence. She took this seriously. Her lovely round Kenyan English and her motherly concern came across when she asked him if he was sure about all of this. "These papers must be in our file, but do not worry, of course we'd get you out if you were sick or...well for any reason. I am so pleased that you'll be able to look in on my friends."

She carefully explained the paperwork of his contract, taking extra time to read it for him, underlining the waivers and looking for him to truly understand what he was signing. She gave him the names of his contacts in Mogadishu, and a very quick overview of his job description. His notebook was filling with the outline of his future. He was listening, writing, and signing, but mostly watching her eyes. With each waiver of his health and safety she'd pause, waiting for the meaning to register. By the time he stepped out onto the path to Yaya, it was official—Max Dubec, *Interim* Somalia Program Manager.

2

Ying, Don's wife, thanked him for the flowers as she swiveled around, holding the bouquet at arm's length. "Nalangu, please put these in some water." An even smaller woman appeared, and then disappeared with the flowers. Ying guided him to the terrace where Don handed him a gin and tonic.

Na lan gu, he rolled the sounds of her name around and watched her as she rested her hand on Ying's shoulder several times during the meal. She stood with one bare foot tucked against the top of her calf, a watcher like the carved giraffe in the corner. Masai, he thought. Her thin shoulder straps crossed bone covered with tight, coffee colored skin, oiled and smooth.

Don was going on about their sojourn, as he called it, and Ying was barely keeping up her end— nodding and putting in her adjustments to the record. Don ordered the events in ascending order: Plumbing wholesale executive, his previous occupation; Hosting a local TV telethon in 1979, raising over $150,000 for medical teams in Thailand; His appointment to the board of Global Aid Partners (Ying inserted that Don's brother had gone to school with Global Aid's founder, Bradley Stokes); Then a list of his many trips to Thailand and some of the disaster hot spots. All of this was punctuated with references to God's leading and direction—a self-conscious faith compared to The Sister of Angelina, who seemed at peace with their humble service to this beautiful, suffering, world.

A ceiling of familiar stars was vaulted above the overhanging branches, as a jasmine breeze slipped across the terrace. The Africa of his dreams came out of the giant atlas that held center stage in his grandmother's serious library. He loved the old maps with Thor's cheeks blowing storms across the deep blue oceans, the greens of the interior surrounding Lake Victoria's blue promise and the snow atop Kilimanjaro. When he was ten, he bought his own atlas and outlined the coast of Africa with a red pen. The swoop over the Horn of Africa was where the pen stopped.

After dinner, Don asked him to come to his study. "A little business," he told Ying. The study was lower on the property, against the shadows of a golf course beyond. He handed Max a piece of paper. "I was able to arrange a flight to Kismayo for you. Have a taxi drop you at Jomo Kenyatta, hangar six. I drew a small map there. Usually we fly out of Wilson, but I found a cargo plane going to Kismayo. I think Rana is around there. Don't know with her. Anyway, UNICEF is expecting you. You can hop on a UN or ICRC flight to Mogadishu from there."

"Tomorrow?"

"They leave at seven, tomorrow morning." He brought out a briefcase and clicked it open. He took out an envelope and pinned it to the desk. "Josie put some things in here for you and some mail for Sharif and Annie." Next, he placed stacks hundreds on the desk, "That's forty thousand, you can leave most of it with Sharif, but always stash a few thousand. Best way to get out of difficult situations, you know."

Beams thrice reflected from Ngong Road searched back and forth across the ceiling. Sleep was waiting for him to slow down, waiting for him to slip consciousness. He imagined his ship disappearing over the horizon, without him this time. As his breathing slowed, he found himself thinking about diving into a cold lake. It was somewhere he'd been one summer, but he couldn't remember where. He was on the roof of a boathouse getting ready to jump into the dark water and he froze, paralyzed, unable to commit to the dive, but he had to, he was next.

3

Giant tails were shining in the sun beyond the hangars, like winged insects hungry for warmth. There was only one airplane with anyone around it, so he figured it was his. He walked through an open gate in the chain-link fence, hundreds of yards from the main terminal—no passport control, no ticket, just a nod to the Kikuyu watchman, and another to the pilot who was looking past him, as if waiting for a real passenger to arrive.

"You're in back," he said, as he tipped his head to the mid-sized cargo plane now aflame with sunlight.

Max found sacks of meal covering the floor two feet deep. There were no seats and only one porthole on each side of the plane. Except for the UN on the tail, everything else was written in Cyrillic. He picked the starboard side for the morning light and sat down on the sacks. The labels said, Unimix, *A Gift from the EEC.* The pilot came in, turned to wave off the ground crew and shut the door. He looked at Max. "Kismayo? Yes?"

"Kismayo, da." The pilot looked at him for another second, then started speaking Russian to the co-pilot as he disappeared into the cockpit. When the engines started, he had an urge to capture the moment, but there would be no picture of his departure, no group to remember their early days, and no reunions. Don French plugged him into an opening, the pilot plugged him into the plane, and the guard at the airport gate took no notice at all.

Time is neither fast or slow, it just is. Rolling out to the end of the runway, he watched the present unfold. The twin engines revved and began pushing into the sunrise. At first, the heat at the starboard porthole was too intense, but as they flew higher, banking northeast, he pressed his forehead into the warm glass. Already the deep green of Nairobi's hills was being overtaken by the dry grasslands. Small farms, each with their own textures and shades of green and brown, staked their claims further and further into the savannah. Then for miles and miles there was only the thin ribbons of roads traversing the uninhabited frontier. In the changing colors below he followed valleys, ridges, and dry riverbeds to where they once overflowed. A line of dust moving across one of the ribbons put his mind back on the present. The plane banked a few more degrees north he caught the long coastline, where the equator and the Indian Ocean meet the Horn of Africa. Below, the coastlands were looking up at the one sound that raked across the sky. He saw long reaches of sand, arcing in and out, breaking the edge of the blue waters, undulating white lines against the dun drab dust and scrub of the desert. The Russian aircraft produced a deafening silence from the illegal decibel levels. Watching the silent crashing of elements and the bending lines of white forming noiselessly off the breaking waves was like a snow storm at night, watching it through the light on the barn, silently burying everything. Alison loved to talk about the magic of water steaming off the southern oceans and rising in mist—then crossing the oceans in a timeless harvesting of life's most elemental inhabitant. Snow was water's highest calling, according to her.

The grinding hollow noise changed in pitch, then the plane followed. As they slid inland, he could see what looked like prayer flags spread out below, stripes going one way, stars and dots laid out on the red earth. These patterns increased, funneling into tracks that turned to roads. Looking back, he could see the tracks fanning out into the bush, as if running from pursuit, hiding beneath the tough little trees or in a dry wadi.

Kismayo's airport is on the marshlands that border the ocean. Once the sea disappeared, he braced for landing. As they taxied past the hollow shell of the terminal building, a swarm of vehicles started coming at them like angry wasps. These were the chopped Land Cruisers of Somalia, the "technicals" he'd seen in photographs— battlewagons full of teen warriors (technical assistants) carrying cast-off Soviet and American weapons. Frozen in the glass, he watched as they slowed down and escorted the plane to some place ahead, like tugs bringing his ship to the pier. A collection of vehicles and a knot of people were waiting on the tarmac.

The engines shut down in a final shudder and the pilot opened the cargo bay door. Max edged around him and jumped out. The rush of thick salty air filled his lungs while he circled around, searching for the ocean's horizon. A forklift roared into sight from the other side of the plane, positioning itself in front of the door. Then a group of Somali men and boys came up behind the forklift to start unloading. A small Japanese sedan sped across the tarmac and up to the plane. He saw the round UN logo on the side door and moved toward it. A thin man, maybe in his thirties, got out of the passenger seat, tucking in his shirt and combing back his black hair. He looked at him. "Dubec?"

"Yes, Max Dubec."

"Good, I'm Jean Paul, UNICEF. Moment, please."

The accent went with the name. Jean Paul stepped out toward the group. It looked like they knew each other officially. Three of them separated from the group and walked toward Max. He looked to Jean Paul, wishing he would come to his side. When they reached Max, two of the men held back, flanking the man with the mirrored sunglasses.

"Welcome to Somalia. I am Ali Nur." He turned and gestured one at a time to his escorts, "Omar Mohamed. Abdi Sud."

"Thank you. I'm Max Dubec with Global Aid." He nodded to the lieutenants. He didn't have a clue who they were, except that the central figure was obviously someone important. The loaders stopped their chatter and watched from the plane.

"I know who you are, and I know your agency. We will see you in Mogadishu. Keep to the south, it's the safest place for you." Max nodded, though he didn't understand the reference to the south. "I have a question for the Americans. Are you planning to invade Somalia? Or will you hide behind the blue helmets?" Ali Nur turned to look at Jean Paul. "I will shoot the first one. Tell them that." Ali Nur took off the glasses and stepped closer. His eyes were dark and watery, a feature that didn't fit with his smooth thin face and crisp white shirt. He held Max in his gaze, as if he was trying to recognize something. The moment passed and his face softened. "You will do well, if you are careful, Max Dubec." After a pause he added, "Rana's house will be free today."

The sunglasses went back on and Ali Nur turned, walking past Jean Paul.

4

Jean Paul turned from the front seat to face Max.

"What did he want? Do you know him?"

"I've never heard of him, who is Ali Nur?"

"Ali Nur is The Boqor's nephew, and his army has just retaken Kismayo from Omar Jess. You just met a warlord. So, tell me what he said."

He'd read about The Boqor. "He told me that Rana's house would be free today. I don't know what that means. Is Rana in town?"

Jean Paul turned back around and said, almost to himself, "Shit, she's got juice." Then to Max, "Tonight you can stay at the base. We're empty except for the journalist."

Max nodded and kept his eyes on the scene at the airport, thinking this was not a place he could just book a ticket and take the next plane home. At the top of the rise the road turned to the right and he could see Kismayo a mile ahead. As they got closer, he saw women and children walking toward them on the edge of the road. They slowed to pass around a large orange Mercedes truck that armed men were loading with furniture. Two of the men near the truck turned quickly, then waved them around with the tips of their rifles. The driver was talking non-stop to the skinny teenager seated next to Max, but he was looking at Max through the rear-view mirror. The road was looking more and more like a main street on market day, except the shoppers were armed.

"Spoils of war." Jean Paul was shaking his head slowly, "Soon there will be nothing left to pay the army. For the next few days the soldiers get to pay themselves, and weed out any threats. This is the second time for Kismayo, but I don't think it will be the last."

Just ahead an older Somali man was being dragged out of a shop by two young soldiers. The terror in his eyes made Max's heart pound. Two more gun-waving boys pointed their guns at their car, the driver hit his brakes and everyone ducked. The two in the street were yelling something as they approached the car with a swagger. Their eyes were bloodshot. The driver brought his head up along with his hands and began to talk back to the soldiers who were now only a few feet away. Jean Paul lifted his head and spoke to the driver who relayed something to the soldiers that seemed to confuse them, prompting one of them to start opening the passenger door. The teenager seated next to Max had his weapon pointed at his door, ready to fire through it if the soldier came any closer. Then the driver was holding the soldier's hand and they were laughing. The other soldier joined in the conversation through the window, across Jean Paul. They backed away and waved the car forward, still joking with the driver.

Five minutes later they turned to the right, and after a few more sandy lanes they came to a high-walled compound, brown and crumbling, with an ancient acacia shading a small crowd outside the gate. After the driver honked twice someone in the crowd banged on the sheet metal gates and they opened into a courtyard. The familiar light blue UN flag was on a pole, not quite as tall as the two-story walls of the house. Several trucks and a handful of people were in the courtyard. The driver was hanging out the window in high excitement, talking to them while bringing the car to a halt.

"Welcome" said Jean Paul, "Fort Kismayo." He fanned his arm around the compound.

The gate locked shut with a grinding screech. Jean Paul waved him to the entry, and said he'd be right in. The driver was watching him, so he held out this hand. "I'm Max." He wanted to thank him, or pat him on the back since they shared that one minute of terror.

"I am Abdi. Kismayo is not good today. Every other day is no problem."

Downstairs the rooms were filled with boxes of biscuits and sacks of Unimix. The kitchen had been converted into a makeshift storeroom. The windows were draped and it smelled of kerosene and dust. A wide concrete stairway went up one long flight before reaching a mezzanine flooded with light, a breeze came through open glass-slatted windows. Jean Paul came upstairs, and went down a hallway to the left. Looking in the first room he said, "You can stay in this one. Hungry? I have some bread. We'll have dinner later. Water is in the filter there."

He motioned for Max to follow him as he climbed through the window out onto a fire escape. He then climbed the narrow ladder to the roof and Max followed. Until now he hadn't been aware of the incessant buzzing in the air. He'd grown accustomed to the mopani beetles, or something like them, in Nairobi, but up here in the canopy of the old acacia he felt their urgency. He could feel the ocean nearby as he scanned across this view of Kismayo's rooftops. "Is that the port? A ship?" he asked.

Jean Paul followed his gaze, "Yes. Business continues."

"Are they bringing food?"

"No, they're exporting goats to Saudi Arabia. Sometimes it's charcoal...I don't think they're coming here empty." Jean Paul scraped over two folding chairs and sat with his feet on the parapet. He lit a cigarette and pointed his sharp bristly chin toward the crowd below. "I can't protect anyone here with just a radio. That's up to our new warlord, Mr. Ali Nur. I've got three months left on my contract...I hope there's still some work left in Bosnia." He held out a piece of paper. "The men at the gate, when we came in, handed me a note from Rana. She'll be here in an hour." He turned to Max, "So, what are you doing with Rana? Is she still with Global Aid?"

Before Max could reply, Jean Paul looked sharply to his right. His eyes were wide. They listened to the sound of several vehicles approaching the gates below. He got up and moved to the other edge so he could look down on the scene moving into the courtyard. A white guy came through the gate, accompanied by shouting and shoving, and soon two armed Somalis were let in with him. From the khaki bush shirt with bulging pockets, he assumed that this was the journalist. The noise swelled as Abdi pushed the gate shut, trapping someone's thin arm, still pointing at those now inside. From up here he could see between the canopy's green vibrating leaves. The mopani accelerated. He felt the pitch rising outside the gate. Stones were now being tossed against the side of the house by children in the streets, one of them pointed at him and more stones came over the wall. Jean Paul had gone down the ladder by the time Max pulled back from the edge. He saw him emerge into the courtyard below, and then hold up a hand to stop the journalist from approaching. He turned to Abdi, motioning him around the corner where the car was parked. The journalist stood by his escorts for a few seconds but started to move toward Jean Paul again. The two Somalis were on guard, but no weapons were raised yet. He could hear Jean Paul telling Abdi to start the car. He heard him call the man Frank. The two gunmen got in. The gate screeched open. Abdi backed out through the crowd and deposited the intruders next to their Land Cruisers. He drove back inside. The gate closed and the crowd pushed forward.

By now Jean Paul and Frank were upstairs, and he was still on the roof. He could hear Jean Paul going off on Frank. "Don't you ever bring anyone in here without checking with me. This is the UN, not your fucking hotel! You don't who those guys are, you don't know anything about this place. If you want be a heroic dead journalist that's your problem. Or maybe you'd like to be kidnapped? There's a story for you. I don't want to be part of the story of how your personally stopped the flow of aid. They threw stones today, but they will do much worse...then you'll have your story—or become the story."

5

Rana stood talking with Abdi and a tall Somali woman whose layers of blue and silver shimmered in the still air. Rana wore a blue head scarf like her companion, but she'd slid it down to her square shoulders. She was younger than he expected. Her conversation with Abdi had the cadence of gossip between old friends. She held his arm right above the wrist, her lips pursed out to show concern, fingers playing on his skin, holding hands, connecting. The Sisters were right—Somalia was part of her.

Hearing Max arrive in the courtyard, Abdi stepped aside, and Rana came forward to greet him. "Ahh, so, you are Max. You're going to Mog tomorrow?" Her handshake was Dutch. Strong and quick.

"Yes, I think so. Thanks for meeting with me."

"I missed your landing, but I heard about it. Not many of us here, so you'll be watched a lot. No problem though. We'll go see the team-house in a minute. We'll walk, yes? Not far. I need to see Jean Paul for a sec. You ready?"

"Five minutes."

"Good! Oh...sorry, this is Saudia."

Saudia held out her thin, graceful hand and he held it like it was a small exotic bird. Her dark eyes were alight and a smile approaching laughter flickered across her face.

Upstairs, Jean Paul was getting off the radio when they entered. He gave her a hug and kisses, this side and that, then he brushed some papers off the daybed and flopped down.

Rana said, "No, I can't sit right now. We're going to move back into our house, and maybe a trip to Labadad Island later."

"Quick trip for Max?"

"Yeah, I need to go there anyway."

There was a large map on the wall over the radio. Max didn't find any islands.

When they left the compound, Rana led the way, greeting some in the crowd as they backed out of her path. He followed closely in the safety of her wake—Rana marching, while Saudia seemed to glide at the same pace. The women talked easily—sometimes slipping into English to include him as they surveyed the damage from this last wave of fighting.

Being outside the compound felt like walking on water—unknown depths waiting for the surface tension to let go. This morning's fear began to fade as they moved with purpose and direction. Rana pointed out the clinic where Saudia worked—its doors and windows still boarded. The buildings in this part of town were mostly cement, with decaying lime plaster. Along the main streets the teashops had brightly colored murals that showed smiling faces enjoying their tea and pastries. The primary colors fit the artwork. Murals on a market showed the same smiling faces shopping, arms full of canned food and sacks of rice. The apothecary's mural had a giant syringe going into a child's arm—more wide smiles. Once they crossed the main road they turned to the right, uphill into a neighborhood of houses with high block walls and metal gates. He heard sweeping inside.

Sand overflowed the remaining sections of sidewalk. The streets were a series of alleyways and it was hard to tell if they were behind or in front of the houses they passed. At the top of one of these alleys they broke out onto the top of the rise and Kismayo stretched out before them. Beyond that, a long white haze hung over the thin slice of ocean that appeared. When he turned around, he could identify the antennas of the UN building to the northeast. The map became clearer. She pointed down the street, past several gates, to where three or four people were sitting against a marigold wall.

"Our office." She passed the people against the wall without a word, only Saudia stopped to talk.

A man on the porch quickly stood and greeted Rana. He waved his arm indicating that something or someone had just vanished down the street. As promised, the house was not filled with soldiers but the front room was filled with mattresses and clothes scattered on the floor. Rana rushed through all of this without a word and disappeared into a back room. "Is fine." she yelled. When she came back into the living room, she saw that Saudia was still outside. "The soldiers...they only took our food, some clothes, and the neighbors' bedding. We're okay, no problem." Saudia came in and said something to Rana while pointing to the mattresses. They both laughed.

"Where do you want me to put all of this?" he asked. After all, it was the team house, and he was on the team.

"Put the mattresses on the sidewalk, against the wall...any decent clothes too, Saudia will find the owners." When he'd cleaned out the living room, she told him that Saudia had gone to the market. "Mohamed is bringing a car around this afternoon but I don't know when. You should go back to Jean Paul's after lunch. We'll pick you up on our way to Labadad."

When Saudia returned Rana filled the water filter, adding two chlorine tablets. He chose a warm Coke, to go with the samosas. They sat on the small veranda overlooking the city. Rana ate in silence as Max looked for a way to start a conversation.

"I met a friend of yours, Lilja."

"How do you know her?" She looked at him.

"I stayed at the Angelina Convent in Nairobi while I looked for a job, and she was there. She's working in Arusha now. She remembered you and suggested Global Aid."

"Lilja...we worked together in Geed Weyn, a big camp near Luuq, long time ago. Another refugee crisis…" She cut herself off and looked at him. "I won't do this again. I'm serious. You can go to Mogadishu and do something good with Sharif. It matters to every person you help, but then...don't stay to see it all happen again. Every time this happens, we get better organized. We can feed and shelter more and more refugees. Armies can count on us to pick up the messes. You see the problem?" She squinted out over the city, closing him off from further questions. "You can find your way back? We'll pick you up in an hour or so. Depends on Mohamed finding petrol." She was already moving inside the house.

6

Finding his way, alone, was exactly what he wanted. The landmarks were simple—the city on one side, the ocean somewhere out on the flat horizon, the main highway, and the antennas on the UN roof—no problem. He stepped out of the house, through the gate, and up the hill to the first right turn. The heat and dust produced a soft edge to the sky, now white and airless over an unseen ocean. As he turned his back to Kismayo, he could pick out the bulk of the UN compound beneath the tallest tree.

When he arrived at the compound the people outside the gate stirred and the talking quieted. An older man with curly gray hair around his bald head yelled over the gate. Max caught the word "ferengi." He'd been called this before and, he wondered what it meant here. He was the stranger, the wanderer, the one out of place, the one to be watched, the one to take advantage of, and the one to make your benefactor. Max came up to the gate and pounded with more force than he intended. Abdi looked past him for Rana, or maybe Saudia, and then let him in. All was quiet inside except the mopani.

He told Jean Paul that Rana's House was free of Ali Nur's men, and that Rana might come by for him a little later. Jean Paul took a seat and put his bare feet up on the radio table. "So, did she say she was staying, or going back to Jilib?"

"No, she didn't say much really. Are there any Global Aid projects in the Lower Juba?"

"Rana has three camps near Jilib. All Somali staff, very well protected too. I assume Global Aid is funding her. Besides that, I think she has a bunch of small projects…personal projects, and a few business ventures. She's more Somali than most Somalis."

"What's ferengi mean here? I think that's what they called me out there."

"They did. It's a Hindi term, foreigner. It's sort of a slur around here, just about everywhere really. Not as nasty as nigger, but used the same way. This side of Africa is India's business colony. They've been making money selling into the world's poorest countries for centuries. While you and the Russians toy with Somali politics. India and China keep her alive. You're all about ideas like democracy, free elections and no corruption. India's about food, clothing, business...who wins?"

Not the people, he thought, but he could see Jean Paul's point, though the muscles of his own exceptionalism tensed. He decided to remain silent about France's reputation in Africa. He used to memorize the maps of Africa where the colors of the countries indicated if they were British—usually blue, or French in pink, lots of colors. Even Ethiopia wore the Italian green despite centuries of independence.

Jean Paul looked at Max. "As much of a pain in the ass that journalist is, we need their reporting to put pressure on the donors, to make them pay attention to what's happening outside of Mogadishu. You're on the UN flight at 10 tomorrow. Don't forget about Kismayo."

7

The road out of Kismayo north ran along the ocean until a junction near Jamaame, where it headed inland following the thick line of trees that hid the Juba River. Rana rode in back with the sleeping Saudia. Mohamed's rifle kept sliding over against his leg—he looked for the safety. Mohamed pointed out the white obelisk that marked the equator; a troupe of warthogs crossing the road; and the name of an abandoned tea shop with broken white plastic chairs scattered around—he'd led these tours before. He thought that Mohamed was about his age, maybe a little older, and was more than an educated, articulate, driver.

Rana leaned forward and said, "You're going to hear a lot about clans, but they're nothing more than handful of ruling families that have kept track of all the cousins and uncles, their enemies, their lands, and their businesses for a thousand years. In all that time the truth's been lost and the myths have grown along with all the old grievances. The Boqor's clan have been in control of this part of Somalia since they moved from the north, maybe fifty years ago. Mohamed, that's correct, yes?"

"No, much longer."

She ignored the correction.

"It's just a question of when you want to freeze the map. Fifty years ago they came to the Lower Juba. Seventy-five years ago they wouldn't be south of Somaliland."

Mohamed concentrated on his driving, and said to the mirror, "Longer Rana, much longer."

He kept making adjustments to his map. The clans and warlords were replacing the rivers and mountain ranges. The oceans were still blue, but the land now held colors that crossed natural barriers and changed abruptly, sometimes erasing generations of families. No hills framed this river, which made him feel like he was on the outer edge of the globe. These new features were now more unpredictable than the rains in the Ethiopian highlands that filled the Juba River. There were only sporadic signs of cultivation—abandoned patches of withering maize or millet, their ordered rows fading. Nature reclaiming a lifetime of work in a single season. He'd grown up with people working small ranches or gardens. Their absence felt ominous.

When they pulled off the main road Rana leaned forward to narrate. "Labadad was a leper colony. Now it's a village of its own. It was started by Mennonite missionaries in the late 50s. I've been coming here since '86. They're immune to the fighting because everyone avoids them—which is stupid because they're not that contagious." He assumed she was trying to reassure him. "I have a few donors that send money, and I help them get the things they need. It's not a big thing."

Labadad was on a tight bend of the Juba where the river almost met itself. They crossed a deeply rutted track, using all four wheels to grind out of the mud. They came to a clearing with two long wooden buildings. Chickens scattered into the thick underbrush where vines were swallowing a rusty fence. Rana and Saudia greeted the children who were searching their pockets for candy. Then Rana signaled him to join her as she walked between the buildings. "You have to meet the Mayor, El Bahb. He's been here the longest—I think half of the people here are his children." El Bahb was the color of the old wood stool he was sitting on. Rana put out an arm to have Max stop ten feet away. "If you get closer, he'll warn you away, he's old school...an Old Testament leper. He likes it that way...the way things used to be. Act like a donor, that's what he wants."

Max put his hand to his chest and bowed to the old man who was looking, but maybe not seeing him. Rana spoke to him in Somali, slow and loud. El Bahb was worn down to rounded ends wrapped in cloth. Max put his hands behind his back, hiding his gift of fingers. A younger man appeared from the shadows of the interior and spoke to Rana. He nodded to Max and they started the tour of the workshops. Several children followed them into the leather shop where they were modifying old shoes, then to a small metal shop. In the sewing room two young girls, their fingers intact, stood up to greet him as they were trained.

When they came around to the Land Cruiser, Mohamed was tying a loop of rope around the branch of a mango tree. Rana said, "Malnutrition assessment. They've got fifteen kids here that we're watching. We've been supplying milk powder." Mohamed was lifting the children very gently onto the scale suspended from the branch. She had Max measure the upper arm circumference of the children using a cloth tape, giving the readings to Saudia. When they were finished, Mohamed made a show of being in a hurry as he put the scale back in the Land Cruiser, shutting the back door just as Rana stopped talking to the mothers, promising to return soon.

Mohamed drove faster now that the sun was over the horizon. It was dark when they sounded their horn at the gate.

Jean Paul opened the gate. "It's too late Rana. You can't be on the road now after dark."

"Never mind," she said. "We had Mohamed."

It seemed like an old conversation that outlined Jean Paul's official concern and Rana's special dispensation as one of the Sisters of Mercy.

She handed Max two envelopes, one for Sharif and one for Annie. "Maybe I'll see you in Mogadishu one day, Inshallah."

8

In the morning Abdi drove Jean Paul and Max to the airport. Rana didn't come by, nor did he really expect her to. She'd done her duty to give a small tour to her new colleague, and that was it. A small UN passenger plane was pulling up to the same place he landed yesterday. He spotted the World Food Programme guy holding his bag, looking at him, then Jean Paul. Max stood there like a veteran relief worker. There were two others getting off the plane, standing together without any bags. Max guessed they were going on to Mogadishu with him. Jean Paul was busy gathering his new guest with no word of goodbye, but Abdi touched his hand to his heart and nodded quietly in his direction. The pilot came around from the other side of the plane signaling the all aboard.

There was one more passenger inside. Max sat on her side of the plane, taking her smile for an invitation. She put down her book and shifted, leaving an empty seat between them. As Max refocused his eyes from the glare of the tarmac, he saw that she was probably South Asian, Indian maybe. He said hello with a British accent, and she returned the greeting in a similar accent. Her green eyes shining in her open, inquisitive face.

"Reporter?" she asked.

"No, I'm with Global Aid." This time without the accent.

"Ah, Rana, then you know Rana…is she here in Kismayo still?"

"Yes, I just spent yesterday with her."

"I'm Hani." She held out her hand.

When he touched her slender hand a scene from a nightmare washed over him. Last night he'd discovered that his fingers were shorter, wearing down. He'd fought with decaying bandages, wrapping them endlessly. He was afraid to look at his feet but he could feel them shrinking too. It was a relief that he could feel her fingers with the tips of his. She held tighter the instant the engines started. He hurried his part of the introductions, "I'm Max, nice to meet you, thank you." He didn't know why he included the thank you.

"I'm with UNICEF in South Mogadishu," she said, now louder.

Her eyes acknowledging the growing sound barrier. They sat back as the plane accelerated into the onshore breeze and lifted over the edge of the Indian Ocean. The plane had four seats on each side, facing each other, an arrangement that frustrated his need to look out the window when flying. He always took the window seat. When he pressed his face to the window between them, she shifted one leg onto the seat in the middle and looked out her window too. He never got tired of watching the world unfolding beneath him. The magic of flight was so familiar, a recurring dream or post-dream state where he'd float over a part of Earth, recognizing the valleys and rivers, anticipating the features yet to appear. His breathing eased as the grinding vibrations chanted an aboriginal poem.

The long curves of the desert's coast stopped at the southern edge of Mogadishu. The abandoned international airport tucked under the wings and soon the port came into view. Two coastal freighters were berthed below. A line of trucks flowed out onto the street. Just north of the port he saw a ship hard aground, the waves breaking against her stern. A minute later the plane took a hard turn out to sea and back again, losing altitude quickly. He shifted back around and grabbed for his pack. The plane touched down as small trees, scrub and goats hurled by. When the plane came to rest at the end of the track three people were waiting next to a Toyota van with a UNICEF symbol.

As people stood outside the plane, Hani came up and touched his arm. "They'll take us as far as the UNICEF office in North Mogadishu, and then they'll arrange a convoy across the Green Line. My office at UNICEF and Sharif's compound are pretty close. I'll get the driver to let you out at your office. I know Sharif will be waiting for you."

The driver signaled for everyone to get in while he grabbed his radio off the front seat. Hani sat between a gunman and the passenger with the green headscarf. They drove away as the driver was still working his radio. The outskirts of Mogadishu began to appear, growing into neighborhoods. Makeshift barricades blocked off side streets, leaving only one way to go. A few minutes later they pulled into a sprawling compound, complete with high concrete walls and metal gates. Hani went inside and he followed. She introduced him to Trevor, the UNICEF coordinator for the North, and then asked about the arrangements for crossing to the southern part of the city. The red-haired Brit rolled his eyes with a hint of conspiratorial exaggeration. "It's different every time, isn't it Hani? I'll know in a minute. I think the Lido's still off limits." The radio in his hand went off and he turned away, giving her a wink as he walked out into courtyard.

He sat next to Hani in the van as they waited for the UN technical to fill up with armed teenagers. The technical led the way, keeping a radio channel open as they raced through Mogadishu's streets. Most of the buildings were hollow—just blackened and broken shells that left enough room between them for this rally to the Green Line. She pointed out the stadium when they reached the high point overlooking Mogadishu. As they passed, he saw the playing field that was filled with makeshift tents and round stick huts with blue tarps. Then he looked out over the ancient port city. The bleached coral buildings looked like the waters receded in some earlier epoch, revealing Mogadishu. He could make out the shapes of minarets and the shell of a cathedral near the seawall. The older buildings never rose past the canopy of the remaining trees. The colors and textures of the old city were encircled by the hollow windows of the newer and taller buildings.

The convoy slowed when they reached the heart of the old city, where the buildings were thicker, with giant pock marks. Light poles were pushed into most of the streets as barricades. The underground wires and pipes had been ripped from the streets, leaving long scars filled with plastics and dust. They were now only a few blocks from the sea wall. Where the wall ended, one of Mogadishu's ancient coral buildings jutted out into the ocean like a lighthouse. The technical stopped but the driver's hand continued to punctuate the rhythm of the radio chatter. They were facing an empty square where remnants of a wide promenade and toppled plaster railings were strewn around like giant bones. Across the square, on a road that came from the lighthouse, another technical came into view, then another van. Headlights were flashed and the radios squawked. The van driver opened the slider. Once everyone got out on both sides, the radios squawked again and they walked quickly across the square. There were two narrow paths slicing through the park. Hani said hi to one of the crossers as they met in the middle, but no one stopped. Once they were in the south van their new technical led them back toward the ocean road.

"That was a good one." she said.

They drove south along the ocean, and past the port, past the road to the international airport at the roundabout just before they arrived at the UNICEF compound. Before Hani was rushed into a meeting, she made sure the driver knew where Sharif lived.

The driver drove him back through the roundabout, toward the port. After a long row of low corrugated buildings, they turned to the right, down a dirt lane, then turned right again, past the backside of the same buildings. They stopped at the end of the alley by a green metal gate. A watchman peeked out of the gate and then opened it while pointing Max's attention to a man at the top of the stairs.

Max nodded to the watchman, saying, "Nabat" in his best accent. Then he looked up and said, "Sharif?"

Sharif nodded and waved him up the stairs. He was as tall as Max, but with his head tilted slightly back, so he could look down his long nose, he seemed taller. Max was struck by his handshake—a Navajo handshake, very light, soft and humble. Considering how handshakes had worked out for the Navajo, he thought it might be more wary than humble. Sharif had a rim of tight gray hair around his coffee-colored head, and a short stubble of the same tight gray hair on his chin. With his large full lips, and glasses balanced on the tip of his long straight nose, he resembled the noble camel.

They were standing on a landing that overlooked the triangular compound. He saw two open sheds filled with Unimix, the two-story building he was in, and another building behind this one. The guard at the gate was looking up at him.

Sharif noticed and said, "That is Maliq, a relation. I have many these days."

As they each took a seat in front of Sharif's desk a young woman came up silently behind him with tea and Danish cookies on a brightly painted tray. He watched her pouring the tea, and then at Sharif—the similarities were striking. Before he could look back at her, she was gone. Sharif looked down his rimless glasses as they went through the news—Nairobi, Kismayo, Josie and Rana.

“So, Max, I know that you want to get to work. How do you want to start?”

“I’d like you to show me the work you’re doing already, and then we can plan on expanding it...if you think we should.”

Sharif nodded, still looking down his glasses.

“That’s good, we can go to a camp soon.”

“Will I have a car?”

“Yes, we have arranged a car and driver, with a guard too, but you should not drive. Most roads have trouble, road blocks, shifta. Your driver needs to be very smart.”

They stirred and sipped, until Sharif pushed his glasses up his nose. “You haven’t done this before. You must be aware that you’re a target—all of you are.”

“Everyone watches the ferengi, right?”

“That’s not a good word for you. Most of the agencies have some good people. It’s not correct for us to use that term for the ones that help us. It’s the country people that say things like that. Mogadishu is very familiar with Europeans, and now Americans too. We need this help, and most of the people who live in Mogadishu know this.”

“I understand, I’ll follow your lead. I have some money from Nairobi, $40,000. Where do you keep it? In the office?”

“$25,000 of it should be with me, you keep the rest for now. Your house will be safe enough.” He wrote out a simple receipt and handed it to Max. "Now we will go to Annie’s and meet your landlord.

9

An old Datsun sedan was waiting at the gate when they came down to the courtyard. They drove back through the roundabout and turned right, across the road from the UNICEF compound. After several blocks of walled-off compounds they pulled up to a set of white gates that opened immediately, closing right behind them as they stopped in the courtyard of Annie's house. Workmen were busy breaking a hole in the wall that separated Annie's yard from what was soon to be Max's house.

Annie came out and greeted Sharif in Somali. They held hands and spoke, turning to Max now and then. She broke off with Sharif and offered her hand to Max. Another Angelina, he thought. He could see her at the table with Lilja and the others. She wore a blue and white headscarf, and an apron over her long dress. Annie took his hand, looking up at him with the same warmth and welcome she offered to Sharif.

"So nice to meet you Max, and thank you for the mail, and this." She held up the envelope that Josie had stuffed with dollars. "You'll stay here tonight, or until your house is ready. Your landlord is there now. Go and see her and we'll talk later." With a nod to Sharif, she took Max's pack inside.

He followed Sharif through the opening in the wall and found the landlord smoking by the back door to the kitchen. She held out her hand—painted nails and rings on most of her fingers. Her English was barely accented, and smokey. "I'm Astur. Excuse me, I've just been to the beach." She pulled her wrap a little tighter. "This is my brother's house but he is in Hargeisa today. Come, see if this will be okay for you. We have lots of furniture stored, so what would you like? European or Somali?"

He only took a second to say, "Somali."

"Good, we have some wonderful carpets."

The dining room had a large mahogany table with raptor talons aggressively clutching the floor. He looked out at the courtyard where a dozen people were waiting, looking up at them—at him. Astur indicated the crowd in the courtyard with her chin. "I know most of their families. They will protect my brother's place—and you of course."

They walked down to the courtyard and he was introduced to the head guard, Hassen Tanzania. He held his right hand to his chest and bowed slightly. Max did the same. Sharif talked to Hassen and some of the others for a few minutes as he listened to the rhythm of their speech. It was quiet in this neighborhood, distant traffic and no other voices. There was a generator running somewhere nearby. Max counted eight armed guards, most of them teenagers. There were also three young Somali women dressed in traditional flowing wrapped layers and bright head scarves worn like crowns. They were pointed out to him as cooks and house cleaners.

A Toyota Hilux pickup was in the courtyard, with a 50-caliber gun mounted over the double-cab. Max was introduced to his driver, another Hassen, Mombasa this time, and his cousin Bashir, who would be riding shotgun—or AK-47. Sharif and Astur had arranged all of this and he was grateful. He was realizing that a property like this came with all of these salaries, needed or not. The house was $2,500 US dollars a month. The guards cost one hundred USD a month each. The women made less. They were all somehow related to Astur or her brother's family.

Sharif turned to him, "This is good with you?"

"Is all of this needed?"

"These guards are protection because they are known to be part of a powerful clan in this part of Mogadishu. That truck is under the protection of this clan. To attack them is to attack the whole clan. You will be safe with them."

"It's good then."

Sharif knew what Max should be doing, so all he had to do was follow. Everything was in place and just waiting for his approval. None of these decisions really involved him except to provide the money, write reports, and get more Unimix. He was led respectfully to each conclusion Sharif endorsed. By the time he made his way back over to Annie's house he was hoping to find a quiet place to be alone in the afternoon heat. He found Annie behind the kitchen, on a small patio. She put down her watering can when she saw him in the doorway.

"I'm so glad to see people coming back to Mogadishu. You'll have lots to do. And you'll be working with one of my favorite people, Suleymaan, Sharif's nephew. Of course, you're hungry, yes? Come, I have some fresh tomatoes, bread, no cheese sadly, but I've boiled some eggs."

He followed her back through the kitchen. She told him he should feel free to have whatever he finds in her cupboards. "It's all a gift you know." Then she whisked him into the dining room. He had lots of questions about Mogadishu and Sharif that Annie could answer, but first he wanted to understand their relationship. Josie had made it sound like he was just supposed to be someone, some American or European, to report to Annie's Swedish agency.

He decided to be direct. "Annie, Josie said I was supposed to assist you somehow, if you want that, I mean. What is it that you understand about that?"

"Oh, I appreciate what they are doing, and I must say that it is good to have you next door. But honestly, I don't have any projects for a big agency like yours. No, I have lots of friends and families here that I know and love. I just help where I can, little things. When I need to go somewhere I ask Sharif for a ride, but that's not been very often lately. No, you don't need to worry about me, just have a meal with me once in a while. That would be nice. Let's give thanks." She bowed her head and was silent. He was uncertain whether she'd asked him to actually pray out loud. He bowed his head and tried to have the attitude of thankfulness. He was thankful but he wanted to tell Annie that he wasn't a Christian.

"How long have you known Sharif?" he asked when she opened her eyes.

"I met him in 1985. A few years after I came here to work in the hospital. It's very close to here. Sharif had just started working for your agency. He has a wonderful family you know."

"I think I saw his daughter at the office, she looked like him anyway."

"Yes, that would be Asha. This fighting has halted the schools, but I'm trying to get her a spot in Gothenburg—the university. Sharif has finally agreed for Asha, but Miriam, the younger one, is tied to her mother."

"I can't imagine what it must have been like. What I saw just driving through the city was crazy."

"It is crazy. People live in the middle of it all, there is nowhere else to go except the ocean. And now they leave for Dadaab in Kenya. I think many will be lost to their country. A whole generation interrupted...Sharif knows how to live here. You follow him, Max."

Annie lived alone. Maybe Rana did too, and tomorrow, so would he—with eight armed guards and two housekeepers and a cook. This was an extreme version of what Don and Ying must have thought about living overseas—the servants and the lifestyle they could never have in the US. The charade was better staged in

Nairobi. You felt like you chose the security company like you would a house cleaner or a nanny. The mowed lawns and gardeners gave the impression of a civil society, with your house on a hill in the right neighborhood. In Mogadishu you just became the paymaster of the armed force that was assigned to you. They guarded the landlord's property, the driver guarded his truck, and the cooks and cleaners spent their time flirting with the boy warriors that lounged about the compound with loaded AK-47s.

That first night, under the mosquito net, as he listened to occasional gunshots around the city, he had a sense of well-being, a hope that he'd be able to play his part here. He remembered little details about what he'd seen today, faces and a few names.

10

The next morning, after a cup of strong coffee with Annie, Max moved through the wall and greeted his staff. He'd arranged to see Sharif around mid-morning, so he decided to walk to the UNICEF office and introduce himself to the director. Hassen Tanzania didn't like the idea of him walking, so he called out to the driver, ordering the HiLux for the trip. Max insisted that he would walk, after all, it was only six blocks to the main road and maybe only a few blocks north from there to Hani's office. There was a growing discussion, then on Hassen Tanzania's command it stopped. Four of them headed back to the shade of the wall and the others went to the gate, waiting for Hassen's signal.

Walking through the alleys of high walls and gates he could felt the eyes of his unseen neighbors on him. The guards stayed ahead and behind, making a box for him, the obvious target. This was not the walk he wanted. Children gathered at the street corners, calling others to see the ferengi. He wouldn't do this again, something could go wrong so easily—Hassen Tanzania was right. The air was superheated where the walls prevented the sea breeze from meeting their faces. The tension steaming off the teenage gunmen turned them into ghosts. They held their weapons ready at each corner, gaining another block, then scanning the houses along the corridors, getting narrower as they neared the road. Just before they reached the main road Hassen Tanzania pulled up. He told Max to go ahead, "We stop here. Too many guns for Afgooye Road. We can't cross it."

"I see UNICEF. Take them back to the house—I'll get a ride. You were right about taking the truck."

"Never mind, no problem. We are waiting for you there." He was pointing at an outdoor tea shop with several UN vehicles pulled up on the edge of the road. His small patrol was already walking that way, fully at ease.

He stood in front of the stream of people moving down the edges of the road. A large Fiat truck, loaded with charcoal, pushed aside the crowd with a wave of exhaust. They swarmed back together as the river's current swept toward the sea. On the road before him was the refugee flow into Mogadishu, from their fields, from their herds of camels—from shallow graves along the way. He was above it all— watching, listening to the urging of mothers and the silence of children. A small girl with a baby on her back looked up at him, then ran to catch up with her mother. It was judgment day—some kind of last days, the end of days. It was families and food that drew them in—clans of cousins and uncles. Here they'd find the remnants of their people and search the hospitals for husbands and children. Vines of relations tangled sharp and twisting a shelter over their heads. A wall to stay behind—maybe one salary for thirty souls. He got looks, stares and pointing, but he was not worth stopping for. He was the white, soulless stranger at the entrance to the city. He crossed the river road and drifted in the current to the UNICEF gates.

Once inside the walls the sounds of Afgooye Road flowed by without the faces. A few greetings later he entered Hani's office, cool and white. A few questions passed by before he surfaced back into the room. "...Yes, I've moved into a house next door to Annie's. Is the head of mission in today?"

"No, Mr. Benswala, George, is not in today."

She asked about Sharif and about his plans for feeding centers. These were the jobs they were here to do—naturally this would be the thing to talk about. He decided that this would be a regular stop, not just for the mail, flight schedules, and news, but to see her.

She acted on his thoughts.

"Do you want to have a coffee? It's just across the road. Your driver can wait here."

"I walked. My house is close, just a few blocks."

"Oh, you shouldn't walk, not these days. This isn't Kismayo."

"I know that now."

"Well, I'll escort you across the road, for a coffee."

11

She introduced him to Hersi, the owner of the cafe.

"Pleased to meet you, Max." He lowered his voice and asked, "Are those your guards?"

"Yes, my house is just up the alley, they escorted me. Is there a problem?"

Hersi looked at Hani.

She explained, "Hersi's trying to have less guns here. It's not safe."

Hersi placed a hand on Max's arm, "Maybe they can leave their weapons with the driver. It makes everyone nervous."

She said, "Your coffee makes them nervous. It won't happen again. Max just came from Kismayo. It's different there."

Hani led him to a table under the thatched awning, against the bamboo screen. Before he sat, he went over to Hassen Tanzania. "I'll be a little while. Could you go back to the house and have the driver bring the truck in thirty minutes? I'm sorry I walked; you were right."

Hassen Tanzania stood up. "Okay, the truck is better in Mogadishu. We'll go back." He signaled Hersi for the bill.

Max said, "I've got it."

Hassen Tanzania nodded, and he saw a faint smile on his face.

After their coffee was served, he said, "That was nice of you, with Hersi, you know."

"Hersi's special, like your Sharif, but older. When I need to find out something, or find out about someone, I ask Hersi."

Max pointed to the sign above the kitchen. "*Shabelle.* The Shebelle Cafe?"

"Depends. Most of the UN and NGO people know it as Hersi's. Somalis know it as Shebelle. My driver, Osman Ali, told me that Hersi and his son used to work at the restaurant on the roof of the Shebelle Hotel, pretty close to where we crossed the line yesterday. The hotel was closed when the government fell and Hersi supposedly found the sign. O said that the Shebelle sign would pop up in different spots around old Mogadishu. Someone would spot the new shop and the word spread until some militia or gangs took it over. Then he opened up Shebelle in Bakaara Market. Right before UNICEF moved across the road the Shebelle sign showed up here. Hersi told me that this is a good place for his grandson, Boutros, to meet 'good foreigners'...like you."

"And you."

Their chairs faced out from the back of the cafe when they first sat down, now they were facing each other.

"So Max Dubec, why are you, a good foreigner, in Somalia?"

"Well, I came to Nairobi to get a job, got the job, and now I'm here. Interim Director for Global Aid, Somalia. Pretty simple. How did you know my surname?"

"Ahh, I know all the names of all the foreigners working in relief. It's my job—or one of them anyway. So, you just showed up in Africa looking for a job? Again, why?"

"The simple answer—to be helpful, doing something useful. I didn't expect to become the project manager."

"You've done this before with Global Aid?"

"No relief experience at all. I worked on ships around South America and Asia. I thought that this would be the best way to see Africa, and maybe, like I said, be useful. That's just between us."

"Our secret."

"Is your last name a secret?"

“Chandra, Hani Chandra, nice to meet you, Max Dubec. Can we do this again? Coffee...without weapons.” She couldn’t help saying it. “I set up a mail slot for you in the lobby. I usually get a break around ten.”

“Thanks for being a friend, Ms. Chandra.”

“We need them, right?”

“We do.”

After she crossed over the road, he continued to watch her weave her way through the people in front of the UNICEF building until her black hair disappeared behind the wall.

12

The green gate opened and Maliq greeted him in Somali, *subax wanaagsan*, encouraging Max to try it. He met Sharif at the top of the stairs and wondered if this was his power position. Sharif took his hand and turned him around, back to the courtyard. "You've been invited to Gaulo this morning. You should see before we make a plan."

Gaulo was in the hollow land east of the airport. The former residence of the Bulgarian Ambassador, and several adjacent properties, was now a feeding center for one thousand mothers and children under five, officially. A small crowd of old men slowly parted when the truck went through the gate. He was expected. The camp commander stood in front of the most severely malnourished children and young mothers, lined up for his inspection, and behind them, the low hum of camp. He didn't want to be here at all—he didn't need to put their faces in his memory to haunt him. The photographs of famine and war were burning images already, images that brought him to Somalia. Sharif introduced him to Farrukh Mohammed, who took Max's elbow in a firm grip and led him slowly through the camp. At one point Max held back, freeing his arm from the commander's grip, trying to get his balance. Farrukh waited, looking at Sharif. He was beginning to see their faces, their eyes watching him. These were the people in the photographs and he was the one they were looking at when the shutter closed. The pictures moved, wavering in front of him, coming to life...but not life. He felt like a passing shadow. The children stood by their mothers silently, the ripple of their attention quickly exhausted. A young woman held out her infant. The little girl's skin stretched tight over her large head and with a tiny heroic effort she looked at him. Flies crawled around her eyes and nose. Farrukh put a hand on Max's chest as he spoke softly to the young mother. She withdrew, melting back into a sea of shrouded women. He knew that all of this couldn't be staged, but it was curated just for him. Did they know he couldn't fix this? Did they think he had the power to change things? Whatever he could do would never be enough.

"Come, they are cooking." He led him to each of the four cooking fires. The women stood back, allowing him to perform. "We have three cooks at each station. They work all day. First, they collect water." He pointed to the empty buckets on the ground. "Then they boil it with the food, stirring and stirring." He pantomimed someone laboring over the cooking pot, stirring and wiping their brow. "Very hard work. Hot all day. You understand? Do you want to take pictures?"

"No."

Back at the HiLux, Farrukh bowed slightly and said something formal. He pictured Farrukh as the proud and desperate generalissimo of this desperate tribe of young women and children. "Please, come and see us again, you are always welcome."

Sharif sat in the back of the HiLux with him. Hassen Mombasa sat in the driver's seat with his door open, but neither of the armed escorts got back in yet. Sharif studied his face and said, "We will talk later...you have seen."

In the following weeks he visited Global Aid's five camps in South Mogadishu, going through the same ritual greeting. Sharif was finally trusting him with his nephew, Suleymaan. Hassen Mombasa was a fine driver, and his English was good enough for directions, but he revealed an impatience, even contempt when interpreting the concerns of the women in the camps. Suleymaan, a young husband with a pregnant wife, interpreted one or two sentences at a time, including Max in the conversation, allowing them to finish without interruption. The requests were always a plea for help for those not covered by the UNICEF guidelines. Sharif said there was an off-book system in place for these, but it needed more of everything. His efforts to locate more Unimix and other commodities brought him into contact with some of the NGOs now returning to Mogadishu. When he heard that ten thousand kilos of milk powder were on offer to any agency able to distribute it, and report back to the French Government, he ran the idea past Sharif.

Sharif said, "Yes, it could be used or traded. Do we need to get it out of the port?"

"It's in two containers right now, but the containers can't leave the port."

"When do we need to take it?

"I don't know. I'll find out. Do we want it?

"Take it. We'll find a way to use it. We'll talk tomorrow. I need to work on this."

Meetings with Sharif often ended this way, with a dismissal. He understood on one level that he was being shielded from the how. Sharif would pose ideas to him, but never talked about how he'd do it. His job was to bring money from Nairobi, get more food, and send the reports. Accounting for the money and budgeting for the future project costs was a calming, regulating, experience that he saved for evenings. Writing proposals and daily reports was best at Hersi's in the mornings.

One morning Hani sat down at his table. "You look very busy, do you mind?"

"No, not at all." He closed his notebook.

"I thought I'd find you here. Hersi says this is your table now...it used to be mine."

"Let's call it ours then."

"Yes, let's. Sitting alone gets old." She put her elbows on the table, and cradled her face. "Why don't you come to my house for dinner sometime? Aren't you getting tired of eating alone in your big house on the hill?"

"It's not much of a hill, and I'm not alone. There are at least ten of us most of the time."

"Good conversations? Interesting stories?"

"None actually. I'd love to, when? I need to go to Nairobi later this week, if there's a seat."

"I'll put you on for Thursday and we'll have dinner on Wednesday. Will that work?"

"Perfect."

13

Most of Hani's coworkers were from Mogadishu, so office talk stayed away from conversations that sounded like life was normal. Her anticipation of a small joy, an evening with a colleague, felt disrespectful. At the last minute, when she saw him crossing the road, she grabbed some papers off her desk and disappeared down the hall. Max glanced at her empty desk as he fished a few notices out of the Global Aid box. The USAID Grant Guidelines Manual he'd ordered was there. He scanned the other notices and when he looked up again, he saw her come into the room—a smile, then back to work. He left without the Guidelines.

During the heated Somali afternoons, he tried to read or write in his notebook under the mosquito net. He used his faded red Moleskine journal to record new names, addresses and ideas. Hani often appeared in the pages, and he imagined an erotic thought bubble above every mention of her name—today she wouldn't leave his thoughts. Maybe he'd gotten ahead of himself, thinking that it might be a date—maybe it was just a meal together. He thought about the first time they met on the plane to Mogadishu—her fingers tightening as the engines started...and another touch when they reached Mogadishu, waiting for the transfer to the south. Since then, there had been numerous touches at the Hersi's, her fingers touching his to make a point, or faux formal handshakes when they met at Hersi's. But she seemed to be aware of a limit to public touching for them, so fingers were quickly withdrawn.

From what he'd observed, Somalis touched a lot. Two men would be speaking, one stroking the chin of the other. Two gunmen walking side by side, little fingers interlocked, holding hands. Even the young women that worked for him, cleaning his house or cleaning the office, touched the boys. That was a bit rougher—pushing, pulling, teasing. He began to see some of the guards, housecleaners and cooks as the young people they were, children growing up in a war-zone, like the hard neighborhoods he'd seen all those years around Manila, or along the coast of Venezuela—the seaport bars and motels that catered to the working girls and boys. He saw a Somali porn magazine left open on the back steps one evening and he wondered how Islam handled the erotic realm. Did they force it underground, into the basements of shame beneath the temples and mosques like the Catholics did beneath their cathedrals? The naked Somali women lived in his thoughts now along with the others—there was no erasing nudity, there was nothing left to uncover. Like the tide, like his ship pulling into Bangkok, they'd climb aboard for a few days, then leave.

These images could have stayed in place, except for her skin, her smell…the way she looked at him. The tips of Hani's fingers now touched him deep in his animal core, stirring life itself. It had been weeks of not having sexual thoughts, and when they did come to the surface, he knew they would pass with some help. That worked for the first few weeks of learning his job. The reality of what he needed to do pushed him far away from that part of himself. Hani was his one true pleasure here—and their connection was always sliding that direction. Now, imagining her close to him in the night, in her house, alone…

When he went back to Sharif's around 3:30 he was determined to finish a supply checklist for the nurse that might come someday. By 4:30 he put his notes and lists away and had Hassen Mombasa take him to Hersi's, so he could walk down to the UNICEF office right at five. She was already in the UNICEF courtyard, when he was dropped off at Hersi's.

Osman Ali drove them slowly through the streets behind the UNICEF compound, toward the ocean. Max saw the airport road on his left. The buildings here were spread out, with containers and trucks behind walls and fences. They pulled into a compound that was once staff housing for airport employees. A row of trees lined the airport's curved wall behind the bungalows, and beyond that the ocean's rhythmic breathing swept across the empty tarmac. Her bungalow was at the end, beneath a green water tower.

She didn't have a cook or a house cleaner, and she shared the guards with the rest of the compound. The other bungalows were also occupied by UN staff, with an Irish flag in one window, and a small Union Jack placard next door. She opened the door and asked him to open all the windows. She went to the bedroom end of the living room as he fought with the kitchen window slats, finally opening each one individually, since the lever proved useless. When Hani returned, she was in jeans and a tee shirt, hair down and not looking directly at him. She joined him at the kitchen window with two cold Heinekens, "We can sit out there for dinner once the sun goes down."

The next thing he knew he was watching himself, hearing himself, tell her that he loved her. The scene was unplanned, unstoppable. He heard himself saying, 'I love you, Hani.'

She said, "I made a curry, with shrimp. George brought them from Nairobi today."

She looked at him, and he wanted to touch the warm brown skin of her neck against the thin white tee shirt. The moment was ready to disappear and he thought he should let it. Instead, he said, "Hani? Can we sit for a second? I want to tell you something."

"What is it? You're not allergic to shrimp, are you?"

She sat on the oriental carpet and pulled over two cushions. "What is it Max?" She was turning her hands over and back again.

"I love you."

She put her head down, but reached out and touched his hand. "I feel something too, but you don't know me very well, and…well, it's this place. I've seen it before."

"I've thought that too. At least, I've wondered," He spoke to her hand. "Being alone here..."

"I think it could be more than that, but..."

He wished he could take back his words. He'd planned to be cool and see how things went. He knew he could be way beyond where she was, that he could have missed it all together. Now she was making him explain how he could feel this so quickly, so irresponsibly.

She stood up and said, "Look, I love what you said, and I want to understand what you mean…but you're so quick...and I need to check on the rice."

He was left on the floor. What did he expect? It was out there now in words, not his best words, or even coherent. What did she say? That she feels it too? He was pushing, again. He didn't know how to act, how to be in love. What did people say? Am I supposed to know the right time, the right words? He stood up and she asked him to slice some tomatoes while she sauteed the shrimp over the single burner gas stove. They worked side by side, overwhelmed by the earlier conversation.

She was confused. Something changed, maybe something fragile broke and the pieces didn't add up. She was really enjoying his friendship, but not expecting more, at least not yet, or like this. Maybe she wanted it to be more but it couldn't be, not here. But then, why not? She liked him...he was different.

Today had felt so different, her anticipation made her feel light. It was the feeling he gave her, a feeling she wanted. She invited him to dinner knowing it could be more than that. And it is, more than she was ready for...and here he was, saying he loved her. So, what's wrong with that?

She brought out her mosquito net from over the bed and stood on a chair to fit the loop over a hook on the patio. Her tee shirt pulled up with her arms, allowing him to see her smooth warm skin surrounding her belly button. A small round table, two chairs, and a shrimp curry, all fit under the net. The cooling dust of the city was aloft in the sunset, making it soft and orange behind them, fading indigo over the sea. The curry was full of spices and smelled like the sea. Every so often she'd take his hand, looking like she was going to say something, but didn't. When they moved back inside, she made a pot of sweet tea with smoky milk. They moved into the living room, using one end of her bed to lean the cushions against.

She said, "Let's not talk about Somalia right now. You must have a lot of stories. Let's share—a little from you, then a little from me. If we pace ourselves, we can fill these long nights together."

They sat side by side, candle burning, legs touching, her bare feet tucked under his calf. They forgot to look for the Southern Cross, as the equatorial night closed in around them. They were the only people in the world right now. He wished.

He shifted and broke the spell, "But it's getting late, I don't want to go—but I should. My guards will be waiting."

"I know, you're right…or, I could have O get a message to them. It's up to you. I'll tell you a story if you stay."

"I said some things earlier, things I really meant, but I didn't plan on doing that, you know, saying everything out loud. This isn't about being alone, I'm used to that...I prefer it...or did until I met you."

She turned to him, now on her knees, looking into his eyes. "Do you have doubts, after what you told me?"

"No, no more than before anyway."

She said, "Okay, here's what I can say. I like you very much. I'd say love, like you did, but that is such a big word...or maybe not big enough. We don't really know each other. I don't know your secrets and you don't know mine. I don't want to be hurt. I don't want you to be hurt, okay? Maybe that is love."

He leaned forward and kissed her.

"Come on then," she said as she got up. "Go get the mosquito net from the patio."

He set up the net, and when she came back, she brought in another candle, setting it on the table next to the bed. She pulled off her jeans and slid under the net, Max did the same. Under the sheets, once the net was tucked under the mattress, she turned to him and said, "Is this okay?"

"It's perfect. Now tell me a story."

14

Hani rolled on to her side, facing him, keeping one foot touching his. "I don't remember anything about India, or moving to Kenya. There weren't any photographs from that part of my life, just my imagination. Hani isn't the name my mother gave me—she called me Meena. I changed it a few years ago…that's another story. Tonight, I'll tell you about Meena.

"I was born in India. I don't know if I have brothers or sisters, grandparents...or any family there now. Over time I've tried to imagine it. Maybe it was a very small village, at the end of a narrow, rutted track. The monsoons used to come right on schedule every year, filling the rivers and washing the plains with the water needed to grow families and food. But after I was born, the rains didn't come at all and the rivers were too low to reach the irrigation ditches. The village withered and the young men, including my father, my biological father, started to leave in search of jobs in the cities."

"Do you remember him?"

"No. He left when I was two. At first, he was able to send remittances but eventually he disappeared. My mother left the village with me as she tried to find him and enough food to survive." She took a breath, "I see her everyday Max. I see her in the women walking into Mogadishu, I see me in their arms, taking my first steps around a refugee camp somewhere. I was lucky.

"My mother took a job as a servant for a family in Meerut, halfway to New Delhi. There she earned only enough money to feed us, she worked as a cleaner, not even allowed to touch the food being served to the family. The cholera epidemic of 1966 struck the region when I was three and my mother died quickly.

The family she worked for initially felt secure living in the walled part of the city. But when the cholera reached into their home they decided to move to Kenya and work in a cousin's shirt factory. I was four, and they brought me with them. My new family was just one of the immigrating Indian families, and as was the custom, they were enveloped into a relative's business.

"I grew up knowing I wasn't really a part of this family. I shared a bedroom with two sisters who treated me like the child of the family's servant. I remember being frightened of them...they would glare and hiss every time I called him Baba. He was kind to me, and treated me with affection, which caused more problems with his wife." She rolled over.

"Tell me more." He whispered.

"Well... I loved school. In class I was one of them, part of the community. I had my blue dress and red kerchief, just like the other children. And I was good at school—better than my sisters. I learned English and Swahili easily, much to their dismay. School was a world apart from everything at home. The teachers were from Kenya and India, some of them trained in England. By fourteen, I was helping with the accounts for the shirt factory, and sitting in on the meetings with buyers and agents. It was my English that made me useful for reviewing documents. My Swahili made me useful in managing the workers.

"My adopted father treated me with kindness, more than oversight. I was allowed to walk between the cultures more freely than his children. I was a valuable employee. Soon after his wife died, he confessed to me his shame in how he took advantage of my mother. He swore that he loved her and begged to be forgiven for not telling me anything about her before now. Without a picture of her I just had this, this shame, this confession that I didn't know how to understand. I tried to imagine it being true, that he loved her, that she felt it too. Maybe she had a moment of bliss in the arms of a lover, maybe she knew something besides loss and shame. I imagined she loved me, huddled in some dark back room. She'd hold me and coo in my ear, rubbing her nose on mine, and smiling." After a minute she rolled back to face him.

"I was 18 years old and under no pressure to consider marriage, which was fine. I dreamed of going to school in London, or if not, the University of Nairobi where I could study medicine or art or anything but business. I started university in Nairobi in 1982. The shirt factory had a store one kilometer west of the university, so I worked there and went to school, living in a room above the store for the first year. I was spending less and less time with the family that ran the store. All of my spare time was spent studying, and having new friendships with other students. University was a place where the tribal and racial boundaries faded a little. Gender didn't matter quite as much. We were dreaming, but it was refreshing to have hope.

"I loved being in Nairobi, especially downtown where the city was full of foreigners. I got a job at Kiberu, a coffee shop in the city—two nights a week. There, I had conversations right out of my study of political science, art, and development. I had a whole new circle of friends. It's where I met Mara, my closest friend."

The candle flickered out. "That's where I'll stop, until you catch up. Right now, I want you to stay in my bed."

They listened to the metallic dripping from the water tower—the ripples imagined as they sank beneath their wonder. She hadn't told anyone her story this way before. She'd never wanted to dwell on not belonging, on not having her own family. Those connections seemed to be for others, but now, as she formed her body next to his in the dark, she wanted to stay close, to be connected. Each time he shifted next to her, she wanted...and wanted to not want him to touch her, to hold her.

He held still, feeling her inches from his skin, listening to her breathing. Her salty aroma and smooth smokey skin had him drifting across her Indian Ocean on an old tramp freighter, with immigrants at the rail, smelling the first hints of a new world. He let his feet touch her, sliding down her legs until he found the arch of her feet. She took a deep, satisfied breath.

15

The heat was building when the sun burst in on them. They looked at each other, side by side, in her bed. Their thoughts colliding in a wordless rush. They stayed this way, breathing slowly, until Max broke off. His impulse was to step back from the edge, but not look away. He went looking for coffee.

Hani dressed quickly, feeling exposed. Her heart pounded uncomfortably as she wrapped her arms around herself. They hadn't made love, yet she still felt an afterglow as she watched him in her kitchen. "Breathe." she whispered to herself. The kettle's whistle released them from the unknown.

"You'll need to be at the office by ten this morning. I'll have O take you to your house after he drops me, and would you deliver a package for me when you're in Nairobi? I'll give you Mara's number, and you can also find her at Kiberu, she still has a few shifts each week."

Max looked out the window of the UN van as it was led up to the field de jour outside of the town of Afgooye. He wasn't registering this territory on his internal map, instead he was looking over new ground in another dimension. Just before the airplane's door was shut, a UN pickup raced on to the field. The pilot waited as they helped a young woman into the plane. She looked around and went right to the head at the back of the plane. The door was missing but she didn't seem to care as she pulled her baggy pants down and sat on the toilet. She looked at them all with a resigned shrug before putting her head down for the two-hour flight. It took a second for everyone to turn away.

When they landed at Wilson Field, he took a taxi to the office. Josie was in Don's office with a file box on the desk.

"Oh Max, you're here. How are you?" He was captured in her embrace. "Mr. French is not here. He's gone."

"Gone?"

"Yes, we haven't heard anything from him, and Ying is moving back to America. Come, I'll make tea. I'll tell you all about it."

She took him back through the office to the kitchen where she talked while the water heated. "He hasn't been in for two weeks, and now Mr. Stokes is coming. I'm sure they'll find another director soon."

"Do you have any idea why he's missing? Does Ying know where he is?"

"He has always been a very private man. He didn't want me to schedule his meetings. One of the last people to meet him here wouldn't even come inside, but spoke to him from the back of an embassy Range Rover. I found this card on his desk. I think it's the person from the driveway meeting."

She handed him the card. Mark Walters, OFDA. On the back of the card, in pencil, was 50k. He tilted the card towards Josie.

"50k? Is that dollars, or tons?"

"It doesn't match in either case. I checked. We don't have any deposits or expenses like that and our food programs don't match that number either. But please, let me know how you're doing in Mogadishu. Is it going well?"

"I think it is. I don't know how I would do it without Sharif."

"You're about to get very busy. Mr. Stokes is bringing some people with him and wants to visit you in Mogadishu. I think they have raised a lot of money for Somalia. You won't be alone after that."

Back at Josie's desk, with Don's office door open, they went over his accounting. He requested an additional $30,000 in cash which she agreed to have by the end of Friday. He gave her several reports and asked her if she thought it would be helpful for Mr. Stokes to have them before he left the States. She started to read the first page then looked up. "I'll have these on the desk when he gets here, I'm not sure where he is right now. Mr. Stokes flies all over the world. It's best here, waiting on the desk along with the current project files. I'm setting up the office so that he can use it when he's here."

"Can I take a look at the Somalia files?"

"Of course, you can use the office while you're here."

He opened the Somalia file and thumbed through it, looking for any WFP information. He saw the name Geed Weyn Farm on a manila envelope and opened it. There were project proposals, budgets and a dozen photographs of Global Aid's refugee camp at Geed Weyn. Some pictures showed the camp in 1982, with 80,000 refugees. An aerial photograph showed the round bush huts covering the area inside a wide bend in the Juba—like a pox on Earth's skin. There was a photograph marked *Staff 1982.* He searched the faces looking for Rana. Lilja was easy to spot, she looked the same. Rana was in a group of three nurses, standing with a few young Somali men. Another picture showed the same place in 1985. There were a few wooden buildings still standing near the river, but all of the refugees and their huts were gone. The large flat-topped acacias stood like pillars in a great empty hall, holding a green canopy over the plain. The first phase of the plan called for fifty, two-hectare farms—a cooperative run by the town of Luuq. The concept was well documented, including notes indicating that some of the ruling families weren't interested in supporting the cooperative unless they had control of who was granted the small farm plots. He also found a handwritten note, dated just before he was hired.

USAID RFP: Somalia Resettlement. Call me. MW

Josie booked him a room at Settlers Rest and told him he could use the van while he was in Nairobi. He parked near the old hotel's service entrance and walked through a well-tended garden on a path that wound around broadleaf ferns and palms. The grass had just been mowed, leaving a fresh green aroma surrounding the wide entrance to the lobby. The main hotel was built with large, squared-off stones, and metal framed windows set deep into the walls. Josie had booked him a room in the annex, close to where he'd parked. The annex was originally built for staff—small rooms with one window facing a tall hedge. It was perfect, he thought. He didn't want to be surrounded by too much luxury, with a suite overlooking the gardens. He did want to enjoy the dining room and bar, and maybe a beer on the terrace at sundown.

Ever since she'd told him that Don was missing, he'd been thinking about Ying. Josie said she was packing up and not answering her calls. He decided to go to the house, and see if she'd talk to him. He'd watched as Don drove him from the Angelina Convent to their house—along Ngong Road, then left at Kabarnet Road. He scanned the houses on the right side, looking for some sign of the French's home. The Land Cruiser was in the drive. The doors were open and so was the front door of the house. Max pulled in and knocked on the open door. "Ying?" Then a little louder after he thought he heard sounds coming from inside. "Ying?"

Nalangu looked out from the hallway next to the kitchen. She recognized him, and putting her finger to her lips, she waved him in, herding him to the terrace. As he waited, he could hear Ying talking to someone. It sounded like a phone call. When she came out her lips were tight. "It's nice of you to come by, but I have no news for Josie, in case that's why you came. I'll leave the house clean and the Land Cruiser will be in the driveway. Nalangu will have the keys."

"Josie didn't send me but she is worried about both of you. Is there any way for me to help?"

"Why do you care? Bradley will find another big donor to sit in Don's office. He'll throw a fit but I don't care. I never liked this place." She paused, then said, "I'm going to have a drink. You can join me, but no more questions." She brought out a bottle of Macallan and two water glasses.

"I talked to him just before you came. Remember, no questions. He's always been so sure of himself, always trying to get in over his head. It's going to be fine, don't worry...that's what he'd say. It'll work out. Well, Africa didn't work out. He was envious of everyone here—the missionaries, nurses in their bush clinics, Sharif, Rana, and Annie. Anyone that looked like a hero irritated him. I know he had panic attacks, mostly in his office. He needs to rest."

Max pulled out the card that Josie had given him and put it on the table—her eyes said it. "I've met him." She picked up the card, and when she flipped it over, the 50k seemed to produce a ripple of recognition. "Thank you for coming today. I know you're trying to help, but please, please let it go. He needs to rest. Before you go, you could bring up the boxes from his little office down there. That would be a help."

Max took the card carefully from her fingers. "Okay. Do you need help getting to the airport? I have the van."

"No thank you, the boxes will be enough."

Don's office was a mess. All the drawers were open and there were piles of papers on the floor. A lamp was tipped over, its shade bent and torn. By the door he found three boxes wrapped with packing tape and tied with twine. He put the boxes on the front porch, said goodbye into the empty foyer, and drove back to the hotel.

16

Max took a taxi to Kiberu in the morning. There were three baristas, and he tried to guess which one was Mara. He ordered his coffee, then asked the server, his third choice, if she knew someone named Hani? The tall Sudanese woman just looked at him, not smiling a bit.

"Why do you want to know this?"

"Because I'm a friend of hers and I have a package for Mara...are you Mara?"

"Please, take your coffee. Sit over there." She pointed to a small high-top near the window. After a few minutes, in which the Sudanese princess kept her eye on him, she took off her apron and sat down across from him.

"Who are you? How do you know that name?"

"I'm Max. I work with her in Mogadishu and she asked me to bring you this package. You are Mara, yes?"

She slid the package closer. "Where do you work?"

"In Mogadishu—I'm with an agency that works with her office at UNICEF."

"American?" She released her first smile, transforming his inquisitor back into the princess at the espresso machine.

"I am."

"How much of a friend are you?"

"She told me that you are her best friend, and she worked with you during the years she was at university. I think you were roommates. Is that right?"

"Okay, okay, you pass. Pleased to meet you, Max. Tell me that you live in California."

"I don't. When I'm in America I live in the Northwest, near Canada."

"Oh, but California, that's where I want to go. You've been?

"Yeah, it's pretty cool."

"Pretty cool. Very American. Do you and Hani just work together, or...?"

"We hang out some too."

"Hanging out...pretty cool. Are you just trying to act like California? I'm just teasing you. I miss Hani so much."

"Me too." He said it before he thought.

"You miss her? When did you see her last?"

"Yesterday." He confessed.

She added it up and pronounced. "You are lovers. Am I right?"

"...We're friends." He'd hesitated and her face reflected it immediately.

"That's cool...but you better not hurt her."

"I would never hurt her. Never."

"I have to get back to the counter but could you come by tomorrow, same time? I have some presents for her."

He decided to walk the ten or fifteen blocks to the WFP office. It gave him time to digest the short meeting with Mara. Her comment, about not hurting Hani, gave him a small shock. There were so many ways to hurt the people you love. His brain was working on a comprehensive vow, an addition to his code.

By just showing up, he got a small shipment on next week's flight. The warehouse manager wanted Global Aid commit to five tons every two weeks. Max agreed, thinking like Sharif—food was power and it could be used for good.

He took a detour to the UNICEF office, in case there were any openings on tomorrow's flight. Again, showing up was like magic. There was one seat, a cancellation just before he walked in the door. His plans for a weekend in Nairobi were replaced by the plan to see Hani as soon as possible. He convinced himself that there was an urgent need for him to return to Mogadishu. Sharif would need time to arrange the trucks and security for a steady stream of supplies, and Bradley Stokes showing up would complicate things too. Good reasons to return.

He studied himself in the mirror as he put on a fresh shirt for dinner. His face in the mirror was like a photograph, but all the other people were missing. Without the others, he couldn't place himself. Images of his family floated behind his reflection. He couldn't see Alison's image, but he felt it. He'd been thinking about what he'd write to his sister, Zoe. Now, looking at the ghosts next to him in the glass he leaned into the nostalgia. A dinner alone, with Zoe as the muse, suited his mood.

He went through the steel framed glass doors into a dining room that felt like a conservatory. The walls had windows down to the table tops, allowing the garden's bright and strange flowers to wonder at the amazing array of the faces inside. A dining room like this is the right place for proposals, anniversaries and some wickedness. He considered the price of this beautiful hotel. Wealth flows upwards, extracted from the earth and the lives of the poor. The wonders of architecture sit on a foundation of abuse and corruption. His thoughts circled back to familiar themes. His notebook stayed open throughout dinner but nothing had been written. What could he write to Zoe? Could he put it into words? Would words ruin it? It was easier to think about work right now.

Work had a schedule, not feelings. His learning curve wasn't as difficult as he'd anticipated. In fact, the work was simple.

17

When Hani saw that he'd booked a seat back to Mogadishu, two days early, she sat down at her desk. She felt sick. This job was a top assignment, a choice she'd made that didn't include what she was feeling. She was prepared for the isolation, solitude, and danger, but Max was a surprise—a discomfort, a disruption.

Twenty-nine—that was the age of change. She was at the point she'd seen in some of her colleagues, a point where careers overtake other plans. She missed her friend and roommate Mara, but found living alone pleasant. Being under guard, listening to gunfire, and driving around with armed teenagers was just part of the job, and the way of life in Somalia now. The time alone after work gave her time to read for the first time since university. It wasn't so bad. Now, her quiet bungalow, the one that housed her Mogadishu self, was no longer enough.

Max was in Nairobi tonight, her city. The place where she'd formed the earlier version of herself. She'd seen the party side of the NGO tribe in Nairobi, and a much wilder scene in Mozambique. That was about coping. In Somalia there were no parties, no restaurants or bars to gather in at night, no doing anything in the open. Somalia made you spend too much time alone. You took home everything you saw each day. One decent bar in a war zone could fix that temporarily.

The books she brought from Nairobi filled in for the noisy bars and restaurants, but they couldn't match the wonder of talking to a living person, telling her story to a man, in the dark, in her bed. It was a rare glimpse of intimacy and intimacy required truth. So far, she'd only told him pieces of her early years. The years that gave you your trajectory. The years you lived with your parents, or without them in her case. She'd worked hard, served others, and was respected by her new colleagues. She hoped that one day she'd be able to become a project manager for another NGO, or maybe find a donor to start her own projects. But that wasn't the whole story. It wasn't only about her success—the story is in the failures. And, failures often happened between colleagues.

Tonight, she sat in her bed with Max's pillow on her lap. She wanted to tell him everything.

18

The entrance to Kiberu had the usual backpacks lining the sidewalk in the morning. Dogs with bandanas waited outside, focused on their traveling companions that milled about the cafe. The bulletin board was filled with messages, photographs of missing travelers, requests for rides, advertisements, and notes from people looking for work. Max's note had been up there once. This morning he bought four kilos of roasted beans, a bagel and a coffee. He waited for Mara at a high-top by the window.

She sat down and placed a shoe box on the table. "Do you have room for this? It's shoes for a boy she knows. Don't be jealous, I think he's twelve. There are letters and other stuff in there, so make sure she looks inside before giving it away—kiss her once for me."

The plane landed in the north, and it was afternoon before he was dropped off at Sharif's. He'd been sleeping in his chair and was still leaning way back when Max came into the office. Sharif looked down his long nose and asked, "So, tell me about Nairobi. Did you accomplish everything you wished?"

He handed him twenty thousand dollars and added, "Don French has disappeared, Bradley Stokes is coming soon, with guests, there's a lot more money for Somalia. And, we're getting more Unimix this week, and five tons every two weeks after that. I think that's it."

Sharif said nothing about Don's disappearance, and raised an eye when Max announced Bradley's plans. Max laid out the schedule for the deliveries, plotting the events on a chart Sharif was using. They decided that the Unimix now in the compound would last for two more months, and the new supplies could be enough to start three more camps.

He was getting ready to leave, when he remembered the Geed Weyn file. "Sharif, what happened to the farm in Geed Weyn? I saw a note about it in Nairobi, something about a request for a proposal. It was just a few months ago. Is there anything happening there now?"

"I've heard nothing. Was there a new proposal?"

"No, just the one from 1985, nothing except the note since then."

"Well, the project never happened."

"I read some of the file. It sounded like the town of Luuq stopped it."

"It is very difficult to design a project like that. They don't like Mogadishu telling them what to do." Sharif came over to the desk where Max was sitting, opened a drawer and took out a file. "Here, this is what we have on it."

He spent a few minutes going through it, finding some of the same maps and photographs. He scanned the faces of the Somalis standing next to Rana.

Hassen Mombasa dropped him at Hersi's a little after five and he joined Hani on the deck. They were in public and, whether it mattered or not, they restrained their impulses. He took out the box that Mara had given him. "I met Mara. I had to pass her inspection, and promise to kiss you once for her."

"She can be fierce. Save the kiss for later." She smiled as she took letters and other small packages out of the shoe box. "The shoes are for Boutros, Hersi's grandson. You've seen him here."

Max placed the bags of coffee on the table. "This is for Hersi."

"Oooh, Kiberu Coffee!" She squeezed a bag and inhaled the aroma.

Hersi refused the gifts two times in the first few sentences, but with every polite word he let his hands touch the bags of coffee, and moved the shoes closer to the edge of the table. He made peace with Hani's gift, and vowed that Max would not pay for coffee anymore. Max took a turn refusing, but Hersi was too good at this.

After Hersi left them, they searched each other's faces—seeing each other for the first time in the new era. She broke the silence, "I want you to come to my house again, you owe me a story. How about tomorrow...just beer and rice, maybe a little chicken."

He reached across the table to touch her hand just to be sure this was all real.

19

His normal table—their table, was occupied by a white guy the next morning. The newcomer nodded to him, and there was a hint of recognition in the gesture. He tried to recall the people he'd seen at the US Embassy in Nairobi.

Hersi guided him to another table near the alley. "From here you can see her as soon as she comes out." Then Hersi looked at the stranger, "I think he is an American. He came yesterday too, wanted that table. This is a better table anyway, except when the espresso machine is working, then it is too loud."

"What's wrong with the machine?"

"It needs parts from Italy. Before, it was every Thursday, Rome-Mogadishu, direct flight. Now it is difficult to buy anything."

"Write down the part numbers or description, maybe I can order it in Nairobi."

"One day soon you should come to my house. My wife misses Americans and Europeans. We used to work in a restaurant in the old city, we met lots of aid workers and diplomats there. My wife Laylo knows English, and she is so eager to talk to someone besides me. You would honor us Max. You can bring Hani, I know Laylo would love it."

Max was honored, "Thank you, I'd love that."

The HiLux pulled up and he started to leave. The American stood as Max passed his table and asked, "Are you Max, Max Dubec?"

"Yes. You are?"

"John Thomas, USAID. Do you have a minute?"

"My ride's here, but I've got a minute. What's this about?"

"Please sit, I'll be quick."

Max pulled out the chair and sat on the edge. He didn't remember him from the embassy, but he had that look—button-down white shirt, early thirties, clean shaven, horn-rim glasses, and an earnest expression.

"We're looking at agencies, like yours, that have worked up-country before. The next phase of our Somalia funding will be to resettle the internally displaced. Global Aid did a fair amount of work in the Gedo District."

Max said, "I was just reading the files."

"We know this proposal. Some of the features of it will need to change, to update of course. Overall, it was a good plan, but it depended on cooperation from the town of Luuq and other power centers in the area. This might be a good time to think about it again, with a focus on resettlement. The leaders in Luuq have asked for Global Aid's help once more. Are you interested?"

"We're pretty busy in Mogadishu right now."

"I understand. And I hear that you're expanding."

"You seem to know about our plans, which don't include Luuq right now, but I'll pass the invitation to our international director. He'll be in Mogadishu in a few weeks."

"Why don't you at least go up to Luuq, and meet with the leaders before your director arrives? I can get you there tomorrow if you like."

"By plane?"

"No, by road. You could be back in three days. Just think about it. I'll be here in the morning, around ten. If you decide to take a look at Luuq, and like the idea of completing the project your agency designed, then I can guarantee the funding."

"Why is this so important right now?"

"To be honest, we need to demonstrate the US Government's support for the principles in the ceasefire. Resettlement is a key to reducing the overcrowding in Mogadishu, which makes it easier to provide security."

"I think it is too early for us to be going out of Mogadishu. I'm the Interim Country Manager, and our only expat in Mogadishu. Maybe in the future, but right now we can't cover it."

"I do know about your agency's plans. For instance, your director is bringing two more agency directors with him, and they all plan to send staff. It could happen in the next two weeks. So, you'll have the staff."

"I need to go, John. It was nice to meet you, but don't count on me in the morning."

John Thomas handed Max his card. "I'll be here in the morning. Maybe I'll have a cup of the Kiberu."

He spent the next few hours visiting two of their camps with Suleymaan, returning to the office before siesta to talk to Sharif about the invitation. Maliq opened the gate enough to frame his thin face. He said that Sharif was not home.

20

Max was waiting for her when she came home. She pulled him into the bungalow, guiding him toward her bed, and held him at a distance. He watched her face rolling through waves of thought, her dark eyebrows forming storm clouds, the light in her eyes shadowed by a typhoon's cobalt sky.

"Are you okay? What is it?" he asked.

She responded with a kiss, then kissed him harder, pushing his head back. She pulled him onto the bed and kept kissing his mouth, pushing into him aggressively. Then she abruptly rolled away and sat on the edge of the bed. "No, I'm not okay, I don't know what I am. Part of that," she patted the bed, "part of that, is my anger. Not at you. Not yet. But I know what this is, this distraction...no, it's more than that, it can't happen here, it doesn't work here. Why did you say that? Why would you push love into a simple friendship? You're already crazy, but I don't want to be. Do you think we can feel this forever, or does it stop when the music ends—when your contract is up, or I'm posted to Timbuktu? I told you that I don't want to be hurt, and this hurts, Max. It's going to hurt you too, and I don't want that because...we've crossed from friendship into something much more complicated. I don't know if I'm crazy in love, or just crazy! I'm sorry Max, I guess this is what they call baggage, this is Meena's stuff…and I need to tell you."

They were sitting on her bed, side by side as she spoke, her words looping through his memories. "When I went to sea, my grandfather told me that a mariner only packs half a sea-bag. Everywhere I went I had to decide if I had room for something I liked, and what I'd have to leave behind if I wanted it. I still have room for your stuff Hani. Maybe I've been saving that space all along."

She changed into a tee shirt and jeans and he opened up the slats. The concrete floor beneath the grass mat at the foot of the bed was the coolest place in the house. He listened as she spoke.

"I thought I had the perfect job in Mozambique. I got to set up a medical team, hire staff and write the proposals. After three months I became a program manager. The NGO was small but well-funded. I lived in a guest house in the same compound with the director and his wife, Justin and Ruth. It was really different than working with UNDP in Nairobi. I had a local staff of thirteen community health workers, and three doctors. We'd go deep into the bush to survey the needs of the small farms and communities that had been cut off during the fighting. I got to talk to people there, to find out how they lived, how they survived. We could act, make decisions on the spot. We had the funding, the staff, and the freedom to say yes. And it made a difference.

"When we expanded the program into the south of the country I needed to stop going out with the teams and make sure they had all the supplies they needed. I started working closely with the director, Justin. I was so naive. I was flattered to get the chance to manage the program, and I enjoyed discussing the daily activities with him. He was a good listener, at first. Then he started to move the conversations to more personal things, telling me things about his marriage. I know, you can see this all coming, but I didn't want to see it. I enjoyed his company…he made me feel wanted...trusted. There's another thing I'm angry about...trust. I don't like being on guard or being suspicious."

“This doesn't end with Justin cut up into small pieces, does it?”

“It could have, but no. And now you’ve uncovered another thing that makes me angry. Sorry, but some things have not changed. Stone the adulteress! No, Justin managed the affair, and the divorce with ease. He now has a new position in a new agency and a new girlfriend. I was in love with him. I’ve thought a lot about it and I can’t deny my excitement when I was with him. We were keeping it a secret, finding lots of excuses to be alone. I always knew where Ruth was. I deceived her. I was awful. But it doesn’t end there. Once Ruth caught us it was over. Justin stopped talking to me, Ruth glared at me like my sisters. Then he tried to have me transferred out of Mozambique. But I wouldn’t go until my contract was complete. Leaving wasn’t a good option for my career. I stayed in Mozambique for two more months. The news was all over the NGO community, and I got looks and propositions. I was the slut. Nobody said it, but it was clear, and I went with it for a while. I was exercising my human right to fuck anyone I wanted, just like the guys. I didn’t need love to make love. At first it was a relief to feel free with my body, at last I could just have sex without all the complications of a relationship. I found a way to jump from my life, a way to stand on the railing and contemplate the falling. That’s what I thought about as we used each other, all the time falling.” She took a long slow breath, “I changed my name to Hani after Mozambique. Mara would introduce me to her friends as Hani, and my old boss, Roger, did too. It’s now my Somali name.”

While she was telling her story he was falling in love with her, falling with her as she showed him her secret scars, or maybe they were tattoos. As she spoke, he stayed as close to her as they could both stand. The wind was still and the heat smothered Mogadishu.

“You’re being very quiet, Max.”

“I still love you both, Meena and Hani.” He wanted to get that out right away.

He was going to say more but she pulled away to face him. The storm still hovering over her eyes. “I don’t need any analysis right now. Just hold me.”

21

The sky vanished, leaving the stars suspended in the blackness as they ate cold chicken and drank Vietnamese beer on her patio. She twirled her bottle in the condensation and said, "Tell me a story in bed, nothing too sad. The sheets haven't been changed since the last time you were here."

Without another word they picked up the remnants of their meal, grabbed another beer to share, and hooked the net over the bed. Inside, with a candle flickering, they relaxed into each other.

He began, "Once upon a time, there was a mad painter named Dmitri, my father, who lived in a condemned house near a university. He was in love with a wealthy and beautiful architecture student named Alison, my mother. He slept in his studio, surrounded faces captured in mid-scream, dark scenes full of hopeless terror. When the room got too full of faces, too loud, he'd have a ceremony and burn them. Alison went with him to the hills above the town, where one by one they threw them on the fire. Honestly Hani, that might not have actually happened, but I've heard them tell this story so many times that it's real. If—when—you meet Dmitri, you'll understand that he might do something like that."

"Does he still paint?"

"Every winter, but no ritual burning that I know of. Dmitri moved into Alison's house outside of town. It had an old apple orchard and a large pasture surrounded by fir trees. I went by the place a few years ago. I could imagine them staring out across the field and talking about having their own land, enough land to grow their own food and build a guest house for travelers. Alison's pregnancy brought her mother and father into the picture. They didn't like Dmitri. The idea that their daughter would end up barefoot, pregnant, living with a communist, drove them to offer her an early dip into her inheritance to bring her back to Seattle. The money came through but she never moved back. She bought 600 acres on the dry side of the mountains, just south of the Canadian border. They designed the buildings and laid out a plan for gardens. He became a good carpenter, with an eye for the bizarre, like the tin Kremlinesque spire on the barn that shrieked in the wind. Alison started making her world into a home for her baby—me. My room was a replica of a fire lookout, with windows on all sides. A fireplace was the core of the house and its massive chimney came up through the center of my lookout. When I was born, Alison and Dmitri were starting to fall apart."

Hani let out a little sigh.

"It happens."

"I know."

"Dmitri filled out the official papers, and according to Alison, he named me Maxx, with two x's. The clerk at the Health Department considered it a typo, or just too cute, and out it went, poof. Alison used to tell me this like a fairy tale. The boy with two x's—about a boy that once had two x's, but then lost one. Sometime the careless boy misplaced it, and other times it was taken by some evil force or someone at the Health Department. The stories were filled with adventures, heroes and villains, as he searched the world for the missing x—searching for a vital clue, a key, a door, or a secret mountain pass...always searching for that lost consonant."

He hadn't thought about that room in a long time. "The afternoon light would flood our reading corner. Alison and I would sit with our backs to the warm bricks and she would read to me. I remember that we could look out on the peach trees Dmitri had planted. He would come by every day to look after them, and wave up to the house when he thought we were watching."

"Were they divorced?"

"No, not officially anyway. They loved each other but had trouble living together. His peach trees thrived and her gardens overflowed. The house was always being remodeled, and fences mended—Alison and Dmitri sharing everything, except contentment."

"That's a sad love story."

"Yeah, it is. Too sad?

"You were loved though, that's not sad...go on."

"Alison's money was a problem. Every few years a major expense would come up, like a new well, an addition to the barn, a goat shed, or another tractor. Alison could pay these expenses easily enough if she could just bring herself to ask for more of her inheritance. Her parents never said it, but it was obvious they were using their money to keep her coming home—a constant reminder that Dmitri was not providing for their grandchildren."

"That part is familiar." Hani said. "In Naivasha the parents are always tearing couples apart over money and grandchildren." She shifted her feet, nudging him to go on. "Tell me about school. For me, that was when I first became aware of the world outside. Did you like school?"

"Alison told me I was un-schoolable by the time I was five. I could read, do basic mathematics and build cool forts in the woods. I didn't know that I was missing school. She thought that school was like a nine to five job, an unnatural way to live. The old money took a special interest in the grandchildren after Zoe was born, offering to send us to the best schools and academies. Alison pushed back, advocating for no school at all. I think that having to run her experiment on her own children made her into a fanatic.

Alison attempted to define the ideal learning environment, which looked pretty much like our ranch. Not just the property, and its natural beauty, but the flow of wanderers that encamped at the edge of the woods."

"Who are the wanderers?" Hani was now sitting in a lotus position, facing him with her hands in her lap. Her eyes were closed.

"Yes, the wanderers, the lost tribe. That was Alison's name for them. When Alison and Dmitri moved onto the land a steady stream of their friends, and their friends' friends passed through. Some of them were on their way to Canada to escape the draft. Others were on a journey or a quest. We must have been on a special map that showed safe houses or free places to crash. The barn was basically a hostel. They'd arrive every spring after the snow melted and set up their camps. Runaways, dropouts, searchers, and outlaws made up the tribe of wanderers that were welcomed seasonally. Dmitri called them refugees—I think internally displaced is more accurate. They were a part our lives, around drum circles and working in the gardens. We'd get to spend nights in the village of tee-pees, tents and old buses that rimmed the aspens. Zoe and I understood from the beginning that we were part of this tribe.

"The aspen forest was my world. Last time I was there I saw how small it was—maybe just one hectare. I knew every tree and the paths that led to secret forts and ceremonial grounds. I gathered stones and made a small pyramid to signal the aliens. When Zoe came into the woods, she pretended to be an alien princess, with special powers."

"That sounds so amazing. My world had no privacy. Our neighbors lived on top of us. Outside belonged to everyone. I want to go to your forest, and have some of Zoe's special powers."

“The wanderers had lots of stories that were part of my education. They treated Zoe and me as peers, without a filter. They openly confessed their failures, appropriate or not. I guess I have a unique understanding of religion, philosophy and sex. My knowledge of history, biology and astronomy were full of aliens and magic. We were revered by the wanderers as little enlightened souls.”

“It sounds like a cult. Was it?”

“Dmitri called it the circle. But...it was really the cult of Alison, I mean, she drew people in. In the eighties the ranch became a kind of halfway-house for people recovering from some real cults. And when the Bhagwan’s cult collapsed, we got lots of refugees from Oregon.”

Hani tilted her head. “Bhagwan? Who’s the Bhagwan? It sounds like a dragon... you had a weird childhood.”

“Bhagwan Shri Ras Nich was a guru from India who built a large cult in Eastern Oregon. Some of his abandoned followers found their way to the ranch They bucked a lot of hay, and built miles of fences while they recovered from utopia.”

“Like resettlement, work programs and a safe place to adjust to the world again.”

“Right, but I think it’s easier to survive utopia, most of the time.”

“Listen Max! That sounds close.” The cadence of the gunshots was sounding more aggressive than the normal Mogadishu gun talk. As she said it, he saw lights moving around behind the airport wall. There were headlights out on the tarmac. The airport would be a big prize, but it would be a battle. Hani quickly blew out their candle and they listened to the war until it moved away from the wall.

She faced him on one elbow, and as the water dripped, and the gunfire cracked in the distance, “When did you leave home?”

“Graduation from Alison’s educational system wasn’t well defined—I think she had a vision quest or some ritual in mind. I had the wandering skills, and was ready to use them. Dmitri’s father that got me a job on a freighter. Alison made me this amulet, and put a small ruby inside. I went up in a whirlwind and ended up here.”

22

The night grew quiet. Hani's head rested on his chest now, listening to his breathing, holding the ruby. "What happened to her? I want to share her with you. Is that okay? I can take dark, or sad, or anything you want to tell me."

He looked at her—insisting on knowing Alison. "She would have loved you. She died last year, when I was living in Venezuela—killed by wasps as she worked alone in her garden. The last wanderer discovered her the next morning. Zoe picked me up in Seattle and we drove over the mountains to the ranch, where Dmitri told us that she was found lying on her side in the decaying garden, covered in dozens of red welts. When I was at The Angelina Convent, I was standing in the garden one morning. The bees were buzzing and I imagined her in her garden. It was so clear. It's late in the fall, after the harvest, when the aspen leaves turn bright yellow, then begin to rust around the edges. The garden was her sanctuary. Inside the deer fence was like this net—the other world ceases to exist. I saw her rooting through the spent squash mounds, their bristly vines like tree branches and their leaves the size of plates, warping over each other, slowly going back to Earth. She stands up, arms stretched out to the side, palms up, head back in the last of the daylight. The falling leaves turn to wasps. They swarm around her and she doesn't move. Then she looks at me, that look I see at the camps, faces from Dmitri's burnt paintings. We see each other, then she lets go and rests her head on a waiting leaf."

Hani was imagining another mother.

He was stroking her hair. "Whatever it was about her that drew the wanderers in, changed when they became more wounded. Zoe felt some of the Bhagwani tried to replace their lost guru with Alison. My sister needed a mother and Alison was being consumed by the wanderers. Zoe named it, *Empathetic Consumption.* Alison took in the pain and loss of her needy disciples. Maybe she was really sick, cancer or something changing her brain, but she wouldn't see a doctor. She needed to be there for the lost tribe. The last wanderer, the one that found her that morning, drifted off when Alison's body was taken to be buried next to my grandmother.

"There was a guy that showed up at the ranch when I was a kid. He told me that contemplating death, at least five times a day was healthy. Now I think about it all the time. I've never been around so much death. To see so many people in a state of mourning, under the cloud of death. I'm the manager of eight thousand mourners, where we supply watered down calories and a thin white burial cloth...it's a strange job. I used to think that death was a moment, an event. Here, I see that moment begins early, and never ends. I don't think there is a God or heaven—I'm not sure about hell."

"I thought that Global Aid was a Christian organization?"

"Well, if Global Aid asked me to sign a statement of faith, or to fully agree with their literature, I wouldn't be here. I think most of their staff are more like the missionaries I met at the Convent in Nairobi—believers. I was hired in a weird, quick interview—no mention of faith. How about you? Do you think there is a God?"

"I haven't been asked that question since university. In Naivasha you believed what your...circle believed. The public schools stayed away from anything non-Christian. Not being different was most important, not offending others was required. University was the first time I had to face what I believed. I ended up with a lot of other people facing the same questions. Education is a big threat to religion, you know. Teaching us to think, to question—to appreciate how flawed so many of man's earlier ideas turned out to be."

"So, what does Hani Mogadishu think?"

"She doesn't think about God. My ideas were shaped by the language of human rights, equal rights, and dignity. Any god that seems indifferent, or unwilling, to prevent such stupid cruelty, that keeps secrets from us, or tells them only to men—that can't be the truth. So, since you asked, I don't believe in God...instead I believe that we need to act, day by day, do good, be kind..."

"Be loved?"

"Yes...and that. But it's hard to do that here."

"We won't be here forever...but, what if we went somewhere new, like Bosnia, or Guatemala? We could be itinerant aid workers."

Hani rolled out of bed and said, "I'd much rather *run* a small NGO...in Africa." She was walking in a small circle, fanning out her tee shirt. She stopped and said, "Are we planning our future? I don't want to know the future, Max. I don't want to imagine being happy, not here. Let's just go step by step." She took off her tee shirt and slipped back in beside him.

23

When Max came up the steps Hersi waved him over. "They've been here all morning." He pointed with his nose at the three Land Cruisers.

"I was supposed to meet the American here this morning. I'm not sure if these guys are part of that or not."

Hersi put a note in his hand. "It's from the American."

Boutros served him coffee as he read the note.

Max, Thanks for taking me up on the ride to Luuq. Omar will take you to meet with Zaynab, one of Luuq's leaders. We'll talk when you return. JT

"Max?"

He looked up.

"I am Omar, Mr. Thomas advised you, yes?"

Max stood up, having to back his chair a bit.

"I remember you from Kismayo." He also remembered Ali Nur.

"Thank you for coming. Zaynab is expecting us today, so when you are ready, we are ready."

Omar's voice was seriously polite. His large head was freshly shaved and he smelled of English Leather. The crocodile on his shirt pocket stared at him. "Have your coffee, then we will go."

"My bag is at my house."

Omar turned and signaled one of those waiting by the cars. "He'll get it for you, no problem."

This was a problem, according to Sharif. Allowing too many people know your business, where you lived, or where you went, could lead to problem. When Omar's guy returned, they started up the Land Cruisers.

Max sat in the back of Omar's black Land Cruiser. He made one last glance in hopes of seeing Hani. The first Land Cruiser took off far ahead of the others and the last one held close on their bumper. Afgooye Road climbed up a gentle rise and then headed across a desert plain.

He'd heard this was called the Mussolini Road. The tarmac stood a meter above the desert, the edges calving when the rains came. The sides of the road maintained a thick border of dusty green bushes, with thorns hidden among the dry leaves. At the bottom of the slope a trail was worn by the constant migration of herders, and now refugees. A small caravan of camels, with their curving slender poles strapped on either side, moved with the current. The road was about one and a half lanes wide, narrower in spots where the edges had given way. The driver avoided most of the potholes, while looking out for goat herds or camels that occasionally took to the road. No one spoke except when the radio squawked, which usually meant another vehicle was approaching. When a vehicle did appear, the road stretched just wide enough for them to pass but no one slowed down.

After an hour on the road the top of Buryo Wayo rose up over the horizon. Max had seen pictures of Ayers Rock in Australia—Buryo Wayo, though smaller, dominated the desert in the same magical way. It stood sentry over the interior, gathering the birds to its smooth red stones. Soldiers and merchants rested among the trees at its base.

"Half an hour to Baidoa." Omar said. "You are fine?"

Max nodded.

After Buryo Wayo the road started to turn to the south and climb above the plain. The highway was broken here and there with detours around missing sections of road. The empty stream beds were washed down to large flat stones layered across wide cuts in the landscape—no sign of water anywhere. The convoy bounced over these in four-wheel drive, slowly climbing a bank to find the tarmac again. At the top of one of these wadis two boys flagged down the drivers. All three cars stopped. Omar rolled down his window and gave the older boy a bottle of Evian. The boy sniffed it, looking at it in its clear glass bottle. He handed it to the smaller boy, who took a sip and handed it back to the older one, saying something along with a wrinkled-up nose. The older boy gave it back to Omar without drinking. Omar turned to Max and laughed, "It's too clean and cold. It is not water to them." The driver got out, unstrapped a Jerry can from the back bumper and poured a better vintage into the boys' gourds.

They climbed another rise and he saw the outskirts of Baidoa. They slowed just a little as they wound through the dusty streets. Baidoa was one story high in all directions. Yards with stick fences and empty buildings gave way to shops and crowds of people under tea shop awnings. The convoy stopped on the shoulder in front of a group of men. A man in a blue short-sleeve dress shirt got in next to Max. Omar introduced Liban as a member of the regional counsel for the Gedo District.

"You are going to Luuq, yes?" Liban asked.

"Yeah, my agency had a project, near there. I'm just taking a look."

"I know it well. Also, I know that Zaynab is pleased you're coming for a visit." He pointed at the dark clouds boiling up in the distance. "Rain, it is coming now. We've waited for two years, now it will be a big rain. Next time you come here all of this will be green. The birds will come back. The road will be gone." Liban laughed at this picture and started talking to

Omar. The edge of the storm was closer. They began winding down an escarpment into a wide valley. Bits of ancient tarmac outlined the twisting roadway. A wall of dust was covering the sinking sun. At the bottom they came out onto a narrow, raised roadbed that went straight towards the storm. The cloud of dust blew past them in an instant—then the rain. He could see the vehicle ahead of them slipping back and forth, trying to hang onto the middle. They all slowed as the windshield wipers ran at full speed. The roadway crossed several culverts where water rushed through. Branches and brush were already constructing a dam that threatened to overrun the road. Going only a few miles an hour, they came to where the raised part of the road met the flat of the valley bottom. What was once a slippery ridge of road became two tracks of water with the center barely lower than the axles. They went on this way, with the water running toward them. On the left, a part of the road was washing away. Omar was on the radio giving instructions to the vehicle in the lead, urging them on. Liban was laughing. "Don't worry Max, Luuq is only a little more. What rain!"

The first Land Cruiser leapt out of the track, sliding violently into the next rut with one side now up on the right bank. Tilted like this, they skirted the washed-out area and tried to get the other wheel onto the center, but the muddy road kept them trapped in the right-hand rut. Liban said, "If you ever see tire tracks going around a big puddle, don't follow it." He then repeated this bit of wisdom to Omar in the front seat. The driver was also talking through the mirror to Liban. Omar was pointing to the right and speaking into the radio. In a rush of words and hand waving he was telling the lead driver to go toward the higher ground and get out of the road altogether. The lead car made a sharp right turn, mud and water spraying as they leapt out of the rut, gunning for the stony shoulder on their right. Next, their car made the jump and pulled up behind them. The last car tried this too, but kept being forced back into the ruts. After a few minutes of trying, they stopped. Their tail was not with them when they came into Luuq a few minutes later.

Two crumbling posts marked the entrance to the town. Zaynab's house was one of the first houses on the left. Runnels of water wound down to Zaynab's door. They picked their way from the Land Cruiser across the mud. Liban and Omar were laughing and pushing each other. Zaynab welcomed them inside, then turned to Max and declared, "You've brought the rain with you, bravo!"

They removed their shoes and stepped onto the worn carpet in the living room. Liban gave Zaynab a big hug, kissing her on each cheek like an uncle. Omar disappeared upstairs and Max could hear him talking to someone. Zaynab's housekeeper greeted Max with tea and a shy smile.

"This is Asha." Zaynab said.

"Nice to meet you, Mr. Max." When Asha said his name, it came out more like Mox. Mister Mox.

Zaynab now fixed her complete attention on him.

Max had a flash of Deja vu.

"I'm so pleased that you have come. Thank you, Max."

She was in her late thirties, younger than his landlord. Seeing her in this decaying elegance, surrounded by the remains of an old river town was disorienting—but then being disoriented was becoming common. He took a chance, asking if she was related to Ali Nur. She laughed and shook her head, "You are good. He's my brother. Do you see a likeness?"

"Something familiar, yes." Max wanted to tell her that she was much more beautiful than her brother, and that her eyes didn't have the look of a drowning man, but he held this to himself. Despite his misgivings about Ali Nur, her welcome felt genuine.

Omar came down the stairs with Ali Nur. Seeing him again renewed his sense of being trapped—a feeling he experienced daily.

"Good to see you here, Max Dubec," His eyes still didn't hold any light, but he looked relaxed, even friendly. Ali Nur spoke to the room, waving his arm around to include everyone. Asha was called out from the kitchen and Ali Nur waved her into the circle. "We will all speak English while you are with us Max, even Asha if she can remember it."

Asha put her eyes on the floor, but Zaynab spoke for her. "She used to be very good at English, she'll remember it again."

Max floated above the evening's conversation, watching the scene that included him. Mostly, he tried to understand this meeting with a warlord and his sister. Sharif had warned Max of the subtle insistent gravity that these ancient families exerted. He came back down when Ali Nur and Liban started having an intense exchange, some in English and some in rapid Somali. Ali Nur turned to Max and repeated what he'd just said to Liban. "Independence will always be met with violence. We get peace as soon as we surrender to the inevitable. Do you know what I'm talking about Max? I think you too have been around the world, am I correct? It's not so big. There's no more room for independence. Somalia must make a decision."

Liban started to speak in Somali, but Ali Nur insisted on English. "Very well, I am speaking to you Max. I don't agree that Somalia has to make a choice." He faced Ali Nur. "I think a handful of big Somalis need to get out of the way. We don't want their independence. That's not food! That's not life! The Gedo has always been my home. The magic of the land is useless without her people. Another year and it will die."

Zaynab cut in. "When Rana and your agency were in Geed Weyn we needed it. You brought us help against the Ethiopians. You were not like the US Government, but truly you were the united nations, Holland, Finland, The Philippines, and your Americans. Liban was there and I worked there with Rana, you know."

Ali Nur said, "Geed Weyn was useful, it's true, but this time camps like Dadaab will be Kenyan prisons." With this everyone agreed. "We will go Geed Weyn, you can see it for yourself."

Zaynab stood up, signaling the end of the evening. She told Max he could have the room at the top of the stairs. "The roof leaks a bit, but it's your rain." she said with a smile.

Max wanted to lock the door. He looked out the window, pulling back the heavy curtains. The kitchen was just below him and the charcoal fire from the oven was sending fingers of smoke through the broken glass. The generator shut down and the light pulsed out.

24

Max had been up since four, waiting for the light. The smell of baking bread was carried on the smoke from below. He heard Asha singing. This feeling of dread was almost familiar enough to enjoy as excitement.

They were waiting for him when he came downstairs. Asha made an American breakfast—fried eggs, fresh bread, mangos and coffee from Kenya. He ate as the others watched. When he finished, Ali Nur said, "Let's go find our friends. We'll use your old technical,"

"Mine?"

"Well, Rana's really. It has a winch that still works. It was the first Land Cruiser Global Aid brought to Geed Weyn. I rode in it many times. You can use it when you're here."

The promise of funds from USAID, and now the promise of a vehicle from Ali Nur was making this too easy. The technical was an old mustard yellow Land Cruiser with the top cut off. When they left Zaynab's the sun was steaming the water from the puddles. Birds flew up around them as Ali Nur drove slowly, trying to keep the water from coming in where the doors used to be. He was wearing yellow rubber boots, blue jeans and a tee shirt. Omar wore a black tee shirt, and a macawis the color of muddy water. His sandals were caked with mud. Liban didn't look like he planned to get out of the vehicle since he still had on his dark pants and was scraping the sticky red mud off his polished shoes with the twig he'd been using as a toothbrush.

The Land Cruiser they were looking for was no longer in the road, but in a mess of ruts and deep mud on the side of the road. A stream of muddy water rushed through the cut in the road. The two men from the stranded vehicle were sitting on the hood, smoking. Omar yelled something across the gap, which brought back an angry response from the men on the hood. Ali Nur joined the banter. One of the hood sitters slid off his perch and waded into the mud at the edge of the new cut. Omar was pulling cable off the winch while Ali Nur fastened a rope to the hook.

"Max." said Ali Nur. "Something heavy…the tire iron, something to throw across with this rope."

Max tied on the weight and coiled the rope in two sections, throwing the loop with the tire iron a second before releasing the rest of the line. He'd practiced this throw many times at sea. A small line would be attached to the larger tie lines when a tug would ease them into a dock. The game was to take out a warehouse window with the monkey fist on the weighted end of the throw rope. This time he was trying not to damage anything. The tire iron hit the mud a foot from the front of the car, bringing a hoot from Liban and a nod from Ali Nur.

Omar paid out the cable as they pulled from the other end of the throw rope. Once connected to the frame they easily pulled it across the wash. By now the sun was at full power, and they retreated back to Luuq.

Their mud caked shoes stood outside Zaynab's kitchen, already baked by the heat of the afternoon. The mopani celebrated in the empty town square. It was going to be just the two of them this afternoon. Ali Nur had Max drive. "That way you'll remember how to get there next time."

He knew the map. The Juba flowed through the town of Doloow, around the wide bend at Geed Weyn, then slowly slithered along overgrown farm lands before it almost encircled

Luuq. They turned off the Doloow road and followed a track that headed toward the river. He could see a break through the trees, and a thick green wall of forest behind the Juba as it rounded the wide bend that was Geed Weyn. A high canopy of thin feathery leaves changed the light—like entering a vast empty arena. He stopped on Ali Nur's signal, and they sat there for a minute without talking. Then Ali Nur pointed ahead to where he saw the shimmering of a tin roof beneath several giant acacias. As they got nearer, he saw a shipping container and four buildings perched on the edge of the riverbank. The track led to the container. Ali Nur got out of the Land Cruiser to greet the guard standing at attention in the shade. He introduced Mohamed Ali. "Mohamed lives here. He's been here since it was a refugee camp, and he's guarded it for you with my help."

Mohamed bowed a little and said," Welcome to Geed Weyn."

The official tour went from building to building. Ali Nur seemed to be going over improvements or corrections with Mohamed in Somali. The kitchen was in the best condition, with a concrete floor, screens on the windows and a long table. It had a covered porch with a concrete patio in front. He was told that the kerosene refrigerator and a two-burner stove would be installed soon. The building closest to the river was smaller than the others, and its parts were being salvaged to repair the two longer buildings. Each of these buildings had a breezeway that separated two living quarters. In the building closest to the kitchen, he was shown his office and across the breezeway, his room. Ali Nur swept his arm around the curve of the Juba, and said, "Your farm."

He followed the river, swirling brown and red, sweeping branches and small trees from left to right. The steep slippery banks were just a couple of meters above the rush of water. The Juba curved around a wide swath of level ground that had some signs of cultivation. It was much bigger than he'd imagined.

Mohamed went to the Land Cruiser and returned with a basket. Asha had prepared chicken and fresh bread, with a Coke for Max. Ali Nur set three plastic chairs and a small wooden table in the breezeway closest to the river, where ate the spicy chicken with their fingers, using a plastic water bottle to rinse their hands.

After they finished Mohamed laid out his prayer rug next to the container and faced Mecca. Ali Nur watched. Nodding with his chin towards Mohamed he spoke quietly, "He is a good man. He'll look after things here until you decide to return."

Max said, "I don't know if it's possible."

"Any way you choose, maybe this place will look better when Mogadishu becomes too dangerous." He appeared to have more to say more, and after a minute he added, "Tonight is a full moon. It will come up right over there." He pointed across the Juba and into the Gedo Forest. "We'll stay to see it before we go back. Until then, we'll rest. There are hammocks in the kitchen. They can be set up here." Ali Nur indicated the metal eyes that were screwed into the corner posts of the breezeway. "You can walk around if you like, there is little danger." With that, Ali Nur went to talk with Mohamed who had finished his prayers.

Max set up the hammock diagonally across the breezeway, giving him a good view of the river and part of the camp. He watched the Juba's surface reflect the passing clouds, going dark and light but never stopping. As the afternoon moved into evening he wandered around the buildings on the edge of the Juba. When he got close to the container, Mohamed came over from where he'd been hiding from the heat. He opened the doors wide and invited Max in. In game-show fashion he pulled back a plywood divider and revealed rolls of irrigation pipe, several foot pumps, mesh fencing and lots of shovels, rakes and hoes. “We are ready for you." He then backed them out and replaced the partition.

The night arrived, and a glow in the east signaled the coming moon. They pulled the chairs to the edge of the breezeway as the last light faded. There were no gunshots and the Mopani had retired. The motion of water pulling at the edges of the river bank made a soft rippling sound that floated above the surface. They stared out into the middle distance together.

“Do you call me a warlord?” Ali Nur asked.

Max wasn’t sure if he had spoken to the Juba or him. After a second, he answered, “Well, that was my first impression in Kismayo.”

“Ahh, Kismayo. What does Rana say, warlord?”

“We didn’t talk about you. But I think she’s under your protection.”

“Protection, yes. Kismayo is under my protection as is the Gedo. It’s my duty.” Ali Nur pulled his attention from the river and looked at Max. “You came to Somalia to help us. Do this project with Zaynab and Liban and I will protect it until the time of warlords has passed.”

The moon rose into a black line of clouds in the east.

25

The ten o'clock break-time was over and Max and Hani were the only ones left. Ever since he'd returned from Luuq he'd been trying to piece together what he was being asked to do. It was an invitation, but it felt like a set-up. He told her about Luuq, Geed Weyn, Zaynab, and in a lower voice, about Ali Nur.

"You're thinking about it, aren't you?"

"It's the kind of project I'd love to try. There's a plan, land, local sponsors, transportation, and funding. And there's a need, or will be soon. Maybe I could hire you away from UNICEF and we could do it together."

"You're crazy, you know that, Max? Anyway, you'll be busy this week with your boss in town. They're booked for Wednesday, in the North. After they're gone, we should go to Nairobi together, I have lots of time saved up."

"And I want all of it Hani. All of you and your time."

"That sounds like a proposal."

"Oh, it is a proposal."

"You *are* crazy."

Arranging transportation across Mogadishu to meet Bradley's plane was going to take some time. He'd need Hani's help getting the UN's approval and he'd need a van and driver that could pass from South to North and back again. The UN had negotiated safe passage for their staff and the NGOs, and for the most part the ceasefire was working, at least in Mogadishu.

There had been a short suspension of cross-town travel because of an incident he'd witnessed. A couple of journalists from Sweden were returning across the city, when their convoy stopped to await the transfer. The cameraman got out of the technical and hoisted his camera to shoot a panorama of downtown Mogadishu. Within minutes a crowd gathered around him. Angry shouts and pushing erupted. Then the escort tried to clear the crowd from around the vehicle, leading to more pushing and eventually shots were fired in an attempt to back the crowd off. By then the transfer technical arrived at the other side of the green line, and mistaking the crowd control for a fire-fight, they took positions, aiming their weapons at Max's escort. The filming continued. The cameraman's partner was holding a microphone toward a group of women when she was shoved to the ground as the crowd surged. Somehow the driver and gunman got everyone back in the technical. They aborted the crossing and drove back to the south as the radios squawked. It was a good story for them in Sweden, but it closed the crossing for two weeks. The Swedes left the next morning from the field near Afgooye. When crossing was reestablished, the routes had been altered and the need to change vehicles on the line was replaced with special escorts allowed to pass non-stop between sides of the city.

The security for these trips was just mathematics. They had weapons exposed, and they drove fast. The UNICEF symbol plastered to the vehicles was meaningless. Every truck, Land Cruiser, technical or van had been stolen or captured so many times that the only true owner was the person driving it now. Watching them drive down the few clear streets you could tell they wouldn't stop—they'd run over anything or anybody that got in the way. There was always a high level of tension. Many of the guards and drivers were younger than him, so he thought this might be an extreme sport for them.

That Wednesday, when Max had made the crossing, the city didn't seem to notice them. The plane was already on the ground when he arrived at the strip north of the city. He saw six passengers finding their bags and other equipment—no large cameras. Bradley Stokes was easy to spot—tall, with his aging athletic head held high.

"Max?" Bradley held out his hand. His face looked a bit puffy.

"Welcome Mr. Stokes,"

"It's Bradley. Good to meet you Max. You're doing a great job here."

"Thanks." Max looked past Bradley as two more men came up to them.

"Alan, Jeremy, I'd like you to meet Max…"

"Max Dubec, pleased to meet you."

"Dubec." Bradley said a bit after Max interrupted.

Alan had a military posture and handshake to match. Max guessed he was retired Army or Marines. His eyes were squinting at the perimeter, gauging his battle zone. He was on alert.

Jeremy also surveyed the terrain. "This reminds me of Oman. I was there for ten years and met a lot of Somalis...here at last." Jeremy was from the American south—his drawl matched his front porch friendliness.

"Do you speak Arabic?" Max asked.

"It'll come back. I know some Somali's speak Arabic. How long have you been here Max?"

"Not long enough to learn much Somali. Only a few months."

"Well, Bradley's been bragging on you, so you must be doing well. Do you like it here?"

"I do…" Max turned to Bradley, "So, we'll be taking everyone to the UN base in the North part of the city before we continue to the South." The van had the only shade, and he noticed the other passengers moving toward it. "Shall we?" Max headed back to the van where the other passengers were already getting in. When he came around the van he saw George, Hani's boss.

"Ah, Max. How are you? I see you have visitors." Max enjoyed talking to George—his clipped British understatements were calming.

"I'm good. I'll introduce you."

George pulled out a few cards. "We've met."

Bradley was going on about his memories of Somalia to Jeremy as the others rode in silence, listening to the loud talker. After about ten minutes the driver and the gunman looked to the left and pointed as a burst of sand erupted about 100 meters away. Everyone looked around. The woman seated right behind the driver was pointing at another plume of sand now fifty meters behind them. Another shell landed to their right, sending rocks and dirt against the side of the van. The driver turned the van around as the radio wailed in Somali. Everyone was bracing for the next blast. Max heard the UN plane heading out over the ocean. Several more shells landed behind them as the driver started to relax his pace. They pulled off the main track and headed away from the ocean, going toward some huts on the ridge.

"It's alright now," the driver said. "They cannot reach us here."

They pulled up to the ring of huts as goats scattered and an old man wearing a Russian greatcoat came out from the shade to meet them.

"It's a mistake, they've stopped now, no problem now," The driver told them.

"Who's shelling us?" asked the women behind the driver. Her companion in the battered safari vest was snapping pictures. "Is this from the North? Is this from Hadji Mahti?" She was taking notes and pointing for the camera guy. "Get this place." She pointed at the old man and the huts.

The driver said, "It is never mind." He was concentrating on his silent radio.

"Look," she told him. "We're being shelled by someone, who is it?"

The gunman opened the side door, indicating with the tip of his rifle that they should stand in the shade by the old man. The camera guy was snapping away as Bradley, Jeremy and Alan followed Max to the indicated spot. George and the woman held back. She kept asking questions until George accompanied her to stand in the shade with the others.

He was used to seeing George start a meeting. He'd stand and wait until the room was his. At the head of a room, or standing on a patch of desert, he was quietly in control. "I'm George Benswala. Our driver here has contacted the UNICEF office in the North. They know we are here. I think we are safe for now."

"I'm Nancy Farare, *New York Times*," said the woman. "That's Neal, my photographer."

Introductions were made all around before George resumed. "There has been a mistake, I'm sure. I've asked my colleague, Trevor, to contact Mr. Mahti for a guarantee so we can resume our short trip. We are only five minutes away."

Ms. Farare was holding out her tape recorder as George spoke. He frowned, but kept on speaking. "Where we are now is safe, and we should only need to be here for a little bit. This happens you know, after all, it's still a war."

Max's eyes stayed with Neal, who was now taking pictures of all of them. Bradley and Jeremy were heading back to the van, returning with their cameras in time to hear the driver on the radio. The driver then spoke to George, who looked at his watch.

"It seems," said George, "That Mr. Mahti himself is coming to apologize for the mistake. He should be here shortly. Perhaps," he said to Ms. Farare, "you can get an interview out of this."

When Hadji Mahti arrived, he came up to George and they shook hands like old friends. He was wearing a white scarf wrapped around his shoulders. His entourage included three new Land Cruisers and several well-dressed Somalis. No guns were revealed. Next, Mr. Mahti greeted the old man in the greatcoat, having received a salute that would not retire until he returned it.

His gaze swept over the group, pausing on Bradley for a second. "I want to apologize to all of you, it is a mistake, but since this war is being ignored so well by the West, not the UN to be sure…" He nodded to George then continued, "we must still be on guard. I assure you that you are safe, and I will do all I can to make your time here fruitful." He addressed Ms. Farare. "I hear you are from the *New York Times*. Any questions?" Neal was clicking closer and closer to him when one of his associates stepped between them. Mahti said something softly and the blockade was lifted, whereupon Neal got within two feet for a close up. He continued to answer Ms. Farare's questions in a brilliant display of savvy and sound bites. The reporter probed him on the war, on rumors of brutality by his troops, on The Boqor and his other rivals. He sneered at the mention of The Boqor, but stayed cool, taking aim at US policy toward Somalia—by which he meant his claim to be the legitimate ruler of Somalia. She pressed on until Mr. Mahti assured her that he'd be more than happy to allow an in-depth interview, if she would agree to let him show her the city, and perhaps accompany him into the countryside. She agreed to the interview, but she maintained that she intended to visit the South as well. "Very well, of course you are completely free." The interview ended with handshakes and a group photo, then George walked back to the convoy with Hadji Mahti.

George had little else to say on the remaining drive to the UN North compound. Nancy and Neal were making notes and Max's people were quiet.

They left the UNICEF compound for the drive back across town after five. George, Nancy and Neal stayed behind. Bradley and the others began speaking as soon as they left the North, taking only slight notice of the modern ruins. Jeremy had a lot of questions for Max, but Bradley kept interrupting with phrases mis-quoted from his reports—guiding the conversation back to the "tremendous opportunities."

26

That first evening, after the roasted camel and spaghetti, Max asked his cook to prepare Somali tea for his guests. He hadn't noticed the radio playing behind the house until the cook's daughter, Hibaaq, came out from the kitchen. Her head was covered with a golden scarf, and without saying a word she held everyone's attention, performing a ritual for the strangers in her tent. The music swirled around her as she poured out cups of tea and handed them to the guests, starting with Bradley, then Jeremy, then Alan. Max caught her eye when she handed him his cup. He gave her a smile and she bowed slightly, lowering her head and backing into the kitchen, with her mother watching.

Alan asked, "Did the house come with this?" he was pointing around at the cushions, table, and carpets.

"I had a choice, so I picked Somali style."

Bradley said, "A little hard on my back frankly. Didn't they have a sofa? That's a nice table in the dining room, so I bet they have some regular furniture. Of course, we'll need a much larger house soon." He looked over at Jeremy and said, "Remind you of Oman?"

"It does. Though in our house we had normal furniture, or western, I guess. We had lots of visitors from the States you know, kinda hard for some people to get down like this." He turned to Max and added, "But I like it, it fits with a place like this...though I might need to pull up a chair before I get a cramp."

Alan said, "I think it will be best to ship in the things you need for a house, make it more comfortable. You said this is the embassy district?"

Bradley spoke up, "Oh yes, the US embassy residences are close, some fine houses...much larger. A few years ago, Mogadishu was a pretty good place to live, lots of restaurants, a UN beach club...and there are great beaches a few miles south of here. I don't think you'll have too much trouble finding a good house in this part of Mogadishu, Jeremy."

"That would be good for our people, you know, to have Christians nearby. I know there won't be any churches, but we could have a small fellowship, or house church."

Bradley shot a look at Max, then said to Alan, "Tomorrow we'll go see Sharif and he can give you a good picture of the situation. I think we'll have a chance to grow our programs quickly. Being back on the ground early, and having a base of operations already functioning, should be a real advantage. Our donors certainly get it."

Alan got up, leaving his tea, and sat at the dining room table. Bradley did too. Jeremy stayed on the cushions and spoke to Max. "So, Bradley tells me that you were hired in Nairobi, a field hire."

"That's right. I was trying to find a job in Somalia, and Nairobi seemed to be the best place to make a connection, I got lucky to find Global Aid."

"Well, you seem to be doing well here, and that's something. It's not easy to find good people to work in a war zone. So, what church do you belong to in the States?"

Bradley tuned in.

"I don't belong to a church."

That stopped Alan and Bradley's conversation. Jeremy nodded his head sympathetically and said, "I see, well...have you ever read the Bible?"

"Some of it, sure. I've read about a lot of religions."

"I'm sure you're a very good person. Coming to Somalia to help your fellow man is what a believer would do. Have you ever considered letting Jesus into your life? I think you'd enjoy having his peace in your heart."

Bradley came over and stood next to Max. "Max came along at just the right time for us Jeremy. Now, I don't know about his background, and any hire is normally screened...a signed statement of faith and all...but I think God has sent him. And I thank God for him. God works in mysterious ways, isn't that right? And, Max is just the interim manager until things get up to speed." Bradley patted Max's shoulder and added, "I'd be glad to have you stay and work with us Max, and I'm sure whoever becomes the Country Manager will be happy to have you on our team."

Max looked up at Bradley, who held his shoulder in a firm grip.

Jeremy processed this, then said, "I'd love to have a conversation with you about faith. I do think Bradley is correct in saying that God has sent you. I find that so wonderful, really, I do. Maybe you'll find the faith to believe that too. I'll pray for you."

Max wasn't sure if Jeremy meant to pray right now, out loud, or like at Annie's, silently—which he'd prefer. Apparently, this time it meant that Jeremy would do it later, without him, which was a relief.

27

The next morning, just before sunrise, Max sat on the veranda sipping his coffee. The next few days would be spent playing host. What could he show them? What did they need to see...to do? He went back inside to talk to the cook who was in the kitchen early this morning. He saw Hibaaq throwing a bucket of scraps to the pack of dogs over the wall behind the kitchen. He'd startled her, she raised her eyes and said, "Everything's hungry." There was a basket of mangoes on the table and the fresh poppyseed bread. He'd stopped noticing the tiny legs and continued to think of them as poppyseeds. He made more coffee.

The van from yesterday's trip was due back at Max's this morning. He'd hired it for the week to accommodate his guests. Hassen Tanzania would lead the detail with Hassen Mombasa's HiLux as the escort. Their first stop would be Sharif.

Sharif set out chairs for his guests, and after the greetings he invited them to sit. Asha served tea as Bradley turned over the conversation to Alan and Jeremy. Max listened as Sharif explained the feeding program, painting a picture of need, and danger. He seemed to have the pitch memorized. Bradley looked pleased.

Their next stop was UNICEF. Bradley pulled Max aside before they got in the van, "You don't need to come, I know my way around this part of town. Your Suleymaan can come though, very bright. We'll take you back to the house."

Bradley and company returned to the house just as everyone was preparing to estivate for the afternoon. He sought out Max. "George would like us to take a look at a new camp near the American School. Do you know where that is?"

"George from UNICEF? Why?"

"I told him we were expanding and he thought it might be a good fit for us. Anyway, I told him we would, tomorrow, first thing."

"I need to check with Sharif first."

"Good, that's right. I'm sure he'll agree. Should be fine."

He couldn't wait for them to leave.

The next morning Max met with Sharif about Bradley's request. Sharif dismissed the idea, saying, "Mr. Stokes makes many promises for us."

After two days of tours and meetings, Max had the house to himself for the afternoon. He blended into the slow-down along with his cooks, cleaners, and guards. A bit of lazy sweeping was going on behind the house and some laundry was being pinned to the line. The guards were at rest against the south wall. Two or three times an approaching car or truck could be heard on their street. He could see that his guards also listened for the van. The usual sounds that accompanied an afternoon like this consisted of the wash of traffic from Afgooye Road, and the breathless buzzing in the trees. All gun shots were read for their direction and distance, and discounted like too much advertising. But if the sounds came from these streets, if the shots sounded too close, the army inside the walls recognized its message at once.

The next vehicle Max heard was the HiLux, but the quickness of its approach registered with everyone inside and the guards grabbed their guns. They came to an informal attention with nervous eyes scanning the walls. The motor was still running outside the gate. Suleymaan pushed through the gate and looked for Max. "They will be coming here."

Max came down from the veranda. “Who? Bradley? Where are they now? Is Hassen Tanzania with them?”

"Yes, yes...your Americans, they are very difficult. They have rented a big house from…” Suleymaan stopped as everyone heard another vehicle come towards the gate.

"They're here!"

Suleymaan opened it to let the van and the HiLux inside. Hassen Tanzania got out and started ordering the guards to be ready. He alerted Annie’s guards too. Bradley looked angry. He came up to Max, pushing past Suleymaan.

“Your man Hassen is causing trouble, call him off. I don’t know what his problem is.”

Max didn’t know either, but before he could find out, they heard another vehicle approach.

Bradley told Hassen Tanzania to open the gate, but Hassen refused. “See,” Bradley said, “He won’t follow orders!”

Suleymaan peeked out, “It’s their new landlord and his men, they can’t be here. Hassen’s right.”

“Max! Let them in. I know them, they’re okay.”

“Not yet. I need to talk to Hassen Tanzania and Suleymaan first…”

“No, you need to listen to me. I’m in charge here, not you or your…” Hassen Tanzania fired his gun three times in the air, then yelled something over the wall. Max heard the people on the outside get in their Land Cruiser and speed away, firing off a few warning shots of their own.

“What are you doing? Why did he make them leave? They’ve invited us to dinner.” Bradley sneered at Max, “You’ve lost control of your people Max. Remember who you work for. You need to fix this!”

Max walked away from Bradley to talk with Suleymaan and Hassen Tanzania. Bradley slammed the door as he went into the house.

“Who were those guys, Suleymaan? What’s going on?”

Hassen Tanzania waited as Suleymaan explained, “The house that Mr. Stokes found for Jeremy is too close to The Boqor’s. Sharif would not want Global Aid working with these guys.”

The clan dynamics were unclear to Max, but he knew that Sharif had strong opinions about where they worked and who they worked with. He thought that Bradley understood this too—apparently not. “How do we fix this then?”

Hassen Tanzania said, “They should go. They cannot be here or we will have trouble. Mr. Stokes would not listen.”

Suleymaan said, “I can have someone drive Mr. Stokes back there.”

“Then what?” asked Max.

“I think they should try and get out of any deal they’ve made...and get out of Somalia too. Please Max...they bring trouble. They are beyond your protection."

Hassen Tanzania nodded in agreement, then went to talk to his crew.

Max went to the house to talk to Bradley.

Bradley was sitting at the dining room table. "This is what I know," started Max. "You made a deal with these guys, and according to Suleymaan, and Hassen Tanzania, they will cause us trouble. They’re not someone Sharif is comfortable with.”

"Look, all we did was rent a house for Jeremy's organization. It's in a very good neighborhood, a big house close to important people...it will be safe there." He started to stand up.

Max held out both hands, palms down, to make Bradley sit and listen.

"Maybe we can unravel this tomorrow, but for tonight you need to return to where you started this and try to cancel or pay off these deals. You cannot be here. I'm not really sure what the problem is, but we need to work with Sharif. I'll see what he has to say. It could die down, but I don't know..."

Bradley stood up. "Sharif is not the director. And you...you take orders from me."

"I have to consider my staff, Mr. Stokes. We're only renting here. Hassen Tanzania and Suleymaan keep us safe, if we listen to them. If we don't, we can't do our work. You need to go back and get out of your agreement. It'll probably cost a few months' rent. Do you have enough money?"

Bradley headed down the hall and started grabbing the suitcases, stuffing in clothes and papers while talking to himself. When he came out, he said, "Give me Global Aid's cash...and think about finding a new job."

Well, thought Max, that's it. He went to his room for the cash, counting out five thousand dollars. The remaining twenty thousand belonged to the projects, not Bradley.

"Bradley snatched the cash from Max and said, "I'll go now, but you and I will meet with Sharif tomorrow."

"Please wait until you hear from me. I'm not sure Sharif wants you to come to the office. Let me see him first. See what the issues are, okay? I'm sorry, but everyone will be safer this way."

After Bradley left, Suleymaan spent a long time talking with Hassen Tanzania. Astur came by just before dark to make certain that the three Americans were gone. Suleymaan left with Astur, saying he'd come by in the morning to take Max to Sharif's.

During the night Max sat on the veranda and thought about where this was going. The gun shots felt closer, aimed at them instead of the sky. It would be best for Bradley, Jeremy and Alan to leave Somalia tomorrow. Hani needed to bump someone and get them out of here. After that, he was pretty sure he'd be fired. What would happen then—to Hani and him. This incident was on his watch, and it touched everyone—the refugees, Sharif, Suleymaan...Annie...maybe even Hani.

He stayed up most of that night in solidarity with his protectors. He'd gone around back to join some of the guards in their evening tea, making eye contact and trying to look worth protecting. Around midnight the rain started, coming off the ocean in a mist. Bales of thin blue blankets sat next to him on the veranda. He listened to the rain and felt it lowering the temperature, coming for those balancing on the edge of life.

28

The clean air from last night's rain lingered. Hassen Tanzania started loading bales of blankets into truck as soon as Suleymaan arrived. He was early. Max had coffee ready in the dining room. Suleymaan's eyes were wide and unblinking as he faced Max across the corner of the mahogany table. Max asked, "What is it?

"They killed Maliq! Your office has been robbed."

"And Sharif?"

"They drugged him with some powder. When he woke up the office was robbed, everything is turned over. Maliq was found by Miriam this morning. They killed him Max!"

On that same fresh morning, Hani arrived at her desk to find three Somali men coming out of George's office. Her sense of dread increased when she was asked to come into his office.

"George cleared his throat, "Hani, dear...I'm afraid you'll need to return to Nairobi for a bit."

"Why? What have I done?"

George tented his fingers as he looked at her. "It's not about you. But it seems that Max is in some sort of trouble…and, well, it would be better for you to be out of Mog for a while. Max has become a bit hot right now, and since you two seem to be close, it could involve you. His director has made some trouble that threatens their work here. So, just to be safe, it's best that you work out of the Nairobi office for a few weeks. I'll see that Max flies out to Kenya soon. You can talk to him there...so please be on this afternoon's flight." George stood up, indicating that this was all he planned to say. In the silent suspension of the room, she felt her world spinning out of control.

She left the office and found O waiting by the van. "Ah, Hani, we must go."

Does everyone know? she wondered. "Wait. I need to talk to Hersi."

Hersi was barely visible between the espresso machine and the thatched screen. His eyes told her to wait. Boutros brought her coffee like every other day, but she didn't notice. Hersi came over after one of the men she'd seen in George's office got up and left.

"Hersi." she said, touching his arm. "Please tell me what's going on, where's Max?"

"I haven't seen him today, but I saw Suleymaan, and there's some trouble. Sharif's watchman was killed, and there was trouble at Max's house yesterday."

"Tell him I'm going to Nairobi, please make sure he flies out today. He can have a seat."

Hersi squeezed her hand. "I look after you both, you're my family. My clan."

Max was watching from the alley with Suleymaan. He didn't want her to see him until he knew what this meant. He peeked from the alley into Hersi's back door. When Hersi saw him, he quickly looked over his shoulder, then hesitated, giving him a sign to wait. After a minute he came back into the kitchen and said, "The American was here this morning looking for you. He says you must meet him at Hodan's by noon. Hani is leaving for Nairobi today, part of the trouble, I think. She thinks someone told Benswala to get her out of Somalia."

"The American, did he leave a note? Did he say why?" Max stopped. This wasn't Hersi's problem. He needed to see George. "I'm sorry Hersi...I'm always bringing you trouble."

"Never mind my friend. Be careful."

Back in the alley, Max and Suleymaan watched Hani get into the UN van. He touched Max on the forearm and said, "She is ready, do we follow her to the plane?"

"No. You follow and be sure the plane leaves with her on it. Then go to Sharif, you're family. Have Hassen Mombasa meet me at the house at eleven thirty."

Max watched from the shade of the wall after Suleymaan drove away, then walked across the road to the UNHCR office to see George.

He knocked on George's half open door. "Ah, Max." He stood up and crossed to the door, closing it quietly and motioning for him to take a seat. "You, my friend, are in a bit of a pinch I take it."

"Quite." he replied.

"I'm afraid your director and his companions will be staying for another day or two, until we can secure safe transport for them. This clan business takes time. But, don't worry, keep your head down for a few days and this should all resolve. In the meantime, as I'm sure you're aware, Hani is off to Nairobi—a good place for you too, I imagine."

"What have you heard, George?"

"Keeping situations from exploding is my business. Sharif's guard being killed this way, only few hours after your director stumbles into a clan feud, is an escalation we don't want to continue. I recommend you join Hani in Nairobi as soon as you can...it will all be here when you return." George stood up and asked him to exit through the back hallway. "So many eyes here, right?"

"So many eyes." Max muttered to himself as he crossed over the road. Walking the alleys back to his house, he imagined being shot in the chest right here, right...now. Until yesterday he was feeling more at home on these streets—beginning to see the battle lines. Now he felt the limitations of his immunity.

Suleymaan returned at 11:15. Max was waiting on the veranda.

"She is in the air. Safe."

"Thanks, Suleymaan...you okay? Have you seen Sharif?"

"I need to go to my home. I can't go to Sharif's right now, I'm best at home today. Are you going to Nairobi too?"

"No, I'll stay in Somalia. I'm going to meet someone at Hodan's. I think he'll have some answers. Bradley, Jeremy and Alan will get out in a few days, but for now they're our problem. I might be an hour at the most. We'll talk later, maybe I'll know something more." He felt there was so much more to say, but it would have to wait.

29

Dr. Hodan ran a local NGO on the southern edge of Mogadishu, where the road crested the hill and bent out toward the west. The last time Max saw her was when he brought a donor from the Netherlands to meet her. A meeting with Hodan was good for a donation of at least $25,000. She had a small refugee camp around her faded blue two-story hospital. The camp was just small enough to grasp the numbers. For the Dutch representative this was comforting—he could count them. Scale was Hodan's genius, and her eyes always matched her beautiful smile.

He was sick the first time he met her. He'd been unable to eat or get out of bed for several days. It wasn't malaria, or giardia, but something a lot of aid workers were coming down with. He was too sick to fly to Nairobi, so he'd spent four days in bed. Suleymaan had been worried about him—or for his job—and brought Hodan by the house to take a look at him. Like an older sister she'd looked down at him, and after getting a few answers to the routine questions, she said, "Homesickness. You should go to Nairobi when you feel a bit better."

Max arrived on time. John Thomas was waiting outside the hospital. "Dr. Hodan has made her office available, let's talk in there."

Hodan's office was in a large store room with one window facing east. Her desk was not set up for meetings, but for work. Besides the desk, the room was filled with old medical equipment; X-ray machines, autoclaves, walkers, crutches, and boxes of expired medicines. She did not turn down donations. She'd hung a framed copy of her medical diploma next to a picture of her standing with Boutros Boutros-Ghali. The photo looked recent. He saw Hodan as a friend. Like Suleymaan, her face was pleasant to look at and her eyes were true. He searched John's eyes. They arranged two chairs, facing each other next to the desk.

"Let's see," he began. "Your project here is in danger from the actions of your director and his friends. Then your warehouse guard was killed. This might not be the end of it, but I can help you keep it together, if you'll let me."

"I think I have it worked out for now, but thanks."

"What I think you have worked out with Mr. Benswala is temporary."

"What does all this have to do with you? Did you have George remove Hani?"

"You need to go to Luuq, today, if you want this to stop. And yes, I thought she'd be safer in Nairobi."

Max's head spun as his gaze wandered around the hot office. He saw sacks of French milk powder behind the door—Hodan and Boutros Boutros watched from their frame on the wall.

"What will make this stop? Is Ali Nur behind this trouble?"

"We would like to fund your farm project at Geed Weyn. Ali Nur will make sure your feeding centers stay open. All of your staff will be protected."

"Is that the deal? Really? If I don't go to Luuq, you shut down our camps, kill the staff...kill me, even Hani?"

"I think you're blowing it out of proportion. Ali Nur isn't making this trouble. He's offering to protect you. To get things done here you've got to choose sides, and right now this side needs you to take advantage of the offered protection. Go with Omar today and start the farm. It's a good project. I've been told that Sharif can run things just fine without you. You need to trust me

Max. Without our help you can't stay in Somalia. If we work together, you'll be able to develop the farm, and maintain the feeding centers in Mogadishu and the Lower Juba."

"Is this really about one agriculture project?"

"That's part of it, but let me lay it out for you."

"Please."

"I think you know that USAID, or OFDA for that matter, are not really interested in beginning development projects while this civil war is going on. What I'm going to tell you is strictly confidential." John leaned in toward Max. "We do have an interest in you being at Geed Weyn."

"Who is we?" Max wanted to hear it out loud.

"Your government." John put up a hand to keep Max from interrupting. "Somalia is at a critical juncture. We're trying to avoid a massive humanitarian disaster on one hand and a dangerous shift in the world order on the other. Somalia is in the middle of both. As far as the US government is concerned both of these dangers need to be stopped. Bill Clinton will be inaugurated in a little more than a month. There are plans in place to send in US Marines under the cover of a Humanitarian mission, but it needs to happen before the new administration is in place. Right now, the Clinton folks are against any invasion plans, but in the interregnum, Bush still has the authority to act."

Max was trying to keep up with the direction this conversation was heading.

"Farah Mohamed, The Boqor, is not a friend of the United States. Ali Nur was his spokesman in New York at last summer's UN conference on Somalia. Since then, he has signaled that he wants our help in displacing his uncle. If that were to happen, if The Boqor is somehow removed from power, then we think Ali Nur would make a more friendly ally.

The Boqor would be a problem for any US troops entering Somalia."

Max thought Ali Nur had been quite clear on his opinion of UN or US troops in Somalia.

"Ali Nur is in a dangerous game, but we have a common goal that makes him a good bet right now. That shift in the world order I mentioned? Well, that is something that both Ali Nur and the US government want to prevent. Radical Wahhabi cells are forming throughout the Middle East and Africa. We see these cells as a larger threat. They've practically taken over large areas in Afghanistan and Pakistan. There are new groups now in Sudan. Somalia is their next target. Right now, these groups are working in Somalia under the cover of a few Saudi based relief agencies. The aid and support they give to Hadji Mahti is matched by what they supply to The Boqor. What they want is a failed state. Even though Somalia's neighbors have no love for Somalia, they, and we, do not want an Afghanistan on the Horn of Africa. Still with me Max?"

"Yep, still waiting to see where I come in."

“The US can act to counter this trend. Working with Ali Nur, to see if he can weaken his uncle, is one way we can provide assistance without a more robust military presence. That takes guns and money. With you operating a project in the Gedo, between Luuq and Mandera, we have a way to supply them under the cover of your farm in Geed Weyn. Ali Nur has agreed to this arrangement. You would be the go-between, and you'd have a cover for importing what Ali Nur needs. He trusts you Max."

"How much of this does Bradley know?" Max asked.

"He’ll know that we’re funding your Geed Weyn project. He’ll also know that it is a special circumstance, and to leave you alone. But it depends on you. We’ll give our assurance, along with Ali

Nur's, that your work in Mogadishu and Kismayo will be able to continue. Sharif is able to keep it going, right Max?"

"How long do I need to be there? How long will this take?"

"By the end of January, you should be free to return full time to Mogadishu, or go home to Washington, if you like. I'll make sure that Hani is safe."

"Keep her out of this, this has nothing to do with her. If Ali Nur isn't successful, and The Boqor comes after everyone that worked against him, can you protect us from that?"

"This is an attempt to stop the all-out destruction of Somalia. If Ali Nur fails then there will be no foreign aid workers in Somalia—just the terrorists. We'll pull your staff out in plenty of time if it starts to go that way. Right now, you don't believe it, but you are in a unique position to change the direction of the civil war here." John sat back and studied him.

"How does this work then. Am I stuck in Geed Weyn as a freight agent for Ali Nur? Is there really a farm project?"

John pulled out a brief, but official looking document for the Geed Weyn project, and the name of his contact in Mandera. "Spend time setting up your base there. Go ahead and start the farm. You'll be able to travel to Mandera to receive the containers of farm and other supplies. We'd prefer that you stay away from Nairobi until the new year. By then we'll know if Ali Nur is our man. If you agree, I'll get your director and his companions back to Nairobi today."

"What will you explain to Hani?"

"I'll look her up in a few days, when I'm back in Nairobi. She'd be proud of you, but she'll never know the details."

Max left the office and looked for Hodan, but she was gone. Omar's Land Cruiser was idling next to the Hilux—his backpack and messenger bag were already in the back seat. He sent Hassen Mombasa back to the house with a message that he was going to be in Luuq for a bit, but that everything else was to keep going. Before they drove away, he turned to the sky, following the sound of an airplane.

PART 2

30

Hani watched the ocean pushing in on Somalia—a view she remembered sharing with Max the first time they met. The circumstances were different when she left Mozambique, but the sense of loss was familiar. Despite George's assurances that her removal was temporary, it felt final. Mara insisted on taking her suitcase as they walked to the bus stop near Wilson Field. It took two transfers to get to Mara's flat, where Hani spent half an hour putting her things back in the drawers and looking at what she'd left behind when she took the job in Mogadishu.

Mara had everything ready when Hani came out to the living room. After drinking a glass of wine in silence, Mara placed a bath towel around Hani's shoulders. Hani let her head rest into Mara's hands as she started combing out her long black hair. Her breathing slowed and she closed her eyes. The silver slicing sound of the scissors danced around her head, making little cries with every cut. Mara will know, she thought, she'll know how far to go. Loss clarifies what's gone—what you want to keep. Max was gone, maybe her career too. When Mara stopped, Hani felt the short bristles, running her fingers over her head, feeling it's new shape.

31

Another airplane left Mogadishu a few hours after Hani's. John Thomas sat on one side while Bradley, Alan and Jeremy sat on the other. As Somalia's coastline disappeared, John carefully, and incompletely, explained the situation. “We need Max in Geed Weyn for a while. Until he’s finished, we, the US Government, will assist you in Mogadishu. That will require some coordination from your Nairobi office, but I believe Sharif can handle things in Mogadishu. We'll be able to check in with Max from time to time in Mandera, just across the Kenyan border."

Bradley objected, "We need our own manager in Mogadishu—Sharif is good...I know, he's been with us for years, but we need our own...own person, staff... international staff. Alan here is going to be our Africa Director in Nairobi, and he'll need to have contact with all our staff, including Max."

"I'm afraid you cannot contact Max for now. We'll see how things go, but he’ll be busy for a while, and we don't want him compromised by any unauthorized contact."

Alan sat forward, "I'm retired military Mr. Thomas. While I appreciate the fact that you've chosen Global Aid for a special assignment, we need to know what *not* to do. And, it seems like Max still needs the cover of working for Global Aid." Bradley nodded approvingly.

“We think that his official status as a relief worker will survive the next few months without any contact. To your first point Mr. Dullen, the less you know the better. Work with Sharif to keep the feeding centers operating. This is the best goodwill you can generate, and therefore the best protection for everyone, especially Max."

John looked at all three of them and said, "This is strictly confidential. Last July we were made aware of a potential US ally in our attempt to de-escalate the fighting in Southern Somalia. A high-ranking member of The Boqor's clan is willing to work with the US to disrupt his hold on Southern Somalia. The area includes Luuq and Geed Weyn. When this first came to our attention we contacted your Africa Director, Mr. French. He forwarded us Max's name. Since Max has been in Somalia, we've been keeping an eye on him and helping him from time to time. Our contact has agreed to have Max as our go-between." John paused to make his point. "Your recent troubles could have been much worse had it not been for his relationships in Somalia. Your difficulties, however, prompted us to accelerate the plan. Our goal is to reduce the danger to our troops, should they land in Southern Somalia in the future. I remind you this is not to be discussed once we land in Nairobi. And, should events proceed as we anticipate, there will be lots of grants available."

"And if things don't go as planned?" asked Jeremy.

"Well, then we have a failed state on the Horn of Africa that would rival Afghanistan. It will be much harder to provide relief for the humanitarian disaster that will certainly follow."

Bradley and company arrived at Settlers Rest as the sun set into a pink haze. As an entry point into East Africa, the hotel offered a view of colonial civility, as long as you didn't linger too long outside the walls and gardens. A twenty-foot-tall hedge screened out the lane that curved beneath it. Inside these walls Bradley relaxed his jaw and rolled his shoulders as he waited on the terrace. Alan and Jeremy sat down, showered and bwana casual.

"How do things look now?" Bradley asked as he scanned the garden. "I love finishing a trip here. It's quiet enough to think. Right?"

Jeremy said, "Well, there's a lot to think about, considering what we just heard...and experienced."

Alan said, "It's best to leave the Max thing alone, Jeremy."

Jeremy took his eyes off of Alan and refocused on Bradley. "Is this common? Have you run into this before?"

"What?" said Bradley

Jeremy whispered, "Working with spies." Then he added, "I think this *Max thing* is tied to Global Aid and its partners in Somalia. My board doesn't like complications."

"I wouldn't assume that John Thomas is a spy. But I don't think you should discuss this with your board, Jeremy."

Jeremy nodded slowly while turning his Tusker around and around on the table. "I understand the need for secrecy." He kept turning the bottle. "So, it was your Mr. French that sent Max into this. Did you know about it?"

"No. Don was in charge. Sometimes you have to act without a committee. It's like Vegas—what happens out here, stays out here."

32

Bradley's flight to London would depart around midnight. He left Alan and Jeremy to dine together while he went to the office for a late meeting with Josie. Alan would start running things tomorrow morning and Bradley wanted to maintain an open channel with her. He needed her updates, as well as her eyes. He couldn't afford another set-back like Don French. He spent fifteen minutes locked in Don's office before he came out and took a chair in front of Josie's desk.

"Thank you for staying late. I wanted to tell you personally that Alan will be taking over as Africa Director in the morning. Hopefully he'll get things back on track, starting with Somalia. So, you know, Max will be out of Mogadishu for a while. Alan will need your help getting up to speed. He'll be spending some time in Somalia until we can get a proper Country Manager."

It was news to her that Alan would be her new boss in the morning. He hadn't made much of an impression, but she didn't really care who used Don's office. Like Sharif, she just wanted someone that wouldn't make trouble.

"Please Mr. Stokes, tell me what is happening with Max?"

"Max will be okay, Josie. For now, he'll work in Geed Weyn on our farm project. He's got a special assignment that I can't share with you right now. I think Don might have known more about this than any of us. What do you remember about the time when Max was hired?"

She came out from behind her desk and took the chair facing him. "Mr. Stokes, Mr. French was not well. He hired Max only a few weeks before he left. It was so fast."

"Do you remember any meetings or contacts he made around then? Maybe USAID?"

"Yes. There was one meeting he had with someone from OFDA. It was the week before we hired Max. I had his card, but I gave it to Max. I believe the same person called once since that meeting. Mr. French was getting very private so I don't know all that he did."

"Do you remember the name on the card?"

"No." It was the first time she'd lied to him. "When will Max be able to come to Nairobi again?"

"It'll be a while, maybe a few months."

"Ahh, that is too long."

"I know. But Max is doing a good thing up in Geed Weyn. It is dangerous for him and dangerous for us to look too closely. Alan knows about Max's situation. He'll keep you in the loop." With that, Bradley stood up. "Could you call me a taxi, I should be leaving soon."

"I can have my husband give you a ride sir. It would be no problem at all." She knew what the answer would be. She'd known Bradley for years and never once had he accepted her invitations to dinner or a ride to the airport.

"No, Thank you. I'll just take a taxi at this hour."

When Alan showed up the next morning Josie had the coffee ready. After a quick tour of the office, he took the same chair that Bradley chose in front of her desk.

"I hear you've kept Global Aid going since last summer. Bradley speaks highly of you."

"Thank you, Mr. Dullen." Josie said.

"Please, I'm Alan, between us. Okay?"

"Very well, Alan. How can I assist you?"

"Well, frankly, I think I'll be learning from you."

"Do you know what's happening with Max, Alan?"

"I'll let you know when I can, but don't expect any real news for a while. I think Max can take care of himself out there. Why don't we go over the project files. I'm making some field visits in the next few weeks."

"I'll bring in the files, Mr. Dullen."

———

Hani spent two days in Mara's flat. She didn't check in with UNICEF, but she called her mentor, Roger at UNDP, hoping he'd know how she could get a ride to Mandera. She was unable to reach John Thomas, whom she suspected wasn't really with USAID. And, she called Josie at Global Aid and set up a meeting. They agreed to meet at the mall on Argwings Kodhek Road, near Global Aid.

———

Josie left the office with enough time for a treat before Hani arrived. She ordered a strawberry-banana smoothie, asking for whole milk instead of the skim milk that was becoming so prevalent in stores where the foreigners shopped. The thin bluish milk looked like it came from weak cows, and she was not on a diet. She took a table on the edge near the entrance and watched.

When Hani walked in, they looked at each other, recognizing a bond. Hani held out the flowers. "Thank you so much for taking the time to meet me."

"My pleasure. I'm anxious to hear what you know about Max. When you last saw him, and what you think is going on. I'll let you know what I've found out...but it's not enough."

She took out a folder from her bag and laid it open on the table. She slid a photo across to Hani. It was a photo of Max taken the day he was hired last summer. Watching Hani's intense gaze and her breathing confirmed what she heard over the phone—there was love here somewhere.

"The last time I saw him was the day before your director came to Mogadishu, last week. I heard there was trouble, but I was forced to leave before I found out anything."

Josie pushed two more pictures toward her.

"This is the camp at Geed Weyn back then. I think the farm Max is developing is just behind these guys."

"That's Rana! Are these buildings still there? Is this where Max is living now?" Hani looked at every face and squinted to see beyond them.

"Yes. According to Sharif this is where Max is now." She pointed to the other picture. "And this is the nearest town in Somalia, Luuq."

Hani looked at the street scene, where drooping trees shaded an open market square. She looked into the faces of the people captured walking and talking. "But won't Max be coming to Nairobi soon?"

"No, I don't think so. But I did find the name of the bank manager in Mandera where the farm account is." Lying to Bradley still felt disloyal, but going through Alan's desk did not.

34

Hani was surprised by the phone call from John Thomas. His voice sounded relaxed as he apologized for not returning her calls. They agreed to meet at a restaurant that she knew.

The restaurant was tucked in a narrow alley between a primary school and a church. A tall hedge lined the patio where light green umbrellas shaded the tables. The sound of children playing drifted through the leaves. She saw him looking directly at her, sitting at a table with his back against the hedge.

He stood up. and held out his hand. "Hani, nice to meet you. I'm John, John Thomas. I've seen you with Max at Hersi's."

When they were both seated John pushed a menu towards her and said, "Why don't we order some lunch? I'm starving, and besides I'd like to make our meeting last long enough so that I can call it a day. It's on me."

She agreed right away, not wanting to engage in a series of polite refusals and then settling for a token meal. She was actually hungry, and the longer they talked the more she would learn. It took until their lunch was served for John to assure her that her position with UNICEF was not in jeopardy. She hadn't asked, but she let him talk while only nodding and answering a few times. John gave the impression that UNICEF was nothing more than an extension of his agency. While he was talking, she was looking at the business card he'd handed her. It was from the Office of Foreign Disaster Assistance, OFDA. Max's farm project was being funded by USAID. She thought that both of these might be covers for something else.

Eating the savory ribs was messy. The barbecue sauce was too good to waste so the conversation was accompanied by the licking of fingers and wiping of mouths.

Last night Hani and Mara talked about how she should approach the meeting. Mara thought she should employ a flirty demeanor in order to get to his secrets. She had lots of advice about men, especially American men, having studied them through films. Hani determined not to let him control this meeting. He was not her employer or in a position of authority. As she watched him eating, with sticky fingers and a stain on his white shirt, she was confident that she could handle this American. She had her defenses up around men like him—well educated and climbing toward some senior position in the home country. They exuded authority even in situations they knew nothing about. Those that started in the Peace Corps were some of the best. If he'd been in the Peace Corps, then he'd be sure to tell her.

They ordered a second round of Tuskers as they were licking the last of the barbecue sauce off of their fingers.

She asked, "What is Max doing in Luuq? I know it's not just an agricultural project. And why does George think I'm in danger?"

John took notice of the new direction and sat up in his chair, his head slightly to one side. "I can't tell you more than you already know. But first I want to know why I should tell you anything. Are you more than just...colleagues?"

"That's none of your business!"

"Hani, I'm sorry. Really, it's just a question of relationship...the more serious, the more I can tell you." The particular tilt of his head this time looked genuine.

"Then, yes. I love Max Dubec. So, can you tell me what he's doing in Luuq?" Having just confessed her love, first name and last, in front of a government representative, seemed official.

"You know about his work and about his trip to Luuq, anything else?"

"Okay." She said as she rearranged her chair. "I'll answer your questions, but then it's your turn to tell me something I don't know."

"That sounds a bit like strip poker to me." he said.

"Well, I would like to see everything you've got...about Max." That came out wrong. Maybe it was the alcohol that was pulling them into a hazy flirtation, or maybe this was needed to get the truth.

He looked at his watch and said, "First, before we go on, if I leave too soon, I'll be expected to return to my gloomy office downtown. Then I'd spend the rest of this afternoon doing paperwork. If we have one more round it will definitely be too late to head back into town."

He was hitting on her. Mara was right. "Okay then let's have another," she agreed.

"Where were we? Ah, yes. Do you know about Ali Nur and Zaynab?"

"Yes, and I know that Max is somehow under their protection. Which, I assume, was why they took him, and me, out of Mogadishu. But why?"

"Has Max told you how extremely beautiful Zaynab is? She's quite a legend you know." The beer arrived and they both took long pulls from the chilled bottles before he continued. "What do you think the connection is between Ali Nur, Zaynab, the farm at Geed Weyn and Max?"

"I don't know. Why don't you tell me?"

"But you do have a hunch or a guess, don't you?"

"All I know is that Max is in some kind of danger and I'm sick of this game you're playing with his life. Who are you anyway? CIA?"

"You don't want to know Hani, really. This may sound hyperbolic, but Max is playing an important part in trying to stop the fighting in Somalia. And yes, he is in some danger. He was also in danger when his guests fucked up in Mogadishu."

"Max is being held hostage in Luuq as a part of your agency's plan, right?"

"You're seeing part of it, but Max is not a hostage, per se."

"Then what kind of hostage is he?" she snapped back.

"Max is not a hostage at all. He made a deal. One that might help bring an end to the civil war in Somalia. If all goes well, and even if it doesn't, Max should be in Nairobi in three or four weeks. You need to be patient. You already know enough—too much really. You can't share any of this, not with Josie or anyone at UNICEF. It's best if everyone thinks that Max is just setting up his agency's farm project in Geed Weyn. We don't want any of this other stuff known...especially who he's working with. The wrong people could connect the dots and that would be dangerous for Max."

"But why Max?"

"Max came along at the right time, and he seemed...well, unattached. We've been watching him and he's done well. Global Aid has history in Luuq, Ali Nur trusts him, so it all fit. Global Aid's not involved in this beyond hiring Max. Really, you shouldn't know any of this. Wait it out in Nairobi, Hani. I'll keep an eye on him, don't worry."

A new sound floated through the hedge. It was the same children's voices, except now they were singing in unison. They stopped to listen.

"Mali." he said.

"Mali? What about Mali?"

"I was in the Peace Corps there." He paused, then asked, "Are you okay? I can't tell you anything else right now, except that the day Max went to Luuq he made me promise to make sure you were safe."

"He did?" Hani's heart jumped in her chest.

"Yep, He was looking out for the feeding centers, for Sharif and Suleymaan, for Rana in Kismayo, but I think he was mostly thinking of you. You can call me again and I'll return your call promptly. I promise." He put his hand over his heart.

As Hani made her way back to Mara's, she thought about telling Josie what she learned, but she wasn't sure that she should. He'd made a point about the need for secrecy. But being patient in Nairobi wasn't going to happen. Max needs someone else watching out for him, and Mandera was as close as she could get right now.

After John watched her walk out of the restaurant, he felt profoundly lonely. He attributed this to the alcohol, but he knew it only let his thoughts roam around more freely. From practice, John was replaying their conversation in his head. Tomorrow he'd need to write up an Encounter Report. His boss, Mark Walters, had given him the task of handling Max, who seemed to be going along so far. Hani might need attention. As he let his memory reconstruct each sentence, he regretted suggesting that her relationship with Max was nothing more than a hook-up. Looking into her pretty Indian face, where the color of eyes and teeth played so beautifully on dark skin, he let himself slip back to Mali. Bamako was different than Nairobi, but it was Africa. The choir he'd been listening to wasn't the party music of Mali, and Hani wasn't someone he knew a long time ago.

35

Max stood just beyond the covered porch of the kitchen watching the stars and listening to Mohamed saying his prayers in the breezeway. Kerosene lamp light flickered through the screens of Yasmin and Xabiib's room—the two sisters that Zaynab brought from Luuq keep house for Max and Mohamed. Yasmin the older, and Xabiib the younger, treated Mohamed like a father, and Max like Zaynab's guest. This evening they'd made evening tea into a Somali/English lesson, including him in the simple pleasure of speech. Being able to watch them talking, laughing, and working around the camp filled up a few hours of the long days and nights.

Max finished looking at the stars as the moon slid lower, touching the branches of the giant acacia that shaded his suite. Mohamed called it Python, after the twelve-foot snake they'd pulled from underneath the building years ago. The reality of his kidnapping, his involvement in the overthrow of a warlord, and the ghost of the serpent beneath him were occasionally eclipsed by the domestic world of Geed Weyn. Guilt stalked his better moods, and thoughts of Hani were saved for the mosquito net in the evenings. Yasmin's radio came on when Mohamed finished his prayers, sending out waves of spiced Somali poetry set to Arabian strings. The Juba River moved under the stars at the same frequency as he settled into his hammock, letting it rock back and forth, suspended. This would have been the time they'd spend telling stories, her skin touching his in the dark.

The mornings here belonged to the birds. Their songs and screeches were matched by their brilliant colors—bright yellow with red under feathers, and the iridescent blues of sunshine on a tropical lagoon. Max made his way down the steep path to the shower on the river bank. He threw a few rocks at the pallet that served as the shower floor, and when nothing slithered out or ran away, he hung his shorts and tee shirt over the blue tarp that shielded the shower from the camp. He turned around to face the other bank, as the barely filtered river water ran over him. Last night's images of Hani were more potent in the morning. He listened, and when he could account for the all the others sonically, he yielded to his memory of her body and her touch.

A squawk from Mohamed's radio silenced the birds. His VHF radio usually just emitted a series of static-like codes. This morning's code was followed by a voice—someone was coming.

Ali Nur arrived driving the promised technical, no other vehicles, no Omar, just Ali Nur. After he greeted Mohamed, he turned towards Max. He'd seen shades of this Ali Nur in Luuq, like a man at home—safe.

"You're here." he said, as if Max had made a choice. "We have a lot to discuss, yes?"

"We do." said Max.

"My sister will be coming with a feast tonight. You will be our guest. I'll come over to your room in a bit." With that Ali Nur went over to the others. Yasmin and Xabiib were standing at attention next to Mohamed.

Max went into the kitchen and got a bottle of water out of the little kerosene refrigerator. He checked on the ice cubes. It had taken two days to make ice, but he'd fiddled with the wick yesterday and got a much better flame. He went over to his office to prepare for the meeting. The desk was covered in old farm documents and maps, and an emergency evacuation plan from 1983. The road-map to Mandera was marked with numbers that corresponded with a few photographs he found in the pocket of the folder. He pulled out his revised list of farm supplies.

When he heard Ali Nur step up onto the breezeway, he re-staged his maps and paperwork, leaving the list on top and sliding the evacuation plan under the pile. Ali Nur knocked on the office wall as he stepped into the doorway.

"We can talk." He scanned the little office, going slowly over the items on Max's desk.

Max moved the conversation to the breezeway.

Ali Nur said, "Is everything good for you? Tell Zaynab if you need anything"

"It works. It's good to have Mohammed, Yasmin, and Xabiib here."

"I'm leaving the technical here...but it is only safe to drive between Luuq and Mandera."

"I have a list of supplies I'll need for the farm."

"Show me."

Max grabbed it off the desk along with a map of the Gedo District. Ali Nur slid out a pair of glasses and looked over the list.

"Other Items?" Ali Nur's finger rested on the line item.

Max wanted to hear it from Ali Nur as well as John Thomas." I know that this farm is just cover...a way to conceal the guns and money you need. I can do this if I know that you'll continue to protect the work in Mogadishu, and the Lower Juba."

"Of course. We've all made a deal that we dislike. Your interests are protected."

"I didn't make a deal. I'm here because of a threat."

"You must play your part. You came to help Somalia, didn't you?"

"What happens if you fail? How does your protection help then?"

"By then Mogadishu and Kismayo will be occupied by your Marines. Agencies like yours will be protected, since one of you might be the son or daughter of a congressman. We can be open Max. It is good to be clear. But this is between us. You need to make a farm here. Everyone must see it happening, they must believe it."

"I understand. So, the list?" Max asked.

"These items are available in Nairobi?"

"They should be," said Max. "The hand tractors are Italian, but they have a distributor in Nairobi."

Ali Nur was nodding, adding up the list in his head. "Then I will have these," he pointed to Max's items, "And, these," pointing to Other Items, at the border in four days, Friday."

"And then I'll go to Mandera to sign for them, right?"

"You know about Mr. Hassen? At your bank? He'll go over the procedure on the Kenyan side when you meet him. The Somali side will be no problem. You'll lead your trucks back here, simple."

Max reached out for the list in Ali Nur's hand. "I'll number the items. Prioritize them. Once the first container arrives, we'll be able to start working the land."

"Zaynab's farm is much more than a cover. You can get a good start no matter what happens.

36

Ali Nur disappeared like everyone else in the heat of the afternoon. Max saw Mohamed resting on a cot in the breezeway of the building he shared with Yasmin and Xabiib. Yasmin was in the kitchen reading. He let the breeze rock him in the hammock. This morning's short talk with Ali Nur had only given him the outlines of his tasks, but there was a hint of hope in what he'd revealed. He thought that if he was expected to drive to Mandera all the time, he could just drive on to Nairobi before anyone would know he was gone. The thought didn't develop beyond that. Not yet, he thought.

Around 5 o'clock Mohamed's radio squawked twice. He saw Ali Nur come out of Mohamed's room. Yasmin and Xabiib came out of the kitchen to help Zaynab unload baskets of food. Ali Nur told Max to unhook his hammock. They'd use his breezeway for dinner tonight since it caught the breeze from the river. Ali Nur brought out a carpet and rolled it out on the deck. They moved the low table from the kitchen to the center of the carpet, then started to gather pillows and cushions to sit on. He told Max to guard the table, pointing up into the tree above them where he could see the troop of monkeys. He saw the first monkey yesterday. By the end of the day there had been eight. Now it looked like a dozen small grey monkeys, growing braver by the hour. Yesterday Mohamed told him, "I'll have to shoot one of them. Then they will all leave. But not yet."

The food came out in a rush. Xabiib was first with a large bowl with rice piled high in the middle. Yasmin was carrying a large platter with fresh tomato and cucumber slices. There was a smaller bowl in the center with hummus whipped up into a peak. Xabiib brought out another platter with triangles of puffy pastry that had a brown meaty sauce oozing out at the corners. The smells were a magnet that drew everyone to their places. Zaynab came out, almost running, with two large glass jars filled with tea. The sound of ice against the glass turned everyone's head.

Ali Nur instantly asked. "Where did you get that ice?”

“I brought this from Luuq's ice plant...it's working again."

Xabiib jumped up and ran to the kitchen, returning with a hand full of forks, spoons, and chopsticks.

Zaynab said, "Choose your weapon, or fight with your hands."

They sat silent until Ali Nur said something in Somali mixed with the Arabic *shukran* that Max recognized as thanks. Zaynab, Yasmin, and Xabiib bowed and held out their right hand, as if to say, ‘You first.’

At first there was no talking but lots of sounds. Max went fork-less, right handing into the hummus with a piece of bread he'd ripped off after seeing Mohamed do the same. Zaynab was telling him something about everything he reached for. The samosas filled with camel meat made this a feast.

Eating together, enjoying the smells and flavors...and even the feel of the food, had everyone flowing in an easy conversation. It was part Somali, part English and a little Italian. Yasmin was supplying the translations to her delight. He was able to follow some of the stories and memories that this meal was evoking. Many of the stories were about the aid workers that lived here ten years ago.

Mohamed told one story that Ali Nur kept interrupting with his own memories of the event. Yasmin's translations, and Ali Nur's English insertions were enough for Max to follow. There was this one American, a very big man named Floyd, who fooled them all. They were unloading a truck that was carrying the building materials for these buildings. It took ten people to lift each of the crates off the truck-bed. Floyd waved them all back as he grabbed the sides of the last crate. He grunted and strained as he pulled it to the edge of the bed, then he squatted down a little, and spread out his legs like a weightlifter. Mohamed and Ali Nur both stood up and struck the pose to illustrate. Then Floyd, with a loud shout, picked up the large crate and lifted it over his head. Everyone gasped, their eyes popping as he took a few steps toward the retreating crowd. Then he threw the crate down. the sides buckled, and everyone could see that it was filled with Styrofoam insulation. Mohamed said that he'd never seen this material before. A few of the Mogadishu Somalis, Ali Nur being one of them, saw the trick and started laughing and clapping at Floyd's show. Zaynab added that Floyd was a real heartthrob for a few of the Somali nurses in Geed Weyn, especially when they learned he had no wives, not even one.

All the ice had melted, and they'd eaten most of the food. Yasmin and Xabiib rose at the same time and started clearing the table. Zaynab reached across to Ali Nur, taking his hand. When he looked up at her, Max sensed a moment of resignation pass between them.

Ali Nur and Max moved the table back to the kitchen. Then Ali Nur said, "Bring out the two chairs and set them under your net. I'll be right back."

Max set up the chairs, with a small table between them. He could hear Zaynab above the other voices and laughter in the kitchen. He could also see Mohamed and Ali Nur searching in the container with a flashlight. Max let the mosquito net drape over the two chairs, and used a few stones to spread out the bottom.

As he waited for Ali Nur he stood on the edge of his deck. The Juba flowed past in a smooth column with moonlight reflecting off the ripples that swarmed around the newly emerging sandbar.

Mohamed pointed it out yesterday, telling Max to watch for the crocodile that liked to pull up there in the mornings. The river kept moving. The stars were too far away to wish on, but the moon connected him to Hani, over the horizon in Nairobi. He turned away from any thought of her when he heard Ali Nur step up onto the deck with canvas sack from which he first produced a hookah. He placed it on the table and then pulled out an old wooden box.

"Smell it Max." he said as he slid the lid back to reveal the aromatic tobacco. “It's Lebanese, apple and some spices I don't know the name in English."

He handed Max a small cellophane package containing a tip for one of the hookah hoses. After showing Max how to attach it he took a few pinches of the tobacco and loaded the brass bowl. Then he extracted a bottle of whiskey from the sack and placed it between them.

Zaynab came out with two old heavy glasses filled with Max’s ice. Ali Nur poured out a good measure in each glass, then raising his glass, but no salute followed. Instead, he searched Max’s face and nodded.

After a few sips, and a few puffs, they fell into a rhythm.

Max asked, “Would you call yourself a freedom fighter?”

Ali Nur thought for a second, “It’s better than warlord, yes? Names don’t mean anything now. My uncle is called The Boqor, a nickname that he is starting to believe. He thinks like an old man.” They took another sip. “Maybe I am a freedom fighter...would that make you feel better?”

Max thought it might feel better to think about it this way, but said, “I’d like to believe that, but it doesn’t make any difference what I want to believe. I’ll feel better about this when it’s over and I can return to Mogadishu.”

"Soon...for now you'll go to Mandera on Friday to get our first containers. Then next week you'll go again. Mr. Hassen from your bank will have all of the documents prepared for your signature. He'll handle the customs papers. Once you clear customs in Mandera you'll drive back to Toobiye, the checkpoint. Mohamed will draw you a map of Mandera. No one needs to look in the containers, but if that happens, they'll see your farm equipment first. You'll have to keep them from looking further."

"I'll try." said Max

"No, you must succeed. You must."

They heard Zaynab loading her Land Cruiser. Ali Nur stood up and watched. "She wants this farm. You can help her, Max."

The carpet was still on the deck after everyone had gone. The radio was playing across the yard as he tucked into his cocoon and drifted into the darkness.

He was in a rubber raft trying to get back to his side of the river. It was losing air, making it hard to row. The current was pushing him further and further downstream. When he reached the bank he couldn't find any place to land, the steep slippery mud walls didn't offer any purchase. Sliding out onto the edge of the raft he lunged for the shore but slipped down into the river. His legs were kicking away imagined jaws as he hung onto the edge of the shrinking raft. He drifted half in and half out and then he saw the children. They were running along the top of the bank. They were calling him "ferengi" and then they started throwing small rocks at him. There were more children and adults now picking up bigger stones. He could see Zaynab and Hani chasing away the crowd. They stood there on the bank as he drifted out into the current. The raft was quickly losing its air as he tried to stuff it under him to keep afloat...he woke up in a sweat. His heart was racing. He'd pulled the mosquito net from its hook and wrapped it around himself, trapping him in the web.

37

Max awoke when the early birds began their concert. New birds and new music would be there each time he stirred in the early light. He envied their freedom, easily floating above the river's drone, calling back and forth in the language of song. He wanted to test his freedom now that he had wheels.

Geed Weyn to Luuq was only fifteen or twenty minutes. The Geed Weyn junction now had a dozen tracks going left to Luuq. At the first checkpoint there was a large stone on one side and an old filing cabinet on the other, with a long steel pipe across the road. He saw a young man coming out of the bush with an AK-47 and an impressive belt of shiny bullets crisscrossing his skinny chest. He held up a hand towards Max as he picked up one end of the pipe and walked it open, waving Max through.

The guard before the bridge gave him a short salute as he passed. He drove into Luuq and turned left into Zeyneb's shady compound. The gates were off their hinges resting against the wall. Several men were welding something and a few others were mixing up mortar for another row of blocks on the wall. Before he got to the front door Asha opened it and welcomed him into the dark interior. They exchanged some Somali greetings, which he was able to extend for four good sentences now.

"Look at you two!" Zaynab said as she appeared on the stairs. "Yasmin is a good teacher, yes?"

He started to greet Zaynab in Somali but she put up a hand and said, "English. Asha needs the practice and I love to speak it. I think there are more words for us in English."

"Okay. Good morning."

"Good morning to you. I'm having some breakfast, join me." She put a hand on Asha's shoulder, Asha bowed and disappeared into the kitchen.

Zaynab wore a sheer sari-like wrap, with a man's macawis. Her braided and beaded hair was wet with drops of water running down her neck. She was barefoot, leaving wet footprints on the tiles. "I had such a good time last night. Really." She sat down in an ornate arm chair and patted its mate for him to sit. "So many memories for me and Ali. Also, for Yasmin and Xabiib. You know, they were there when it first opened. Xabiib was only 8 and Yasmin just 14. They are orphans from the Ogaden." She closed her eyes and let her head rest against the chair. "Those two would follow the nurses around when we did our visits in the camps. Xabiib was so afraid of the white people. I'd have to carry her if they got too close. Yasmin took to Rana and the others right away. So, we always had a double shadow."

"Where have they been since the camp closed? Do they live in Luuq?"

"When the camp started to break up, in 1983, we adopted them. Not officially, but Somali style. They came with us when we moved back to Mogadishu."

"We?"

"Yes." she said, nodding her head a little, "Aldo was here then." Zaynab stood up with a sigh and pulled her sari a little tighter with a look at him. "I'll go help Asha with our breakfast."

They sat at a small table off the kitchen. Asha never said a thing, but listened intensely, her face reacting to everything Zaynab said.

"My husband, Aldo, is Italian. We grew up together in Mogadishu. Our families knew each other and did some business together. His mother and father came to Somalia after the Second World War, sinking their fortune into the colony." She looked at him. "You know, having you here, back at Geed Weyn, has put me in a mood. I'm so lonely for the memories of those years, when Aldo and I, and others too...Italians, Brits and Somali's all went to the cinema together, or played basketball and spent days on the beaches. Do you know the Lido?"

Asha did, he could see her face feel the ocean breeze.

"I know where it is, but it is too close to the Green Line. I think the beach club is actually part of the North now."

"North or South didn't matter then." She swept her hand over that idea. "From the Old Port to the Beach Club the Lido would be filled with people strolling in the evening breeze.

"Ah Max. We watched our country slip into this chaos. There was a window of time after the Russians left when we'd meet in the cafes along the Lido and talk of revolution. There were students, professors and many others agreeing that it was time to overthrow a corrupt regime. What did we know? Of course, we were ready to question our parents—it's the way, yes? But our families and clans pulled us in. Our fathers were business partners negotiating on the construction of the New Port, their biggest contract ever. They'd invested their bribes already, so talk of revolution was not well received. Everyone knew it was just a matter of time before another civil war. Many Italians moved back to Italy, but Aldo's family had too much at stake. They believed they were too big and important to be caught up in this, they thought it would pass. Besides, they had very little left for them in Italy. Aldo was seen more and more like one of them, not one of us. There were suspicions and tensions in our families' relationships too. Everyone was making secret plans to escape or survive. It was in the middle of this that Aldo and I decided to get married. We moved away from restless Mogadishu and settled in Luuq." She paused before adding, "We were so heroic and clever back then."

Zaynab and Max were back in their chairs in the living room with two glasses of ice tea sweating on the delicate mahogany table between them. She opened up her arms to the living room and said, "This is Aldo's house. And you're working on his farm."

"Your husband's farm...your farm?"

"Oh yes. The papers you have, the maps and all the planning were Aldo's project at first. Aldo said that he'd be fine with a modest income and maybe a farm someday. We were like your missionaries Max, wanting a better world, but we did not have the time. He is a good man. We've gone back to just being good friends. Though, he does still tease me like a lover—always Italian. Staying married is a convenience that he says will make it easier for him to rescue me when the time comes. His family finally quit Somalia in 1980, leaving the remnants of their holdings to Aldo and me. They didn't want to watch how things would end. Aldo went to see them for Christmas the next year and never came back. He sent for me but I never left. I was too busy. The Ogaden War had just started and we had more than a quarter million refugees in this district alone, more than a million in the country. I signed over Aldo's farm to the new Somali Refugee Agency and soon we had 80,000 refugees on the bend of the Juba. I volunteered in Geed Weyn and found my new friends Rana and Utja. Ali volunteered and convinced others to join him in proving that they were patriotic Somalis. It was either that or join the army. At any time, a truck could roll in to pick up replacements for the fighting. Those bright, beautiful boys would run for cover, crowding into the kitchen.

"It's been a long time since Ali and I have been this close. He always tried to protect Aldo and me...Okay! You came for a reason, not to hear me talking about the past. I don't know why it is so easy to tell you my heart. Maybe there are just too few beautiful young men left." She laughed.

"I wanted to talk about the farm, to get your help organizing things. But wow, It's your farm really."

"We can do something good, and maybe it will last this time...maybe not, but what else is worth doing? You've seen all that we saved from Geed Weyn, yes? Well, we won't lose what you bring us now. I want this for Aldo too."

They spent the next hour planning out a much larger farm. When they were finished Zaynab walked him out to the technical and he asked, "Have you heard anything from Sharif, or about the camps in Mogadishu?"

"Ali paid for the burial of Sharif's cousin, and he's helping in other ways. Don't worry, you're doing the right thing." She kissed him on the cheek and added, "You're a good man too."

38

Mara shouldered Hani's backpack as they walked the few blocks to Kiberu. For all the time they worked or just hung out at Kiberu, there'd always been backpacks stacked near the entrance—now one of them would be hers. The WHC Land Rover pulled up a little after 6am. The Irish girl got out and ran into the cafe. Hani forgot her name and hoped she wouldn't need to introduce her.

"Hello, you ready?" Before Hani could respond the Irish girl turned to Mara, and held out her hand, "Hello. I'm Brin."

"Oh, sorry. Brin, this is my friend Mara. I'm ready,"

"Find him." Mara whispered as they hugged.

Brin introduced Hani to Sylvie and Anita before they pulled away from the cafe. Sylvie woke up long enough for the greetings then went back to sleep. Anita was driving with Brin in the front passenger seat. She draped an arm over the seat and said, "So, Roger at UNDP said you were going to meet someone in Mandera—someone you worked with in Mogadishu."

"Yes, and thanks for giving me a ride, the timing's perfect."

Brin had black spiky hair with red tips. Anita had the same short hair, but without the highlights. There were places on both heads where the clippers uncovered white skin. She tried to imagine that party. Brin was turned so that Hani could see the field of freckles spread across her tipped-up nose.

"We'll have to talk to keep Anita awake. Absolutely no sleep last night. Do you drive?"

"Sure, I can take a turn. I know this part of the road up to Isiolo. I grew up in Kenya."

"Ah, Great! Do ya hear that, Anita? More drivers!" Turning back to Hani she asked," Why don't you take us out a ways then? Anita really won't make it much longer."

"Sure, I got at least three hours of sleep. You talk and I'll drive."

Anita pulled over, switched with Hani, and was asleep in seconds.

"She's from the Netherlands." Brin started. "This is her first overseas assignment." Brin looked back at Anita asleep with her head on Sylvie's lap. "She's a lot of fun and good at her job. Definitely enjoying being away from home. And Sylvie, our Italian princess. Just kidding, Sylvie's great. She's not here for the money, that's for sure."

"Did she work at UNDP? I think I recognized her from the time I interned."

"Yeah, she was there. How funny, did you work with Sylvie?

"I didn't get to know her really—I just remember her as this beautiful Italian...princess." They laughed. It was rumored that Sylvie was an heiress, and she was treated like it. Even crumpled up in the back of the Land Rover, with Anita's head resting in her lap, she still looked tall and regal.

"We'll spend the night in Haburwein with the Imam and his family. You'll love the kids and Nura, his wife. They're Somali. That'll leave seven hours for the last leg to Mandera tomorrow."

"How often do you make this drive?"

"Every three months we get two weeks to recover." She looked back at the sleepers, "Don't we look it?"

"R&R."

"Yeah, but not much rest."

“What’s it like working with Women’s Health Cooperative? I heard it was an all-female organization.”

“Yeah, it’s great most of the time. R&R is a break from that too. At first it was just a few medical teams, seconded to one or two small NGOs in Lokichogio. They decided to go out on their own, thanks to some very nice donors,” she cocked her head towards the sleeping Sylvie, “We’re kind of a sisterhood.”

Driving out of Nairobi, through constant road construction, was hard on three hours of sleep. About an hour out of Thika, Brin took the wheel. The traffic had thinned but was still being regulated by a few heavy lorries grinding towards Mt. Kenya in the distance. Hani drifted into a green and undulating world of dreams. When she awoke, she saw that Sylvie was now driving, and that Mt Kenya was right beside her out the driver’s side window.

"Hey." said Sylvie, "Remember me? UNDP?"

"Yes, of course. I do...Brin said you were now senior staff with WHC. That's great."

Hani wasn't really into rehearsing the same topic that she fell asleep to. She had the outline of Sylvie's story from Brin. It was hard to feign interest but she tried. Sylvie didn't go on too long, and Hani took this as a courtesy. When sleep and road travel mix its only restaurants, bathrooms, and beds that mattered.

Sylvie said, "We'll stop for a meal in Isiolo. Maybe twenty or thirty minutes more. After that it's another five hours to Haburwein and a real bed. This is my favorite part of the drive. After Isiolo we'll leave this paradise and enter Kenya’s Northern Frontier."

Hani rested her head against the half open side window, letting the wind comb through her new short bristles—feeling the cool all the way down to her scalp now. This was where she wanted to bring Max. Coffee plantations and tree farms checker-boarded the valley up to the edge of the reserves. In her sleepy head she could see him growing old with her on these slopes. Maybe tending an orchard like the ones he said surrounded his home in America. The sky was changing from an alpine clarity to a white haze as the road went down into the spreading plain.

Like many of the villages and towns along the highway, Isiolo greeted you with garbage. Everything seemed to get pushed out to the edges. Plastic bags and bottles tumbled in the wind, glistening in drifts against broken fences and disintegrating huts. The stench from the tannery and slaughterhouse made an impression too. Marabou Storks hopped out of their way as their Land Rover pulled in for petrol.

Disorder was swept further and further into the back streets as they came into the center of Isiolo, where trees arched over the road and shaded older buildings. Anita, now fully awake, started to wrap a scarf over her head. "Not for Allah," she said. Brin tousled her red spikes.

They pulled into the walled drive-court of The Hunter Hotel and Bar. There were half a dozen Land Cruisers and Land Rovers with UN tags. Once they were seated on the veranda, they took turns using the bathroom. Anita said it would be the last one until Haburwein. It took a few minutes for the bumping and grinding of the road to dissipate. Though they were still sitting, the absence of motion, rushing air, and motors made this variation of sitting a relief. Stretches, like yawns, were infectious.

Anita ordered a round of Tuskers, the mixed grill (Halal), and a large platter of pom frites. The recognizable pieces of meat went first, then some speculation about the remnants. There was no second round or relaxed digestive pause after lunch. They made another pilgrimage to the bathroom before they folded back into the Land Rover.

Anita took the first leg, back out onto the main road, then a right turn—Isiolo disappeared fast in this direction. The remainder of that day they pushed their way out into a vast open scrubland. She thought they passed three or four small villages, but they made little impression and she wondered if they were a mirage. Heat was building, making shimmering pools on the roadway. They were pushing the Land Rover a bit harder now, to reach their stop by dark.

As they approached Haburwein the angle of the light finally released the blue in the sky. The red dirt started to make shadows, and the little old bushman trees finger leaves were flooded with green. Then she saw the camels and several people slipping through the bush. She thought she saw a grenade launcher among the poles strapped to the side of one of the camels. The sky began to burn red in the west, giving a pink glow to the large castle clouds over Haburwein's white mosque. They were traveling slower now, trying to avoid sending clouds of dust into the open market beside the road. From this side of Haburwein they could see the same road winding out toward blue hills. They'd covered their heads and accepted, for everyone's sake, that they should try and blend in as much as possible. It was a relief as much as a concession to be your own shadow.

In the warmth of the Imam's bow, she felt his respect and acceptance. His wife and children stood in the arched doorway.

Once inside the guest house, Ibraham, the Imam, left with the two boys. Nura led them down a hallway and opened the door to their room. She pointed to the small bathroom and told them that the water tank was overflowing so they could use all they needed. Nura's girls watched as Brin and Anita brought out hair ribbons, watercolors, and candy. Sylvie brought out a large book, tied with a yellow ribbon. The girls—little and big—gathered around the book with its bright pictures of women dressed in traditional clothing from all over the world. Sylvie had one of the smallest girls on her lap as she talked to Hani. "This is Alil, Nura's sister's child. She was orphaned and living in Dadaab, the big camp south of here."

39

As the sun set, a scratchy recording of the call to prayer came from the mosque across the courtyard. Nura got up and gathered her little girls and their presents. Once Nura closed the door, Brin started running water in the little sink. She took her head scarf off and her blouse before coming back in the room to dig out a washcloth. She stripped off her thin strapped tee shirt and threw it back at her pack before she returned to the sink and started rinsing her head and neck, wringing out the water over her firm little body, until a small pool formed at her bare feet. Anita too removed her clothes, joining Brin at the sink. Hani watched, then began to pull away her layers until she too stood naked with her sisters.

Sylvie sat on the edge of the bed with her blouse open and Hani saw the familiar scars that meant cancer. When she slipped off the blouse, she looked at Hani and said, "It's been three years and I still miss them. On R&R this time, they dared me to go with them to the nude beach near our hotel." Brin looked over her shoulder and winked at Hani. "At first, I wouldn't let anyone see me naked this way. You know, the unspoken questions and stares just reinforced my loss. And, to young girls, these scars are scary, they know the monster that clawed them off, and they'd wonder when it would come for them. But as I watched, covered up, I just saw bodies, all kinds of them walking around with every shape and size and color…so, it helped. And, yes, I walked across the sand naked and free. It actually felt…erotic." Sylvie joined the standing bath. The scars on her sun-tanned skin cut across her chest and into her arm pits. She put her arms over her head and twirled around behind Brin and Anita and said, "Now I don't care." Hani felt a surge of pure arousal seeing herself naked with them.

She knew the beach Sylvie mentioned, or one like it north of Mombasa, where Mara dared her to go bare in front of others. It was just before she left for Mogadishu. Mara said the rule was to leave all clothes in the car, so Hani grabbed her book and draped her towel around her neck, covering her breasts, as they walked out to the beach. She tried to match Mara's steps, hiding in the shadow of her spectacular shimmering body, the body everyone was watching. Hani sat with her book in her lap next to Mara, who laid on her stomach, stretching out her long dark body on the pink sand. She tried to see the words, but she just saw her breasts instead of the pages, feeling the eyes of strangers judging and comparing—just like she was doing. Swimmers came out of the water facing the sunbathers, then walked across the stage, parading large and small, firm and sagging symbols of gender. Since nothing was covered, nothing was secret. Men and women, children and grandmothers, wrinkled old grandfathers and stunning bodies like Mara's blended together after a quick look. She watched a group of women slowly walk into the waves. Three generations of bodies huddled together, giggling and splashing in a circle. Hani stood up and went to the water's edge and splashed the salty water on her hot skin, then turned to face the beach with her head back and her hair blowing in the breeze. She felt eyes on her once secret body, and wanted to get through the self-conscious seconds of nudity, to find the joy in being seen—even enjoyed. She swam out by the circle of women and floated up and down with them on the rolling sea, covered, then uncovered by the waves. She'd rarely experienced this intimate connection with women other than Mara, who shed clothing the minute she came home and walked around topless without a thought.

In the dark days of Mozambique, Hani had used her breasts to attract, then short-circuit the undressing eyes. With her nipples poking through her light tee-shirts, finding a partner was extremely easy. She didn't remember their faces or their bodies, it wasn't about them. The lights might have been on or off, she didn't remember, just the tension building, and then release, then building again. She feared that she'd turned something on, or off, that might be permanent, that she'd gone down so far that she couldn't find her way back. She did remember having sex with a woman from Norway that last week in Mozambique. The foreplay was slower, more comfortable, but she still had to finish herself. Now, standing alone in front of the mirror, she didn't recognize this body. She'd lost a little weight in the two years she'd been in Mogadishu— her nipples had darkened a bit and she thought a little pubic maintenance wouldn't hurt, but her once proud, weaponized tits, still pleased her. She weighed them in her hands and thought about Max.

They froze when they heard a knock at the door, reaching for the nearest towel to cover themselves. Nura, with a smile and a wave of her hand, said not to worry. Her little girls had their hands over their smiles and their eyes wide with curiosity. Nura asked Hani in Swahili if they needed anything, and said dinner would be ready soon. Brin and Anita let the girls help decide which top to wear, and they delighted in helping them wrap their heads in the latest fashion. They loved Hani's Mogadishu style.

40

After a quiet dinner they returned to their room which was beginning to cool in the night air. The ceiling fan cut through the lamp light, strobing it overhead. While Hani was brushing her teeth Nura knocked softly on the door before peeking in. Seeing Hani at the sink she crossed over and, in Swahili, asked her to bring Anita to come see her husband. Anita was listening and came to stand next to Nura. "Anita. Nura says that we need to come with her to see the Imam."

"Really? Ask her if this is about her girls. No, wait. Never mind. Will you interpret for us?"

"Of course."

As they left the room Sylvie and Brin reached out to let Nura's hand touch theirs. Nura waved off Hani's attempt to cover her head as she led them down a back hallway and entered Nura's apartment. Ibraham motioned for them to sit and have tea. Nura served as they settled on the cushions. Nura and Ibraham exchanged a few words in Somali before he spoke to Hani in Swahili, while looking intently at Anita.

"Will you speak for us Hani?" he asked

"I will." she said. Still not sure where this was going.

"Please tell Anita," Nodding at Anita as Anita nodded back. "That I have read the papers she gave me." He spoke slowly, used to the rhythm of translation.

"We have both read it," said Nura.

Ibraham said, "They want to teach this in our primary and secondary schools, but these are Kenyan schools, not everything is right for Somalis."

"It's not just Kenyan, it's the voice of all women. It should be the voice of all men too." Hani didn't have to worry about the tone. It dawned on her what they were talking about. Her gut tightened and she had a floating sensation.

Nura saw this in Hani's face and said, "Yes, we are talking about that, the cutting of my girls. Ibraham is saying that it is the time for Alil, she's already nine."

"Oh, Oh." She reached over and braced herself with a hand on Anita's knee. Anita covered her hand with both of hers as she looked back at Ibraham.

"Imam, you can stop this here in Haburwein. You can show them that the Koran doesn't teach this."

"Please, in this house I am just Ibraham. One man. One man with daughters who one day will be wives. Even if I don't want this for them, their husband's families will expect it—it is the way here. My words, even the Koran's words, can't stop this."

Nura touched her husband's cheek with one of her hennaed fingers, tracing the imaginary channel where his tears could fall. Hani recognized this Somali gesture as a way to soften someone, a way to touch their heart, or even a way to say, I love you.

He said, "My mother, my sisters and my wife have all had this ceremony."

"It is not a ceremony Ibraham, it is abuse and torture!" Hani thought this might come across without translation. Anita asked in a softer tone, "What does Nura say? I know that you must know what happens to these girls. If they don't die, there will still be the pain, and infections and fistulas. Peeing or menstruating is painful. It doesn't need to be this way."

Hani took her time with this translation.

When she finished, Nura picked up the argument, speaking to her husband in Swahili. "I don't want this for our little girls. And I don't want husbands that would want this for their wives. I don't want in-laws that would demand to inspect your daughter's vagina to make sure she was mutilated like I was." Ibraham sat face to face with Nura, her eyes holding him mute. "I have lived in shame since I was eight years old, in a culture of shame and violence and I won't have them live like that too." Then Nura took her husband's face between her hands and said, "You would have loved me so much more if I was complete, Habibi."

Hani quietly translated this for Anita while Nura and Ibraham continued to look into each other's eyes. For a minute Nura and Ibraham forgot about their guests as he spoke to her in a tender voice, his hands now on hers as she cradled his face.

Ibraham took a cleansing breath and said, "Thank you Anita, and you too Hani. It is a difficult subject to discuss, even though it has touched so many lives. It is clear that it is an evil."

After Hani translated this Anita pressed a little more. With her hands open towards the Imam, she asked him, "What will you do? Will you let the schools teach this? Will you protect your daughters?"

He squeezed Nura's hands as he lifted them from his face. "I will seek direction." was all he said.

They left Ibraham alone on the floor as Nura walked them down the hallway. At the door Nura took Hani and Anita's hands in hers, and with tears in her eyes said, "Maybe, maybe our girls will escape the cutting." Then she added. "He is a good man... and he hates evil."

41

A line of clouds hung above the blue hills, allowing the night's coolness to linger. Max took his coffee back to the breezeway, scanning the dirt for any sign of a python. Xabiib came up with two boiled eggs and some fresh bread she'd toasted over the gas burner. They heard the clank of a jerry can against his technical. "Mandera?" she asked.

He tried to put together a good sentence in Somali, but it sounded like, "Yes, me go, Mohamed go, Mandera." Xabiib said it properly and then he repeated it. She nodded her approval.

Mohamed sat in the passenger seat with his AK-47 cradled in his arms. At the Doolow Road he casually swept his arm to the right. After Max made the turn Mohamed's arm pointed straight ahead. He was able to go about twenty miles an hour on this section, which he figured would get them to Mandera in a little over two hours—Mohamed said it would take four. Mohamed's needle now pointed hard to the left where a set of rutted tracks headed down the embankment. He was between first and second gear, grinding in and out until he decided to just roll along in first. At this pace Mohamed's estimate was looking optimistic.

An hour passed where neither of them spoke. The track wound through an insistent forest of short flat-topped trees that blocked the horizon. Mohamed's hand came up, palm down, as he patted the air. Max slowed as they rounded a sloping curve before they came to a wider opening. "Time for prayer."

The tracks encircled an ancient puddle where the trees thinned. He'd seen this place in one of the pictures from the file, *Near*

Toobiye. When they stopped Mohamed walked straight into the forest to relieve himself, then took a bottle of water to the other side of the road to pray. Max used the facilities and then pulled out his map and tried to pinpoint where they were. This track would abut the road coming down from Doloow, and then run parallel to the Dawa River until just before Mandera.

Mohamed finished his prayers and looked over Max's shoulder at the map. "We'll be in Toobiye soon. I'll stay there until you bring the trucks." He knelt down, and used a twig to draw a map in the dust. It looked pretty easy—into Mandera on the only road from the border until the junction with the El Wak Road. The bank was on the left, just a few blocks. "You can't miss it, right here." He stabbed the ground. "You have money?"

"Yes,"

"You need to pay here, and here. When you leave you pay again, here, and here." Mohamed poked a hole in the sand at the Passport Control, and the Customs. He reached under the seat and pulled out a handgun. He slid the clip out, then back in. "You won't need this. Inshallah." He put it back under the seat.

Toobiye had several sagging buildings, and a few round huts beneath a green canopy facing the Doolow Road. Mohamed got out while a dozen people watched from darkened doorways. Max slowly turned left out onto the road to Mandera, then drove along the Dawa River just beyond the band of trees on his right. When the trees thinned a fence came out of the forest and he saw a small refugee camp with a large white tent. He didn't recognize the logo. Beyond this he saw the Kenyan flag flying over the border station with two identical buildings—Mohamed's holes in the dust.

He rolled up slowly with his passport ready. Seeing just one uniform he thought the two one hundred-dollar bills tucked into the last page might be too much, but when has a bribe ever been too much? The officer thumbed through to the last page of the passport, barely acknowledging the transaction. He stamped the passport and handed it back and pointed to hole number two. "Customs."

There were three uniforms here. He didn't know the standard way to pass a bribe to a customs agent. The agent asked about his vehicle license and missing tags. Max explained that he'd only be in Mandera for a few hours. One of the uniforms, who couldn't have been more than sixteen years old, came out of the building and started to poke around the technical. He looked in the basket and tapped on the jerry cans. The officer at the window told him that he'd need a temporary license as he handed him an envelope. The only thing that Max had to put into it was the two hundred dollars he had left for this part of the crossing. The envelope went back inside the building and the window closed. Max could see the problem developing. He tapped on the window to get the agent's attention. "Excuse me sir. I'm afraid that I've left one of my papers with them by mistake." He pointed back at the Passport building. The agent just stared at him, then closed the window. Soon the young officer that had been inspecting the technical, ran out the back door and over to the first building. When he came back a few minutes later, after some counting and discussion, an officer came out and wrote 1600 on Max's fender with a thick piece of chalk. He pointed to his watch, then the fender.

The Kenyan military occupied a small base on the right side of the road and the guards at the gate were taking a long look at Max's impotent technical. He could see the intersection ahead so he pulled into a tea shop that had a white Land Cruiser parked in front.

As soon as he pulled in a tall Somali teenager approached him. "I can watch it for you," he said. "I watch this one too." He pointed to the other Land Cruiser. Max fished out a ten-dollar bill.

"How much for an hour?" he asked as he held out the note.

"It is enough."

He had that look, like Suleymaan—polite, good eye contact and good English. It was a snap judgment, but he'd come to see that most of young people working with the foreigners were educated and honest. This was what their education was worth now, translators and fixers. He didn't mind overpaying for the protection—without friends, even the ones he paid, he'd be lost.

"I'm Max." He held out his hand.

"I am Yusef."

"Do you work with them?" He tipped his head toward the only other people in the tea shop.

"Sometimes, but I can work with you too. I can get what you need in Mandera. You can trust me."

Over Yusef's shoulder Max could see the three aid-worker types looking at him, so he nodded towards them, and they returned the nod.

"I'll be back in an hour."

"No problem. I'm watching it for you."

Max walked along the once paved road until he reached the El Wak Road. No vehicles drove towards Somalia, but trucks and cars jammed up before the intersection. He turned left and walked on a broken sidewalk past the shops and bars that lined both sides of the road. The shops sat a few steps above the sidewalk with front porches filled with Manderians. The talking hushed in a wave as he walked past them. Before he'd gone a block the wave had informed the next block that he was coming, and behind him he heard the chatter increase. The patrolling Kenyan military seemed to produce the same disturbance in their wake.

At the end of the third block there was an open lot, then the bank. The building's aluminum and glass door had the straightest angles he'd seen for days. He entered through the portal into a cool, mechanically whirring world. There was a young man in a short-sleeve white shirt leaning on his elbows at the one teller window. No one else was in the lobby. He showed his Global Aid card to the teller and asked to see Mr. Hassen. The teller came from behind the counter, through the half door that needed a key to open. He led Max to the right side of the lobby where he knocked on the door, announcing, "Mr. Max Dubec, sir."

Except for the picture of President Moi, the room was unadorned. "I am Ahmed Hassen."

Max took a second to respond, wondering about what part this banker was playing. What did he know? Mr. Hassen offered him the one chair in front of his metal desk. His white shirt was pressed and clean, while Max's best shirt, the one that Xabiib ironed last night, was wilted and no longer white.

He pulled out his passport as proof of his identity and Mr. Hassen recorded the information in a ledger. Max noticed a blue folder pinned under Mr. Hassen's left elbow and asked, "Is that my account?"

Mr. Hassen put his hand on it and hesitated, "Yes, I assure you all is in order."

"May I see it, please?" The banker/co-conspirator looked at Max for a second before sliding the blue folder across the desk. Max scanned down to the balance, $98,750.00 USD. The next paper was an invoice, marked paid, from a freight broker in Nairobi; $48,007.00. He went down the list of items in the shipment, there was no sign of any "Other Items." After a bit of shuffling Mr. Hassen handed him a manila envelope with the documents for Customs. He went over each step, which paper for whom, etc. When he finished Max decided to see if he could actually access some of this money. "I'd like to withdraw $10,000 in US Dollars from my account. Do you have that much currency here?"

Mr. Hassen, who was preparing to stand up, slumped back down in his chair. "Well, yes. We have the currency. Is this for project expenses?"

"I am able to access my account, correct?"

"Yes, of course. As far as I can see you are the authorized signer." Mr. Hassen looked like he was going to say more, but instead he excused himself and went out to the lobby. Max could hear him talking to the teller. After a few minutes he came back into the office and said, "He's getting your money now. You'll need to sign for it of course. I've sent word to the drivers—they'll be waiting for you at the border in thirty minutes."

"Until next week then." Max offered his hand, and Mr. Hassen gave it a short shake.

Max went over to the teller's window and watched him feeding hundreds into a counter. He did this four times before he banded the cash in two blocks of $5,000. Max put one in each front pocket and crossed over to the other side of the El Wak Road.

He walked back with his hands in his pockets, holding on to the cash. He hadn't even thought about the possibility of the money until he looked at the account balance. The original Geed Weyn proposal was only for fifty thousand dollars. Now there was a lot more money involved, and a lot of that would need to be cash— his mind was racing around the cash in his pocket. Yusef was sitting on a stack of pallets next to Max's technical when he returned. The Land Cruiser was still there, and they were still drinking beer.

"Hey, Yusef, do you want something to eat or drink?" His eyes lit up. "I'm buying." Max figured it was better to share the table with Yusef—the aid-workers would ask questions. He kept the conversation on Yusef until the trucks arrived.

Max drove up beside the first truck and got out. The driver held out his hand, waiting for an answer. Then he swooshed his hand towards the border, then he used his index finger to circle like tires going forward quickly. Max was now standing on the top step looking in at the driver and his family. Three children and maybe two wives, looking like they lived on the road. The driver was laughing at his children's fear of Max. The two small boys were peeking around their mother with wide eyes. Seeing himself in the large side mirror he understood. Max stepped back down and took a look at the two trucks with twenty-foot containers chained down on the flatbed trailers. He wondered how they'd make it through some of the wadis.

They cleared Customs and Passport Control without a request to inspect the containers. He headed out onto the Doolow Road and found a pace in second gear that kept the trucks in sight. At Toobiye there was a guy sitting on a metal chair in the middle of the road. He slowly dragged the chair to the side of the road as the trucks pulled up. Mohamed came out from one of the huts and Max saw a woman's silhouette behind him. Mohamed walked around the trucks, pulling on the thin metal seals and checking the chains. "No problems?"

"None. Very smooth. No problem."

After Toobiye he crawled along in first gear. The speed didn't matter now, he knew where he was going. The sun was quartering in on them as he pulled his ball cap lower to shade his eyes. At least he didn't have to follow the trucks that were stirring up the soft red dust. As the sun began to lower through the treetops, a strobing rhythm of light and shade matched the cylinder beat of the trucks. If it was really this simple, this easy, to fulfill his side of the deal, then he thought he could do it a few more times. He'd go and see Zaynab tomorrow and find out if she had any news from Sharif in Mogadishu. He'd push them to do their part. He resolved to make the farm work. He could at least lay the groundwork for the irrigation and other infrastructure needed for a real farm sometime in the future. This touch of euphoria was highlighted by the world around him being flooded with the colors of the day's last light. What had been dried out and faded was now filled with shadows and definition. He could feel the sun retreating.

They stopped at the wadi they'd crawled out of this morning. Mohamed got out to survey the drop off with the truck drivers. They took turns with the two shovels, digging down the ridge as the sun set. It was dark when they resumed. Their headlights sweeping back and forth through the forest until they saw a light in the kitchen, and then another in the sister’s room.

42

Hani woke up in the damp little room before the prayer alarm went off next door. She shared a single bed with Sylvie, which required spooning with as little contact as possible. Hani lifted the sheet up over Sylvie's shoulders before she dressed and went outside for air. A band of low clouds hung above the blue hills in the north. She thought about Max out there, over the horizon.

Ibraham crossed over to the mosque, and a few minutes later the call went out to Haburwein through four metal horns on the corners of the mosque. She thought that the ancient chanting was enhanced by the scratchy recording. As the others got dressed and repacked their bags, Hani started to pick up towels and washcloths, then scooped handfuls of water from the sink onto the floor, pushing it all towards the ceramic toilet pad on the floor. Alil slipped into their room and told them that breakfast was ready in the kitchen. She took Anita's hand and led them down the hallway.

Nura had bread, jam, and tea set out on the low table. She also had a guest whom she introduced as Miriama, a teacher from the government primary school in Haburwein. Anita let out a little shriek of surprise. She introduced Miriama to her friends. Miriama had written to lots of agencies looking for help with her idea for a project in Haburwein and other towns in the frontier and Anita was the only one to write back. They were speaking English, with Miriama speaking rapidly and using her hands. After a bit Anita came in to get some bread and jam, and take a sip of her tea. Miriama held out a small black notebook to Hani and said, "Please, may I have your contact information?" She was pointing to an empty spot on a page filled with names and numbers. Some were highlighted in yellow and pink, somc had bold black rectangles boxing them in, and very small notes dancing around them.

"Sure, of course. Hani, Hani Chandra."

Miriama wrote the Somali word for Hani, XANII. Hani gave her Mara's address and phone number, as well as a number for her department at UNICEF. Miriama and Anita huddled again before she stretched herself toward the door, needing to leave. She kissed and hugged everyone in the room and promised to keep in touch with Anita. She put all that excitement back under her headscarf and ran across the courtyard and past the mosque.

Brin said, "Wow! She's great. She's perfect Anita."

Anita agreed, though she looked a little dazed. Nura got big hugs from everyone before they left, and she made Hani promise to come back. They filled up the Land Rover at the edge of town before they settled in for the seven-hour drive to Mandera.

With Brin at the wheel Hani sat in the back with Anita. "Hey, what was all that about with Miriama? Do you work with her?"

"I do now." Anita said. "It's the first time we've met. I left a letter for her with Nura when we came through here two weeks ago. I am trying to start a project for women in the frontier and someone like Miriama, a teacher, would be perfect."

"FGM?" Hani asked.

"Oh yes, how can it not be about that. But it's more."

"Is this through the Cooperative?" Hani asked.

"No, but Sylvie is helping me put it together in my spare time. I just finished the proposal on break. I can show it to you if you like?"

"It's good Hani." Sylvie said from the front seat. "You should read it. Anita needs to send it to UNICEF anyway. It would be great if you could help us get it to the right person. Even if they don't fund it, it would be good to have them endorse it."

Hani had reviewed lots of proposals. When Anita handed her the working copy, she scanned down the contents listed on the second page. She could see that this was not a formal submission in a typical UN format but more like one you'd send directly to donors in the American style. She flipped through the pages, checking off the elements: Executive Summary, Problem Statement, Objectives, Methods, Staffing, Funding Sources and Reporting. In the back were assumptions and fact sources. The pictures that followed went from beautiful images of women and children in the Frontier, to clinical images that threatened to burn into your memory if you looked too long. Hani had seen FGM materials before, but now she layered them over Nura's girls.

She flipped back to the title page and placed Anita's proposal on her lap. "Before I read this, I want you to tell me about it. Not everything, but the parts of it that make you believe that you can do what you're proposing. If your donors believe you, they'll be more willing to believe this." Hani had both hands around Anita's proposal.

Sylvie agreed and nodded to Anita. "She's right. You can't rely on just that." She was pointing at the proposal on Hani's lap.

"Try this," said Hani. "I'm already very sympathetic, and I already think that the problems you aim to correct are real problems. So, let's say that I am a donor with similar projects after my money. I need to hear it from you." Hani was pointing to Anita's heart. "Start with why you care."

Anita looked at both of them pointing fingers at her and said, "Fine. Okay. But it won't fit in there." She tapped the proposal on Hani's lap.

"That's okay. It's in there. It's in all those words." Hani said this as her finger scrolled down the contents of Anita's proposal. "You never know who you're talking to, or which of the things you say touches them. The real proposal is spoken first."

"See if you can do it before Mandera," Brin called out from the driver's seat.

Anita sat quietly for a little bit, gathering her thoughts and looking for a place to start. "I am a Muslim woman," she said. "But only by birth. My parents came from an Albanian town in Macedonia, Gostivar. which meant that the Orthodox cathedral was the center of life, despite the large Albanian population. My father was a mathematics professor at the local university. His Macedonian co-workers made much more money, and even got housing allowances so they could afford to live on the Orthodox side of town. When his visa came through my mother, who was his student in the beginning, leapt at the chance to run away to Europe with him."

Sylvie raised an eyebrow.

Anita defended them. "What I'm saying is that they were educated, they grew up in a backward and hostile community and they wanted something better. Okay? Are you guys sure you want to hear all this?"

"I do," said Brin.

"Me too," said Sylvie.

Hani added, "We have lots of time. Think of it like you're seated next to that sympathetic donor on a plane for the next four hours."

"Anyway, so my parents moved to the Netherlands before I was born." Anita said. When she paused it gave everyone time to wonder if Anita's mother was pregnant before or after they moved.

"In Holland my father couldn't find a position at any university, but he taught mathematics at a technical school outside of The Hague. My mother walked dogs for a living. The

Dutch are crazy about their pets. She finished her degree after I was born, but she still walked the dogs. She told me that she appreciated their natural honesty."

"I like dogs more than people sometimes," said Sylvie.

"Thanks!" said Brin.

"Not you guys. Really! Keep talking Anita."

"We lived among Muslims, Muslims from everywhere. Lots of Indonesians. My father never attended the mosque after he moved to Holland. My mother made lots of friends with the help of the dogs. The streets in the neighborhoods of The Hague are filled with dog walkers introducing themselves and their dogs. My parents were becoming more a part of The Netherlands than our Muslim neighbors. One of my school mates was a little girl from Egypt, Umma. I remember that when we were nine, she started to wear a head scarf all the time. She became quieter and more serious. When I asked my mother about the headscarf, because I wanted one too, she told me that I didn't need a head scarf, or any other covering. She mentioned the word circumcision but I didn't understand what she meant. I wanted to fit in at my school—soon many of my friends would be covered"

Anita closed her eyes. Sylvie reached over the seat and stroked Anita's hair. When Anita opened her eyes, they were wet. "Umma started missing a lot of school days, so I volunteered to take her the lessons. Umma's mother was frightening to me. She was completely covered, Afghanistan style. I could barely see her eyes behind the screen of her head covering. She didn't speak Dutch, but she let me in to see Umma. Umma was in bed so I sat next to her and started to show her the lessons. She stopped me with a finger to her lips, and after hearing that her mother was in the kitchen, she pulled back the covers and lifted up her skirt to show me what they'd done. Her vagina was bruised and bleeding where they'd sewn her labia together. They only left a small hole for her pee. She took my hand and had me touch it and it was hot and swollen. It was angry red, I almost fainted.

"Umma pulled her skirt back down. She didn't say anything, but I could see that she was in pain. I just sat there. I was nine. I didn't know what to say. I was so afraid of Umma's mother that I panicked. I had to get away from there so I told Umma that I had to go and I ran out of their house. I didn't stop running until I got home. That night I told my mother what I saw and she took my hand and led me up to her bedroom where we talked for hours. The word circumcision didn't describe what I saw. My mother held me as I sobbed, I was sick to my stomach so she put me to bed where every time I woke up, I'd see either her or my father sitting on my bed, touching me. The black hijab floated in my dreams.

"Nobody talks about mutilating their daughters, they use the word circumcision. A word that in Europe brings up several images. The Muslims that brought the cutting with them hide behind this culturally sensitive shield. After all, the snipping of the foreskin didn't really hurt that much for the baby boy. Besides, it gave them a little head that some women prefer." Brin and Sylvie looked at each other.

When they stopped in Wajir to refuel, Brin insisted on driving the next leg to El Wak, even though Anita would be the next driver in their routine. Brin didn't want to interrupt Anita's story. They did stop about fifteen minutes out of town for a bathroom break on a little rise where they could see several kilometers in each direction. Anita hadn't spoken since Wajir—they were all too busy thinking about girls and women they knew. Hani was thinking that in Naivasha, a town full of gossip and scandal, she'd never heard anything about cutting. She thought about those girls with their little heads covered, having become women so cruelly. It was a big secret.

Once they were back up to speed, Anita picked up the story. "I walked to school along the street where Umma lived. It was a few blocks out of my way but I was drawn to it. Afraid of her mother, but worrying about Umma, I looked for clues. Curtains open, curtains closed, or a shadow of her mother at the open door. My fear and fascination made it into a dark fairytale where Umma was being tortured and held captive by an evil witch covered in black. I don't know if it happened like this, but I remember her father seeing me on the street and trying to warn me away with his eyes. We got rain that night, so in the morning the fog was lifting off of the sidewalk as I made my way past her house. There was a black tradesman's van parked where it blocked my view of Umma's window. The Imam came out of the house cradling Umma's body in a white sheet. The van pulled away with Umma and disappeared into the fog."

Hani saw the street in her mind. She saw it as a little girl would see it. All of them were imagining from their own memories of being little girls. There was a moment of silence for Umma that lasted ten kilometers. When Anita finally spoke, it snapped them back from that place of grief.

"A few days before Umma died my father went to the local Imam. He never told me what he said to him, but the day Umma died my father went to the police to report the abuse and neglect. He wouldn't let the police interview me until they provided a counselor and allowed my parents to come with me. By the time they questioned me the newspapers caught the story, reporting that it was a tip from someone in the Muslim community. So far, the Imam hadn't talked to the media, but the neighborhood was roiling with the suspicion and accusations. My father saw what was coming, so after my interview at the police station, he drove us to Utrecht to stay with a Macedonian family my mother had met. I never slept in our house again.

"I was out of school for a month while my parents turned their lives upside down, starting over in a new community. I remember it being sunny and bright there. It felt like a different country, a foreign place where there were few headscarves and you couldn't hear the call to prayer. The black hijab was fading from my thoughts. When I was twelve years old my mother went back to school and got her nursing degree. She started working in a women's health center that had many Muslim women and girls as patients. She didn't run away like I did, but she found a way to fight back."

The proposal sat in between Anita and Hani. Anita was letting her fingers run up the stack of papers as she said, "I followed my mother and became a nurse when I was twenty. By the time I started working with my mother, the clinic had developed a series of small outreaches that addressed the FGM issues for women and girls across Europe. She went to Scandinavia and France, even to Italy to talk about the clinic's community approach to combating the ignorance and cruelty of the practice. In here," she said tapping on the proposal, "are many of the same programs, big and small, that could work in Kenya and maybe even in Somalia." Anita's hand slid over to touch Hani's knee. "So, that's why I care...and why I think I can make a difference."

In El Wak they stopped at an Indian restaurant that featured pictures of the food, faded grey and pink, on their menu. The chicken curry was everyone's choice. By adding a lot of spice Hani could make the curry taste familiar. Brin said that they were only two hours out of Mandera, adding, "This is our neighborhood. El Wak is where we start our break and where we end it."

When they got back to the Land Cruiser Brin pulled out a pack of cigarettes. Sylvie and Anita took theirs, and Brin offered one to Hani. "We don't smoke on break, just up here. I know that's sort of crazy, but it works for us, right?"

Sylvie, let out a stream of blue smoke. "Besides, if you don't smoke no one thinks you can take a break."

Hani took one and joined the circle for the ceremony.

A few kilometers after El Wak the road forked. The sign on the road straight ahead said, MANDERA. They turned left.

"Landmines," said Sylvie. "Don't know if it's true, but we always go this way."

They were traveling on higher ground, on a course for a small ridge with a backbone of rocks. On the right the land sloped off towards Somalia. Anita was driving now as everyone else was drifting sleepily, their clocks resetting to the rhythm of the long hot afternoon. When Anita downshifted at the edge of Mandera they all returned to the present. Brin began to point out the key features of this part of town to Hani—the gas station that had a good mechanic, the worst restaurant in town, the corner where the money changers did business. Hani looked into the spaces between the buildings to see rutted winding lanes with groups of people in front of the shacks and tents. The road started to jam up, trucks and cars stopped and started, with people and animals crossing through the traffic.

The El Wak Road ended in the center of Mandera. Brin pointed out the road that led into Somalia. "See the flag? That's the border."

Hani looked over her shoulder and saw two trucks with containers rolling toward Somalia.

43

Hani watched for landmarks when they turned away from the center of Mandera. The streets became alleys that wound through a neighborhood with bungalows buried in vines. They'd turned five times, and on the last turn to the left she saw a two-story house at the end of the road. It looked like an observatory with its white Quonset tent on the roof. The road went up a small rise and ended at Swedish yellow gates with a small WRS logo sticker. Anita gave the horn two light taps. A large round head with short grey hair peeked out and his face broke into a broad smile as the gate swept back.

"That's Sam," said Brin. "He owns the house."

They pulled into the courtyard and before they stopped Sam was opening Sylvie's door. He gave her a big hug, which she returned. Then he hugged the others, until he got to Hani. "So, who are you?"

Brin broke in, "Sam, this is Hani. She's with UNICEF in Mogadishu."

"Jambo Hani. Have you travelled from Nairobi with these sisters?"

She nodded the obvious yes.

"Then you get the same welcome home." He put his arms around her and she felt the strength and protection he offered.

Sylvie walked over to the side of the house to look at the new construction. Sam, seeing this, told everyone to come and see. "It is not finished yet," he said in a hurry as he rushed to be the first to enter. He pointed to the shower that was tiled up to the shower head—clean white squares without grout. The flat roof was laid over beams of pine that let in light from the spaces between the rafters. A washing machine stood across the room with its back off and wires dangling out of the freshly painted block wall behind it.

"Does it work?" asked Anita, still looking at the shower.

"Of course. The water tank is full too," said Sam. "I'll pick up my tools and you can be the first to use it."

"Wow!" said Brin. She turned to Hani and said, "Sam just started this shower room when we went on break. We have a shower and a washing machine!"

"It's nice, yes?" Sam appealed to everyone in the room.

Anita was already heading into the house to drop off her bag and grab the first shower. Sam started collecting his tools, and by the time she returned he'd swept it out and hung a bright orange tablecloth over the doorway. Brin explained that while Sam was fast at new construction, he had little time or vision for fixing up the existing interior. Of the four bedrooms on the second floor only two of them were occupied. Brin opened the door to one of the empty rooms where Hani could see the beginnings of a renovation. Paula had one of the good bedrooms and Sylvie had the other one. She followed Brin up to the rooftop where she was shown her cot next to Brin's and across from Anita's. Both ends of the large tent on the roof were covered with mosquito netting, allowing the treetop breezes to blow through. The three cots were all on one end, with a long folding table dividing the space, leaving room for camp chairs and a low coffee table at the other end. The remainder of the rooftop patio was open to the sky.

They took turns using the new shower and unpacking. After Hani's shower she put on a clean tee shirt and the same jeans, hoping that Sam would hook up the washing machine before Monday's meeting at the bank. When she put her book and glasses on the night-stand between the cots and slid open the top drawer just a crack, a pink vibrator instantly caught her eye and she closed the drawer. She had a drawer next to her bed in Mogadishu, a simple piece of furniture that, from time to time, struck up a conversation with her. Even when closed, the drawer's erotic spirit whispered to her until she opened it, knowing that she wouldn't resist for long, only just long enough to prolong and enjoy the anticipation. Since the first night Max had been in her bed, the drawer stood slightly open.

She poured a glass of water from the water filter and walked out onto the patio in front of the tent. When the sunlight faded that one extra degree, she could see the rooftops of Mandera, and the forests beyond, fading into layers of muted greens and smokey blues. The people of Mandera were moving beneath the smells and sounds that filtered through the canopy. She stood at the parapet, letting the wind blow through her hair. Sam sat on a metal chair in the courtyard below her.

Sam got up from his chair just as Hani heard, then saw, a white Land Rover turn up their road. It sputtered to a stop next to the one she'd ridden in for the last two days. She watched as a woman, whom she assumed was Paula, got out and after a few words to Sam, disappeared into the lower floor of the house. Conversation, laughter, and footsteps got closer. Sylvie introduced Paula, who was eagerly looking at Hani, asking with her eyes why she was there.

Anita broke in to release Hani from her gaze. "The shower is wonderful. You should definitely take a shower." Paula didn't hesitate, except to reach out and grip two of Hani's fingers. "Welcome Hani, we'll talk, but the shower! How great!"

After Paula headed for the shower, Brin quietly said to Hani, "Finnish."

They spent the evening under the stars. Dinner was almost an afterthought—gin, rice and beans, more gin and some chocolates from an Italian grocery store in Nairobi. Paula and Sylvie were talking about work details and Hani tried not to listen.

Paula suddenly turned to her and said, "Sylvie said you were looking for someone, who?" The lack of a segue was maybe a Finnish thing, but then most of the people she knew were going back and forth between languages, omitting the little softening gestures and careful approaches.

"I'm looking for a friend of mine who is working in Luuq. So Mandera is the closest I can get right now." It was all true.

Paula's face took on the look of a dog sniffing at a new scent. "Luuq isn't safe they tell me. We have Somalis from Middle Juba and as far up as Luuq saying that there will be fighting again. Very soon. What kind of project is it?"

Everyone was listening so she told them a version of the truth. A version that stated that Max is a colleague from Mogadishu. And a version left out that he might be in some danger after he was taken to Luuq by one of the warlords. A version that told the truth about the farm at Geed Weyn, and a version that left out the killing of Sharif's watchmen, probably by the same people that took Max to Luuq. So, as far as they knew, Hani was here because she missed Max.

After Paula went to bed Sylvie asked Brin for a cigarette, whereupon they all stood up, including Hani, and moved over to the edge of the roof. The brief lighting ceremony brought their faces close to each other and in the flickering flame they were sisters performing last rites of another day. Hani said, "I need to add a few things to what I said."

Brin touched her hand, "You don't need to explain anything."

"I think I should though. My friend, is in Luuq, and there is a farm project...but he's sort of the hostage of a warlord too. It was his only way to protect all their camps in Mogadishu."

"He was kidnapped by a warlord?" Sylvie was unprepared for this.

This detail, she realized after saying it, was really the whole story. "His agency used to run a refugee camp there in the early 80s... he knows them...the warlord is from the Luuq region. But there was some trouble in Mogadishu and he was taken to Luuq. I had to leave too. UNICEF moved me back to Nairobi. I'm worried about him. I just want to know that he's safe."

Sylvie squared to her, "You're not thinking of going to Luuq are you? Please say you're not."

"No, but he's supposed to come to Mandera sometimes and I thought I could find him. But now I see how much trouble that might cause."

Sylvie said, "Maybe one of the other NGOs in Mandera has seen him, or knows about him. Should we ask?"

"Thanks Sylvie—all of you, but I am meeting someone on Monday that might know something. Maybe after that."

Anita said, "Sam will help you Hani. He knows Mandera. You can trust him. Really."

Brin asked. "Do you have a picture of him?"

She went over to her cot and found the picture Josie gave her.

"He's a lot darker now, and his hair has grown out. That was taken last July, in Nairobi. I met him right after this picture was taken."

Anita and Sylvie looked over Brin's shoulders, all of them looking into Max's eyes to see if he was good enough for her.

Sylvie said, "You tell us when and how we can help."

"Thank you. You could let me volunteer while I'm here. I would love to be busy."

"Of course," said Sylvie. "We'd love to have you."

Hani stood at the parapet for a while after everyone else had gone to bed. She missed her work in Mogadishu and was afraid that UNICEF might not want to send her back to Somalia. Maybe she could get herself seconded to WHC. She breathed the smoke that floated through the treetops. Max was close, but just beyond her imagination. She woke up several times in the night trying to remember where she was.

44

The squawk of Mohamed's radio sent a shock wave through him. Maybe an attack was coming, maybe Ali Nur's plan had been discovered, maybe they were coming to seize the trucks. He heard new voices, children's voices replacing the morning birds.

"It is Zaynab," Mohamed announced when he saw Max in his breezeway. “She's coming now with the.... machine to unload the trucks."

"What kind of machine?" He watched Mohamed searching for the English word. "Crane? Loader? Forklift?" and with each word Max tried to imitate the machine.

"It is that one."

“A loader.”

"It's an old one from the Italians, very slow. It will take them an hour to get here from Luuq."

Max saw Xabiib bringing his coffee to his breezeway so he hurried back to conceal the notebook on his desk.

"How did you find Mandera?" she asked as put the tray down on the edge of his desk.

"Mandera was fine. no problems. But a long day."

"Today will be a big day. So many people will be with us. Very busy." With that she hurried out.

He was also looking forward to a full day of work. The farm, he thought—get something good out of this. He wanted something to do besides escorting trucks across the border. In his notebook he’d drawn up a calendar, complete with x'd out days and Mandera days. At first it was intended to be an organizing tool, as well as a bit of paperwork that made him feel that he was managing something. But with so little to do the calendar seemed more like days scratched into the prison walls. Paranoia also edited his thoughts. The slightest chance that his notes could bring danger to Hani, kept her name out of the journal. Recording the daily activities went beyond the farm. He was detailing all the players and the circumstances of his kidnapping. The secret notebook felt disloyal, which was crazy. His loyalty belonged to the camps and his staff in Mogadishu—to Hani. They were the ones he was working for, and they needed him to do whatever he was doing here.

The truck driver's camp stirred when they heard the loader grinding through the forest—judging from the sound it would be just turning off the Doloow road. As he looked in that direction, he saw Zaynab's Land Cruiser emerging from the forest. She pulled up in a cloud of dust, and went right over to Mohamed. There were no greetings but lots of pointing. Mohamed hurried to keep up with her as she headed into the truck drivers' camp. He watched this from the doorway of his office. He'd gotten up to join them, but instead just stood there leaning on the door jamb. He liked Mohamed and Zaynab, but wondered whether they would defend him if Ali Nur's plans failed—or even if it succeeded. Xabiib, Yasmin, and Mohamed were his watchers as much as anything. And Zaynab...he suspected that she had a spell she could use on him—the familiar lure of an older woman. At times he forgot that he was not a part of this clan, not a family member, but just a stranger that was useful for now.

The drivers' children were running around the circle of talkers, stirring up a small cloud that ringed the meeting. The women in the driver's camp stayed by the small charcoal fire they were tending, unconcerned with the matters that were animating the talkers. The loader came through the forest like a rusted yellow rhinoceros and he walked out to greet it with the others.

Zaynab came up to him and said, "We need to put the containers over there." As she pointed to a place closer to the river. The farm plans that she held were now well worn and filled with notes and small side diagrams. He could see that other hands had made changes too.

She pointed out the loader operator and said, "That's Macmud, the Colonel. He will be our farm manager. The others," she pointed out the two young men leaning on her Land Cruiser. "They will also help on the farm. All of them will stay at Geed Weyn and work on the farm."

The loader started pushing dirt into a ramp, first digging out a sloped area for the trucks to back into, then piling up that soil into the beginnings of a ramp. Everyone was watching. As Max stood next to Zaynab he asked if she would be staying long enough to talk.

"Oh yes, there will be time today. Are things good?"

"Things are fine, I just need to know that things are good in Mogadishu. That they're being protected."

She turned from watching the loaders mesmerizing prehistoric dance and took his hand in both of hers, "Liban has gone to Mogadishu to keep an eye on Global Aid, not to worry. This is a good thing Max—this farm that you're helping begin." One of the trucks started up its engine, blowing out a thick plume of inky smoke.

They suspended their conversation as the main event was about to begin. The ramp was almost up to the truck bed now. The truck backed into the soft dirt as the loader pushed more dirt up to the bed. The chains that secured the container had been released and Macmud's two helpers were feeding the chain through the eyes on the end of the container. Macmud slowly guided the loader up the ramp. He tipped the loaders bucket forward a bit until his helpers could hook the chain on it. Mohamed relayed the signal now between the driver and the loader. The loader started to lift up on the end of the container. The added weight sank the loaders front tires deep into the fresh ramp before the container raised up a few inches. Mohamed, looking back and forth rapidly between the driver and the Colonel, signaled the driver to slowly pull out just as the loader pulled backwards. The container broke free from the truck bed with a loud screech.

Zaynab ran over to the spot where she wanted to place the container as the loader dragged it in a wide arc until he lined up with where she was standing. She waved it into place. By now the second truck was backing into the ramp. Macmud's helpers were unhooking the chains. The next container slid off easily and she guided it into position, leaving enough space between the two containers to add a roof and more storage.

Mohamed came over to Max after the loader shut off its unmuffled engine and handed him two hundred dollars. "Give it to the driver." He was indicating the driver of the first truck who was beginning to gather his family into his cab. "It's for the chains, and their silence."

Yasmin brought out two plastic bags filled with food for the truckers. Goodbyes, waves, dust, and they were gone.

Everyone that was left started to move towards the compound, where Zaynab was waiting. She was waving everyone in closer, hands inviting them all forward. She introduced Macmud and his two helpers, formally making them part of the camp family. Except for Max, they all knew each other. She'd introduced Max as the project manager, and she announced Macmud as the farm manager. The titles sounded the same, but he imagined it had some subtle difference in Somali.

The Colonel shook Max's hand, then put his other hand on top of Max's and said, "Macmud, please to call me Macmud."

Looking an old scar cut into his closely shaved head Max imagined the machetes flashing and slashing as Macmud fought his way through his enemies. The plans for the farm were now under his arm.

Zaynab took Max by the elbow and turned him toward his house. "While we wait for Omar we can talk."

The afternoon quiet was beginning to the sounds of sweeping and Yasmin's radio. The swirl of the Juba flashed faintly on the walls of the breezeway as they pulled up the camp chairs to the edge of the deck.

"Mogadishu is the same. Your camps are fine. Sharif is fine. You don't need to worry. Macmud. He is a good man. He was very good to Aldo and me when we needed to leave Mogadishu. He is trusted."

Max listened to her go on about the farm for a bit, before he said, "I need to speak to Sharif."

"You cannot right now. In a few weeks it will be different, but right now it is important to wait." She paused then added, "Your Mr. Dullen has come back to Mogadishu, so I think he'll be able to keep things going with Sharif."

"Alan Dullen?"

Zaynab turned towards him and lowered her sunglasses. "Not to worry. We are watching over your business in Mogadishu. We need it to look like nothing's changed. If Alan is a problem again, we can take care of it. It's only been a few weeks since you've been gone. Liban is protecting you in Mogadishu. For now, that is a very good protection, believe me."

She slid her glasses back up her straight nose and turned back to the river. She was wearing soft leather riding boots, jeans and a white tee shirt from the 1981 Pan African Games. He'd seen the same logo on the bullet ridden walls of the stadium in Mogadishu. Back then he imagined Zaynab had been a stunningly beautiful young woman, laughing and arguing with friends at a cafe on the Lido, or sitting on her family's balcony overlooking the leafy city and the Indian Ocean beyond.

"I need this to work." She said it like a prayer.

"I know. Me too." He added the amen.

45

Omar arrived near the end of siesta, so instead of ending the rest with a lazy stroll over to the kitchen, or putting on a fresh shirt, the camp came to life in a hurry. Omar was not quite a family member, and his presence altered everyone's pace as they responded to his frequency. His soldiers drove their truck over to the containers while Omar pulled up in front of the kitchen. Max placed the notebook under his cot and went out to meet him.

Omar steered him out toward the containers and said, "What have you brought us?"

Mohamed had a long metal rod fit into the loop of tin that sealed the container. With a nod from Omar, and a brief look towards Zaynab, he snapped the seal. Just inside were two crates that spanned the whole width. Max recognized the Italian name on the label and directed the soldiers to drag the hand tractors to a spot between the two containers. The soldiers looked to Omar before they agreed to move his equipment. There were long white plastic pipes in several sizes and #3 rebar that were as long as the container. Max helped the soldiers drag them out and place them in a stack on the outside of the container. Macmud was counting it all as they stacked them. Next there was a wall of cement sacks about five feet tall. Omar told the soldiers to remove enough of the sacks to allow them to pass behind the cement. He knew the layout.

The soldiers brought out a long case and Omar pried off the lid—pulling out an old AK47 covered in kerosene and grease. He nodded his head appreciatively, and with a flick of his head the soldiers went back in and retrieved a smaller wooden case.

Omar fit the curved clip and handed the gun to Mohamed. Macmud and his helpers were now unloading the cement, sack by sack, Macmud carried the first of the 94-pound sacks, then left the rest to the helpers. Deep in the container Max detected an organic grass smell. The soldiers started carrying out bales of khat, placing them next to Omar's Land Cruiser. He picked out two of the bales, the only ones with blue twine, and put these into the back of his Land Cruiser—ordering his driver to stay with the car. He pointed to one of the other bales and had it taken over to Mohamed's container.

By the time the cement was removed they'd started on the next container. Max helped clear the path for Omar's soldiers to retrieve their loot. After an hour Macmud said they'd leave the rest, which was a clear relief to his helpers. Besides, the smell of food was now compelling them all to finish.

As the crew loaded their plates with roasted goat, he watched Zaynab and Omar next to his Land Cruiser. Omar passed her a small package. Omar said his goodbyes as his soldiers bowed to Zaynab and sent looks to Xabiib and Yasmin.

After Omar's band left, Macmud and his helpers followed Mohamed to find a place to sleep. They'd been debating the use of one of the containers for living quarters. Zaynab had plans for a small village of traditional huts around the fields and had drawn a good sketch of one on the side of the irrigation plans. The rest of them sat in front of the kitchen, content to linger as the darkness brought in the quiet. When Mohamed returned, Yasmin brought out two lanterns. Xabiib got up and cleared the plates before the crawly bugs came in for the light.

Zaynab was quiet as they all settled into looking at the circle of light—tired and full, perched at the beginning of the farm. The talking and dreaming of the farm was now a series of immediate tasks. She looked from one face to another, fixing each face in the commemorative photo. He watched Yasmin looking back into Zeyneb's eyes, nodding. Then looking at Xabiib the same way. Once completed she looked long into Mohamed. He figured that anyone surviving the past decade in Somalia had a deep bond. Next, she turned to him. He could feel the warmth of her attention—splicing his image into her inner clan. He returned her look, and nodded when he had taken a few deep breaths. Still, she held him, not moving off just yet. A little smile emerged, made slightly eerie by the lamp light shining from below.

Max was also putting today's images into memory. He was just able to clear out the surrounding chaos of the real situation and look at this circle of friends, co-conspirators, and founders of a farm on the Juba. Since he'd been in Somalia, and especially since he'd been in Geed Weyn he'd been flooded with memories. Maybe it was because everything was indeed memorable, and getting more so every day—the lurking danger pushing out the petty. Now his amygdala was pumping a steady dose of adrenaline that made memories brighter and faces more beautiful.

After Zeyneb's gaze left him, he continued to look into that middle space where she'd just been. He wandered to a time when he'd sat in another circle, with someone boring into his unwilling self with their magic spell. He felt no such defensiveness about Zaynab's attention, but his earlier experience with a magic eye played out like a hologram between the lamp and the darkness. He'd seen Alison and Dmitri hold a circle with their stares. Theirs was a benign cult, with a few rituals and rites meant to welcome strangers. He'd been included in several of these meditation or healing circles, he'd felt their power, his mantra low in his chest joining with the others. The warmth of Zeyneb's gaze was like Alison's. He remembered it as breathing, like the sea, in and out, connecting you to everything.

He thought about Rebecca, his first taste of love one magical summer. She lived in the Wilbur Hotel. Max and Zoe spent a few days at Wilbur more than once. The homeschool network included lots of religious groups, all united in their need for independence with a degree of paranoia. The hotel had been closed for years until a small Christianesque cult talked someone into letting them occupy it. Rebecca called him at Alison's a few months after they broke up."

"Max, you've got to come and take me away, please."

Her voice had an urgency so he left right away. The two-hour drive wound out of the hills until it met the Columbia River, there he turned east, up the draws and onto the soft rolling wheat fields. When he arrived, she gave him a kiss and a long hug, whispering her thanks into his ear. Her body was tense. "You ready to go?"

"After the circle." she said.

"Okay. What's going on. Why don't we just leave now?"

"Not yet, please."

He hadn't seen Phillip in several years. But here he came, dressed in white, walking down from the hotel porch where he'd been watching them.

"Max, Max... well it is so good to see you." Phillip held Max's shoulders, looking into him like they do. "How are Dmitri and your mother? I haven't seen them in a long time?"

"They're well, Phillip."

Rebecca said, "It's Levi now, we're getting new names. And we're moving to Belize."

Alison had little tolerance for guys like Phillip. He was a typical spiritual seducer—Alison's term—small hands, small feet, full lips framed by waves of dark hair, and dark cloud of a beard—

eyes looking out from some unknown distance. He thought Zaynab had slightly masculine features.

"You're in time for the circle. Join us."

They followed Phillip—Levi, into the dining room and the circle. Rebecca stayed at Max's side, holding onto his arm. They sat three quarters of the way around the circle, clockwise. Phillip raised his left hand, then slowly let it float down, so that by the time it landed the circle was quiet and all eyes were on his lap. Levi, as the high priest, started to speak in tongues. Others did too so that a low hum began to reverberate in his chest. Max knew how to enter the circle's collective consciousness, or how to appear to. He kept his knee pressed against Rebecca as an anchor, as much for himself as for her. As the humming took on a chant like cadence Levi raised up his arms and brought his hands together over his head, then, when everyone was watching him, he gave a short sermon on love and the purity of anything done in the name of love. He finished, by looking at each person, one at a time, especially the women. His gaze was trying to break in, he came around the circle slowly landing on Rebecca, he waited for her to look at him. Her knee pressed into him as she fought off the intrusion. She looked into Levi's eyes for 30 seconds, then Levi broke off and looked past Max. Rebecca was vibrating.

When the circle broke up Phillip invited Max to stay for a meal. Rebecca answered yes for them. They watched as two women went into Phillips room on the second floor. "Okay, he'll be busy for ten minutes. Ill grab my thing and meet you by the orchard gate."

Max waited a full ten minutes, then drifted off across the courtyard as if he was looking for something in his car. She was waiting by the orchard with a small green suitcase. They drove off without a word until they started driving along the river toward Alison's.

Max pulled out of that memory as the circle broke up. He needed to escape, but with Hani this time.

46

In the dark, five AM quiet, Hani went down to the shower room and stood beneath the cool water. At first the water shocked her awake, then her skin recalled the heat of the afternoon as the water washed over her head, and down across her shoulders. She turned her back into the stream and breathed in and out, slowly counting out her two-minute allotment of stored water. Sam had figured that if everyone limited their showers to just two minutes it could last a few weeks. Water deliveries were getting more costly since the UN had contracted most of the water trucks in the region for their growing camps in Dadaab.

She returned to the roof-top patio to let her hair dry as she watched the eastern horizon go from deep blue to the yellow of the curtains she once had in her kitchen. She hoped to disappear into Mandera like a coastal Somali from Malindi, with her head covered and her hennaed fingers holding the edge of the sari.

Hani and Sam had talked under the stars on the front steps late Saturday night. She'd shown him the picture of Max, and as he looked at it, she found herself confessing her fears and her hopes. He only asked a few questions, the kinds a father would ask. He insisted on accompanying her to the bank. "There are lots of new people in Mandera these days," In fact, 'all the new people,' was a theme with Sam. He felt something was building, citing the increased military presence, refugees from the middle Juba and the presence of Nairobi Somalis like Mr. Hassen. "You have your business with the bank in private, but then we'll go see some of my people. If Max has been here, we will know it."

———

As they approached the main intersection Sam loomed larger and she took her place at his side, just a half pace behind, letting him forge a path through the crowded market and along the row of shops. When they reached the end of the shops, he indicated the bank with his chin. The clean white building wasn't clothed with the dust and grime of its neighbors—it would be invisible in the Nairobi, but here it seemed to be spying on the frontier city along with the troops and officials so recently interested in this edge of Kenya. Sam's paranoia seeped into her imagination.

Sam pointed to the low-slung bar across the street, "I'll be over there when you come out,"

The aluminum handle on the glass door was still cool. The air conditioners whirred in the white space that reminded her of the office in Mogadishu. She approached the counter to speak to the young Indian teller. "Good morning, I'd like to see Mr. Hassen please."

"Of course. You are?"

"Hani Chandra, I'm with UNICEF."

The teller wrote her name down on a scrap of paper, then continued to stand at the counter as if she wasn't there. When she continued to stand at the counter, he looked up impatiently and said that she could wait over there, pointing to the set of chairs and a table with magazines. She wondered if anyone had ever waited at this bank before. Once she sat, the teller placed a call to Mr. Hassen. He'd turned away and spoke quietly into the phone so that she couldn't hear. The droning machines set up a thrumming that vibrated in her chest. She breathed in to the count of seven, then a slowly exhaled in-sync with the electric motor. A telephonic beep brought her back to the moment. A few words passed over the line before the gatekeeper knocked on the office door to the right of the counter, opening it halfway, and announcing her before stepping aside. "Hani Chandra with UNICEF to see you, sir."

"I apologize for the wait Ms. Chandra. Please." He was standing behind his desk as he greeted her.

"So, how can we assist UNICEF Ms. Chandra?"

"Thank you for seeing me. This is actually a personal matter."

He sat back down.

"I'm looking for a colleague of mine. I believe that Max Dubec is a customer of yours." He relaxed just a little less, his eyes narrowing as his mouth pursed. She continued, "I know that he is working out of Luuq, in Somalia, and that his bank account...actually Global Aid's account, is with your bank." She knew that her information was correct.

Mr. Hassen's expression continued to cool, dimming the light in his eyes. "You've come from Nairobi to ask this for UNICEF?"

"No. I've come to see Max. And, I was hoping you could help me get in touch with him."

"Well," he said, sitting up now with his hands folded in front of him on the empty desk. "I cannot discuss the clients of this bank."

He was about to go on when Hani interjected, "I have the account number here, maybe you could tell me when he was last here, or when you expect him again?"

"I'm afraid I can do neither. A banking relationship is a private matter as I'm sure you can appreciate. I do hope you find what you're seeking, but this office cannot legally, or ethically, assist you." He stood up indicating that the meeting was over.

"Thank you for seeing me anyway. And when you see Max, please let him know that I am in Mandera. You can do that, yes?" This made Mr. Hassen stutter a quick repeat of his wall of client protection. She walked past Mr. Hassen and across the lobby. The coolness of the room revealed how flush she was feeling. The eyes of the teller followed her. She thought perhaps this young Indian would be easier to get information from if she found him away from the bank. Mr. Hassen watched her cross the room and waved as she reached the door.

Emerging into the real Mandera, she breathed in the heated sweet and savory, fresh and rotten. A trickle of sweat rolled down her temple as she shaded her eyes against the light. She wished she could hear the conversation she was certain Mr. Hassen was having with someone right now. Well, she thought, it's started.

She squinted across the road, looking for Sam. She spotted him and they made eye contact. She waited for the herd of goats being driven down the highway. Before she reached him, he'd started walking toward the main intersection. She came up beside him following in his wake. They didn't speak until they turned and went down the empty road towards the border. Sam told her that he'd found someone who might have seen Max last week, and they were going to see him now. She felt light-headed and wished to get out of the sun. There was no sidewalk on this descending last stretch of Kenya's frontier. The border station was now only a few blocks away. To the left was an army base and to the right was a row of tea shops and retail aimed at the incoming Somalis—a business plan that hadn't really worked out. Sam pointed ahead to a tea shop, one with a couple of Land Cruisers. Hani thought UN, or maybe CARE, until she saw the small Norwegian flag painted on the door, then the NRC logo. These were her people.

They walked into the small courtyard and under the sun shade. A box fan was dancing on the bar top with a rhythmic rattle. This was a much rougher copy of the NGO bars and tea shops in Nairobi or Lusaka, but it did carry on the tradition of license plates from around the world tacked to the walls and roof rafters. Sam led her to a table where a young Somali sat before a plate of chicken and rice. He looked up at her, then to Sam, and stood up to greet her. Sam introduced her to Yusuf.

"Please, you should finish your meal," she told him.

"Tell her what you told me." said Sam.

She sat down across from Yusuf and held out her picture of Max. "Have you seen him?"

"Yes, yes, that's him," he said looking back at Sam and nodding.

Sam said, "Good. I'll get something to drink and you can talk. Do you want anything Hani?"

"Oh, I have what I wanted—news."

Sam went over to the bar and got a Fanta.

Yusuf started, "I saw him last week, I think it was Friday. He parked his technical right over there and I watched it for an hour. I watch for the UN and others. I will watch for him again. I was looking for him today."

"Was he well? Did he seem good to you?"

"Oh, very well. I want to work for him. I can find anything he needs. Ask the other NGOs, I could be a good help."

"I'm sure you are. Did he tell you about his project in Somalia?"

"No. Well, yes he did say he was working on a farm outside of Luuq, Geed Weyn...the old refugee camp."

Sam came over and sat down. "It's best to leave that. She needs to know when you think he'll return."

"I'm here today waiting on him, maybe tomorrow." Yusuf looked at Hani and added. "Do you think he will need my help? I would go to Somalia, I'm okay there too."

"I don't know Yusuf." She looked at Sam, searching his face for a clue about how much to ask or reveal.

Sam said, "When you see him again, I want you to come and tell me. Don't tell him about this yet. You know you must be careful. Maybe someone follows him, we want to watch him to be sure. Okay?"

Yusuf's face puzzled over.

"It's okay," she said. "Don't worry. We just want him to be safe. I am his friend and Sam is my friend too. You can help us. Just be sure to tell Sam, okay?"

Yusuf finished mopping up the last of the sauce with a piece of bread. He pledged his caution, clearly hoping it would lead to a job. Hani knew these young Somalis. Educated in the northern frontier as a Kenyan resident but always a Somali threat. There were camps for them, not futures. Employment with an NGO was a way out. As her hope mixed with her sympathy for Yusuf's situation, she gave him a hug. When she walked back out to the street, she looked down the road to the border. She could have stayed all day just watching the road winding off to the left on the Somali side. That would be the path to Luuq, to Geed Weyn, and that was where her eyes lingered.

She caught up to Sam who had started walking slowly, deep in thought. "I believe he is telling the truth, and that he'll come to me with news of your Max. Don't worry, but be patient." Hani, now in step with Sam's pace, nodded, not wanting to interrupt his thoughts. "I will tell you what I'm hearing about Somalia...and about Luuq and its clans. I have been listening to the wind with an ear toward the Gedo, and I have heard rumors about Ali Nur, and his uncle. They say The Boqor has gone to Beledweyne with his artillery and most of his army. I think, in his uncle's absence, Ali Nur is holding the space north of Jilib and that he wants to keep control of Kismayo. What I also hear is that Kenya is trying to seal off this part of the border forcing any future migration towards Dadaab. Soon our border will be closed." He added quickly, "That might not happen Hani, I'm only trying to figure out why this, and why that. Be patient, we will connect with your Max when he comes to Mandera again."

47

Mark Walters called John Thomas as soon as he got off the phone with Mr. Hassan. "Damn it John, this Hani needs to be controlled! She's in Mandera! She's been to Hassan and he's getting nervous. I want her back in Nairobi today! Get her out of Mandera, now!"

John's first reaction was admiration—she was determined to find her lover. He could only wish for that kind of love. Mandera would be hard to work out on short notice, but he looked forward to getting out of the office and maybe seeing her again. She'd been in his head ever since their lunch last week. Her search for Max seemed so much more noble than the agency's mucking about in the Somali clan fighting.

He found his favorite pilot at a Celtic bar near Wilson Field. Jimmy Leary was just settling into an afternoon of drinking when John came to get him.

"There's no fucking way. I'm not going anywhere today, and tomorrow it will be the same answer. Find someone else."

They'd already had half a dozen assignments together. The company didn't trust him without a minder, so besides John, a number of embassy staff, under the cover of cultural exchange or trade related assignments, got to ride along, making their time in Africa seem full of adventure. In truth, what he did was routine for a pilot trying to make enough to retire in Portugal. John noticed that he'd put on a bit of a gut. At forty-two Jimmy was only five years older than John, but he'd aged in the African sun, a bit run down and overweight. His round head was highlighted by bright little eyes.

"Come on man, it's time to go to work. I'll buy you a night of drinking when it's over. Right now, I need you sober."

"Nope. It's me day off and it might last a week if I'm lucky. Besides, you can't make a round trip to Mandera in a day unless you leave at dawn. There's no way I'm flying the frontier at night now that the Kenyan pilots are patrolling the line." He didn't object when John slid his pint to the other side of the table and sat down. "What's in Mandera anyway? I don't want to know."

"Look, we can spend the night in Mandera somewhere. Fly back in the morning. It will be worth it."

"I know an Irish girl up there."

It was only a matter of time. "See, we could see old friends and have a nice Ethiopian dinner. Mandera's lovely this time of year."

"So, what's in Mandera?"

"A woman, and she needs to come back to Nairobi as soon as possible. Mark insists."

"Ah...it's a woman. So, what's she done to Mark?"

"I don't think you need to know more, but it will be a chivalrous mission. I'm not sure you'll be rewarded by the damsel, but you will be rewarded."

"It will be dear John Thomas." And with that he left his beer on John's side of the table and stood up. "Why are you still sitting there, it'll be dark in five hours."

An hour later they were taxiing down the runway in the Pilatus Porter. It would be three hours without talking since Jimmy didn't provide headsets.

48

Max smelled the freshly turned earth, familiar and inviting. The clank of shovels first alerted him to where he was when he opened his eyes. His dreams had been a puzzle, the pieces not fitting together no matter how many times he tried. Hani showed up sometimes, but she always was out of reach, she couldn't hear him. It was taking longer and longer to fall asleep since his subconscious escape planning was too intense to lure peaceful slumber. It wouldn't let him tiptoe away from the real world, down the hall to sleep. The one thing that did bring him peace in the night were the occasional bird calls. Their otherworldly songs took him away, floating over everything with the casual confidence of the birds.

Max walked out from the containers, following the path of the rebar dragged through the dust. The Colonel and his helpers were digging out a platform halfway down the river bank for a pump station. The loader was building a path sideways and down across the bank. Macmud would bite a bit of dirt each pass, going just far enough out to avoid tipping into the river. Max watched until he'd carved a narrow road down to the platform. He scraped it level and retreated up the new road to where Max was standing. They nodded to each other.

By the time Zaynab arrived, Macmud and his helpers had forms set up for the concrete at the pump pad, and had started digging the irrigation canals using an ancient transit to determine the grade. Rebar stakes with strips of white cloth arced in a line that encircled the bend in the river. Around ten the loader shut down and Macmud and his helpers sat in the shade of the raised bucket smoking or chewing. Yasmin brought out tea and fresh bread. The diesel fumes and dust hung in the air, giving thc horizon a blue hue that followed the Juba downstream. Max felt that he could be anywhere in the world right now, anywhere where people grow food, live by rivers and see their plans turn into reality.

———

By afternoon, Zaynab and Max were covered with dust and crusted mud. They'd walked the full length of the farm picking up handfuls of the red dirt and letting it crumble through their fingers. She joined Max on the breezeway as the camp quieted down to its slowest heartbeat. She sat next to him, boots up on a five-gallon bucket, her arms draped over the arms of the plastic chair.

"I heard from my brother this morning. Your supplies were very welcome. He's looking forward to a few more from you."

"I heard talk on the radio that the US might land in Somalia soon."

"Everybody talks...I don't know what they're going to do. But I think they'll do it soon."

"Would that be a good thing for Luuq? The US in Somalia?"

"You like it here? You care about Luuq? You have a place here someday, maybe a statue in Luuq!" She laughed and poked his leg with her finger. She looked out at the Juba, sat up a bit, then turned to look him. "I won't leave Luuq until this farm is working." She continued to stare at him. "If they take too long to come ashore there will be a big problem for Somalia. It is the only way right now to stop the fighting. They must come soon. And, yes, Ali Nur knows this too." She added, "Take another twenty thousand dollars tomorrow. We'll have lots of workers here in a few days.

49

Early the next morning Max had quick breakfast, while Mohamed waited in the technical. On this second trip he found the map laying out more clearly. After a quick pee stop before Toobiye, they rolled into the checkpoint where Mohamed got out. Max saw Mohamed's friend waiting by the same hut.

His study of the map revealed that the road between Toobiye and the Kenyan border ran parallel to the Dara River. It was here, between Toobiye and Mandera, that he could easily trek overland into Kenya without being seen. This would be the only place he could escape without someone being able to see. But then what? He was hoping to have enough time on this trip to take a taxi out along the Kenyan side of this stretch.

Once he crossed the border he drove very slowly up to the tea shop, scanning the army post across the street. Yusuf was waiting when he parked.

"How are you Yusuf?" Max said as he shook his hand.

"Very good. I knew you would come back today, just like you promised. You are good?"

"I am. We'll have lunch after I get back. I might be a little longer this time." Max looked at his watch. "Maybe close to one o'clock. Does that work?"

"I'll be here. Thank you, Mr. Max."

"Just Max, okay?" With that, he grabbed his messenger bag and walked up the road toward the bank.

Having been here once was enough to make his walk to the bank routine and novel at the same time. The landmarks rolled out in front of him, familiar and predictable. He wished that his skin was not so foreign. He wanted to walk down this street and see what people were doing. He wanted to have a beer on one of these porches with the old men telling their stories.

The bank was routine. Customs papers and manifests were handed over like the first time. Max again wished to see the account balance and activities, and when he was through, he requested an additional thirty thousand in US currency. And again, after an uncomfortable pause, Mr. Hassen called out to his teller to prepare the withdrawal. This was no regular bank. It was clear to Max that this particular branch had a lot of US currency. He doubted that he'd be able to get that much foreign cash out of a branch in Nairobi without waiting a few days. He thought that he should ask for more each time to see if there was a limit. This nagged at him the rest of the day. His name was on the account. He was taking the cash out, in his name, for way more money than he could justify with the farm. Even though the cash didn't feel like real money, there was a real trail, and it led to him. Mr. Hassen said the truck would be waiting by early afternoon.

There were two taxis across the street from the bank, and he picked the driver that spoke the best English. Pulling out his map he pointed at a road that went out of Mandera, toward the Toobiye checkpoint, but on the Kenyan side.

"Yes, but where do you want to go out there? There's only goats and cows out there. No one lives there."

He told the taxi driver he just wanted to visit the three corners where the countries came together.

The driver shrugged. "There is nothing to see. The border control is not there."

"That's okay, I just want to see the countryside." Max pulled out a twenty and they started to drive through the town heading north.

There didn't seem to be a direct road out of town on this side of Mandera. They drove past the camp he'd seen from the road. WHC was stenciled on the white Quonset tent. The driver turned left and right down streets and alleys until they reached the ragged edge of town. A narrow track led out into a field and then into the forest. The bigger and deeper forest was on his left, following the Dawa River. On the right there were footpaths leading toward Somalia. Max watched the taxi's odometer to see where they would be in fifteen kilometers, that was where the road would be only four kilometers from the Somali border, and about ten from Toobiye.

Mr. Hassen placed another call to Mark Walters before Max had made it across the street. Walters then picked up the sat phone on his desk and dialed John Thomas. When a phone rang in the little tea shop, Sam turned to look at the white man on a SAT phone, sitting alone. The mind-game of figuring out where someone was from, what that accent was, who do they work for, etc., ran in his head. He recognized most of the expats, and could date their service in Mandera to the color of their clothes—by the time your white shirts turned the color of the Dawa you were a local. This guy's shirt had the slight pink white of a Nairobi laundry. The SAT phone meant government, probably American. Yusuf walked around the back of Max's technical, blocking off any direct view of the stranger's eyes. There was a triangle of peripheral staring.

Sam could see the truck driver walking about, tugging on the chains and looking at his watch. Max's taxi pulled in behind the waiting truck. It wasn't unusual for everyone to be watching the activity on this stretch of road, but Sam was amazed at this American with the SAT phone, his lack of tradecraft. He was intent on what Max was doing, completely unaware of being watched. Yusuf looked to Sam, but Sam kept his cover. The taxi drove off and left Max talking to the driver before he walked up to the tea shop where Yusuf was waiting. Then he spotted John.

"I'll be right in. I need to talk to this guy for a minute."

Yusuf walked past Sam's table, still playing his role, and took a seat at the next table, sitting back-to-back with Sam.

"Hey Max. You look right at home out here." John kicked a chair out for Max to take a seat.

"What are you doing here? Here to check up on me?" His first thought was about the money he'd been syphoning off. Did they know? Of course, they knew, but did they care?

"I just wanted to see if you were doing all right. Looks like you'll be pretty busy this week. Do you want something to eat?"

"No, I have plans already."

"Oh, with Yusuf? Good kid."

"You've met the one person I know here, except for the banker. So, how many more? How much longer?"

"It won't be long, maybe a few more weeks."

"Have you seen her?"

John thought that Max might not know that she was in Mandera, but he doubted it.

"She misses you Max. You're a lucky guy."

"Did you tell her when I would be back in Nairobi?"

"I told her that I would keep her informed."

John was beginning to think that Max really didn't know Hani was here.

"Look, I've got to go back before dark and I've promised Yusuf a good meal this time. Please tell her that I am coming as soon as I can." He reached out and touched John's forearm, Somali style, implying a contract between them.

John's eyes softened under the touch. "I'll tell her Max. I will." As they shook hands John asked. "Where did you go after the bank?" He held on to Max's hand a bit longer.

"I had an hour to kill so I took a drive around town. I was seeing where a few of the NGOs were. Remember, I'm just an aid worker here. Are you going back to Nairobi today?"

"Probably, I might be back soon though. Is Yusuf your guy here?"

"I think so. He'll know when I'm in town."

"Good, 'til then." John walked out and got into a taxi.

Max walked back through the tea shop and sat down across from Yusuf. John's appearance in Mandera reassured him on one level that he was not forgotten out here in the bush. It also brought up feelings about Hani that he wanted to think about later, when he was alone. The money didn't come up. He looked at Yusuf now and saw something was wrong.

"What is it?" he asked.

Yusuf said, "Max, this is Sam. He wants to speak with you. I know him, you can trust him."

Sam was in the process of joining their table. Max had a stab of fear. Sam didn't smile and Max thought that he was getting held up, or that maybe this guy was a spy for Ali Nur. He pushed down his panic and nodded to Sam.

"Why do you want to speak to me? Are you a friend of Yusuf's?"

Yusuf cut in, "Sam is a very good person. I know him."

"You are Max? With Global Aid? And you work in Luuq. Right?" Sam asked.

"Yes," said Max, looking back and forth from Yusuf to Sam.

"Who was that man you were talking to? American?"

"Sam, nice to meet you." Max held out his hand as a way to slow down the interrogation. He was uncomfortable telling him anything, especially about John and what that led to. "What is it that you want to talk to me about?"

"I cannot tell you unless I know some things. I know Mandera, but I do not know you or the one you were meeting with. Whatever you are doing I think it could be dangerous and I don't want anyone hurt, so I need to know if you are safe."

Max was curious about the meaning of, safe. "Please just tell me what you want. I'm safe and I'm not in any more danger than anyone else right now. What is this about?"

Sam whispered, "Hani."

Max quickly looked at Yusuf, but he'd never mentioned her to him. He looked back at Sam. "Do you know her?"

"Yes."

"Where is she? Is she here in Mandera? Is she okay?"

"Yes, and yes."

The truck driver walked up to the tea shop and was now standing by Max's technical. He didn't come in but waited for Max to see him there, then he pointed to his watch and sent a pleading look at the sun, and then back to Max.

Sam turned to see this and then looked back at Max.

"When do you come back?"

"Where's Hani, I want to see her, now."

"I think you must go back to Luuq soon, yes? Next time, plan to stay overnight. Hani will be waiting."

"But, where is she staying? Who is she with?"

"Look Max." Sam's expression softened as he leaned forward on his elbows. "I am watching out for her. She is staying at one of my houses, with three very good European women that I care for. I take care of Hani like the other sisters. She will be safe. But you had someone follow you today after you left the bank, and then the American came looking for you. I don't know who else is watching you so we cannot lead them to my house. I will figure out a way for you to see Hani next time you come. Yusuf will watch."

Max pulled out a hundred, and gave it to Yusuf. "Thanks Yusuf."

When they were all standing, Max remembered the lunch. "I'm running out on lunch again…"

"It is never mind," said Yusuf.

Max shook Sam's hand. Again, feeling jealous of someone else's proximity to Hani. Once on the road he drove at the truck's pace, picking up Mohamed and his friend at Toobiye. It was dark when they reached Geed Weyn.

50

"Let's go John Thomas!"

"Plenty of time Jimmy, we'll be in before six, right?"

"There's a storm coming in this evening. Looks like you didn't find the girl."

"Nope. She might be back in Nairobi already. Maybe we'll come back. Did you find yours?"

"I did."

"And?'

"And, I might be willing to come this way again—with or without you."

He wound up the powerful engine and they taxied out to the west end of the tarmac. Without stopping, he turned the nose into the east and within ten seconds they were airborne. Instead of heading south he took an extra circle over Mandera, picking out the WHC tents before straightening out for Nairobi. Seeing Brin in her natural habitat was a shock. Until now he hadn't thought about what she did, or where she worked. He'd underestimated her, he thought. No, it wasn't that...no, he'd never seen her at all. He'd never wondered about what she did, or why. This Brin, the girl that kissed him eagerly before he left, this heroic version, was a person he wanted back in his life. Her fierce Irish beauty attracted him—a salty and satisfying beauty that demanded equality.

He had a feeling that the woman with Brin was the person John was looking for. He tried to stay out of company business and just fly the plane. Without headsets he didn't have to listen to them talk, but he did see faces.

Wilson Field had a large fleet of airplanes dedicated to Somalia—The Red Cross, UNICEF, NGOs, and always a few foreign government planes. A lot could be learned from the pilots and ground crews. After they landed, Jimmy and his helper spent two hours preparing the plane for another flight. He arrived at The Lion's Den a little after eight in the evening, and ordered a large steak with potatoes. Princess, the owner and cook, sat down at his table when she served the meal.

"The word is that the Americans have decided to land in Mogadishu soon." she said.

"Who says that?"

"The South Africans." She pointed with her chin at the group of men all dressed in white short-sleeve uniforms. Jimmy knew most of them and nodded when one of them looked up and noticed him.

"The journalists were with them in Uganda today. When they returned, that one over there, has not stopped tapping on her computer." Again, with the chin she indicated the back booth, where Jimmy could see the legs of a woman and the light from a laptop screen. He knew those legs—The Guardian.

"Princess, keep this warm for me, I need to see her. Bring us a little whiskey would you dear?"

He pushed aside his meal after he poked one last bit of potato into his mouth. Princess gave him a look, but he stopped her. "I'm only hunting for a little information."

He waited for the whiskeys to be served at her table before he walked over. "May I join you? Unless you need both of them."

"Go away Jimmy. I've got to finish this by ten."

"Oh, that's okay. I'll just sit here real quiet and sip one of these." He slid into the booth.

Katherine Toland broke a little smile as she reached for the whiskey. She shoved it at his glass, almost knocking it over. "Cheers. After this you've got to let me work, okay?"

He swirled his glass and took a small sip. She did the same.

"Princess tells me you were in Kampala today. What's the news?"

"You'll read about it tomorrow. Until then it's mum."

"You know, I could, but I'd never hear the news that wasn't printed. Only you can tell me that."

Katherine relented easily, knowing that he wouldn't stop pestering her until she gave him something. He was someone you wanted to keep happy, since he'd fly you where no one else would. "I was in Entebbe actually, with the British Ambassador and various spooky types from London. Also, there for the meeting was the US Ambassador to Somalia, with his straight men. Honestly, these guys should be in the movies. NATO had a representative, along with Uganda, and Kenya. Ethiopia was out because of the Eritrean problems. I think Ethiopia is betting on a future Somaliland in the north to solve its internal Somali issues. You won't read about that."

Princess brought two more whiskeys.

After Princess left, he asked, "Did they decide to go into Somalia? That's the story, right? There's a betting pool among the pilots at Wilson. I'm down for Saturday."

"You lose."

"When? Where?"

"Pick up a real newspaper tomorrow morning. Dateline: Mogadishu."

"Do the warlords see this coming?"

"Oh yes, they see it and they welcome it."

"You can't tell me they've become partners with their invaders? Wow, that's not going to happen,"

"Don't forget the two million Somalis facing starvation, you cynic. Food aid will pour in, instead of Somalis pouring out to Dadaab."

"So, what's your angle on this?"

"Well, the part I'm supposed to be writing is about the coalition. Coalitions are all the thing, you know. Of course, it's mainly the US going in with the UN endorsing it all. They really had no choice. The Foreign Office is going along to keep an eye on Kenya, and the French welcome the use of Djibouti. The Boqor and The Hadji are part of the coalition. They win."

"How so?"

"Look, they've been fighting for more than a year, they're both worn out. There's little left to steal from each other now. So, they negotiated for territory held, and the boundaries patrolled by US troops. In a few months they'll regain their strength, having controlled the movement of food aid outside of Mogadishu and Kismayo. Here's the best part though. They've both agreed to turn over a whole list of weapons. Can you imagine them really doing that? Honestly, no one believes that the US will stay in Somalia very long. The warlords are hoping to replace all their supplies once the coalition collapses." She drained her glass and said, "I'm so fucking tired of this part of the job, Jimmy. I'm becoming a messenger for the official line. My editors are getting unheard of access to the military. Do you know that there will be film crews and press invited to the beach landing? All arranged by the coalition. Guaranteed to be a safe excursion for all."

"Sounds too good to be true, peace in our time."

"Well, on the bright side it could be peace *for* a time."

"What's Kenya doing in this coalition?"

"The way I see it is that Kenya pushed this now because so many Somalis are crossing into the Frontier. Dadaab might be able to handle sixty thousand refugees. They've already started another camp around Dadaab to double that. They don't want them getting past Dadaab. They never have. What they do want is a piece of the massive humanitarian budget, and the millions from illicit trade in sugar and khat. No matter how much fighting and destruction continue in Southern Somalia, the trading goes on."

"I won't need the morning paper now."

"I've got to finish this up now. If you're still around later…"

"I'm heading out now my dear. Let's go have a nice dinner some night before you go to Mogadishu."

"That assignment has gone to the Ambassador's niece, Shelley. I'm sure she is very experienced."

"Like hell, right?"

"Good night, Jimmy. Call me."

51

Sam gave Yusuf a phone number and told him to call when Max was back in town. "Just leave a message with the person that answers. Don't use any names, just report that you're ready for *lunch.* I'll take it from there."

Sam drove to the WHC camp, hoping to find Hani with the sisters. Before he got to the camp he turned right, into an alley with several bungalows on either side. The house at the end of the row had a long porch and wide front steps covered in flowers. The brightly painted bungalows sat in the shade of overhanging trees, with gardens in various states of riot. This block was once the living quarters for a mission to Somalia, and the big house at the end of the alley was once the meeting hall—some still called it the sanctuary.

He went up the steps and knocked on the door, calling out. "Tessa! Tessa, hello?"

"Samuel...come in." She was as bright as her flowers, wearing a brilliant yellow headscarf, and earrings with small iridescent blue wings dangling around her bare shoulders. She'd been a teenager working for the missionaries as a house cleaner, and Sam was general handyman around the mission as a young man. He bought this property, one piece at a time, after the missionaries left and she'd lived here ever since. She put together a tea with fresh fruit and thin wafer cakes, his favorite. Her eyes took in his grey hair, and the stubble on his chin. That giant round head held a smile that gave her warmth.

Ever since Sam met Hani, and found out that she was searching for her lover, he wanted to see Tessa. As she sat there in front of him, he watched her, she was still the girl he first kissed. He could see past the years to that slim Ethiopian figure now aged to maturity. The years hadn't bent her over, or dulled the brightness in her eyes. He could see the brushstrokes if he looked closely, but from here, the picture was one of a comfortable beauty that made his chest ache.

"Have you been well?"

"Yes, yes, I've been good. I should have come by more. But I'm very busy with the women from my house."

"I see them most days on my walk. Sylvie brought me a present from Mombasa, see?" She turned her head back and forth, showing off the earrings. "I miss them when they go away. There's a new girl with them now, Hani. You have too many pretty women in your life now, no wonder you don't come by."

It was meant as a joke, but, like most humor, it had the sharp edge of something true. He'd planned to ask Tessa for a place for Hani to meet Max, but now this request felt thoughtless.

"What is it, Sam?"

"You know me...yes, there is something I wanted to ask you."

"Well, then ask me, Sammy."

"Hani is here in Mandera looking for her boyfriend, who's working in Luuq. He might be mixed up in something dangerous, so I want to be careful how they meet. I was thinking that this would be a good place."

"You want them to meet at my house?"

"No, not this house but one of the bungalows, maybe the green one."

"Of course. Bring her here whenever you need to. I'd like the company."

"He might be here on Thursday or Friday. Someone will call you saying, *it's time for lunch,* or something like that. Then call me at this number." He handed her a business card with a number written on the back. "I'll only bring him here when I'm sure no one is following. This needs to be very private. It's the best way to stay out of danger."

"You are so dramatic."

"Things are changing. Not like it used to be." Sam reached out and took her hand. "I am afraid for Mandera, for the Frontier. Borders won't stop this." They sat together until a breeze slammed the screen door.

Tessa wrapped her long arms around him as he stood one step below on the wide stairs. "Come back soon Sammy. Promise, or I won't let you go."

"I promise."

The visit with Tessa reframed his day. His lips still tasted sweet. The renewed idea of love...of loving Tessa again, displaced the paranoia that had been growing in him. The highlight of every day had been seeing Anita, Brin, Paula, and Sylvie home safe every night. Hani was now one of them too. All of them were so brave and free. No, he thought, they are young, like Tessa and me long ago.

He walked into the WHC tent looking for Sylvie. The office end had two rows of folding tables and a half dozen white plastic chairs. Sylvie was typing away on a laptop when he came in.

"Sam, welcome. Do you want tea or water?"

"No dear. Do you have a moment to talk?"

"Yes, naturally. Sit."

"You need to know some things so you can all be safe." To the question in her eyes he quickly added, "It's not a big problem, but Hani." He lowered his voice and looked around. "Her boyfriend might be in some danger, and that might come to us, to you and the Cooperative."

"What kind of trouble?"

"I don't know, but he has people watching him in Mandera. He has U.S. Government people meeting him. He takes trucks across into the Gedo. All of it says danger. But Hani wants to see him. So, I've asked Tessa to let her stay at one of the bungalows for their rendezvous."

"Have you met him?"

"Yes, I came to tell Hani, but I wanted you to know why she'll be gone for a few days."

Sylvie suddenly remembered Brin's visitor. "We had a visitor this morning. He's a friend of Brin's, a pilot."

"Where's Brin?"

Sylvie pointed. Over the top of the canvas partitions, he could see Brin's spiky hair. Even at this distance her freckles could be seen dancing across her nose.

"Brin!" Sylvie yelled, then pointed to Sam, and waved her over.

When Brin came over, he asked her, "Did your friend say what he was doing in Mandera?

"Who, Jimmy? He flew some American up here for the day."

"Did he see Hani?"

"Hani? Jimmy did, sure. Why would that matter?"

"Was an American with him?"

"It was just Jimmy. Hani was working with me when he came in. What's going on Sam?"

"How well do you know this pilot?"

"Jimmy? I've known him ever since I came to Kenya. Irish, you know, we've dated. I think he is just a pilot. He flies all kinds of people around, independent. Do you think he was looking for Hani? That's crazy Sam. He just said hello to her, the rest of the time he was talking to me."

"A coincidence then?" asked Sam.

Sylvie said. "Yeah, pretty sure...anyway it is a good thing for Hani to be away from here for a while."

Brin looked at Sylvie. "Where's she going?"

"She's going to stay at Tessa's until she meets with her boyfriend."

"Wow." Brin was shaking her head.

Sam got up and said, "I really don't know if there's a problem...but there are lots of little clues. Let's just be careful. Yes?"

"Of course. Thank you." She pointed toward a group of women in the shade and grabbed his wrist. "Don't frighten her Sam."

Hani quickly excused herself and walked with him away from the group.

"Is he here? Did you see him?"

"Yes, he was only here for a little bit." He was going to explain but her face fell,

"He's gone? Sam?"

"He's coming back in two or three days, and he'll be here for one night. He had to go today, but he'll return to see you."

"He knows that I'm here? You told him?"

"Yes. Now, I have a place for you to stay, with Tessa. I'll bring him to you there. It will be the safest. Okay?"

"At Tessa's?"

"She is happy to have you. We're very old friends, it will be a safe place."

By sunset she'd moved her few items into the green bungalow. She sat with Tessa on the front porch talking and listening to the thrum of traffic beneath the percussive monkey beat and bird calls. The equatorial winter evening was cooling, green to blue. Tessa listened to Hani's story, her mind wandering through her own odyssey.

Hani awoke in the night to the sound of rain on the tin roof. She listened, feeling alone and safe. The alone part was an orphan's constant companion. The safe part was the clean sheets and her new friends. Louder drips were now coming from the house's gutters, pouring streams of water into puddles that were spreading across the yard.

She got out of bed, with her blanket wrapped around her, and sat on the porch where the rain popped and banged over her head. The trees shook off the water with every breeze, adding layers of beats on top of the seeping sound of fresh earth. She went inside and shook out a cigarette from the pack that Anita gave her when she left, along with a copy of her proposal awaiting edits.

52

John waited two hours for Mara to come home, and when she did, she wouldn't let him in. "Hani's not home right now, I'll tell her you stopped by." Then she shut the door in his face, slowly, but firmly. He could hear the bolt slide and the chain being secured. He returned to his office and was surprised to see so many people still at their desks. Mark was back from Kampala and asking for him.

"Enter." Mark barked through the closed door. He was digging through a file cabinet, pulling out a wad of folders and putting them in a banker's box. Without looking up, he said. "Close it down. Pull your guy out and close any accounts. I'll handle Hassen."

"There are four more containers heading for Mandera right now, three of them will arrive on Thursday we've got to get them all out of Kenya by Saturday."

"Fine, close it after that, just don't keep any more of our money in their account." Mark looked at him. "Did you know that your guy is taking our money. Hassen said that he's grabbed more than fifty thousand dollars in cash so far." Then he leaned forward, looking into John's eyes and asked. "Did you find the girlfriend?"

"Nope. She was there alright, but I think she's back at her friend's apartment by the university. I'll be sure by tomorrow."

"I want this wrapped up. I hope I don't have to worry about your guy up there, or his girlfriend. You let that little thief know that he can keep the money as long as he keeps quiet. But if he starts talking, his girlfriend might have to convince him to shut up." Mark drummed his fingers. "You know, maybe your larcenous aid worker should keep working the farm for now. Keep him in Somalia until we see how things turn out."

"I don't think he'll go for that. He's going to want to move freely pretty soon. We can't make him stay. Can we?"

"No, of course not. But he could find a good reason to stay put for a while. Let me know as soon as you find the girl, okay?" Mark came around the desk and put his arm around John's shoulder. The awkward move tensed both of them. "Stay on this John, you're doing a great job. When are you scheduled back to the States?"

"February sir."

"Maybe I can get you out by Christmas, would you like that?"

"I guess, sure."

With that he slid out of Mark's arm and went back to his desk. It was midnight and he was wired. He took several files and put them in his briefcase. He didn't head back to his apartment, but found himself driving toward Mara's.

53

When the rain started in the middle of the night, pinging off the rooftops and containers, Max felt the camp stir. Within a few minutes he could hear Xabiib and Yasmine on their breezeway, laughing. The Dyer rains had finally come. This was a mixed blessing. The farm work had started without counting on the Deyr at all. The field work and ditching would be stalled if the rains continued for more than two or three days. While he was in Mandera, Macmud had cleared and planted a quarter hectare with a variety of the new seeds, at least that patch would be able to take advantage of the rains.

He didn't join in the celebration. Ever since he witnessed what rain could do to the roads, he dreaded it. Having a passable road felt like the door was open. Once the roads washed out, the door closed.

Before dawn he noticed that the rains had stopped. He could hear the early bird's excitement. The dampness made him wrap his blanket up around his shoulders. When he came to the kitchen, he found them all listening to a Somali broadcast on Xabiib's transistor radio. Yasmine gave him an update. "Your Americans have landed in Mogadishu. They were like monsters coming out of the sea, and then the planes and helicopters swarmed into the airport."

She was excited. Mohamed looked worried. He guessed that old Macmud had seen this all before as he got up and roused his helpers. He could see by their boots that they'd already been out in the fields.

Yasmin summarized the news he missed. "They are going to make sure the food aid is safe, even outside of Mogadishu. Hadji

Mahti has stopped his war with The Boqor. And the Deyr too!" She danced a little two step and then covered her mouth.

He went over to Mohamed, "Hey, is everything okay?"

Mohamed looked up, slowly translating the question before he replied, "Billii's suffering the Malaria."

"I'm going into Luuq today for fuel, can I get you something? I'll see if Zaynab has some Primaquine."

———

The Juba River was flowing hard under the bridge at Luuq. When he pulled into Zaynab's he could see Omar's black Land Cruiser, and Asha in gumboots, washing away the red mud by throwing pails of water over it. When she saw him, she pointed to the front door, then took another pail water and tossed it over Omar's Land Cruiser

Zaynab and Rana were standing in the open doorway.

Zaynab said, "Look who we have in Luuq now!"

"Hello Max. It's been a while. You're starting to look the part."

As far as looking the part, he thought she had him beat. "Are you coming out to Geed Weyn?"

"I'd like to."

Zaynab insisted, "Of course you should visit, see what Max is making."

Behind them in the doorway he saw Omar with a towel around his thick neck. He didn't smile or offer a greeting. Max tried to break Omar's glare. "Your container is still on the truck. Macmud will get it off this afternoon."

Omar said, "I will come out. Don't open it."

Max noticed how Zaynab and Rana both stiffened when Omar appeared behind them. He felt like he'd interrupted something. They didn't invite him in, or even offer him water.

There was an uncomfortable vibe and he wanted to stay away from anything that might delay meeting Hani tomorrow. Remembering the Primaquine, he asked Zaynab if she had any.

Rana asked, “Who’s got Malaria?”

“It’s for Billii, she came back from Toobiye with us yesterday. Mohamed thinks it’s Malaria.”

Rana walked Max to the technical while Zaynab went to find the medicine. “I remember when this was a new Land Cruiser, with a roof and a windscreen.”

“When you come out to Geed Weyn I’d like to talk to you. I don’t want to talk around here.”

Asha came out with four bottles of mineral water and some Chloroquine.

“How old is this, Asha?”

He waited as Rana checked the label, then handed him the pills. “I’ll come out later today and check on Billii.” They watched Omar backing his Land Cruiser out of the steaming courtyard.

Max drove up the neck of land that kept Luuq from being an island. The road turned into a street without sidewalks, and alleys leading off under the green canopy. He saw Omar’s Land Cruiser on the right side of the commons, at the fuel depot. He was sitting at a rickety tin table with a bright red can of Coca Cola. When Max pulled up, he heard the town generator chugging away. The depot was an empty lot between the generating station and the tea shop that only served Samosas and Coke. If the generator was working the Coke was cold.

Two boys were hauling a jerrycan towards Omar’s car. Max signaled them to fill his too, and then went over to sit with Omar. Another Coke came out and Max slowly pulled the tab. He was looking forward to dining out in Luuq, such as it was, but sharing this little reward with Omar pretty much ruined it. His dark presence hung over the lack of conversation. Max tried to think of something to say to him, but he didn't want to ask any questions that might arouse suspicion. In his darkest thoughts he believed that Omar would be the one to pull the trigger, if it came to that.

"Macmud will pull the container off this afternoon."

"You said that already."

"We're going to pull it next to the others."

So far Omar hadn't looked at him, at least he hadn't turned his head, and Max couldn't see behind the dark glasses. Finally, he spoke to the space in front of him. "Now we will see if you keep your promises." He got up when the boys came to the table and he handed them some Shillings.

"How much do you give them?" Max asked.

Omar turned to him. "Do you have Shillings? Or just our Dollars?"

"I have some Shillings."

"Give them three hundred. It is enough."

Before Omar got back in the Land Cruiser, he took a cloth from the glove box and wiped off the fuel that had splashed.

With Omar gone, he asked for a Samosa and another Coke. He recognized a few of the locals, and naturally, they all knew who he was. There was a light breeze up in the trees, and a few times it drifted through the depot. Diesel, kerosene, charcoal, dust, and the smell of cooking, hung in the heat. After years of sailing into port cities, he recognized this feeling—knowing where a hole-in-the-wall bistro was, a bar on the beach, and someone that knows your name. Luuq knew his name, and who he worked for.

54

Rana came to Geed Weyn with Omar that afternoon. Omar, straight away, went over to the container, which was now sitting beside the other two. Rana headed into the kitchen. Omar approved the breaking of the seal but Macmud was struggling with the thin braided cable that stretched instead of snapping. Omar stepped up to examine, then pulled out a pistol, pointed the gun at the cable and fired.

Macmud lifted the latch and swung the doors open. The floor of the container was soaked with diesel fuel that was seeping from several of the barrels. Max could see that most of this container was not for the farm. Omar directed Mohamed to get the barrels out of the container right away. The bales of khat, wrapped in plastic and tied with twine, were moved into an empty corner in the first container. Max saw three bales with the blue twine. Omar was taking stock of the crates that remained in the new container, shifting them into similar shapes and opening one of each.

Rana was greeted with shouts of joy and hugs from Xabiib and Yasmine. This compound had been her home for more than two years. The three of them, hand in hand, started walking from building to building, starting with the kitchen, then to Max's.

Rana asked, "No python?"

"No, no, no...it is gone." They still took the step onto the breezeway quickly.

Rana stood looking at the Juba filling from last night's rain. "Max, Is he good? Do you like him?" She stayed focused on the river, as they gave their assessments.

First Yasmine, "We like him very much. He is different from some of the others."

Then Xabiib, "Very kind. I think that he is lonely."

When the gunshot went off, they all looked toward the containers and waited, listening. They waited until they heard normal talking before they relaxed.

Rana remembered Billii, and asked where she was. She crossed through the garden and knocked on Mohamed's door. Billii was sitting up, still analyzing the gunshot. She was soaked with sweat, her thin shawl sticking to her narrow frame. A light came to her eyes when she recognized Rana, but she was too exhausted to do more than smile and touch her face. Rana kissed her forehead and went into Geed Weyn nurse mode.

"Did Max bring you the Chloroquine? Did you take it?" Billii nodded, making a face that everyone knew. Then Rana turned to the sisters and said, "Bring mineral water, and ice, if you have it." They looked at each other and became Rana's assistants once more.

Max hung around the containers, watching Omar. He tried to look busy, helping uncrate a water pump with Milindi, the mechanic. Macmud's helpers could fix anything, with practically nothing. They were thrilled with the American water pump, but less impressed with the Italian hand tractors. They'd been working on old Italian machinery all their lives. Omar came out of the container and looked at Max, then closed the doors on his weapons. He handed Mohamed a padlock.

Omar motioned for Max to come over. "I'm not staying. Take Rana back to Luuq before you go to Mandera. We'll get these soon. Mohamed will be watching."

There was nothing to respond to, so Max nodded and wished him, "Safe travels." To which Omar looked confused.

As his Land Cruiser sped off, he could feel the tension release.

Mohamed was closing the doors to the container where the khat was stored, but he didn't lock it since that's where Milindi stored his tools.

Billii was seen in the hammock on her breezeway for a while. Rana had given her a cool sponge bath and plenty of fluids. In the kitchen the three women talked and laughed in Somali. Mohamed went into the kitchen to get some water for Billii. Max could hear more laughter and Mohamed came out with a big smile. Max was on the outside of all of these friendships. Even Rana's relationship with Hani predated his arrival in Africa.

He sat at his desk going over a hand drawn spreadsheet for the farm. With the new salaries that Zaynab wanted to pay, that still left over twenty-five thousand dollars of un-programmed cash. If he left it all with Zaynab, he could defend his actions. But, if he was forced to escape Geed Weyn, he'd need lots of cash—it felt like theft from any angle. He put the accounting back in his farm folder and walked onto his breezeway.

He heard Milindi still working by the container. He walked over to where Milindi was pulling nails out of pallet boards and stacking them up for future projects. The container with the khat was open, so Max went inside. He saw the blue twined bales and felt Omar's eyes on him. When he was sure that Milindi was still wrestling with the rusty nails, he picked up one of the white twined bales. Looking over his shoulder and listening for Milindi's hammer to screech out another nail, he picked up one of the blue bales. It was similar in weight, but felt flat and hard on the underside. Tipping it over, he poked his finger through the thin plastic and came up against metal. As he continued to prod the size and shape, he discovered that it was a box. It was too quiet, then he heard another board being placed on the stack. Max put the bale down, having first repositioned a layer of khat and plastic over his discovery.

When Rana came over to his breezeway, he was thinking about the boxes hidden in the khat. It had to be money. Nothing else made sense. The idea of taking it fascinated him, like looking at a serpent. Rana was sitting next to him now, watching the Juba in force, swirling around the crocodile sandbar and carrying branches out of the highlands.

"It's strange being here without eighty thousand refugees. This bend in the river could make a nice farm."

Max asked, "What's going to change now that the U.S. is in Mog?"

"Mogadishu should be quiet for a while. The whole area around K4 belongs to Boqor's clan. As far as he's concerned, UNICEF belongs to his clan, the real fight will move to the Middle Juba now." She shrugged. "I don't care to know any of that. Honestly, I just want to be left alone to work in Jilib."

"You're in Ali Nur's circle, you're part of the clan. Right?"

"Look Max, you have to have family here. Zaynab and Ali Nur have been my family. I think you're making too much of it, it's just the way it is. All those young men and women we trained here in Geed Weyn, they were from the most modern generation ever. When it started to crumble, the only place they knew to seek refuge was their clan. If the clan is going to fight, you're going to fight. It really didn't matter how progressive they were, they were never far from extinction."

"Is that what happened to Ali Nur, and the others? Did they all end up as fighters and clan leaders?"

Rana took in a short breath before she answered, "Some of them, yes. The ones that didn't get killed."

"Why does he protect you?"

"Not just me," she said, turning to look at him. "He tries to protect all of Gedo, and that includes you right now. For Zaynab he would fight to the end, and since she wants this farm, he'll fight to make that happen too. He works with your government just so he can protect us. There's a lot you don't understand!"

He knew that was true.

"Okay," she said. "I'm sorry. Being back in Geed Weyn...actually being in this exact spot."

The sun set into the forest and he stood up to stretch, "I've got a bottle of scotch that Ali Nur left."

She came out of her thoughts. "Perfect. But first I want to check on Billii. I'll bring some bread, and I have cheese from home." When she said this, they both heard it—*home.*

Rana pulled out her flashlight and walked through the garden to check on Billii. With the door open, Max could see all of them sitting vigil. The lantern light illuminated their faces behind Rana's silhouette in the doorway.

When Rana returned with the bread and cheese, Max poured out two glasses of scotch and handed her one. They clinked and sat quietly, the lantern light waving shadows overhead.

"Max, bring out your mosquito net if we're going to sit here."

He unhooked it from over his bed and stood on his chair to attach it to a rafter over the two chairs. They scooched their chairs closer and leaned a bit toward each other to avoid exposing skin to the bloodsuckers. The lamp light had its own circus of insets intoxicated by the magic glow. They tucked their legs up on their seats and watched as the occasional scorpion or camel spider cruised around the light.

Rana spoke from somewhere in her memory, "Before this house was built, we all slept in tents. I shared one with my friend Utja right here. All those modern Somali boys living close to all those European and American single women was a problem. And not just for those beautiful boys, some of us were young and very naive. We had no idea what signals were being sent, neither of us did, I'm sure. We all worked with two or three male nurses that we were training. Ali Nur was one of my trainees. His sister Zaynab worked in our lab with Marilyn." Rana was looking back into time, names and faces surprised her as she told her story. "One night our tent was broken into. A knife cut through the side of the tent that faced the river. I woke up and Ali Nur was pinning my shoulders down, he ripped my shirt open. We looked right into each other's eyes. We were both terrified. Utja screamed and he was gone. Neither of us said we saw Ali Nur, it would be too damaging, it might even stop our work. No one was hurt so we just went on. Since there were no witnesses, nothing came of it. Ali Nur disappeared that night and the next time I saw him, years later, he was leading a small militia that ran Jilib for his uncle Farah."

Rana thanked him for the refill of scotch, then added, "Even though there was no proof, and no accusations, it was clear that Ali Nur was suspected. Why else would he leave so suddenly? The only other reason could be that he'd been pressed into the army that very night, and no one believed that—especially Zaynab. By the time Ali Nur reappeared in Middle Juba, Geed Weyn was closed and WRS was doing agriculture work around Jilib. There, in Jilib, and as far as Luuq, Ali Nur had some power. For Global Aid it meant that we could move and work freely. Staff came and went through the late eighties, but I made Jilib my home."

"So, you worked with Ali Nur in Jilib? That must have been weird."

"It's a bond to share a secret."

He wasn't sure if she meant with him, or with Ali Nur...or both.

"Do you feel at home here? However that's supposed to feel?"

"There was a small window in time, right after Geed Weyn closed, where I found my heart beating in tune to what I was doing, and where I was living. A blue moon. For a few years things were okay, then things changed, slowly at first, then fighting swept down the river. I'll probably never feel that again. If you stay too long you won't fit either"

55

John parked in front of Mara's for several hours. Mark's suggestion that Hani could be used to force Max into staying in Luuq, was too much. He always suspected this moment might come. But this wasn't what he signed up for—not this directly anyway. Leaving the agency now seemed right, leaving Hani and Max in this situation did not.

In the morning he drove over to Kiberu, and when he spotted her taking a smoke break with two other women, he got out of his car, closing the door hard enough for the smokers to look in his direction. Mara stared at him, then excused herself from the group and walked across to confront him.

"What the hell do you think you're doing? You can't stalk me. I'll call the police."

John backed up a step and put up his hands. "Whoa, I'm not stalking you. I need your help."

"Help how?" Mara was standing her full six feet, eye to eye with him.

"Depends. If she is in Nairobi then it's easier. But, if she's still in Mandera I need to know now."

"I don't know where she is, or why it matters,"

"So, she's not at the apartment?"

"I don't trust you. You've done something with her friend, and now you want to do something with Hani. No way am I helping you. Now leave or I will scream, and they will believe me when I tell them you tried to assault me. Go!"

"Okay, I'll go. Please Mara, if you see her tell her to find a safe place to stay."

He handed her his card, scratching out the official numbers and writing a new number on the back. She grabbed his arm with a grip that stabbed into his muscles.

"If I know where she is, why shouldn't I warn her that you're looking for her?"

"Go ahead, warn her. I want her to know I'm trying to help her. I'm not the one she should be afraid of."

She released his arm and turned over the card a few times.

"Is this your number?"

He nodded.

She walked back to Kiberu without looking back. She waited just inside the door until she heard his car drive away. After work she made a call to Josie at WRS. They'd never met, but Hani knew her, and Max worked for them. She couldn't think of anyone else to turn to.

The WRS office wasn't quiet that day. Alan was still in Mogadishu, and the news of the Americans landing in Somalia had spawned a lot of interest back in the States. Josie was stacking up notes on Alan's desk. She was getting calls from other US based NGOs asking about conditions in Somalia. She was informed that two different NGOs were sending a small team to go into Mogadishu and they needed her help in arranging it. They cited assurances of her cooperation from Bradley Stokes.

There were no seats for Mogadishu on either ICRC or the UN flights. Josie even called a charter service but was told that they could not fly to Mogadishu until at least next week. She booked hotel rooms and sent off answers to as many requests as she could. When Mara's call came, she almost didn't answer. She wasn't surprised to hear that Hani had gone to Mandera. Mara told her that she traveled there with three women from WHC, Brin was the only name Mara remembered. Josie called the UNICEF office in Nairobi and got a contact number for WHC in Mandera.

56

John was fairly certain that Hani was still in Mandera, which meant finding Jimmy and making another trip north before his access to Max was officially cut off. His diplomatic ID allowed him to drive out to the plane, where Jimmy was in his Lufthansa mechanic's coveralls, with his hands on his hips and a small cigar in his mouth. His tools were spread out on a blue blanket, and another blanket was draped from the engine compartment.

"Hey Jimmy. What's wrong with her?"

"She's never been better. Just finishing."

"I'm going to need a lift tomorrow, Mandera again."

"Can't do it man. I'm going to spend most of tomorrow tuning her. Not ready for the frontier yet. Maybe the next day though." John didn't detect the usual surly negotiation.

"Okay, we'll make it Thursday morning. I'll be here at sunrise." He wasn't serious about sunrise, only wanting one of Jimmy's typical comebacks. But there was no comeback, just a thumbs up.

When Jimmy finished putting his tools away, he stripped out of the mechanics suit and drove down to the Lion's Den on an old red Honda 90. He spent the next two hours trying to get in touch with Brin. Princess let him use her office, so he sat in there, with his feet on the desk, slowly sipping Princesses best Irish whiskey. There was a time when Jimmy and Princess were talking about running this place together. After he'd invested twenty thousand dollars, she ended up with the new kitchen and a debt she'd never have to pay off, except in food and drink.

He finally got through around sundown. First, he spoke to Sylvie, he remembered her from the other day, she was obviously the boss. After another minute Brin came on the line.

"Ho, Jimmy. What's up. Miss me?"

He was unprepared for her voice. He'd been thinking about her, and imaging her in every way he could, but her real voice was so much more satisfying, he took a second to reply.

"I do actually. I'm coming up on Thursday, same cargo, same mission. Look dear, I think that your friend Hani is the person my American is looking for. Is she still with you?"

Brin froze, then said, "No. She's moved on."

"Good then. Don't tell me anything else about her."

"Is this serious Jimmy? Is she in trouble? Is someone trying to hurt her? Shit, Jimmy. Fuck!"

"Hey, hey, hey, I won't let this guy get close. Okay? He's a good guy, just works for some real shits."

Sylvie had been listening to Brin's end, she took the phone, "This is Sylvie, please don't bring your American here."

"That's the thing Ms. Sylvie, he's going to be looking for her in all the NGO offices and camps. He's pretty sure she's still in Mandera and he thinks she'll be hanging out with you aid types."

"You're not telling him?" Brin asked, their heads cheek to cheek.

"Not my business. But she's your friend, Brin, so I wanted to warn you guys, okay?"

Brin took the phone slowly out of Sylvie's grip and turned a quarter away. Sylvie matched the quarter on the other side and took one small step.

"Thanks Jimmy. I still want to see you, come and get me when you can ditch the American."

57

Thursday morning, after a number of attempts to contact the WHC Mandera station, Josie got a call back from Sylvie. Sylvie confirmed that Brin was one of her team, but she hesitated to confirm her whereabouts. Josie, sensing that Sylvie could be trusted, told her that Max, a friend of Hani's, was an employee of Global Aid, and she knew that Hani travelled to Mandera with Brin and others from their agency. "All I want is for you to get a message to Hani, if you see her."

"I can take a message...and, if I see her, I can pass it on for you."

"I think you know how to find her, so please tell her that someone named John Thomas, from OFDA, is looking for her, and he might come to Mandera to find her. I think she should be warned. Okay?"

Sylvie waited a long pause before replying. "I can do that, of course."

"Thank you. Please be careful."

The second warning.

Sam grilled Sylvie about everything Josie said, having her go over the message several times, until she stopped him. "I think she is telling us the truth. She knows Hani's in Mandera, and she wants us to deliver a warning. We're already on it, right? Hani can't be found. Right?"

Sam said, "Tell the others to completely deny that Hani's still here. He might already know that you brought her from Nairobi, but say that you haven't seen her since, and that she probably went back to Nairobi. You don't know anything about Max."

Since Hani moved to Tessa's, the sisters of the co-op spent the evening discussing the rendezvous Sam was arranging.

Brin said, "I think it's so cool, I mean, she came here to find him, and now they're going to be together."

Anita said, "For one night. Do you think she'll stay when he's back in Somalia? Maybe she'll stay longer. We could use her, you know?"

Sylvie was about to answer, but Brin broke in. "Hell no, she should go with him."

Sylvie said, "To Somalia, to Luuq? It's way different than you think Brin."

"I'm not talking about Somalia, no, they should run off together."

Anita looked at Brin, "I think Hani loves this work, really. Max is probably here for the same reason we are. Why couldn't they work here together?"

For a few minutes they all listened to their own thoughts. Would they leave with their lover? They thought about who they would have left with, and what that would mean. Not many couples did this kind of work.

They agreed to trust Brin's Jimmy, and the woman from Max's agency, Josie. There were mixed opinions about Max.

58

This morning, when he went to refill his coffee, he saw Rana standing out by the river's edge, looking at the freshly laid concrete slab where the pump would go. When he came up to her, she didn't turn to greet him. But, spoke over the Juba, "It would be so amazing if this all worked. If they left us alone. If this farm survives the next year, it would be one of the best things to happen for Luuq. I think then, Zaynab leaves, if she can."

"To Italy, to Aldo?"

She tipped her head to one side, "You know about this?"

"I've spent some time with Zaynab. She's told me a lot of things."

"They like you Max. But this will never be your project. This belongs to Ali Nur for now. So, if it makes it a year…"

He gave Rana a ride back to Luuq before driving to Mandera. Mohamed was not coming today, an absence that said more about his feelings for Billii, than it said about how much Max was trusted. Mohamed told him that three men would be joining the trucks in Toobiye, on the way back. "One of them is Billii's brother Abukhater, or AK."

After he let Rana out at Zeyneb's, he drove back across the bridge, past the road to Geed Weyn, and up the Doolow Road. Landmarks were now subconscious, freeing him to plan their future. That's what it felt like today, he could see the end of this weird captivity. He'd been rolling around the idea of just a few more trips, just another week maybe. He didn't know if he could stay in Africa, but he couldn't leave Africa without her. She'd spent most of her working life in the UN and NGO world, and he wondered if she would go away with him.

When he approached Toobiye, he rolled past the checkpoint, nodding to the person he now knew as AK. He drove slowly on the next stretch, estimating that fifteen minutes at this pace would be across from the spot he'd reconnoitered on the Kenyan side. He slowed down on a straight stretch, then stopped. Looking all around, he got out of the technical and started collecting rocks. There weren't any big rocks, so he made a row of little ones just outside the tire tracks. He got back in and backed up about fifty meters, he could just make out the line, unnaturally straight. It was a place on his map now.

Max's arrival in Mandera followed his normal routine. Once he was clear of the border, he checked in with the ever-ready Yusuf.

"Where is your friend Sam?"

"He is waiting for me to tell him you are here. He won't come if the American is watching."

Max thought it would be pretty easy to spot someone watching him since there were only two other people in the tea shop right now. After Yusuf left to make the call, Max had some tea and put his feet up on the metal railing that enclosed the patio—just another aid worker taking a break.

59

Tessa and Hani worked in the flower beds lining the alley. Tessa was especially concerned that Hani shouldn't disturb any of the mushrooms just erupting from the moist red earth. The ringing phone stopped Hani's breath, and she hardly took another until Tessa returned to the garden.

"He's here?"

"Yes, I think that's what, *ready for lunch*, means." Tessa rolled her eyes and added. "Samuel's code words. But I do believe he is right to be careful. Anyway, I called Sam and he's going to see your Max."

Hani looked at herself, twigs in her hair, mud on her hands and knees. She took a big breath and looked at Tessa, women to women, their eyes looking into a human mystery.

"You should use my bathroom Hani, more room to get ready, yes?"

Sam got Tessa's call just before noon. Before that call, he'd received a call from a friend at the airport. A plane with the American had just landed. The pilot and the American then walked over to Mandera General Insurance, across the highway. Sam's friend had earned his Shillings.

When Yusuf returned, he moved Max to a dark corner of the tea shop. He dug in his pocket and pulled out a hundred and slid it over to Max. "Here, this is yours."

"No, Yusuf, you earned that, I need your help. Keep it please."

"Oh, no. I have the hundred you gave me. This is the American's. He wanted me to call him when you came this week. But, I didn't. I thought I better take his money so that he doesn't need other watchers, yes?"

"Brilliant, perfect." He slid the hundred across the table. "You earned this one too." Sensing that he had more to say, he asked, "What is it Yusuf?"

"Do you have a job for me, maybe. I can go to Luuq with you, or if you set up an office here, I can run it when you're gone."

"I'm almost finished with my part of the farm Yusuf. I would hire you if you were in Mogadishu for sure. But I can't hire people for the farm. Sorry. How about Nairobi? Have you thought about getting work there? Most of the NGOs have offices there. I'd give you a recommendation for the NGO I work with. My friend has contacts at UNICEF and UNDP in Nairobi, maybe she could find you a position. What do you want to do?" As soon as he said it, he realized what a clueless western question this could be.

Yusuf had an answer ready. "I will go to university, and have a job. Then I will have a wife, and we will move to Canada before we have children, and I will send money to my brothers and sisters."

"That's a great plan. I'll help if I can. You better let me watch for the American now. He might want his money back if he finds me here and you didn't call him."

"But I need to wait for Sam, he told me."

"Okay, but maybe you can watch from somewhere else, I'll be fine. The American is not a problem for me."

Yusuf agreed and took up a position down the block.

60

After the call from Tessa, Sam had hired a taxi and drove by the airport. On his second pass, coming back into town, he noticed a blue Nissan sedan pulling out onto the highway from the insurance office next to the Mandera's terminal. There were two white men, the American was driving. He followed them to the small UN office in town, and waited until they came out five minutes later. From there they drove to the WCH camp. He watched as they walked into Sylvie's tent. When they left, they passed right by him. He followed at a distance until they headed out of town, in the direction of small camp, run by a Belgium based NGO. He waited for a while, then went to see Sylvie.

Sylvie, Brin and Anita were huddled together around Sylvie's desk when he came in.

"So, what did they say? Do you think they know?" Sam asked.

"Well, Jimmy knows for sure, but he didn't let on. Only a bit of a wink. Didn't say a word," said Brin.

To Sylvie, Sam asked. "What did they say?"

"Well, John, the American guy, said he needed to find Hani for her own protection. And, if we knew where she was...and I think he knows that we all know each other up here, we should give her this note."

She handed Sam a sealed envelope with Hani's name written on the front.

Anita spoke up, "I don't think it means trouble Sam, I think he really wants to help her...he sounded...he sounded honest." She knew that sounded stupid, but it was her impression...and Brin agreed.

The answers were probably in the letter in his hand, but it was sealed. Opening a sealed letter, addressed to someone else, was like stealing. It was the thinnest of trusts, the lock, just a piece of paper.

61

Hani kept her shower to two minutes, considering this the Mandera way. The water was cooler than usual due to the new rainwater in the rooftop tank. As she combed out her hair, she kept looking in the ornate mirror propped against the wall in Tessa's bedroom. With the door open she could see her full self for the first time since she left Mara's. Tessa saw Hani staring at herself in the mirror, wrapped in a green towel, trying on one of Tessa's topaz and black headscarves. She backed quietly out of sight. Hani missed this person that she saw turning and watching herself. Mara was always twirling and parading outfits around the apartment, and every time she went out it was very important to get it just right. Hani got this a little bit, but since she met Sylvie, Anita, and Brin, she realized that they had this natural beauty, unadorned, even utilitarian. This beauty was evident when they worked. Their clothes didn't matter, their fresh un-powdered skin radiated with life and energy. She hadn't allowed herself to recognize it in herself until now. She decided on jeans, and a tee shirt.

Tessa brought in flowers and fresh white curtains to make the little green bungalow live again. Sam had come by twice since Hani moved in. He'd fixed the gate and raked the whole lane, the smoldering brush pile behind Tessa's house sent a domestic incense floating through the canopy. Hani was walking from Tessa's, back to the green bungalow, when she saw Sam walking up the alley toward her. She looked beyond him but didn't see Max. Instead, he handed her an envelope with her name written on the front.

"Who's this from? Is it from Max?" She didn't want a letter, she wanted Max, here, in person.

"Not from Max. From the American that Max works with. He's been looking all over Mandera for you."

She read it slowly, tipping her head to one side. It was handwritten in a hurry, so she read it carefully, twice.

Sam couldn't help himself. "What is it Hani? What's it say?"

"I know this American. He wants to meet me. He says it is urgent and it's about Max and me. But he doesn't say what it's about. Oh Sam... I just want to see Max and have all of this over with."

"Hani, Max is here, and this American doesn't know that you are here in this place. I still think we can get Max here without anyone seeing. But, since you know this guy, do you trust him?"

"No."

"Then we will keep you a secret for now. Let me take this to Max" She handed him the note. "Soon Hani. Be patient."

62

Sam came through a back door into the tea shop and appeared at Max's side. "Hello Max. Are your trucks here too?"

"Trucks are here tomorrow. I came to see Hani today. Is it safe?"

"I just saw her ten minutes ago, she is safe. Who knows you're here? Have you seen your American friend yet? He's in town too." Sam looked around the now empty tea shop, then handed him the envelope. "She's already read it."

Max slipped the note out of the envelope and went to the bottom of the note to find John Thomas's name. Going back to the beginning he read the three lines twice. "Did he find her?"

"No, don't worry. He hasn't seen her, and he doesn't know where she is. But what is this warning about? Do you have any idea?"

"No." Max was processing quickly. "I need to see him before I see Hani. You're sure he is still in Mandera?"

"Yes, I know what car he is driving and where he goes. Wait for him here, this where he expects to find you."

"Are you sure he doesn't know where she is? You're certain?"

"Yes, I am sure for now. But, Mandera is not so big, she cannot stay hidden for long."

John ducked in under the awning, and adjusted his eyes. He spotted Max at the back and took a seat. "How are you? You're a day early."

Max took out John's note to Hani, pushing it toward him. "What's going on? Why are you looking for her?"

John took a moment to pick out his words. "I think that you're both in some danger. The project is being shut down as soon as you deliver the last container. After that I think you should get out of East Africa."

"If the project is over then why can't I just go back to Nairobi, and then back to Mogadishu? And, why is Hani in danger? She has nothing to do with this thing."

Again, John took a second to form his response. In seeing this, Max was alerted to a change in John, something different in his manner.

"This operation was run secretly, and I mean it was a secret from most of the people that would need to approve it and it's being buried as soon as we clear the containers. It would have been stopped already but that would leave some loose ends. And, loose ends are dangerous."

"What are you telling me?"

"I'm telling you that anyone that knows about this is in danger. You, me, and Hani. Even though she doesn't know everything that's going on, she might know enough, or they think you told her." John put up his hand to stop Max's protest. "I know you didn't tell her anything, but she's figured out some of it already. So, she needs to get somewhere safe, before you deliver the last container."

"Why don't I just go now? I'm in Kenya legally."

"If the containers don't clear customs by Monday, they'll be re-inspected. A real inspection this time. The containers for Somalia have a time stamp on the papers. Anything authorized before the US landed in Mogadishu is still allowed. After that, the new customs rules for Somalia take effect. Once those containers were sealed, the clock was ticking. Your name is on the papers, they'll be evidence of weapons smuggling. No one's going to come to your defense."

"What about you? Are you getting out, leaving whatever agency you work for?"

"I might have too, but I know lots of names. And they don't know if I haven't kept notes or copied documents. In some sick way it's a guarantee of a nice promotion, if I play along. I think the loose ends here are you and Hani."

"Why are you telling me this? Bad conscience?"

"Yeah, I guess. You're trying to do the right thing in Mogadishu, and even in Luuq with the farm. I know that, but things have changed, now I'm trying to help you stay alive. It's that serious. And, I'm completely jealous of you and Hani too. To be honest, I don't know if I'd be up here right now if it wasn't for her safety. You guys deserve a chance to get away from all the shit that's going to rain down if this gets discovered."

"So, if the last container gets in the project is terminated, right?"

"Yes."

"If, then, everything's cool, no customs problems, nothing in the press, everything's quiet. Then will I—we—still be in danger?"

"I wouldn't take a chance Max. There's one other detail. The Boqor, you've helped his latest rival, Ali Nur. You'll never be safe in East Africa as long as he sees you as his enemy."

"What does that mean for Sharif? Isn't everyone I work with in danger too?"

"I don't know Max. Sharif might be okay in Mogadishu, the troops will be guarding agencies like yours. I can't see very far into Somalia's future, but Sharif, and anyone that's survived the last two years in Mogadishu must know how to stay safe. Max, the point is, we need to make a plan to get you out as soon as the last container crosses into Somalia. And, we need to get Hani out before that."

"Do you have that plan?"

"The beginnings of one. I have the pilot. I'll meet you here tomorrow morning at nine, before you see Hassan for the customs papers. I'll bring my pilot and you two can make a deal. I hear you have some cash. Good for you."

"I'll be here at nine."

"So, you know where she is?"

"Not yet. Don't follow me John, we're watching you too."

63

Sam reappeared a few minutes after John Thomas drove away, and to answer to his unspoken question, Max said, "It's okay. He's not the trouble."

"Who is then?"

"Well, it can come from two directions—the US Government, and The Boqor."

"Only a Somali warlord and the US Government?"

"Two Somali warlords, including Ali Nur. It will just be a few more days. I'm meeting a pilot in the morning, at nine. Hani and I will be gone by Saturday. Sam, you've been so kind to help her."

"It is nothing. She's one of the sisters—the bravest people I know."

"Is she working with WHC?"

"Yes, while she was looking for you, she insisted on working."

"I think it's safe Sam."

They drove through the back streets, crossing over the El Wak Road twice, then winding in a circle until Sam was satisfied that no one was following. They drove back toward Max's escape route and the WHC camp. The taxi pulled up to a stop on the edge of a quiet rutted lane. Sam turned from the front seat and told him that he should get out here and walk to the corner, turn right, halfway down the street, turn into an alley with a pink bungalow on the left, and a blue one on the right. Walk down the alley until you come to a green bungalow on the right, that's where Hani is. "I'll come by in the morning. Now go."

Max slung his messenger bag across his shoulder and started walking to the corner, once he rounded it, he could see the faded pink bungalow peeking around a broadleaf hedge. He thought that he must be three inches taller than most of the people that walked along this path. The overhanging fingers kept grabbing his cap. With the cap in hand he came to the alley. The blue bungalow was identical to the pink one. A resinous smoky haze hung in the canopy, softening the light. Two more bungalows on the right side, then the green one.

He saw her. She was sitting by the front door, under a covered porch. He stopped and observed her, as if watching an elusive wild creature in her natural habitat. Her head snapped up, catching a scent—she turned and looked directly at him through the vines and leaves. He looked over his shoulder to see if he'd been followed, then ran up to her as she floated up into his arms. He felt something break inside. Only her arms holding him, and her fingers, each one of them, touching and caressing him, reminded him that he was still in his body. He kept his face tucked in her warm neck, breathing in her scent. His nose lightly gliding back and forth over her soft warm skin. They barely moved as they stayed in that embrace, hidden from each other's eyes until their bodies reconnected, remembering and anticipating sensations.

After time restarted, her nose nudged inquiringly at his ear. He answered back with his nose at her ear and they slowly let their heads slide apart enough for their noses to touch each other. Their eyes unable to focus, breathing the same air. She whispered, "We should go inside."

She brought him to the end of the bed and sat down. He got on his knees, looking up at her. "Hani. It's true. I love you."

She put her hands on his face, holding it, then let his head rest in her lap. When the trance eased, they found themselves on the bed in each other's arms. Their lips touched each other lightly at first, then slowly letting their bodies speak to each other until words could form again.

———

Max got up first, brought to the surface by a bird's call that pierced his dreams. She rested on her stomach, next to him, her legs flexing a little then relaxing. The sun was nearing the point where it falls over the edge—time was still in force, and not enough of it. The deepest secret of life itself was theirs to enjoy in this moment, but it had to yield to the matter of keeping alive. She twisted out of bed and looked at him over her shoulder, their eyes met and she asked, "What is it? What are you thinking about?"

"I want to stay right here, with you, forever. But we can't."

She put a finger on his lips, "Wait a little, I'll be right back."

She put her jeans on and slipped out the door. She ran lightly to the end of the lane and up the steps. Tessa wasn't looking at her, nor was Hani looking into Tessa's eyes. Tessa handed her a basket, and they let their foreheads touch like a kiss. There was no need for words with all the other senses being so exposed. When she came back down the lane Max was watching from the covered porch. His heart was pounding, and the air in his lungs had an intoxicating sensation that made him breath in deeply to prolong the pleasure. They were in a jungle, the only people in the world. She was the forest queen, bringing him something in a basket. She put the basket on the wide railing and reburied her head in his chest for a second then said, "Tessa has made us a small feast, Sit and we'll talk."

They arranged the pillows and she placed the food on the table, including two Tuskers. She tucked her bare feet under his legs on one edge of the wicker loveseat, and rolled the cool wet bottle around her shoulders. They were still in the subconscious world of appetite and instinct when the first mosquitos found them—after a few swats they took the magic under the mosquito net. They hurried to bring in the food, and drape the net around the whole bed. Being together like this was so much easier than going back into the world of time and trouble. Later in the night with the moonlight filtering through the leaves, they started to face the future.

"To be safe you'll need to go tomorrow...somewhere far away. John thinks there's a good chance that you and I will be the loose ends, the uncontrolled piece of their plan. They might've already planned to silence me, but you've added another option, according to John. If you leave in the morning, they'll only have me to worry about. They still need me for one more container on Saturday. I'll be gone before they know it."

"Does it have to be that way, really? I want to have my job back some day. Actually, I want to work with the women here, the Cooperative is very cool, and I could work with them...I want you, and this…I want it all." They were sitting up now, leaning against the cane headboard. Any idea of sleep was gone. They looked at each other for a while, their fingers touching and tracing out their thoughts. She said, "Don't you want to go back to America?"

"No, not America. Not for a while anyway. I want to be where you are, and I'm not finished with this work…"

"You just started. Do you want to do this...well not this, but some type of relief work? Is that what you want to do?"

"Something like the farm in Geed Weyn? Yeah, something small, good work, honest work…okay, what I'm doing is super dishonest...maybe evil."

She leaned into him. "They might have killed you, and Sharif and Suleymaan if you'd refused...you know that right? Global Aid is still feeding thousands in Somalia. You've kept it going because of this."

"Right now we have one option...maybe two, but first thing is to get you away. How about Rome? I'm meeting John's pilot in the morning. I have enough money to get us both out of Africa, and if we're careful it can last for a few months. I can get more."

"Whose money is it?"

"I think it starts out as US taxpayer's money, but now it's Ali Nur's money too. I don't think the taxpayers will ever know about it, and the people running this operation won't file a complaint since they're the ones that really stole it. But Ali Nur, Omar, and others will be looking for any sign of us."

"How much money?"

Max reached for his bag next to the bed and pulled out his stash of dollars and his notebook. He placed ten thousand dollars in her hand, and said, "This should be enough to get you out of Africa, and then we'll meet in Europe after in a few days. Inshallah."

"Everything changes now, doesn't it?"

"Yeah, it's already changed." He handed her the notebook. "Keep this safe. I was planning on sending it to Zoe, just in case…in case something happens to me. The last thirty pages are notes about the farm and the names of all the conspirators, Mr. Hassen, John Thomas, Ali Nur and Zaynab. Evidence…just in case. If you can decipher my hieroglyphics, you'll find yourself in the earlier pages."

She put the notebook on top of Anita's project proposal and touched the money. "So, how much money besides this?"

"Another $30,000 from the bank, and maybe lot more sitting in Geed Weyn. It's all separate from the farm money and I think we could find a better use for it."

"I know a project that needs the money." She pointed to Anita's proposal on the bedside table. "It doesn't take a lot of money to make a big difference, even the $30,000 would fund three projects this size."

"Exactly! I've thought about doing something like that, funding small projects until the money's gone. Maybe I'm trying to justify it all...It's pretty dangerous too."

After they talked about the money for a few minutes, they looked at each other, surprised at how they could be so cavalier about stealing. They took turns reminding each other that it was a rational and pragmatic decision. There were so many good ways to spend it.

"Rome?" There was resignation in her question.

"It's a good place to start." Tomorrow turned into today. "Once you get to an international airport, outside Kenya, you can buy a ticket to Rome. Call Zoe, her number is on the first page of the notebook, she'll be our contact. Leave a message for me when you get anywhere safe."

"Do we really need to leave Africa?"

"You don't have to do this. I mean, you don't have to leave Africa forever, just until we know no one is looking for you. I don't really know how we'll know that though—it's sort of a mess."

"Max, I came up here to find you. To find out if this was real, you and me. And, it is, I'm in, in for all of it. Do you have a map?"

He pulled out a Michelin map of East Africa and laid it out on the bed. She leaned in as he used a small flashlight pen to draw a line to their future. She pointed to Lake Victoria and the town of Kisumu. "I could take a ferry to Uganda and fly out of Entebbe, direct to Rome, three times a week."

"I'll run that idea by the pilot, see what he thinks."

"I won't see you after tonight, will I? Not until Rome. That sounds so impossible, so far away."

He took off his necklace with the ruby inside and put it on her. "Take this with you."

Their dreams worked in concert, distorting reality and frustrating their plans. Always they were too far from each other, always there was another trap, another hurdle, always too slow, and then it played again, and again. When he opened his eyes, he was looking directly into hers. They heard Tessa's screen door open, her footsteps, then in the patio, something on the table, then footsteps retreating—Screen door closing. Hani got out of bed and held out her hand. He took it and sat up on the edge of the bed and pulled her to him.

PART 3

64

Hani sat with Tessa on the steps as Max walked down the lane. He didn't look back. They'd made their plans, they'd made their promises, and somehow, they believed that they would find each other again. Sam let him out at the intersection. Yusuf was talking to someone next to a UN Land Cruiser and he waved at him before turning back to his conversation. Max found John and the pilot at a back table.

John stood up and put his hand on Jimmy's shoulder. "Max, this is Jimmy. You two make your plans, I don't want to know anything, okay? I'll be over there." He took his coffee and sat out by the parking lot. Yusuf moved his conversation to the other side of the Land Cruiser.

Jimmy's eyes scanned Max, "I don't work for them. I'm independent—I just want you to know that. Now, where does she want to go?"

"Kisumu, Lake Victoria. Today."

"I'd have to take on fuel in Marsabit and stay overnight in Kisumu, then the fuel for the way back."

Max put two thousand dollars across the table. Jimmy counted it with the edge of his thumb. "Should be enough."

Max asked, "When can you be ready?"

"Have her at the airport by noon." He scooped up the bills.

"She'll be there."

"John tells me you're needing something too."

"I need to get out of Mandera tomorrow afternoon. I might be in a hurry."

"I can get back by noon. You keep that for now."

He met Sam at the intersection and filled him in on the details.

Sam said, "They will all want to say goodbye. The sisters."

"She's ready to go, there'll be time. Thanks Sam. I'll be back tomorrow, then gone."

"Inshallah."

"Indeed."

Max walked the few blocks to the bank. Maybe only one more time, he thought. It seemed like it would take way too long, and there didn't seem to be enough time. Mr. Hassan went over the paperwork quickly, then, without being asked, he turned his ledger so that Max could see the balance—seven hundred and thirty-three dollars. The easy cash was gone.

When he left the bank, he saw the clouds gathering in the east. The wind was sweeping up dust into the air, puffs of red earth pushed ahead of rain somewhere. He could smell it. Hani would be flying with the wind to her back today, God's speed. He wondered if that was an appropriate prayer.

He waited for his trucks at the tea shop, alone. Even Yusuf wasn't hanging around. John was somewhere in Mandera. Sam was gone, watching somehow. When he heard the airplane, his heart throbbed, he felt it up in his throat. Then he saw the Pilatus Porter bending overhead and waving its wings as it headed out west.

65

Max followed the fading sound of Hani's plane. By tomorrow she should make it to Uganda, by Sunday he hoped she'd be having lunch at a sidewalk cafe in Rome. Then, he'd see her in the cafe, like she was at the green bungalow. Max stood up to break the spell. He needed three trucks, with three containers, and three good drivers soon or they'd be very late getting into Geed Weyn.

Yusuf showed up around lunch time with his sunglasses and a new white scarf flowing around him. He looked the part of a technical assistant, minus the AK 47. "When do you come back?"

"I'm just turning around. I'll be back tomorrow."

"She is gone, Ms. Hani?"

"Yep."

"Will you see her in Nairobi? Or back in Mogadishu?"

"I'm not sure where we'll meet really. But yes, I hope to see her every day of my life."

"They're coming."

He heard the trucks lumbering down to the staging area by the border. He said goodbye to Yusuf, giving him another hundred dollars. "See you tomorrow, I'll need you for sure. You've been a good agent for me."

"No problem."

Max drove slowly down to the lead truck. The driver was chewing a stalk of khat, and it didn't look like his first of the day. He was hoping for older drivers, ones with families in the cab. He looked back to the other two trucks and saw that these guys were a set. All in their early twenties, all Somalis. He could feel the wired effects of the khat and whatever else they were consuming. He hated to bring them into Geed Weyn.

At the customs station he carried out his role, handing over the papers and walking around the container with the agent. Today, a uniformed soldier accompanied them. The date of entry, on the form said today, the twelfth of December. The soldier insisted that the ninth was the cut-off date for pre-inspected items bound for Somalia. The agent, the one he'd been bribing for the past two weeks, was arguing with the soldier, pointing out that the pre-inspection certificate was valid until Monday. Max eyed his friendly agent and saw his thumb and forefinger rubbing together. He asked for the clipboard and clipped two hundred dollars under the top paper, leaving the edge of each bill visible.

When the soldier saw this, he took the clipboard and walked to the second truck, and started the routine over. Slowly walking around the container, banging on the side like he could detect something from that, then looking to the dates, staying with the formula that had gotten him his first two hundred. Max asked to see the papers, and put three hundred dollars under the top paper. He then clipped the papers for the third truck on the top of the stack and gave the clipboard back to the soldier, signaling with his hand that that was all. Five hundred for the three trucks. The soldier examined the three bills under the paper, turning so the agent couldn't see his take, then he shrugged and walked away with the cash. The customs agent looked after the soldier with obvious disgust. Such open corruption! He shook his head to say, '*What can you do?*' Max gave the appropriate counter-shrug.

On the road to Toobiye Max kept an eye out for his line of rocks. Several sections looked right, but no stones. Then, as the forest on his left reached the road, he saw them—it was a possibility.

AK was waiting with his troop when they rolled into Toobiye. They each took a truck and climbed into the cabs, ready to ride shotgun all the way to Geed Weyn. After a few minutes, when everyone should have been settled, AK got out of the lead truck and walked up to Max, he looked angry. The issue was nap time. It seems that the drivers needed more time to sit and chew. He indicated to AK that they'd stop in thirty minutes, somewhere deep in the bush. Somewhere AK and his guys knew the terrain and could watch the drivers.

They were making good time according to the wadis and trees that were now familiar. Even with a rest stop they should make Geed Weyn before the sun sets. He stopped the trucks on a straight stretch where he could see them all lined up. AK and his guys got out of the trucks and found the shade of trees. The drivers gathered at the first truck, still chewing and talking loudly. Their boomboxes all playing different songs, all of them grating on Max. AK's band seemed bothered by the music too. Finally, one of AK's guys shouted for them to turn it off. It didn't go off, instead they turned it higher. AK went up to the driver with the loudest music. He stood before him with his rifle held low, both hands on the weapon. Words grew louder, then the driver grabbed for the gun. They pulled back and forth. Everyone was yelling. AK's guys had their weapons pointed at the other two drivers. One of the drivers had pulled a handgun. No one was backing down.

Someone fired directly at the first driver. The bullet caught him in the chest, slamming him back against his truck, his eyes looking for a hand to pull him back to life, then he slumped to the ground, blood erupting on his tee shirt. Everything stood still for less than a second. The other drivers ran into the bush behind the trucks and AK and his guys went charging after them. Max waited until AK came out of the bush and waved him over. Both of AK's guys walked back into the open with their guns shouldered. One of the drivers had escaped.

AK went up to the body and declared it dead, ordering the others to drag it away, pointing to an animal trail that cut through the thicket on the edge. The blood-soaked sand was brushed over with some twigs. AK climbed up into the cab of the first truck and tried to start it. He called the others over, and after a few minutes the truck fired to life. The others each took a truck. The rest of the drive was very slow, with only AK managing to figure out the shifting pattern for his truck. They stopped a few times for further driving lessons, but most of the time the trucks just crawled along behind Max in first gear. They reached Geed Weyn after seven.

Mohamed asked several times about the truck driver in the bush and wanted to know exactly where this all took place. AK and Max described the place, saying that they could easily find it again. Billii had recovered enough to come out and greet her brother. The talk was all about the big battle.

Here was a loose end, Max thought. He spent a few minutes talking to Mohamed, before he went into the kitchen, where Xabiib had prepared him a meal of rice and beans. As he sat over the hot food, he tried to put together the day where he had started in Hani's arms. He thought of her, hoping she made it to Kisumu, and would be crossing Lake Victoria in the morning. He tried to imagine her waiting in the international departure lounge in Entebbe, Uganda, heading for Rome.

In the dark, he found himself re-living the killing, seeing the eyes, remembering, or thinking he remembered, an interruption in time, a cosmic acknowledgement of a life ended on earth, like it mattered. It didn't have to do with who died, good or bad, justified or not, it was just a little less life in the universe. He'd felt it before at his grandmother's grave as she was mechanically lowered into a very neat rectangular hole. It was raining and he was part of the family that was seated under a white tent. Everyone wanted to leave, to have this over with. Max felt a skip in time, a wink, as his grandmother disappeared below the wet earth.

Mohamed knocked on the wall, asking to enter Max's space. He got up and stood face to face with Mohamed. "AK and his guys will go back to the place of the killing before first light. If the road is safe then you can go. The missing driver will try and walk out to Kenya. His papers are in the trucks so he'll try and cross in secret near Toobiye. Omar is bringing drivers and they'll take these trucks straight to Bardera. They are ours now."

"Is Omar coming now, tonight?"

"I don't know when."

"Am I still going to bring the last container out of Mandera?"

"Oh yes, Omar was very certain. He wants the last truck. He'll have a new driver waiting for you in Toobiye, and that one will go down to Bardera too. You just need to bring it across."

"Can we get the farm supplies out of the trucks before they go?"

"I don't know. Right now, these trucks and these containers need to leave Geed Weyn. I'll ask Zaynab in the morning."

After Mohamed left. The radio squawked a few more times, lanterns went dark and the only sound was Xabiib's radio coming through the garden growing between them.

66

When her view of the white tents receded, she turned to look over the dry hills that stretched out before her. She was pretty sure that Max couldn't see more than one or two moves ahead either, but they'd agreed to push into the future together, and somehow that made sense. She held one end of her scarf pressed against her face, breathing in the lingering scents of Max and her friends.

She tapped on Jimmy's thigh and put her hands together and mouthed the words, "Asante sana." Then in English, "Thank you." They looked at each other for a long time before he nodded and turned back to his thoughts. They arrived in Kisumu as the setting sun glanced off the lake while they curved over the small city. He insisted that they stay at a favorite place of his on the lake.

"Is it close to the ferry?

"I'll get that all set up after we get to the villas."

"I can do that you know."

"Yes, I'm sure you can...I, I just thought it'd be better if you're not seen too much. This is a border town like Mandera, lots of eyes, and you're very easy to notice."

They drove for fifteen minutes along the shore, skirting the city center with its four and five story tourist hotels—hotels that she'd been longing to get through the door, find her room and flop on the bed all alone. The road ended at freshly painted white concrete archway. The circular drive was covered in crushed pink shells like the seaside villas north of Mombasa. Except here, the ocean was replaced with a large quiet lake that was hiding behind the reeds and tall grasses. The lobby was placed in the center of a ring of cabins, not quite villas, she thought. When she finally got to her own cabin, she was able to capture all of the relief that flopping down on a hotel bed could ever offer. Looking up at the ceiling she wanted to wait right here until Max came—carve his name and hers into the beam overhead so he would know he was on the right path.

After she showered, and for much longer than two minutes, she dressed in lightweight pants the color of the shells, with an indigo tunic and a black silk scarf that was long enough to wrap up over her head and across her face. The ruby hung over her heart. Jimmy said he'd be back for drinks. She went to check out the restaurant. As far as she could tell they were the only guests. He'd mentioned that it was some kind of private club for fishing. She counted six staff and heard more voices coming from the kitchen. Besides voices, there was a beautiful aroma that was coming from a wood oven. The smokey lake air was so familiar—the roasted fat, the smell of thick crusted bread, and the vaulted sky above. She took a seat on the edge of the patio, nodding to the bar keeper. This was a job that she might have had if she'd stayed in Naivasha. A wave of nostalgia, almost Deja vu, brushed past her close enough for her to hold on to it as she ordered a Tusker.

How could she leave Africa? Rome, the city Max suggested, would be cold this time of year, too cold for the picture she was seeing of two lovers finding each other by the fountain. No, there would be too many layers of clothes, warm hats and gloves in December. Africa was so big and warm. Surely they could find a corner to hide in until, well, until when, or what? She would feel so much better if that place was still Africa. She'd never been to Europe or the Middle East, and never dreamed of going to America. Those places lay beyond the curve. Dakar, Capetown, Abidjan, or Accra might be far enough away from the reach of a Somali warlord, but not far enough from the US government.

She sat on the edge of the rustic elegance of Africa. The silverware and the glasses were engraved with the words, "Guru Club," in a gothic font. And, somehow Jimmy Leary was a member. She heard a car door close. Then she saw him hurrying through the lobby and striding toward her across the bristly kikuyu grass.

"I'm sorry to have kept ya Hani. There's been a few changes around here. Took longer than I thought. Are you okay, settled?" He caught the bartender's eye and soon two more Tuskers appeared. The sun had set and a pink hue dyed the warm grey haze over the reeds. Black birds with curved yellow beaks clung to the heads, swaying back and forth, keeping time to the wind and invisible waves.

"You're going fishing. Tomorrow morning, 6 AM."

She waited for the punch line that would explain it.

"There's no ferry to Uganda until March. Repairs or something. But I found a guy that has a fishing boat, used to charter to the club here. He's expecting you early so he can reach Entebbe before dark."

"Can Max use the same route? Is this possible?"

"Oh, for sure. He's making enough to be very helpful, but he won't go near the official entry docks. You might have to wade ashore and walk up the beach a piece."

"Tell me about this place, Guru Club." She was pointing at the engraving on the water glass., "But first, can we get a menu? I need to eat."

"Oh, sorry, no menu here. It's a common meal, a traditional Guru Club standard. It's still Friday, so it will be fish."

"Fish? I smell beef, roasted, fat, juicy meat."

"Well, that must be because there is no fish right now...we get the same as them." Jimmy was indicating the staff now lined up behind the kitchen. "Roast beef, potato, onion. Once upon a time, they had great feasts here, always lots of fish, and when the fishing dried up, they'd fly them in from the coast or Europe."

"So, what happened? This place seems abandoned, and not up to the scene you just described. Who owns all this?"

"Well, it's a secret everyone in Kisumu knows, so, I'll tell you." He repositioned himself in a storytelling pose, leaning back with his hands caressing his belly. She'd never noticed it before, a little round ball. Just before he started, the dinner arrived. "I don't have any idea what kind of a '*Guru*' they're talking about. It's a secret that belongs to the few partners left that retired in some wet coastal town in England. I am pretty sure there weren't any actual gurus amongst the members." Two whiskies were added to the table as he continued. "It's owned by Zumu Petite, an old law firm in Nairobi. They've got properties all over Africa, the Gulf and Europe. I'm sure most of the new partners don't even know this place exists outside of a ledger entry. For some reason the budget can't be touched, and the annual pay increases are the source of considerable discussion in the local economy. It's a happy bit of forgetfulness for these folks. And for me every once in a while."

"So, are you a member, or staff?"

"Sort of a special vendor I guess."

"So, helping someone escape is a regular occurrence?"

"As you have witnessed, it's what I do. But you're trusted until you're not...or until someone you shouldn't have helped, suddenly wants to tie up all the loose ends. I keep my eye on who's running for office, or who's getting married, or who's becoming famous for their wealth. One day Zumu Petite will want to clean up the books, and one day one of the senior partners will need to scrub the past, and that's me, along with anyone that ever helped them do whatever they shouldn't have done. You and Max should be okay in a few years. In time you can stop looking over your shoulder. You could blend back into the UN world but I don't think your Max should come back to East Africa anytime soon.

"What happens to John, John Thomas?"

"He'll be fine. I think he's covered his ass. If he's smart, he'd leave too. You know, John is doing Max and you a huge favor. Makes me think he has a soul left. I say you get out of Kenya tomorrow, then leave for wherever...don't wait for Max in Uganda. I'll get him this far, I will."

She was tired, but she wanted to stay awake long enough to take in all the air Kenya had to offer. She wanted the smoke in a bottle, the red sticky dirt in a bag, and the future without fear. But, most of all she wanted Max. Max anywhere, Max in America, Max in India, and maybe someday Max in Mogadishu again. A breeze combed through the reeds.

67

Max was aware of Omar's arrival during the night. Hushed conversations near the kitchen were in his dreams. He followed the rhythm and tones until he fully comprehended where he was. There was nothing he could do at this hour. He recounted his cash, wondering where they could find a cheap enough place to hole up for months, or longer. He flew over the familiar maps—tracing the coastlines, searching to for a safe harbor.

The last dream before his morning birds alarmed him, had him on an old steamer, the kind that his grandparents would travel on between Southampton and New York in the 1930's. He was at the railing as confetti and streamers were raining down on the dock below. The ship was pushed out into the channel. He was trying to find someone on the crowded dock below, someone that he had to say goodbye to. Yasmine's face, and Xabiib's, along with Mohamed and Zaynab stood scanning the deck, but they couldn't see him waving both arms, back and forth over his head. Zoe was there, and Alison too. Dmitri was leaning against the warehouse wall, watching Alison. Just before he surfaced, he remembered that Hani was on board.

The far ridge was struck by the sun's first rays as the trucks started up, setting off the chickens. He was waiting at his desk when Xabiib brought coffee.

"Good morning." But her eyes didn't smile.

Max asked, "Is Omar still here?"

"He's leaving soon." She stood in front of his desk, looking down. The eyes would tell the truth. He noticed how thin and airy she appeared. Even now, as she turned to leave, she simply spun on an invisible bearing and caught a zephyr that blew across his breezeway.

Omar. Ever since the fuel depot in Luuq he sensed that Omar was on to him. His dark searching eyes could see subterfuge and conspiracy. He could smell fear and deception. Lies were his mother tongue. His presence in Geed Weyn was like the low pressure preceding a storm blowing through the desert. There was nowhere to hide, it would wash away everything in its path. Max walked across the compound, past the kitchen, scanning the interior in his peripheral vision. No Omar, no Mohamed, no Macmud. He could hear them near the three confiscated trucks. He headed for the technical parked behind Mohamed's container and as he climbed in, he felt under the seat and touched the barrel of the gun. He started it up and backed out slowly heading toward the fuel drums next to the containers. Omar and the others turned when they heard the technical start, Omar continued to watch as Max began filling a jerry can from the barrel. Max looked up and raised a hand in greeting. Omar stared for a few seconds before turning away. He finished filling the technical, and added a full jerry can to the bumper rack. The trucks were pulling out and Omar was standing with his hands on his hips, facing the river of dust that was billowing beneath Geed Weyn's canopy.

Max walked back to his quarters, avoiding Omar. He left the farm plans and maps on the desk. He left his flip flops on the floor and a pair of shorts draped over a chair. He'd made these choices before, fitting in months of memories into a backpack, giving away or burning the rest.

He heard Omar talking outside the kitchen. Max felt an internal metronome taping out the beats until the next action erupts on stage. The talking stopped, he listened for Omar's footfall.

"Max!"

"I'm here...Mohamed told me the plan. Bring the truck as far as Toobiye. There will be a driver there. Right?"

Omar was looking around the little office, then at him, "Then you'll come back here." Omar moved closer and Max wondered if dogs could really smell fear.

"I'll come back here and then return to Mogadishu since this is over. Right? Or, maybe to Nairobi first."

"What about your farm?" There was a sneer beneath the surface, a taunting in the question.

"They don't need me once all the equipment is here. Is Ali Nur coming today?"

"I don't know. You can ask him about your future when you see him." He walked across the deck and peered into the bedroom. He squinted, making his nose wrinkle in disgust before heading for his Land Cruiser.

Mohamed came over with last minute instructions, and a recap of the planned rendezvous in Toobiye. Max listened, keeping his eyes down. Mohamed touched his chin, "Listen to me Max, be careful today." Then he reached out and shook his hand. Something he'd never done before. They watched Omar's Land Cruiser disappear through the forest. Mohamed said he'd need to wait until ten before he could go. By then the three trucks will have past Toobiye on their way to Bardera, and the all clear would be relayed. After Mohamed left, he listened for a squawk that might signal Zeyneb's arrival.

At ten Mohamed told him to go. He took his messenger bag, and the basket of food Yasmine prepared, and walked over to his technical. Mohamed was in the kitchen and Macmud and his crew were at the far end of the ditches. The door to the container was ajar and the green smell invited him in. He looked at the kitchen again—still no one. He slipped into the container. The bales of khat were stacked three high at the back. He flipped over the first blue twined bale and dug out the tin box wrapped in packing tape. It would take too much time to unwrap so he dug out the other two boxes and replaced the bales. He took a second to listen before he came out of the container. He started the technical and didn't look back.

The overgrown track he'd first driven on with Ali Nur was now a wide dusty roadway, sometimes taking different routes around the old acacias. At the junction of the Doolow road he stopped. He decided to wait ten minutes, hoping that Zaynab would appear. Three hours—that was a clock in his head. Three hours and he could be flying out of Mandera. Waiting here was asking for delay at best. Then he heard it. Definitely a vehicle, just one. When he saw the dust trailing above the still invisible car or truck, he knew that his dust would also be easy to follow. He slowly backed his technical off of the road, but there was little cover.

Large Italian sunglasses reflecting out the windscreen allowed him to exhale. He'd been trying to see into the approaching Land Cruiser, the sunlight illuminating its expanding interior and hiding him for a few more seconds. Zaynab was squinting into the sunlight. He nosed the technical out to the edge of the road. She drove up beside him and rolled down the window.

"You're off then?"

"Last truck. Zaynab …"

She interrupted, "Will you come back?"

"I'd like to be leaving now that this is done. Omar said Ali Nur would need to clear it. Do you think he will?"

She took off her glasses and leaned out her window, arms resting on the edge of her door. "Don't come back. Don't wait for my brother. Go find her and don't come back to Somalia.

You've done what you can for Sharif and your camps. Ali Nur cannot help you in Mogadishu. So go." She paused, then added. "You know, my uncle is searching for Ali, and your Americans are helping. Your country is no different than mine."

68

Hani kept her eyes on Jimmy as the boat quietly slipped away from land. The sun was rising fast as she raised a hand to him before the boat rounded an island of reeds jutting into the channel. The captain pointed to a bench on the port side, and turned away before any greetings. He'd been poling out from the wharf and now was fiddling with the two-cylinder diesel engine mounted in the center. It popped to life with a gasp and a perfect smoke ring, drifting open mouthed until it was lost in the morning air. With the boat now under power the captain turned to her with a smile revealing a row golden teeth. He wore a Somali macawis and a thin blue sweater over his narrow shoulders. The end of the tiller was in his hand, guiding it with his thigh. "We will see the shore by nightfall miss."

"I'm Hani."

"Adam, I am Adam."

"Where will we land?"

He looked back over the bow and focused on things far away. He didn't seem to hear her. The little motor was banging out a steady beat. Their wake like ribbons in the sunlight fanning out behind them.

She pulled out a section of a Michelin map that showed East Africa from Somalia to Uganda. The UN base near the airport in Entebbe was on the east side of the peninsula. Adam's finger poked the map, startling her. "Here. It is shallow." He pointed to an arc of beach north of the airport. Hani's map shaded it green, meaning a park or game reserve—she hoped it was a park. Just then the lake shore folded back and they motored out onto the real Lake Victoria. Looking back Hani could see what she thought to be the lake was only a shallow inlet. This water, deep and serious, was as big as the ocean. The fastness of Lake Victoria was so different from her impression from maps. The inland sea beneath her and the dome of the African sky above her made her journey seem so impossible. She didn't feel buoyant. Two people might never find each other in this. And if they did, they'd join the tribe of fugitives. But Max could change his mind, or be killed. Maybe the sea will open up and swallow Adam's little boat? Who would even know or care?

She took a few slow breaths, until she could feel her heart slow down. She found herself staring off like the fisherman, squinting off into the distance, scanning the edges. She put her nose up into the ten-knot breeze and diesel fumes, and soon she was seeing clearly. The next steps, yes, just the next steps. Wade ashore, dry off, look like a UN worker on break. Find the posting board somewhere on the UN campus and get a ride to...where? She'd stopped to make sure she wasn't talking out loud. The sound from the diesel motor was loud enough to mask normal conversation. The percussive vibration was in tune with her voice in some harmonic parallel. She tried it out, singing an Indian tune from the last film she saw with Mara. She curled up on the bench and watched the world spin. They were floating in the air. The little engine was chugging them steadily all day, keeping them afloat and then aloft.

When Adam quieted the beast, they landed in the water and she awoke. The wake caught and pushed them into silence. The stars spun overhead and she searched for the southern cross. A sliver of moon rested on the edge of the deep sky. Adam pointed over the bow to a shore full of lights, then two dark patches. He cut the engine and started to test the depth with his pole. Hani had her backpack wrapped in a plastic bag, and her shoes tied together around her neck. When the pole showed less than a meter, she removed her pants and let Adam help her into the water. It was only twenty or thirty steps to the narrow beach. Behind that a black forest. The sandy lake bottom oozed as she stepped carefully, feeling for broken glass or rocks.

Adam was waiting offshore until she waved him off. She heard him start the engine, then he was gone. She stood on the beach adjusting to the light. The brightness of Kampala tinted the northern sky, while beyond the airport she could see into the deep night sky. She thought of Adam, sailing over the water. He would bring Max over Lake Victoria. An angel, sent to bring lovers together...like a Bollywood film.

69

Max rolled through the familiar wadis, past the crooked tree that hung over the road and under the low canopy. It opened and closed, sun and shadows alternating. When he could get an extended look overhead, he saw long ribbons of clouds that looked like contrails. Waves of fear and euphoria were washing over him to the pace set by the rolling and bumping track. This would be his best, or only chance to escape. Zaynab clearly thought that his time was up and that her brother had become a disadvantage.

Besides the imagined watchers, there was the driver that escaped. When he rounded that bend, he saw fresh tire tracks circling at that exact point, then heading back towards Toobiye. He rolled slowly past the scene, images lingering in the trees. He passed the place where Mohamed liked to stop—thirteen kilometers to Toobiye. How cool could he be, would he be, if faced with a roadblock. That'd be normal enough, but today he didn't know how he'd react. Each piece of potential danger stood up to challenge his hope. Each one needed to be pushed aside. The faces of Toobiye were turned in his direction, watching him drive slowly past where the road block was abandoned. The metal pole was still resting on a concrete block, the other end in the dust. He rolled past and turned toward Mandera. As Toobiye receded, he shifted into second gear. Each curve let out onto another piece of the road he'd forgotten about. The big trees were now moving away from the road, and a large grass field was on his right. He watched the trees, knowing that when they came closer, he'd find his markers.

The next time he looked back he saw a Land Cruiser, an old one, keeping pace with him. It must have come from Doolow. When he'd round a bend they'd disappear, then they'd be back, no closer, but definitely too close to think about driving off the road or making a run for the border. Out here, someone chasing you would not stop for the invisible line. There was no way to know if someone was really following him. They weren't chasing. Max considered speeding up. He couldn't believe that it was an unrelated matter, that it didn't mean trouble. It did mean that the official border was his next stop, so he settled in for all that that might mean. There would be a few hundred dollars, now an established routine—there would be the minutes on the edge of his nerves, heart pounding, forced nonchalance while they took his papers. He counted on a consistent level corruption.

Through an opening in the trees he saw the flag. A wire fence came out of the trees and raced him to the border. He sped up. When he turned onto the apron of the border station, he didn't see his pursuers, but they'd successfully herded him to the official Kenyan police. On three sides the razor wire was coiled along the two-meter-high fences. Five hundred-dollar bills passed in through the sliding glass window, along with his passport. Customs would be next, and he watched to see if Passport Control tipped off Customs about the increase. Max didn't care, he'd be glad to pay a thousand dollars to be across. He could see the road that went up past his tea shop. The regular Land Cruiser was there, but from this distance he couldn't see if Yusuf was waiting in the shadows.

A soldier slowly walked out to the gate in front of him. It opened, letting him enter the customs area. The gate shut behind him, now he was completely enclosed. Max recognized the agent. He tried to say something normal, but couldn't do it before the man's hand reached out for the papers. The agent stared at Max while his hand deftly picked the bills out and put them under the customs rate book on his left. His eyes stayed focused on Max. "Do you leave today?"

"Yes, I'll have one truck for Somalia. That's it."

"We close at three today. Enjoy your stay."

The pen opened and Max rolled into Kenya, legally, sort of—he had the entry stamp. Mandera was growing. He noticed the army base lined with new tents, and trucks carrying soldiers arriving at the gate. At the crossroads he could see, and hear, the commercial chaos of trucks, cars, goats, cows, and people, lots of people. On his side of the street, the tea shop looked so much the same that he felt a spike of paranoia. Too quiet? Breathe, he told himself. He parked at the tea shop, turned off the engine and took another breath. This was getting crazy. Caution was fine, but this low-level panic was turning everything into a sign of danger. He tried to feel the relief—tried to believe that he was closer to being with Hani.

Yusuf was waiting beneath the bamboo screen that shaded the bar. The regular NGO table was down to two women, Korean, he guessed. Max glanced over at their door logo, UNICEF. He didn't see Sam, John, or anyone else he knew. Yusuf said they should take the technical to the tire shop. Sam would take him from there.

"I need to go by the bank first."

"But there is no time!"

"I need look like I'm collecting the last truck. It will buy me a little time. Where is the American?"

"Sam knows."

When they got to the tire shop he saw Sam's regular taxi, then Sam. Before he got out, he passed one thousand dollars to Yusuf. He put it in his hand, and folded his fingers over it. "Get to Nairobi. Find Global Aid's office and speak to Josie. If you want to get a job with an NGO she can help."

"I will repay you. Really, I will, once I get a job."

"Never mind, you earned this." He turned to Sam, "I need to walk up to the bank, check in with Mr. Hassen. He needs to see that today is no different."

"Quickly Max. Mandera is hot now. War is seeping in on us."

"Is the pilot back?"

"The airfield has just been closed to all civilian traffic. Your pilot is there now and your American is trying to get permission."

He left Sam waiting at the tire shop and walked the three or four streets up to the bank. He came up from behind the bank, and scanned the parking lot and bar across the street. He wanted to be seen at the bank. Mr. Hassen was leaning on the front counter when Max walked in. He looked at his watch. He swept his arm toward his office and gave a slight bow. Papers were signed and fees were paid, leaving a negative balance, though Mr. Hassen didn't seem to care. He stamped the customs forms paid in full, and handed him the papers. There was a brief handshake, but no goodbyes.

He walked back to the tire shop and grabbed his bag, feeling the extra weight. He thought about just handing one of the boxes to Sam as a thank-you. But it wasn't a gift. It was stolen and it would be trouble for anyone caught with it.

"You'll wait at Tessa's until the American comes from the airport. Be ready to go." Sam added, "Brin will meet you there...she's leaving with your pilot too."

After a few more turns, Sam drove up to Tessa's lane from the opposite side he expected. This was the last place he'd seen Hani. His heart raced trying to grasp the idea of catching up to her by tomorrow. He could feel her slipping further away to Uganda across Lake Victoria, to Rome or somewhere. Maybe she was leaving a message to Zoe right now. He didn't want to lose her out there.

He sat in the same wicker loveseat that she was in when he first saw her. Tessa sat across from him, stirring a cup of tea. Brin walked up the lane and joined them. She put down her pack, gave Tessa a kiss and introduced herself to Max. After a second, she gave him a kiss on the cheek. "You better find her Max." She was Zoe's Irish twin.

They heard a car stop, then a door closing and steps coming quickly up the lane. John stopped at the little gate. He nodded at Max, then turned to Brin. "Where is Sylvie?"

"At the house I think, why?"

"Do you have a key to your Land Rover? Can you get supplies from the clinic?"

"What's this about?"

John looked at her, then to Max, then back to Brin "If you're going to fly out of here today you have to make it look like a medevac. That's the only way any non-military flights are going to be allowed to fly. Jimmy's waiting."

Brin caught on right away, it was like they had a plan for this type of evacuation. "I'll get Anita to drive. I'll be the attending, and Max the patient."

"I'll be waiting near the gate to be sure they let you in. You've got an hour to be on the tarmac. What are his symptoms? I'll be asked."

Brin put her hand on Max's forehead. "He's burning up, probably highly infectious." She poked his stomach and felt the glands on his neck. Maybe he's nauseous too. Diarrhea maybe. Don't worry. We'll be there on time."

"I need Max for a few minutes."

Max was trying to figure out what was just decided. John sat down and finished the last of Tessa's cookies. He reached in his pocket and pulled out an envelope with a string closure. He tapped it a few times before handing it to Max. "That's the last favor I can do for you. And probably my last for anyone, officially."

Max felt the passport shape and weight. "Have you heard from Hani? She should be in Entebbe by now."

"I don't think I'll hear anything. You guys are on your own. You might want to buy Hani one of these too. You should assume that someone will want you out of the way. If this ever gets investigated, you'll know a lot of the details. We'll see if Clinton wants to look backwards."

Max put the envelope in his pocket without looking at it. "Thanks."

"Thanks for what Max? I've gotten you into this, this is just a way for me to feel better. Besides, I really hope you and Hani find Shangri-La. Good luck." John glanced at Tessa's house. They could hear Brin and Tessa scheming. "I can't wait to see how sick they make you look."

"Me too. I'm afraid they might actually make me sick."

John walked away and Max walked up to Tessa's.

Brin dashed out of the door and took the steps two at a time. "I'm off to get Anita and the Land Rover. I'll bring you some scrubs. You're going to be a sick staff member, our first and only male nurse, okay?"

"What have I got?"

"Very high fever. Tessa's working on that. And we're going to give you some red scabs on your face. You'll look way too sick to touch. Go see Tessa. I'll be back in ten minutes, be ready."

Tessa's kitchen was anchored by a large table heaped with freshly dug roots, flowers, and large green leaves. Besides the recognizable vegetables and mushrooms there were long stringy roots and purple carrots with pointy beards. Pots and kettles hung from the low ceiling. A little gas burner was set on a block of stone, a foot off the floor. Narrow French doors opened onto a patio covered in vines. There was a long table against a clapboard wall where water jugs and basins sat. Tessa brought him through the kitchen and out to her patio. She pointed to a green chair. "We'll wait for Brin. I've made you a tea that will help you achieve a very good fever."

"I thought we were going to fake it." The thought of drinking her concoction made him feel sick already.

"Oh, well, it won't make you sick, it'll help you fake it for few hours. Your kidneys will feel better though."

"You and Brin are enjoying this."

Tessa smiled and patted Max's arm. "Oh Brin. Yes, she's running away with her lover. It's been good to see life go on, to see you and Hani and Brin follow love. It won't be easy, but it's good to know love early. We'll miss them both. Now, we need to make some pox."

He watched her chopping the purple roots and putting them into a shallow dish. A spoonful of hot water was added, and a pinch of something brown and powdery was sprinkled on it. It turned bright red.

When Brin returned, she threw Max some pink scrubs. "Here, change into these. They're Sylvie's."

While he changed, he asked her. "Do you know where you and Jimmy are going?"

She was sniffing the tea and making a bad face. He couldn't tell if she was acting for his sake, but it looked like something that Zoe would do. "Portugal. That's the plan. How about you and Hani?"

"We don't know. I think we'll meet up in Rome and decide from there. Portugal sounds good."

"Don't you want to go home? To America?"

"Not yet."

Tessa came out to the patio holding the dish of the red root paste.

"Here, we'll try it out on your arm. Turn it over, I want that tender white skin."

She took a bit of the paste on the end of an awl, and dabbed it on three spots. It had a little burn to it and Max looked up at Tessa.

"Too hot?"

"Not too bad. Are you going to put this all over my face?"

"And your arms too. It will be very convincing."

"And the tea, is that really necessary? These spots look pretty real."

He watched the three spots get a small red circle around them on his skin. The burn didn't get too bad. Then he saw each of the red dots harden off and grow a scab like skin. When he touched one it held on to his skin. Tessa also noticed this and called Brin to see.

"Wow. That's perfect. What do you think Max? Ready to get really sick?" Brin was holding the cup. "Ready?"

"No. But yes."

He pulled his face away from the steaming brew and took a breath.

"Better to drink it all at once."

He swallowed it and kept it going down. It didn't have the taste to match Brin's face, but it had a whiskey burn. Tessa had him turn his face up to her so she could apply the scabs. Brim was working on his arms.

"We should go soon. How do you feel?"

"I think I'm sick enough. Are you're finished with my pox?"

As soon as Max said it, he felt a wave heat pushing beads of sweat through his scalp.

Anita backed the Land Rover up the lane and was opening the back doors as he was led out in Sylvie's scrubs. He was definitely feeling the fever along with a slight euphoria. They arranged him in a stretcher, swaddling him in a white cloth that resembled the burial cloth they used in Mogadishu.

Anita leaned in, putting her face close to his. "Hi Max. I'm Anita. Give Hani a kiss for me. I'd give you one, but you might be contagious."

Anita drove while Brin sat in the back attending to her patient. Max was burning up, but the sensation wasn't completely uncomfortable, like being in a very hot sauna. The euphoria continued to mask his apprehension. He barely noticed when, at the airport checkpoint, he saw John and a Kenyan soldier looking at him from the open back door of the Land Rover. The next thing he remembered was being buckled in behind the two front seats of an airplane. He thought he could smell Hani.

"You set there, mate?"

He blinked his okay and watched as Brin gave Jimmy a long kiss. The engine roared and the tail swung around. In his mind he was a part of this machine. The thrust of the take-off rushed through his head just before he passed out.

70

Mr. Hassen watched as they loaded a stretcher into the airplane. He'd rushed out to the airport after the driver of the last truck showed up at the bank when the border closed for the day. From the insurance office, near the front gate of the airport, he'd watched a WHC Land Rover drive out onto the tarmac and transfer a stretcher onto the airplane. He checked with the airport operations office and learned that the flight was some kind of medical emergency, heading for Wilson Field in Nairobi. He drove to WHC. Mandera continued to swell with the Kenyan Army jamming the streets and erecting roadblocks at the main intersection. The air-conditioning in his Toyota sedan blasted moldy air into his face as he crawled through town.

Sam expected visitors. Waiting in a taxi near the camp, he watched as Mr. Hassen parked and went inside the big tent. Sylvie was prepared to fend off inquiries, having prepared a medical record of her emergency patient. Mr. Hassen couldn't really understand the diagnosis that Sylvie read off the chart, it being some of the most convoluted Latin she could muster. They didn't know a Max Dubec.

Mr. Hassen drove back to the bank—every bump and slow pedestrian was in his way. This wasn't his first time bending the law or even erasing certain evidence, but it was his first time doing it for someone like the US government. When he returned to the bank, the blinking red light on his desk phone wanted answers. “Where is our truck? What’s happening up there?” He recognized the voice of Mark Walters.

“The plane that brought Mr. Thomas to Mandera should be in Nairobi soon.”

“Is he there?”

“Mr. Thomas? I didn’t see him get on the plane. There was a nurse, the pilot and I’m sure it was Dubec on the stretcher.”

“What the fuck is going on up there. This thing is over, I told you to shut it down. You leave a message on this number if you find Dubec or Thomas in Mandera. Can you get the truck through customs?”

“Not without the consignee. It’s bonded in Dubec’s name—Global Aid.”

“Fuck, fuck...FUCK!”

“Mandera is becoming a garrison town Mr. Walters. The army will be into everything. Your truck will be opened on Monday unless you can find a way to stop it.”

“You make sure that container doesn’t get inspected. If this comes back to me...I’ll find you. You don’t want that Mr. Hassen. If I was you, I’d take my money and hide.”

“There is the matter of the final installment. I did my part.”

“We’ll see. Take what you got and destroy any records. Any of this reaches me I’ll come looking for you. Do you understand?” The line went dead before he could reply.

Mr. Hassen got up and looked out his office door at the driver, still waiting by the air conditioner. He waved him into the office and shut the door. Next, he called the teller from his phone, telling him to close the doors of the bank on time then leave, he’d be staying late and would arm the security system. The driver waited patiently, which is a big part of driving trucks across borders.

After the doors were locked, he sat down across from the driver. "I need you to take the truck and container away from the border crossing tonight. You won't be going in just yet."

"Where do you want me to take it? I need to return to Nairobi by Monday."

"That won't be a problem, it's just that I need to find the consignee. I'm sure he'll be available by tomorrow. Maybe you could leave the container and trailer and I could arrange another truck and driver to take it into Somalia?"

"I already have the papers, and I won't get paid unless it's delivered."

"If I might, how much will you be paid for this load?"

"Two hundred and fifty dollars, plus mileage and fuel."

"Okay, how much is the trailer?"

"I can't sell it to you, it's not mine!"

"Trailers get stolen sometimes in Somalia. I'm sure it's insured enough for the lessor to be made whole. But for your trouble I can offer you...ten times your rate—twenty-five hundred...US dollars? Does that seem fair? But you'll need to move it away from the border. I'll show you where I want it parked. Shall I get your money?"

By dark Mr. Hassen had deposited the trailer two or three kilometers out of Mandera. He let it be known to one of the taxi drivers that hung out across from the bank that there was an abandoned container out that road.

Mark Walters was unable to reach John. After his call to Mr. Hassen, he drove out to Wilson Field. He was headed for the controller's office when he saw the plane coming out of the dusk, land and taxi to a stop. He hurried back to his car, and showing his credentials to the gatekeeper, drove quickly toward the plane. He recognized Jimmy, but only saw one other person get out of the plane. He got out of this car, leaving the door open and was coming at them with his fists clenched. Jimmy looked at Brin. She wouldn't like this guy and he knew she could go off if Mark puffed up anymore. So, with one hand on her shoulder, he picked a target for his fists, and considered where this guy might keep his gun.

"Hey, where's your patient? Where's John?"

"Had to drop the aid worker in Marsabit, too sick to travel. John's still in Mandera. I'm going back to Mandera for your Mr. Thomas tomorrow. You'd have to check with the clinic in Marsabit about the aid worker. If he's better we could pick him up on our way back. Your call I guess."

"Go get him and the aid worker, then call me on this number. I need to know you've got them."

"You got it."

Jimmy grabbed the card and went back to get their bags. Brin stood there as Mark walked back to his car. She kept looking at him, catching his eye as he rounded the airplane and headed for the gate. She turned as Jimmy dropped her bag at her feet. "I'm just buying time. John doesn't need a ride from me, he's going overland to God knows where. He'll be okay. Find himself a bunch of real honest CIA of FBI types and defy that prick to make a move."

"Is that guy CIA?"

"Maybe. Could be something else. Something slimy and dirty."

Walters went through the building without seeing anyone. He took the stairs to the third floor, two at a time. Once he made it into his office, he locked the door and started making a map. He scribbled out a fairly accurate Kenya, then it's connection to the surrounding countries. Next, he dotted in the airfields he knew of. On the side of the map, he listed names, then drew lines to their locations. He started to shade in parts of the map where he didn't have contacts. He listed other names, officials, a retired Navy Seal, and a few low-level clerks that would love a little work. He then connected the names to Nairobi, Mandera, Marsabit, adding Naivasha to the list as he remembered Hani.

For the next hour he spread out his net, calling as far as Addis Ababa, Djibouti and Kampala. In each of these he asked them to keep an eye out for Max and Hani. All he would say was that they needed to be located soon, for their own protection. He also made contact with Sterling, a colleague in Kampala. He'd agreed to check in with the UN base out in Entebbe, as well as keeping an eye on the half dozen small airstrips surrounding Kampala. They spoke a common language full of hints and euphemisms.

71

He opened his eyes when the plane began to descend. He was still strapped into the stretcher with his head behind Jimmy's seat, looking directly at Brin. She was looking to the right, in the direction of their turn. He was trying to guess when Jimmy would feather it out and he'd feel the ground rolling underneath him. It came with a hard bump and he was glad that he was strapped down.

Brin said, "Hey, you're awake. How do you feel?"

"I can't move enough to tell."

Jimmy came around the airplane and opened the door. He looked in at Max, "You feel well enough to walk around? We'll only be here for thirty minutes."

"Yeah. Please."

She had reached over him, and released the strap over his legs. "Be careful when you stand up."

He felt blood rush to his head.

"Woozy?"

"Yeah, a bit. I really have to pee."

"Okay, let's stand you up. You'll have to do the rest yourself. Unless you need a nurse's assistance."

"I've got this, but thanks."

The field at Marsabit was bare and flat, with a hint of green around a solitary mountain. He saw tree tops and roof tops a kilometer away. When Max went to the other side of the plane, he saw a pickup coming toward them. He didn't care.

After he was finished Brin asked, "How are you feeling now?"

“I’m a little thirsty, but not bad. What did you guys give me?” He was picking at one of the red warts on his arm. He felt his face too.

“Here, I’ll get some water. I think those will come off in a hot shower.”

Brin dug out a bottle of water. “It’s pretty warm.”

He took a sip, then she pulled out a bandana and poured some of the water on it. She handed back the water, but took his wrist in her grip and started rubbing the wet cloth on one of his red spots. The bump softened, then Brin picked it off, leaving a red blotch on his arm.

“I don’t know how long that’ll last. Let me get a few more of them off’.

“Try a few on my face.”

“Good idea. You don’t want to go around looking like this.”

“What time is it?”

“It’s about four. About an hour more in the air. You’re going to have to sit so I can reach your face. You can work on your arms.”

He sat on one of the wheels as she poured more water onto the bandana and started on his face. Four o'clock, by now they’d be looking for him.

“Oh good, these come off your face just fine. They’re only stuck to your whiskers. Except these.”

She touched his nose, and the skin just below his eyes.

“I don’t think these will leave too much of a rash. You’re pretty sunburnt. Don’t you use sun block?”

It had been a long time since someone else washed his face. Maybe this is what people liked about hairdressers, or barbers, he thought. “So, tell me what was in the tea.?”

“Well, Tessa said it was some sort of tonic. She said it was something you’d give to induce a fever in order to hurry a sickness along. I'm pretty sure she added the good stuff to keep you relaxed. You were very relaxed. Do you even remember anything about the airport?"

"No, not really."

"Well, you were a perfect sicky. The army guy jumped back and covered his mouth and nose when he took a look at you. These are coming off okay." She was picking off the bumps on his face, making him wince when they took the whisker with them. "Almost got em. The ones on your arms though...do you have a long sleeve shirt? That'll scare someone."

"I've got what I was wearing before I changed into Sylvie's scrubs. I had to leave most of my things. I can buy something in Kisumu, or when I get to Uganda."

"Maybe Jimmy's got something. Not the same size, but you'll want those covered up til they heal. Pretty good disguise though, right?"

"Yeah. You guys did good."

Jimmy signaled that it was time to get back in. "Max, there's been a change of plans. I would have told you sooner, but you were really out of it man."

"What changed?"

"Not going to Kisumu. We were allowed to take off for a medevac to Nairobi, if I don't show up, they'll start looking. But we're going to drop you off in Isiolo. I don't think you want to show up in Nairobi, right? Listen, when we drop you in Isiolo I want you to go to the Hunter Hotel, get a room, and call this number. I'll call him when I get to Nairobi—to verify your story. Okay?"

Max took the card. "Who is this guy? What's he going to do? Does he have a plane?"

"Okay, in order. He's a friend that owes me a big favor, and he's going to get you to Kampala-Entebbe. In a plane."

"Tomorrow?"

"I hope so. You still have some dollars? It'll cost as much as first class to London, but you might get to Entebbe before Hani leaves."

"When do we land in Isiolo?"

"One hour. I'll only have a few minutes on the ground so you'll get a taxi to the Hunter, right downtown.

Brin sat forward, allowing Max to crawl over and into the jump seat. Before Jimmy fired up the plane, she leaned back, "You'll find her Max. I know it."

No you don't, he thought. You don't know it. It was a knee jerk reaction that he'd learned from Alison. Someone saying that would get a look, or a short lecture. He always thought Alison should just let it go. "I will. I know it too."

"When you get to Isiolo you'll be met by a doctor, and a wheelchair. Once outside the airport you can ditch the doctor and take a taxi. Change taxi's once then head to the Hunter. By the way, Hani had lunch there when we drove up from Nairobi. The restaurant is top notch."

The ground below was flat and sprinkled with old trees that topped out flat, spreading their longest branches over their claim to whatever water their roots could bring up. He had a vague notion of where Isiolo would be on the map, the part that was starting to turn green. Mt. Kenya's high snowfields were on the horizon.

He tapped Brin and asked if there was any water left. She took a small water bottle out of her pack and handed it to him. She watched him drink, then put her hand on his face, rubbing one of the little rashes beneath his eyes.

When they landed in Isiolo, Jimmy stopped on the apron. He turned to Max. "I'm not turning her off. As soon as I stop, next to the ambulance over there, Brin will open her door and you'll get out. Walk away from the plane and then wait for them to come to you. As soon as they have you, I'm rolling. I don't want any questions and there's not much light left."

Jimmy gunned the engine to start a roll toward the waiting ambulance. Brin opened the door on Jimmy's signal. He turned away from the prop-wash and walked clear of the airplane. He kept walking until he saw the man with the wheelchair start to move toward him. Jimmy gave him a thumbs up then swept his tail around, blowing the blanket off the wheelchair and up into the sky. He watched while the blanket was recovered and shook out. He heard a plane lift free of Isiolo, as the man motioned for him to sit in the chair. He pushed him toward a hearse-shaped Peugeot. When they stopped, the pusher came around and squatted down. "I'm Doctor Josiah. What's going on? How can I help you?"

"I'm Max." As soon as he said it, he regretted it. He hadn't looked at his new name yet, the passport was still in his pocket. Maybe it didn't matter, but he thought he'd better start thinking about disappearing. "You know, being out of that airplane makes me feel a lot better. I think I need to get some air, just sit here for a bit, if I may?"

Dr. Josiah's wide set eyes were sincere. With his head slightly turned to one side he looked truly interested, and trustworthy. "Well, okay. But I'm interested in these spots on your arms. Where have you been? Did you have a doctor look at these?" He'd taken Max's arms and was turning them to see the spots.

"I was just in Marsabit, and Mandera. I was in the care of an NGO up there. One of their nurses is on the plane that brought me here. She thought it was best for me to rest here before going on to Nairobi." He thought he'd better stop with the story and see if the doctor was going to let him go.

"What did she think this was?"

"She was sure that it was an allergic reaction. It was hard to get a breath for a while. I guess I panicked a bit in the airplane. But I feel much better now. May I stand up. I've been crammed in for hours."

"Okay, sure. Let me help you up, slowly."

"I'm definitely going to get an allergy test when I get home."

"Please, sir, I need you to at least get into the ambulance to take you off the tarmac, and I insist on at least listening to your heart and taking your blood pressure. I have to make some kind of record. You know, to get reimbursed for my expenses."

Max wasn't sure if this was his way out. Offering a bribe might be offensive, or required. He agreed to get in. Dr. Josiah folded up the chair and got in the driver's seat. He drove very slowly around several parked aircraft. Once they were outside the gate Dr. Josiah waited. Max took it as a meaningful pause, and he thought he knew the meaning. He'd fiddled out two hundreds from the roll in Sylvie's scrubs, they had nice deep pockets. "How much do you charge for meeting me at the airport, and for examining me?"

"Oh, you won't pay more than twenty Shillings. It's not very much, no?"

"But you charge the Kenyan health service, don't you? How much do they pay for this?" He knew he was in proprietary territory here. Dr. Josiah was thinking of a number, Max thought he could feel the calculations ticking. In Somalia the number was almost always one hundred dollars. A hundred for a doctor, a hundred for fuel, a hundred for a rifle. Salaries too, one hundred dollars a month for guards. It made it easy. "Here. Will that cover it?" He put the two bills on the center console.

Dr. Josiah looked at the bills, but didn't show any surprise or alarm. The sound of his calculator stayed constant, ticking.

"That covers it—the medical part, you know, the ambulance, the out of office visit and the consultation. I presume, Max, that you don't want any record of this. Is that correct?"

"That's true. I just wish to have my privacy. I'm glad to pay for your services, and I can pay another one hundred dollars to keep this between us. Please, I'm not in trouble or dangerous, it's nothing like that....it's a matter of...love." Another wave of Tessa's potion flooded him with peace—the good stuff was still working.

Dr. Josiah nodded, then looked at Max, his expression warmed back into his sincere and trustworthy doctor self. Max handed him the hundred.

"I'll drop you near a taxi stand, but before you leave, I want to do my duty, medically."

"Ah, the blood pressure and stethoscope thing. Sure, that'd be fine. Thank you."

His blood pressure was predictably high enough for Dr. Josiah to wag his head a little. Max convinced him that he'd get it checked out, but Dr. Josiah handed him his card and made him promise to check in with him before he left Isiolo. Max promised. He got out of the ambulance and waved goodbye. Standing there he noticed a few people looking at him, just staring. He walked over to a bench and sat there until this current set of witnesses would be replaced new ones.

The Hunter wasn't very far from the taxi stand, less than a kilometer. His taxi pulled into a crowded drive-court, on the corner of a busy intersection. The courtyard was surrounded by eight-foot-high stone walls and shaded by large Eucalyptus trees—more Nairobi than Mandera.

He slung his messenger bag over his shoulder and walked into the lobby. While he waited at the front desk, he noticed how weird he looked—the pink scrubs, and a Somali shawl wrapped over his shoulder. He felt the envelope and realized that he didn't know who he was now. With a nod to the desk clerk, he stepped out of line and headed into the bar. The aromas drifted out every time the swinging kitchen door slapped against the wall. He took a booth and slid a Canadian passport out of the envelope.

72

Rodney Macadam (DOB 13/7/1967, 6'1" 177 pounds) looked at himself in the photo, then leafed through to see the stamps. There was a notecard in the back with bullet points.

- Mother's Maiden Name-Sarah Andersen, 22/2/1942
- Father-William Henry Macadam 26/7/1940
- Get another Passport soon!

Getting the room was routine—the new passport number recorded in the registry, the key in exchange for a deposit, and sideways glances from the other guests passing through the lobby. His room was on the second floor, depending on who's counting. He went to the window and adjusted his compass. The last light was to his left. A note card from the hotel management informed him that local calls could be made from the room and international calls from the concierge's office. He dialed the local number. A man picked up on the fifth ring. "Yep?"

"Is this Mike?" No reply. "I'm a friend of Jimmy Leary. He gave me this number. He'll call you this evening from Nairobi to confirm this. I'm at the Hunter in Isiolo and I need a flight to Entebbe tomorrow morning."

"Name?"

"Max."

The line went dead. He considered calling again, but decided on a shower first. When he pulled out his old clothes, he could smell Geed Weyn. It was this morning's smoke, and the perfume scent of the New Blue Omo that Xabiib overused. The red spots on his arm were still visible, but the ones on his face, except for under his eyes, were completely gone.

He waited another fifteen minutes before he called again. It was picked up on the second ring. "Okay, Jimmy says you're okay. I'll come to the Hunter. Ten minutes."

"I'll be in the bar."

"See you in a few."

He'd stacked the three tin boxes on the night stand and started to unwrap the top box. He opened the lid and found exactly what he expected. He took only a few seconds to remove the tape from the others and spill out the cash on the bed. The pile was a lot bigger than the $40,000 he took into Somalia when he started. He guessed that it was over $100,000. He quickly stuffed it into his bag and covered it with his underwear and a wet towel. He locked the door and went down the curved stairs.

Brin said that Hani dined here. He imagined he was going down to meet her. Just a few more steps, make a deal with the pilot, call Zoe to see where Hani is, then find a place to disappear with her. He stopped at the front desk to make an appointment for an international call around eight, then walked into the bar. The table he wanted was at the far end with a good view of the entrance. The French doors to the patio were all closed now, but a few diners remained outside with blankets on their laps.

He glanced at the menu and ordered a steak, medium rare, and a Tusker. He'd spent a bit of time in Geed Weyn thinking about what he'd order when he got out. The food was good at Geed Weyn, but there wasn't much variety—he was tired of chicken. When the beer came, he asked for an order of the frites he saw going by on a tray.

The dining room was only a quarter full, maybe eight tables, with three men at the bar. Max guessed tourists, guides, local business people and maybe a few aid workers on their way to

Sudan. From what he could hear, one table was Dutch, several British conversations, some Swahili, and he couldn't decide if the table closest to him were speaking German, Swiss German, or maybe they were from Austria. The guessing game brought him to the question of the pilot's accent. It definitely had an American laziness to it. Max pegged a newcomer at the bar as his pilot. He couldn't hear his conversation with the bartender, but he could tell they were acquainted. He turned around, looked right at Max and walked over to his table.

"Are you looking for a pilot?"

"I am."

He sat down and put out his hand. "I'm Mike."

Max hesitated, then took his hand. "Max. Thanks for meeting me." Now he figured he'd told enough people his name he wouldn't be too hard to find him. Looking at Mike, he still wanted to confirm that he was really Jimmy's friend. His paranoia always seemed to come just a little late. "What did Jimmy tell you about me?"

"He said you might buy me a beer if I met you."

"Okay." He signaled the bartender.

"Also, he said you were in a big rush to get out of Kenya. Sounded interesting, plus I owe that bastard a lot. I'd do anything for him."

"I hope that includes a flight out of here first thing in the morning."

Mike cocked his head to one side, then righted it. "Big hurry? Someone looking for you? Somalis? Hey, Jimmy gave me a quick background. I get it. I'm married to one."

"Married to?"

"A Somali. They can be a lot of beautiful trouble. So, you were in Somalia? NGO? Which one?"

"Global Aid. I was in Mogadishu, then Luuq."

The beer came and Mike spent a few minutes lost in thought, taking a big gulp, then another.

"Can you fly me out in the morning?"

"I think so, but I'll need to check a few things first. Entebbe could be a problem for me. I can get you close though. Because this is for the Irishman, it'll come in around...eight hundred bucks. Deal?"

"Agreed."

"Now let's talk about Somalia. You were in Luuq?" Mike appeared ready to just to sit and talk now that deal was done. Max thought he'd enjoy a conversation with him, but he still had a call to make, and stacks of hundred-dollar bills to count and ponder. The money cast a shadow—fingers reaching out to him from an evil place. His food arrived, vanquishing the dark spirit. Mike reached over and helped himself to Max's frites. "I spent a lot of time flying in and out of there in the eighties. Did you live in Luuq? The town?"

"I was about ten klicks out the Doolow Road."

Mike seemed to be remembering it from above. "Geed Weyn!"

"Yeah. Geed Weyn. When were you there?"

"Must be...'83, I think. That was big camp with lovely nurses. What were you doing there?"

"I sort of had to be there."

"Look. I don't want to know your shit, you know. Sorry if I asked too much. But I know the people Jimmy usually works for, which means you're in some kind of trouble. I don't need to know...unless I do. So, do I need to know anything else?"

"Someone might come looking for me, which you probably guessed already, but if we can fly out in the morning it should be okay. I'm just a paying customer, right? Isn't that how it works?"

"As long as they don't shoot me down, you're just a customer. But hey, I'd do anything for Jimmy."

"I've got to make a phone call in a few minutes, but I'm free after that, I'm buying. Order something to eat. I should only be ten or twenty minutes."

"You sure?"

"Yeah, I'd enjoy a conversation."

"Right then. I'll check on our departure."

———

The concierge dialed Zoe's number and handed him the phone. He discounted the first two rings, thinking that these weren't ringing in Zoe's apartment yet. He imagined the phone coming to life in the Seattle morning. Zoe's old apartment building had a turret on the third floor, facing west. Last time he was home they'd watched the sunrise reflected in the glass towers downtown. He lost count after six rings. Then the line came to life, but the tone remained electronic.

"Hi, not home, leave me a short, short message. Bye."

Zoe's voice lit up his face. The concierge looked at him quizzically. Max gave him a thumbs up and he left the office, quietly closing the door.

"Zoe, it's Max. I'll try again...Did you get a message from someone named Hani? I need that message. I'll try again. Zoe...I love you...I'll try in the afternoon, your time…" The machine timed him out.

He found the concierge at the front desk. "Do you wish to make another call, sir?"

"How late will you be available?"

He shrugged. "Someone will be here, no problem, sir."

He took a few minutes to run up to his room and count the money. He could feel Omar's outrage at the discovery of the theft.

Had the search already scoured Nairobi? Were they in one of the cars pulling into the Hunter? His impulse was to hide it, to keep it in the dark, unable to signal its location. One hundred and seventy-five thousand dollars would be hard to silence.

Get through? All good news?"

"Nope, I'll try again later. How about you? Things set for tomorrow?"

"It won't be early, around ten. I'm waiting for a call from Kampala about a field close to Entebbe. You can get a taxi easily from there. If that works, you'll be there by afternoon."

There was another beer on the table and Mike was eating prime rib.

"Where did you get that? I didn't see it on the menu."

"Friday night. Prime rib at the Hunter. They had a little left. That's right, you're new here. Well, next time." Mike was in the zone. He'd secured a good price, and paid Jimmy back part of some big favor. He looked satisfied.

Max asked, "How long have you been out here? As long as Jimmy?"

"Before Jimmy. I came out in 1978. What's that, fourteen years? Yeah, well."

"So, you know Rana."

"Sure, Rana and a whole bunch of nurses. Those were the best of the bad times for Somalia. It seemed bad at the time, but now it's really fucked up."

"You're a private pilot for hire now?"

"Oh Max, what can I say? I'm like my own NGO now, without the money, or the logo. I'm a humanitarian enterprise. So, so much more than a pilot for hire. You see, you're a human in need. I'm not trying to use you or convert you, no...this is a joint venture to alleviate your human suffering."

"Well, that's a good fit for me right now. Who were you flying for in '83?"

"Jeez, that'd been the Jigjiga boys, '80 through '84."

"Jigjiga? Like in the Ethiopian town?"

"Ahh, you know it?"

"Know where it is, never been there."

Mike sat back and looked at him "Let's get out of here. You don't want to sit around your hotel room alone all night. I know a place near here, a private club—very discrete, promise."

Max really wanted to hunker down in his room and wait for the morning—wait for the sun to rise on the day he might take Hani's hand and fly off to the future. He was just starting to feel the relief of being away from Luuq and Mandera. The tension was seeping out of him, as was his energy. "I really need to sleep Mike. I've had a long day, starting in Luuq."

"Whoa, Sounds like it. Look, it's not yet nine, I'd have you back by eleven."

"What time do I need to be at the airport?"

"I'll pick you up around nine, maybe later. You'll get a good rest."

"Okay." He watched as Mike finished his prime rib, soaking the bread in the juices and licking his fingers with pleasure. Mike was built on a different scale, like 7/8th. The proportions were perfect, his head, his arms and hands, all perfect, but a different scale. Max didn't want to lose sight of the man that was going to get him out of Kenya in the morning.

They left the hotel on foot and turned right at the gate. Max was thinking that this might be a mistake. He hoped Mike was careful, but then he must be, he was a pilot, all of the ones Max knew had enough cowboy to be fun, but a serious side as well. Mike was leading the way, past a dozen side streets that got narrower and narrower. They turned right into a lane with a canopy of intertwined limbs, hung with large green teardrop leaves. He smelled the weed at the same moment Mike knocked on a white wood slate gate. It cracked open, a woman's head peeked out, looking up and down the lane, resting on Max for a second. She had short cropped hair and large loops in her ears, Kikuyu style. She kissed Mike and moved aside for Max to enter. Mike pointed him to a table in the courtyard against the wall, then went over to a table where several men were using an ornate hookah. When Max sat down, a young girl came over to his table with a bottle of water.

"Hi, what can I get for you?"

"I'll wait for him." He pointed to Mike, who had taken a seat, and a turn on the hookah.

"Cool. He's good people." He hadn't heard that phrase in years. He liked the all-encompassing simplicity of it. "I'm April. This is my family's place. You're an aid worker?" She'd had taken a seat. Her eyes scanning the yard, not looking at him. Her hair was in long braids, with thin leather strips woven in. Definitely not Somali, but having the same grace and

confidence.

"Yeah."

"Where did you work? I know lots of them working in Sudan. Is that where you worked? Maybe in Loki?"

"Somalia."

"Is that where you met Mike?"

"No, I just met him. You ask a lot of questions."

"But there's so much to know."

"You're right. I have a question. Don't have any trouble from the police?"

"See the man talking to Mike? He's on the council. And that guy that just came in? The doctor."

"Dr. Josiah?"

"You know him?"

"He's my doctor, actually."

She stood up and hailed the doctor. Dr. Josiah looked at Max, "You're feeling better, I guess?"

"Almost fully recovered." Max rolled his sleeve up and in the dim light the spots were invisible.

"Um, um...good. Still, I am puzzled. The symptoms are not consistent with anything I've ever seen." The smirk on his face blossomed into a wide smile. He turned his head toward the table that Mike was visiting. "But I think I figured it out. I believe you will recover fully from this. Don't worry, we have a deal. I'm just relieved to have an answer so I don't have to keep thinking about it. Can't let things go."

Mike came over and greeted April with a quick hug of her shoulder. "Get us the little hubbly bubbly, the blue one. Thanks sweetie. You're going to be taller than your mother." He turned to the doctor, and said, "Doctor."

"Mike. How's your son? Better?"

"Bashir's good, so I'll send you a chicken."

"I'll let you get back to your business. And Max, you can consider this our check in. Good luck."

"Asante sana."

Mike unwrapped the hashish and carved off a piece for the hookah bowl. He looked up at Max.

"He's your doctor too? Have you been here before? I've never seen you in Isiolo. I am curious."

"Mike, for now, at least for a few days, I'm not Max. I'm Rod, from Canada."

"Okay. Shit. This is serious stuff...Rod. Right? No worries, I don't care."

"Ask Jimmy about it sometime. He knows a lot of the story. It won't matter in a few days. I've just got to reach Entebbe by tomorrow."

"All's good. Let's just have some of this and see where it leads."

He hadn't even thought about getting high in Africa. He'd heard the stories of prison and even executions for possession. But here he was, taking his turn on the hookah. April's matter or fact explanation of the club's exemption, and the presence of Dr. Josiah, seemed good enough reason to enjoy his brief stop in Isiolo. They smoked in silence, drawing in just enough air—focused on the small red glow until they looked up and saw each other. The hashish had washed over him in a rush. Max fought off an initial burst of paranoia by rebuilding his surroundings and tracing himself to this spot. It was still Friday, and this person across from him was going to fly him to Uganda, to Hani. He looked around the garden, at the tall walls, at the canopy lit from underneath, like the moon rising beneath clouds. These people were his friends, and his doctor was here. He asked, "The Jigjiga boys? Was that the outfit you flew for?" he'd been rolling the name, Jig-jig-a, around in his head.

Mike picked it right up, "The CAI... yeah confusing letters. They're gone now, but it was pretty nuts Max...no, Rod. I like Max better, but it'll be Rod. I'll practice. Rod…that was my first gig out here, and it was really wild. At the time I didn't know anything about aid work, but it was way different than I'd imagined. I'd grown up listening to missionaries preach in my church back in Schenectady, New York. That's what I wanted to be, an MAF pilot. Going to the deepest jungles and landing on mountain tops. Real hero thing you know. I'll bet you're not that different, I mean, how'd you got interested in being a missionary type, right? Global Aid is a Christian NGO, right?"

"I'm not a Christian, they didn't even ask me that. I know that that's how they advertise, or raise money, but it was feeding people. Not missionary work."

"Oh, and what's missionary work? Feeding the hungry, healing the sick. Yes you were. Whether you believe or not. We're all on a mission...Rod. There I remembered it."

"All I mean is that I never went to church and I don't believe there is a God."

"You sure?"

"No, not certain. I'm not sure of much really. But God, Heaven and Hell seems like a story, something told to children when their pets die."

"Well, there's a lot of weird shit I've seen. I'm not certain either."

"Back to Jigjiga. How's that connected to CAI?"

"Missionary kids, the boys, Jason and Geoff were from Jigjiga. Their dad was the headmaster of the missionary school out there. The boys became the star players when a group of churches in America decided to start Christian Action International, CAI, as a Baptist alternative. The old man had a thing about the Southern Baptists. Jason was the Country Director for CAI in Somalia when I started flying for them. Lots of money, really nice aircraft. I was twenty-six, flying a twin engine. The boys were just in their early twenties, like 20 and 22. They were good kids...we were all trying to be good kids."

"What was Mogadishu like then, in the early eighties? Rana talks about it like it was, like you said, the best of bad times."

"I'll tell you, but I don't want to hear your version of what it's like now. I don't want that picture. I hear about it most days from my Fatima. She's been shunned by her clan, but she sure gets all the latest news."

The idea that Mike's Somali wife was tapped into the Somali web, reminded him of the need to get beyond their diaspora as soon as possible. This also threatened to turn down the growing euphoria he was trying to enjoy. The promise of a temporary escape offered by the hashish and Mike's company was hard to hold onto.

Mike looked up at him. "You got someone? A girlfriend, wife, lover?"

He waited to see if Mike had posed a rhetorical question. Mike waited.

"I do."

"Then look at everyone like that. Like they have lovers. Like they all want someone to love...someone to love them back. You'll really see them and understand what we all really want—what we all really need."

Max remembered waiting at a stop light when he saw the woman in the car ahead of him. Her face reflected in the side mirror, thinking her thoughts, living her full and complex life. A whole universe of connections and relationships that were intertwined and as meaningful as anything in his world. That she might be lonely, hurt, overjoyed and anticipating something right then, one car in front of him. The rest of that day he'd stared at others in a sonderous state. If he could just become part of Hani's universe forever. But life is complex, and a dark corner of his universe was lurking. How could he just walk away from Sharif and Suleymaan, the feeding centers? He needed to talk to Josie. He needed to explain the circumstances. He needed to be forgiven. He just needed to explain it to Josie. She'd understand love, he was sure of it.

"Hey there Max. You okay?"

"Yeah...So, why did you stop working for the missionaries?"

"It wasn't working for me any longer. It didn't match my picture anymore. It was probably me...a bad picture. Not really bad, but not right somehow. We lived well, flew off to retrieve ice cream from Djibouti. Took donors on tours, and smuggled in supplies for officials. All this was in the name of spreading the gospel. I was out on the edge of my church's prayers. I'd prayed for missionary pilots and now I was one, and I wasn't in any need at all. We had the best houses, planes and Land Cruisers. I had to return to the states every six months to speak in churches, to raise money for our work. We were always pressing for more and better aircraft, which somehow was going to make the difference. I'd have to show how more planes produced more souls, not easy, but I tried. We imported everything we needed from Europe and the Middle East every week. It didn't fit. It just stopped being true. I couldn't ask for prayers anymore, and I didn't want people like my dad working their ass off to support me anymore."

"But CAI and others did the work, right? I mean they set up feeding and medical programs just like the non-Christian NGOs, didn't they?"

"Oh, for sure. Your people at Global Aid and the others all had good programs, and good staff. It wasn't the actual work, but the bullshit that it took to get it funded. Do you have donors Max? Shit, Rod?"

"No, I was hired and paid, just a job."

"That's better. For you, I mean. But where did the money come from? Are you on a grant, USAID, or UN funded? I'll bet it's the church donor, the wealthy donor and the widow's mite all in the name of saving souls. Did you save any?"

"Is that really a thing? Saving souls? Sure, I get the idea, but it was never the point I thought. Feed the hungry, right? I've seen the advertising, it talks about reaching out, about shining light, etc. It didn't affect anything we did. We were like the others, working inside the UN guidelines...which didn't include saving souls."

"Forgive me Maa...Rod, but there are others out there quietly, and economically, doing the work of relieving suffering and providing real assistance, both short and long-term. They're saving souls every day. I worked alongside them for years. Your Rana became one of the quiet ones, that's what I call them. You might not ever know what they've done, or how many they helped. They're doing it without the planes and Land Cruisers, they live on the other side of town from K4 and the NGO neighborhoods. They take local transportation, go to local shops, get invited to weddings and funerals. Some of them are Christian for sure, but you wouldn't know it. I think they're all Buddhist in their hearts frankly. But they won't judge you for loving whoever you love."

Annie told Max once about some Canadian Mennonites that lived on the North side of Mogadishu. They were part of her tribe. The quiet ones that Mike was talking about. He'd never been invited to a Somali wedding, but in Geed Weyn he felt like it was possible to not always be outside the circle. Global Aid and the other big agencies didn't try to be quiet about their good deeds—they needed to raise money, advertise and promote. The aid workers he'd met treated the reality of large-scale fundraising with contemptuous appreciation.

Mike put both hands on the table and said, "Right now I fly for small farmers, and ferry sick people. You'll see, my plane smells like goats this week, next week who knows. If you come back this way, I'll have you out for dinner. Fatima would love to talk to another American to see if I'm normal."

"You think I'm the standard?"

"Doesn't matter, it's just that she can't believe we don't have clans. Maybe we have 'em, but not like Somalis. We're a people Max, a big noisy bunch of world conquerors. We're fat, loud and rich. Most of us are movie stars too. You know the thing that puzzles Fatima the most? Our families. Somalis have strong connections out to their distant cousins, and their cousin's cousins. I've got a mom, dad and a sister. Grandma's gone, so are the aunts and uncles. Nobody writes or calls—maybe on Christmas, or a birthday, if it got on their calendar. It seems normal, right? Same for you? Just a tight little clan of three or four, right?"

"My sister and my dad now. I've barely met my cousins. Some of them never."

"Good, then you can tell Fatima that's how it is. She just can't imagine how lonely we must be. Really, she pities me...which makes her feel a little better. It's fine with me. She wants more children, but not until it's safe for her to return to Somalia. You can tell her that too, that it's not safe, and might never be."

"Well, if I do come this way, I'll take you up on the invitation."

"Good. I'll be here. You're like a part of my clan, more of a sub-clan, the expatriate diaspora." Mike slowly pushed himself up with a groan, then he offered Max a hand, pulling him to his feet. "Time to get you to bed, like I promised."

Max started to fish out another bill but Mike objected. "No, no, this is part of the first-class service."

Back in his room at the Hunter, he took another shower and sorted his few clothes for the morning. He peeked at the dollars again. As long as they stayed on the bottom of his bag, covered with a tee shirt and a pair of shorts they seemed harmless. With the light off, he watched the headlights reflecting on his ceiling. He tried to imagine Mike's life here in Isiolo, and he wondered if he could really disappear from his past and change cultures.

The lights on the ceiling crossed from two directions, intersecting then fading away.

74

Hani sat down on a tree root, having scanned for snakes. She put on her shoes and stuffed the plastic bag back into her pack. Her underwear was still wet but she put her pants back on and started walking along the shore toward the airport lights, looking for a path inland. She knew from the map that Kampala Road ran out the peninsula, with side roads leading to main road. Her back story would be as close as she dared to her real story. The UN part was easy but explaining her being in Kampala, looking for a ride off the continent, that needed some imagination. She was going to play it that she was on holiday, just wanted to take a break and visit friends in Europe. She hoped that no one from her Mogadishu office was there, but even then she'd have a true enough story to tell.

When she came to the end of the beach, she was confronted with a concrete wall that went right to the water. The wall had sharp glass teeth embedded on top. Behind the wall spot lights aimed at the corners of a compound. She went along the wall, going inland. The path led along another wall, this one shorter, but also showing its teeth. There was a break in the wall where she saw a lane that ended in bright lights.

At the corner of Kampala Road, she looked to her left for a place to eat. She saw signs of familiar restaurants, looking like stretches of western Nairobi all lit up and busy. She crossed the road and started walking, looking for an outside cafe, looking for her people, UN people, NGO people. After passing several bars and nightclubs spraying music out into the night, she saw an outside bar under a thatched roof and lanterns hanging over the six or seven tables. The bartender's dreads were the colors of the ANC. She caught his eye and after a few nods steered herself to a table on the edge. A few patrons noticed her, but only for a second.

"What can I get you dear?" The waitress's dark Spanish eyes stood out on her pale skin.

"Steak Frites please. And, a Tusker. And, water too, with gas. Thanks."

"Right. Are you waiting for someone?"

Hani smiled, "No. No one else." She checked her impulse to clarify, but it was true, she was alone.

When the food arrived her hunger awoke, the aromas overcoming the stale air from the lake. Her thoughts about a shower and clean clothes waited as she felt the savory food giving her strength.

The waitress brought her more bread to go with the sauce. "You were hungry. Can I get you anything else?"

Hani considered, then asked if they had coffee, fresh coffee.

"I'll drip you a cup if you like."

"That'd be super, thanks."

When the coffee arrived, the waitress looked at the empty chair. "Do you mind?"

"Not at all. Maybe you can help me?"

"Help you how?"

"Well, I need a room for the night."

The waitress put out her hand. "Karin."

Hani took it. "Hani, nice to meet you."

"Try the Ace. two or three blocks, on the lakeside. It's got a giant Ace of Hearts on the sign. It belongs to his brother." Karin flipped her head towards the bartender. "Raffe, call your brother for Hani here, see that she gets a good room for the night, will you?"

Without a word, Raffe, dialed, waited, said a few words in a Rasta tinged Swahili, then hung up. "Whenever you're ready, miss. I can give you a ride if you like."

"Thank you, really. I can walk, but wow! Thanks."

———

The Ace was in transition—a two level motel looking a little worn and signs of long-term residents occupying the cottages on the lakeshore. She was hoping for at least one real hotel night on this trip. She wondered if there was a Ritz in Rome. The shower was weak, but the water was hot. She ran it completely out while showering and washing a few clothes. She'd take another shower in the morning after the little tank under the sink recovered. Kampala Road was bright and busy until well after midnight. She heard the distinctive grinding of C130's sweeping over the Ace all night and at three in the morning she was ready for Earth to spin into the new day. She didn't know how different Entebbe's UN base would be. Nairobi's base had grown a lot since she first started there during college, but it was not nearly as big as Entebbe's. Maybe it was stricter here, more signature and stamps. In Nairobi you could always get a ride around Africa. Even European flights were possible if there was room. But then she'd always worked closely with the director, or program officers. No one knew her here.

75

At sunrise someone knocked on her door. The owner, Raffe's brother, stood on the second-floor walkway. "I have a message from Karin. They offered to make you breakfast this morning at the bar."

She looked down the street to where the bar was, and then back at the hotelier. "Is it too early?"

"Oh no, they have been there since five. A bar at night, a coffee house in the morning—very smart."

The morning commute was flowing toward the airport and UN base. When she arrived at the hedge in front of the bar, she saw that most of the tables were occupied.

Karin saw her and sat her at the end of the bar. "How was your night? Coffee?"

"Is it always this busy?"

"We get em coming with caffeine and leaving with alcohol. Raffe keeps trying new things."

"Well, it seems to be working. Yes, Coffee, thanks."

Raffe came out of the kitchen and put a plate of basted eggs on a bed of roasted potatoes in front of her. "Try this. Tell me what you think. Do you want bacon? You eat bacon, yes?"

"I do, yes, please. And, I want to thank you for getting me a room at the Ace. It was very nice. You're both very kind to a stranger."

"You never know about strangers." He said this with a theatrical glance. "Maybe you're an angel. We never know."

"I can assure you that I am not, but I think you and Karin might be."

"You are on a journey. Am I right?"

Hani paused, blinking back tears. "I am. Is it that easy to tell?" She thought that her backpack gave her away, or the fact that she needed a place to stay—pretty stranger like. But Raffe suggested more than a trip.

"It is just a guess, a hunch. Tell me if you like the eggs this way, I'm thinking of adding it to the menu."

The morning crowd disappeared a little before nine. Karin took off her apron and sat down on the other side of the bar. "So where are you off to today?"

"To the UN base, see if I can get a ride to Rome."

"Oh, I should have introduced you to Marcel. He was just here. I'm pretty sure he's the one to talk to. I hear it's not so easy now."

"I used to be the flight coordinator for UNICEF in Mogadishu." As soon as she said it, she knew it could lead to more questions.

Karin didn't ask any, but the look on her face invited Hani to say more. She let it drop, asking instead. "Are you staying another night?"

"Yeah. I don't think I'll find a flight today, but maybe."

"Well, I don't think the Ace is too busy. Do come by and let us know what you find. Maybe Marcel will be here tonight. I'll introduce you. Couldn't hurt. Raffe is barbecuing ribs this afternoon. You should come by for an early taste."

"That sounds really good. Thanks."

Raffe came out of the kitchen when he saw her start to leave. "How was breakfast?"

"It was great, thank you. Oh, I almost forgot to pay."

"Never mind, it wasn't on the menu yet."

"Well, it should be. Hey, I was wondering if you had a phone, I need to call someone this afternoon. I would pay, it's an international number."

"Sure, no problem. I've got it hooked up to a computer so I can make calls for free. Most of the time it connects, and when it does it's much better than the local service. Come by this afternoon and we'll try to get one for free."

There were several taxis parked along the road, the drivers standing around, smoking and laughing. She got in the taxi at the head of the line.

It was further than she thought. She had the map committed to memory, but the driver took her through a residential section of Entebbe and not along Kampala Road. The taxi pulled into a large parking lot filled with containers and charging forklifts dancing to their monotonous chirping.

She entered the building and stood in front of the directory. Flight Operations was on her right, down a hallway and across from the bathrooms. The morning coffee had reached her bladder, which gave her a reason to hide in a stall and quiet her nerves. Concealing the truth was not comfortable. She went over her plan to request a seat on a deadhead flight to Rome. It was almost always a favor to be given a free flight, even for project coordinators. In her position it usually required your supervisor's approval. She thought that she should have told Roger in Nairobi her situation. He'd understand. He'd cover for her. She could call him. As she washed her hands she looked into her eyes in the mirror. She looked guilty. She tried a few other faces, casual, innocent, but her eyes didn't change much.

She pushed open the Flight Operations door and came into a large room filled with people at desks. There was no reception desk, meaning that if you were here, you knew who to see. She stood there scanning the faces, waiting for someone to make eye contact. Several people noticed her and went back to their papers. At the last row of desks, she recognized a young Sudanese man she'd met in Nairobi. She remembered him, but she couldn't come up with his name. It was something English, like William or Robert. While she was standing, deciding if he would be a good start, he got up and walked toward her. "Hello, you're from the Nairobi office, aren't you? Hani, right?"

"Yes, I thought I recognized you."

"It's Robert. So, are you working here now?"

"No. I'm with UNICEF in Mog. It's good to see a familiar face. There are so many people here."

"Yeah. It's busy. I think I prefer Nairobi. How's Somalia? That sounds crazy now."

"I've been out of Mog for a few weeks. I missed the landing. I'm sure it's chaos at my office. Sort of glad I missed it actually."

They shared a head shake and then a pause. "What are you doing in Entebbe? There are a few more of your Nairobi colleagues here."

She took another look around the room. "Actually, I'm trying to get a seat going north, Rome."

"Good luck. It's not easy. They're using more charter companies now, and they don't allow free rides to NGOs or UN staff."

Robert looked around for a second, then pointed to a narrow hallway to his left. "Take a look at the board. The UN planes are in blue, the others in red. You'll need to talk to Marcel, if you can find him. He's not here right now but that's his assistant, Rohanna."

"Thanks Robert, really good to see you."

Memories of Robert were starting to surface. Her sense was that she'd seen him at a very bizarre party in Nairobi. A party that was followed by a week of unsettled tension in the office. She recalled that nobody looked at each other, and everyone ate lunch alone. She wondered what Robert remembered.

She stood in front of the large white board that listed the flights in and out. A number of flights had no information other than PRIVATE and a tail number. The UN planes had every box filled out. Seating Capacity was next to AVAILABLE. Looking down this column she saw two flights with a seat. Going backwards she found the DESTINATION column. Niamey and Djibouti.

Robert had given her an answer, she didn't need to have a free ride this time. Flying out on a private charter would really reduce her exposure. There'd be records of course, but you'd need to know where to look. She left the building and started walking toward the airplanes. She was hoping that the security here was lax. She put on her UNICEF necklace,

Ugandan military guards were posted at the opening in the fence, not the UN police. She slowed her pace, looking for anyone outside the fence that might be going in. She'd tag along, act like she was part of the team. Two people had just gone through, and from this distance Hani didn't see the guards checking ID. She decided to have a smoke, giving her a reason to be loitering this close to a protected zone. She watched a pickup go in with a wave. After a few more people passed through without stopping, she put out her cigarette. All they could do was say no, unless they were looking for her. She got a disinterested glance from the gatekeeper and started walking out to find the charters. There were only three that looked big enough to make the jump to Rome. No one treated her inquiries as improper, but no one was going to Europe.

She walked back to the UN base and took another look at the big board. On the far-right side she noticed the bulletin board, scraps of paper with things for sale and people looking for other people. Hani went back into the main office and asked the woman at the first desk for a scrap of paper and a pen, and wrote MX HN @ACE, then dated it. Looking at it up on the board she thought it needed something else so she drew in a very small heart between their call-signs. She left by the main door, looking to see if Robert was at his desk. He wasn't. On the ride back to the Ace, when they came close to the shoreline, she looked for her fisherman-angel.

76

Hani checked in with the front desk at the Ace. As she waited, she could look right through to a small apartment. Raffe's brother waved, and then turned to someone she couldn't see. A young girl came out and smiled at her. Hani asked if she could have her room for another night, or maybe two. The girl looked back into the apartment, then back at her.

"Yes, of course. I'm Mattie. I made your room up while you were gone."

"Oh great, thank you Mattie. I'm...well you know. Pleased to meet you." She felt that this bright-eyed girl had something more to say, so she smiled and waited.

Mattie lowered her voice and asked. "Are you a friend of Karin's? Oh, I shouldn't ask, I know. I think she's really nice."

"She is very nice, I just met her yesterday. Raffe's nice too. They've both been very kind."

"Raffe's my uncle."

"He would be a good uncle. You're lucky Mattie."

"I know."

Hani said goodbye and went back to her room. As she walked up the outside steps, she could see the lake through the forest of fronds that were swaying back and forth. The offshore breeze was so different here. In Mogadishu the salty air carried the spices of India inland to mingle with the charcoal smoke. The salt was missing here. She felt the cool air though, reminding her how much she would have loved this climate on that coast. Right now, she just wanted to be alone, safe in this room. The alone felt much better knowing that she had made friends here, and that when she got tired of being alone, she could just walk up the road and be welcomed.

At first, she sat on the edge of the bed thinking about washing a few more clothes, but she wasn't sure if they'd dry in time. The air was humid and there was no fan in the room. She leaned back onto the pillow and listened to her fears making their case. Soon she was staring out, suspended over her life, watching images of Somalia, of Max. Movie clips of her and Max at her little house by Mogadishu's airport. The Bougainvillea hanging over her tiny courtyard framed Max as she watched from her kitchen window that first night. Other clips played, out of sequence, but always circling back to Max.

She rolled over and took out Max's notebook to find Zoe's number. Scrolling through the three pages of names and addresses she followed him around the world. Venezuela had the most recent entries before Africa. The back pages had Max's record of his time in Geed Weyn, evidence…in case. Compared to his journal entries, which were practically indecipherable, the notes from Geed Weyn were clear and detailed. She flipped back to July and August and saw her name on almost every page, but his words raced across the lines too quickly to read without slow decoding and assumptions. Some sentences were almost a flat line without protruding consonants to hint at the meaning. X'd out lines, missing words, arrows, small drawings, underlines and clouds drifting in the margins was like a map of his world. She was able to decode the first few entries—his first thoughts about her. In the frequency of his words, the missing key words that would connect it all, (the interrupting parenthetical doubts in another voice added another layer) and in it all she could see him falling in love with her. She read on for several more pages, just letting her mind follow the rhythm of the stream, comprehending beyond individual words. In this hypnotic state she held the beating ruby in its pouch, pressing it to her breast.

A low flying cargo plane roared overhead, bringing her back to her room at the Ace. It would be after 1am in Seattle now—time to call Zoe. She thought about writing Zoe's number on a blank page in the back of the notebook, and there she found, in the sleeve, a postcard of Daisy's Bar, Puerto Cabello, Venezuela. Nothing was written on the back. The Spanish style, columned terrace faced the sea with a long arcing beach on the left and a black rock seawall on the right. She tore off a small corner of a blank page and put it in the pocket of her jeans. They were getting pretty bad, but they'd have to do. She took the last almost clean tee shirt out and tried it on. She wished that she still had her Bob Marley tee shirt, Raffe would like it. She still had no idea what to say to Zoe. She had no idea when or where she was going. Maybe it was safe enough at the Ace for now. On the way out she saw Mattie was on the bottom step.

"Hi Mattie."

"Hi, I'm going to Raffe's, with you."

"Oh, have you been waiting for me? I'm sorry."

"Well, a little. But it's no problem. My father says I can go to the barbecue, if I'm back before dark. I really want to talk to Karin, and you too, about working for the UN. That's what I want to do with my life."

"That's great. Does Karin work with the UN?"

"Not now, but she did for years. That's where she met Raffe. He worked for a local NGO."

"Mattie, I left a message for a friend. My boyfriend really. Anyway, I left the message that I would be at the Ace, if he even sees the note. Will someone be here if he comes in late?"

"Sure, I'll leave a message on the desk. And I'll tell my father. What's his name?"

"Oh, if someone asks for me. It will be him. Okay?"

Mattie looked at Hani for a second, processing the nameless boyfriend.

"Yeah, I'll let Papa know. I'll be right back."

When Mattie returned, they started walking down the edge of the road. Mattie was leading, looking for the first place she could safely cross to the other side of the road. The sidewalk there would allow her to walk next to this mysterious Indian woman. Hani also wanted to walk next to Mattie, she felt bad about not being honest with her. Once they crossed, they both turned to each other. Hani spoke first. "Mattie? Mattie, I'm sorry I didn't tell you his name. Really, but it needs to stay secret for now. That actually sounds even weirder now that I say it."

"Oh, don't worry. I like mysteries. I really don't need to know his name. But if he checks in, I'll need a name, you know, any name."

"If he comes. I mean it's a slim chance he'll see my message, but if he does come, he'll give you a name. I hope you get to meet him."

"How did you meet him, your boyfriend?"

"We met in Mogadishu, no...actually we first met in Kismayo. He was just going into Mogadishu to work with an NGO. My office at UNICEF was close to his house. So, I saw him all the time."

"What's he like? Is he like you?"

Hani knew what she was asking. "He's an American. Tall, blond and his eyes are blue, like the sky."

"That's cool."

They were following the scent of the barbecue. Mattie was forming another question, which she did with pursed lips and a wrinkled nose and said, "I don't see why that's such a big deal."

"What, that he isn't Indian?"

"Or that Karin isn't black, isn't African? It was a big problem between my dad and Raffe for a while. Did your parents allow it?"

She stopped in front of the bar and faced Mattie. They were almost out of time to have any more private conversation, and she wanted to really answer the questions of a fifteen-year-old girl. She remembered being fifteen. "Well, in my case I didn't have parents to protest. I was an orphan. But I know the Indian community in Naivasha, where I grew up, fought against mixed marriages. They'd even kidnap the guy or girl and hide them in another city. Lots of broken hearts. He said his family in America is very progressive, which I think means that it happens all the time but it's pretty different in the smaller villages in Kenya and Somalia.

Maddie nodded, "The thing is, around here, there are so many churches, tons of missionaries. Marrying one of them is good way get to Europe or the States. That's what I've heard. I know one girl that worked with a missionary in Kampala. She got pregnant and they sent the guy back to England. She's still here, living with her mother and their son. She's my age. She always talks about when she's leaving, but it never happens."

"Yeah, I know stories like that too. Listen Mattie, I'm sure Raffe has made your path a lot wider than most".

"I'm lucky, right?"

"Absolutely."

She gave Mattie a hug. It was the first human contact since she left the sisters in Mandera and it felt good.

Raffe peeked out from the backyard, wearing an apron and snapping his tongs. "Come on in, we're back here. Hey Mattie. You talked that old man into letting you out?"

"I've got to be back before dark. That's so lame. Talk to him, please?"

“We’ll see, we’ll see. Come on.”

Raffe led them to bar stools that were turned to face the barbecue. Karin yelled hello from the kitchen and Raffe went over to check on the ribs. When he opened lid a cloud of smoke billowed up, and Hani could hear it sizzle.

“The first batch will be ready soon. Hungry?”

They answered, “Yes.” at the same time.

Karin said, “Raffe’s been working on setting up your phone call. He called a friend in Florida this morning. There’s a delay, like at the Post and Telegraph, and it cuts out sometimes, but it’s free.”

“That’s so nice of you guys. Thanks.”

“Raffe, I’ll watch those. Hani wants to make that call now.”

“Okay, let’s give it a try. It worked earlier. Florida, USA.”

Raffe handed the tongs to Karin and she snapped them just like Raffe as she walked over to the barbecue. Mattie jumped off her stool and joined Karin.

Raffe led her through the kitchen and into a small office. He had wires running everywhere. Most of his computer equipment had their covers removed, so that the circuit boards, motors and fans were visible. He pulled out an office chair with a missing back. “Sit here. So, where are you calling?”

“Seattle, USA.”

“Oh, good. Do you have the number. You know it’s like two in the morning on the west coast, right?”

“I know, but that’s probably my best chance to find her home.”

“Okay, let’s try it.”

Raffe hit a few keys, then reached for the paper with the number, narrating his moves on the keyboard. “First, we’ll need an internet connection.” The audio was coming from a small speaker on the desk. Hani listened as the familiar set of beeps and tones reached out into the ether for someone to notice. It was a moment that she knew well. When the first computers started showing up in her office there wasn't a technology department, Hani and other support staff set up the machines and started figuring out what they could do. She knew what came next. She held her breath, and tried to will a response. The beeps fell into a long line of pinging, then she heard the pick up on the other end. It was a slightly different tone, but still in the secret language of ones and zeros.

"Good, good. Now I'll…" Raffe was typing in an address. "Come on, come on...So, once I get connected to this site, I can dial the number. There's another way, but this is what worked this morning." A website flashed up on his screen. "Here we go." Raffe carefully pecked at the numbers, but stopped before the last one. "Okay, as soon as I hear it ringing, I'll go outside so you can talk. Good luck."

He hit the last digit, then hit enter. There was nothing for a few seconds then it rang. Raffe backed out of the office, leaving Hani frozen, hoping she could open her mouth when Zoe answered. With each ring Hani tried to imagine Zoe waking up in the middle of the night, it would take her a while to get to the phone. It rang again and again, each one more desperate. Hani counted seven, then eight. She didn't know how to hang up, but she didn't want to miss any of the rings by going out to find Raffe. Then someone picked up.

"Hi, not home. Leave me a short, short message. Bye."

She hadn't counted on this, but she'd left plenty of detailed messages before. "Hi, my name is Hani Chandra and I'm trying to reach Zoe Vermillion. I'm a friend of your brother, Max. He asked me to leave a message for him. Please tell him that Hani is in Entebbe, Uganda, at the Ace Hotel. He will be calling today or tomorrow. Thank you...I'm looking forward to meeting you. Goodbye."

She sat there until the message machine gave a final beep, then silence. Hani had put a lot of hope into speaking to Zoe, she wanted to hear her voice. She wanted to make a connection and begin weaving into that part of his world. When she came back to the bar Karin and Mattie both sent inquiring looks. Hani shook her head, and they frowned. "Don't worry, you stay right here. We can call again after the rush. We'll get through, I'll try another service, or I can drive you to the Post and Telegraph if you like. I'll make you a plate of ribs." Raffe knew where some of the basic answers were found.

77

The morning sounds increased, along with the light seeping into his consciousness. Max dressed quickly and went down to the lobby in search of the concierge. He needed to focus today, and not be distracted. Last night was careless, and he was pretty sure that by this morning someone would be looking for him. It wasn't fear. He'd known a lot of that as recently as yesterday, but this arousal was much clearer, more optimistic. It held a promise that was much greater than mere survival.

Upon seeing Rod, the desk clerk made a call to the concierge. He held up his hand, his face beaming with a broad smile. When he placed the phone down, he said the concierge was on his way. "Can I bring you some coffee while you wait?"

Max picked out a safari chair in the lobby. The thick dark leather was slung from top of the back, to a rail under his knees. The brass fittings were pitted, and the wood was cross hatched in a less exact fashion than the work he'd seen in Somalia. The carvings flowed along for a while then lost focus. His coffee arrived, on a wooden tray with hot milk, sugar and a piece of yellow cake. The waiter used his foot to drag over a small folding table, the chair's mate. The coffee was poured, and a small butter ball was dropped in. After drinking his coffee, and taking the little cake in one bite, he grew uncomfortable waiting in the open— an obvious target for anyone to see and remember. He looked up and caught the desk clerk's eye. With a quizzical tilt of his head, he silently asked about the concierge. The clerk barely moved his hands, palms down, wait, soon maybe. Max watched the few people up this early—mostly staff. That's who he'd ask if he was looking for someone.

The concierge was apologetic. "Please excuse my delay. I see that you've had your coffee, very good...shall we?"

"Are you wanting the same number? America?"

"Yes. Should be around four in the afternoon."

The concierge placed the call, then handed him the heavy black receiver. Max nodded and the concierge left the room. On the fourth ring Zoe picked up.

"Max? Max?"

"Hey Zoe."

"Oh Max, how are you? Where are you?"

Max waited, hoping she wouldn't start speaking.

"Zoe, say, over, and wait for a few seconds, there's a delay. Over."

"Okay, now, where are you, and who's Hani? Over."

"Did you talk to her? What'd she say? Over."

"She left a message. Are you guys together? She said that she was at a hotel, I think so anyway, the message was hard to hear. Entebbe, Uganda...I looked it up. Is that where you are? Over."

"She's in Entebbe? At a hotel...she didn't say which one? Are you sure? Over."

"It was hard to hear. I could definitely hear the word hotel, before that it sounded like *A* hotel. Over."

"Is that all she said in the message? Over."

"Maybe it was just the connection. She said she was looking forward to meeting me. So, you're bringing her home? Are you coming home? Over."

"I can't right now. I need to meet her soon, maybe today. If she calls again, find out everything you can, tell her I'm going to be in Entebbe today, later today...Zoe, you'll love her. I love her."

"I didn't hear your over...but I'll talk. I'm supposed to work in the morning again, but I'll see if Rebecca, remember her from Wilbur? I'll see if she can cover for me. Do you think she'll call again? Over."

"Thanks, ZV. I do think she'll call again, I told her to leave me messages until we meet up, it's the only way we can find each other. Over."

"Okay, I'll be here tonight and tomorrow, what time is it there? Over."

"I'm ten hours ahead, it's about seven in the morning here. I'll let you know what's going on as soon as I can. Thanks for sitting by the phone Z, I miss you. Over."

"I'm happy for you, tell Hani I love her too. I think I will, she had a beautiful accent, sounded sweet. Bye. Over."

"Thanks Zoe...I love you. Bye. Over."

And it was over. He sat there, holding on to her voice, and missing home. He puzzled over which hotel she meant, but she was in Entebbe, and he was going to be there today.

At breakfast he picked out a table on the patio that had a good view of the lobby. The table was partially obscured by a small palm that he could see through—paranoia rising again. By eight, he was back in his room, fully packed, and pacing. The Hunter was on a busy corner, cars and trucks accelerating in four directions. Each one slowed or stopped at the intersection, giving him time to guess which one was coming for him. He couldn't see who got out of the cars. When he saw the wrinkled old Land Rover lurch into the Hunter's auto-court, he knew it must be Mike. He didn't wait. He grabbed his bag and went to the top of the stairs, where he saw Mike's legs, tall leather boots, and the same khaki shorts that he'd worn last night. It was Mike's voice, chatting with the desk clerk.

"Ahh, good morning, Rod." He gave Max a little wink.

On the way to the airfield, Mike said that he'd gotten permission to land at the private field near the town of Kajjansi, halfway between Kampala and Entebbe. He planned to refuel in Eldorat on the way there so that he could drop Max and get out of Uganda before too many questions were asked. Max was taking this in, fitting the time puzzle together. At the security gate for private pilots Mike danced through the questions, leaving out any mention of Uganda. Max showed his ID and it passed the inspection with a few back-and-forth glances, picture, face, picture, face.

Mike's airplane was of the same vintage as his Land Rover. The aluminum body was dented, wrinkled and patched. The engine housing was folded up and the headless backside of a grimy pair of overalls was bent over the edge. "Stay here. My friend's a talker. Don't worry, it's just a little maintenance, he should be finishing up by now."

Mike got out, walked up to the plane and started talking to the overalls. Max couldn't hear what they were saying, but he could hear the deep rasping voice of the headless mechanic. Finally, the man's head came up and turned toward Mike. The greasy welders cap, sat atop a black face ringed with a white beard. He looked over at Max, then back to Mike. They seemed to be arguing, but it might just be their style of communication. There was a tenderness in the hand that Mike offered as the old man came down the little ladder. The mechanic took Mike to several places around the plane and pointed, Mike nodded, and they'd move to another spot. Back at the engine he had Mike climb up the ladder and take a look, while the mechanic continued to talk, low and insistent.

Max could predict the result of this conversation. He'd spent most of the last seven years speaking his truncated, reverse English. And, at the same time trying to use all his senses in deciphering the new words that came back. His intuition was pretty good at making meaning out of Somali or Swahili. It was the faces with all of their wrinkles and ticks, the eyes revealing emotion, the mouth tight or loose. This looked like an old routine.

Mike came over. "Okay, look. He's going to give me grief if I don't do a few things before we fly. Don't worry, it should only take an hour. I've just got to get a few parts for Edgar. You can come with me or wait over there." Another airplane landed. Mike pointed to an open shed with a picnic table, between two hangers.

Max was deciding which way would keep this moving forward. He decided to keep his eyes on Mike's airplane. "I'll wait over there."

"Don't worry, I'll get you there."

Max sat at the picnic table between the hangers, watching Edgar. Of course you have to wait, he thought. It's an art. The ability to squat beneath a small tree or bush and slow down your body to the point of being suspended between consciousness and a dream. The heat lighting up a dark primordial region of the mind, a place where monks and Sufis rendezvous. He'd practiced it on restless afternoons, when the breeze would stop and his hammock was too much cloth. He'd squat on his haunches like the Chinese dock workers when they worked, ate and slept. He'd face out over the Juba. Let his eyes glaze over without focus on some middle place that could reflect his mind. Occasionally he found that dimension, where you're two places at once, then no place at all.

He turned when a black Suburban drove up to the terminal. No one got out. After a few minutes a man, white, sunglasses, white shirt, and a blue blazer on his arm, came out of the terminal and got in the back seat. The Suburban rounded the drive and drove past Max, the tinted windows reflected the two hangers framing him. A few minutes later Mike's Land Rover came through the gate and drove out to the plane. Mike got out and waved him over. Edgar was looking through the box of parts that Mike placed on the hood. Edgar was pinching up screws from the bottom of the box, holding a part that looked like a lobster, several wires hanging off of it.

Mike turned to Max. "I saw one of ours drive by. Did you see it, the Suburban? They looking for you?"

"Maybe. How do you know it's ours?"

"It sure looked like it. The tinted windows, the diplomatic plates."

"Where do you think they're going? The hotels?"

"There's only a few hotels to search, and the Hunter'd be my first choice." Mike turned to Edgar. "How soon can you hook that up? The other stuff will have to wait. I need to be up in ten minutes."

Edgar shrugged his shoulders and started up the ladder, mumbling to himself.

"Okay Max, get your stuff in here. We're going to get in the air before they can get back, just in case."

Mike parked the Rover on the far side of the hangers. Max brought over his bag, and slung it into the cockpit. Mike started a quick inspection of the plane. When he got around to Edgar he said. "Come on man, five minutes."

Edgar pulled up, holding a pair of wrenches, "Start it."

Mike swung up under the wing and slid into his seat. He handed a headset to Max, then closed his door. The engine cowling was slammed shut, and snapped down. As soon as Edgar retreated beyond the wing tip Mike hit the starter. The engine gave a weak groan, turning over slowly, then it coughed twice. He tried again, this time it fired. He tested out his controls, wagging his tail before he released the brakes. They circled over the outskirts of Isiolo, before flying parallel to the main road. Mike pointed to the roof of a black vehicle heading towards the airport. Through the headset Max heard Mike laughing. "They're too late. Do they know where you're going? A phone call can beat this plane to Kampala, you know."

"Did you file a flight plan?"

"Got to. You're a game hunter scouting out the area around Turkana. Listed Eldorat as a stop. If they're serious they'll have all the obvious fields covered."

Max turned to look out the window. He felt the chase, even up here where he'd imagined he'd find relief. Whoever was looking for him, if they had the manpower, could just stake out all the airports and wait for him to drop into their hands. The freedom of flight became a trap. But they could only guess where he was going. "What do you think?"

"Well, I could drop you in Bungoma, it's not an obvious choice. Close to the Uganda border. As long as you can get a ride it'll be the best way to arrive quietly. You still got money? I can give you a small discount."

"I have enough."

"It's about an hour and a half from here. Is that where you want to go?"

Max turned back to the window, pressing his forehead into the glass. The vibration driving home the idea that this wasn't over yet. "Bungoma then."

78

The late afternoon crowd was loud and full of laughter. It was guilty humor, an ashamed humor, meant to hide the unforgettable scenes and stories of loss and death. How can life be truly enjoyed after a day of touching even the edges of a disaster—the human heart needs to feel something other than despair. Over time these colleagues become your family, knowing what you know. She heard the tables filling up and she missed it.

Raffe brought out two plates, reminding Mattie that she'd need to get home in less than an hour. Her face fell. "I'll talk to the old goat. Maybe he'll let you work here when you're sixteen. I could use your help."

That instantly lifted her face into a smile, her eyes dancing with the thought.

Karin ducked her head over the back bar.

"Hani, there's someone you should meet. I'll bring her back." She disappeared, then came back leading a woman that looked so familiar. "Hani, this is Rohanna. Remember I said that Marcel was the one you needed to contact at the UN, well…"

"Oh yes, I saw you today at the base. Robert pointed you out. You work with Marcel, right?"

"That's me. I remember seeing you as well. Nice to meet you. You know, someone was looking for you this afternoon. He talked to Robert. The guy was old, an old tough Brit. Not the boyfriend type."

Mattie got up and offered her chair to Rohanna.

Rohanna put her hand on Mattie's shoulder, "No sister, you stay. I'll grab another."

Hani was feeling the shock of this revelation. Her pursuers so far had been invisible, if they were real at all. Max said to be careful. Now, it was a person, a Brit. The way Rohanna said, 'an old tough Brit' suggested the face that she was imagining. "What did he say?"

"I didn't talk to him, just Robert. But he knows you're in Entebbe. Karin tells me that you need a ride to Europe. Are you running from this guy?"

"I'm trying to get to Rome, I can pay."

"But not on the airlines, right?"

"I'd prefer to, oh, I need to…"

"Whatever, look, might not be my place, but...I didn't like that guy, don't think he's your type, you know. I'll help you if I can. Marcel doesn't care about the charters."

Hani said, "I talked to some of the charter crews today. Nothing to Europe."

"Did you talk to the crew from Belgium? They're headed to Khartoum and on to Cyprus. From there you can find lots of flights to Rome."

"I thought they were leaving today?"

"They are, in about two hours. Their logistics officer is meeting me here in a few minutes. You want to talk to him?"

"Sure." Two hours, two hours...Max might be here today. And the Brit. Maybe he saw the note on the bulletin board, maybe he figured it out, and was waiting for her at the Ace?

"Stay here, I'll ask him a few questions when he gets here. If he's open to taking you I'll introduce you. Okay? Don't worry, he's alright." She stood up and took a second to look down at Hani. "I get it. I don't need to know but I get it."

"Mattie. I need to give you a message for Max. That's his real name. I don't want to write it down. Okay?"

"Oh yeah, for sure...What's the message? I'll wait for him."

"I don't know what to say right now. Hey, you're going to be late, it's almost dark. I was going to walk with you, but I…"

"I know. There's a good spot on the walkway by your room where I can see the office and the street, I'll wait for you there."

"Mattie, I love you, thanks."

Mattie reached over and squeezed her hand, then went into the kitchen to hug her uncle. She waved at Karin as she left the restaurant and started down the sidewalk. As Mattie crossed the road Hani thought she looked much older than fifteen.

With every arriving customer, some of whom Hani could see, she tried to pick out the one that Rohanna was meeting. She knew a lot of the UN flight crews. Most of the logistics people she knew, at least the older ones, had a few side hustles going. The voices were mixing with the music, but every once in while a shout, or crack of laughter, would reach her ears. She wanted to go out there and be part of it all but the thought of a silent Brit, skulking in the corner, kept her out of sight.

Raffe came out with another beer for both of them, and sat down, wiping his brow. "Man, so hot in there. Karin's working it for you. You'll see."

"I don't want to leave! But I really need to. It's so fast."

"You still have time to finish the ribs on your plate, and I'll send some with you for your travels." He took Mattie's chair. Even if she wanted to be alone, she knew they would have never let her sit by herself and suffer. After a few minutes of watching new orders being spun around the carousel, he went back to the kitchen.

Karin leaned over the bar and tilted her head toward the front. "They're talking about you, Ro's on it." She held out crossed fingers.

Waiting for another flight, one that would take her directly to Rome, was now out of the question.

When Rohanna came back, she sat down, and laid out the deal. "Okay, he'll get you on the flight tonight, five hundred US dollars. Will that work? I didn't know what your budget was, but that was the going rate."

"Perfect, thanks Rohanna."

"Call me Ro, that's what my friends call me."

"So, what do I do next? I've got to get my things from the hotel, and…"

"They're leaving at seven, little over an hour. Marco will need your name so you can get through the gate. Take a taxi to the UN building where I saw you today. You know where the planes are. Do you remember the Belgium one?

"I can find it."

"What do you have for ID?"

"This." She pulled out her UN necklace. "And my passport."

She wrote down Hani's name and the Kenyan passport number. "Marco will make sure the guard lets you in. Don't pay them til you're on the plane, and don't get off in Khartoum. Marco says you can slip off in Larnaca, but Khartoum is looking for a reason to frustrate any relief to the south, better to stay out of sight when you're there."

"Ro, I don't know how to ask this."

"Go ahead dear, what is it?"

"There might be someone else that needs to get out this way. I left a message for him on the bulletin board at your office. Can I tell him to talk to you about flights? I don't really know if he'll see any message I leave for him, but…"

"I'll do what I can. Tell you what. You write to me someday and tell me all about it, for now...you get to a safe place, and if I can, I'll help your boyfriend too. Do you have a picture?"

She slid the picture of Max out of her passport.

"Looks Danish."

"American. His name is Max, though he might not use that name, you know."

"Promise you'll write, sounds intriguing. I better get back to Marco." She gave a thumbs up to Raffe, who had been leaning over the bar.

Karin came back. "Got it worked out?"

"I think so. I've got to go though, I have to get back to the hotel, then…"

"You'll be back. It's going to be okay Hani. I know it."

"I'm leaving a message with Mattie. I'll make sure she tells it to both of you too. There's so much I want to say, but it'll have to wait. I hope I can come back to see you, to repay you for your kindness to a stranger."

"We are fully paid, no worries."

Hani walked, then ran down the street to the Ace. She saw Mattie sitting in a folding chair and reading under the light outside the room.

Hani rushed up the stairs and opened the door. "Come in, sit while I pack."

She fished out the picture of Max again and handed it to Mattie.

"That's him?"

"Max, yes. So, he might to come to Entebbe. I'll keep leaving messages for him from the next place I land, but in case I can't get through, and, if he finds my message, and figures out I'm at the Ace he'll come here looking for me. Introduce him to your uncle and Karin. Tell him that I got a flight to

Khartoum and on to Larnaca, Cyprus. Tell him that I'm still trying to get to Rome. Tell him that I tried to call Zoe, his sister. Oh, that's too much."

"No it's not, I can remember that."

Hani folded her shell-colored pants, but before she put them in her bag she asked Mattie, "Do you want these, I think it will be too cold for them in Rome? You should see if I have anything else you want...I'd trade you for a sweater."

Mattie's eyes sparkled. "Oh, I have lots of sweaters and warm socks. Do you need a warm hat?"

Hani dumped out her bag and started making a pile for Mattie. "We'll trade."

"Cool, I'll be right back."

"Hurry, please."

When Mattie returned Hani tried on a few things as she tried to have her message include everything. "Okay, I'm sorry, this is all so fast. Please tell him about the Brit. That's really important, he's got to be careful. Oh, and, tell him to talk to Karin, or Raffe about the charter flights...about Ro."

"Don't worry, I know what to say. I hope I meet him. I hope he comes here, really. I'll tell my dad to watch out for anyone looking for you or Max. We're sort of used to secrets, being a hotel, you know?"

"Right, I guess you would be. This secret is really serious, at least for a few more days. I'll try and find a way to let you know it all worked out."

"It will, it will."

It made her nervous to hear people say things so positively. Things didn't always work out. If they did then there wouldn't be refugee camps, droughts, or floods, there wouldn't be famines or wars. She'd spent her short career trying to fix things that went terribly wrong. Hani had thought that her life was immune from these calamities, but only by the thinnest slice of luck. Somehow, she'd managed to escape real pain, or real danger. There was always a way out, until there wasn't, and that might be now.

She walked to the taxi stand, her bag so light for a trip to Europe. The weight just underscored the basic needs she had, some clothes, a lot of money, and some new friends to remember. None of it is hard to carry. Not like the refugee mothers, holding an infant in one arm and a hand holding on to a frightened child at her side. She refused to cry anymore until she found Max. She could see the restaurant and Karin busily serving her expatriate clientele as the taxi pulled out onto the Kampala-Entebbe Road.

The night lights glowed redder as she approached the airport. The taxi dropped her in front of the dark UN building. She started walking out across the lot towards the lit-up tails of the C130s. A fuel truck drove past her and through the gate. She showed her UN ID, then folded out her passport for the guard's inspection. With one step back, the guard ushered her onto the tarmac. She saw someone standing by the plane—it didn't look like an old Brit. She waved and picked up her pace. Marco offered his hand at the ladder. The back ramp of the plane was closing. He guided her to a sling seat in the cavernous belly, its engines whirring up as soon as the ladder was pulled in. She couldn't hear what Marco was saying, but the gesture his fingers made reminded her of the five hundred dollars part of the deal. He traded her some bright orange ear protectors for the cash, and climbed up the metal steps into the cockpit.

The sensation of lift seemed to stretch gravity. A potent flood of adrenaline washed over her...saying this was the end, and the beginning. The overwhelming sensation faded as the plane leveled off. Marco, peeked back down from the cockpit to check on his passenger. She took a second to respond, giving him a nod and smile, before he retreated. Her relief was becoming physical, closing her eyes and calling for deep breaths, the vibrations massaging her body.

79

The arid highlands beneath him gave way to the patchwork of small farms in a wide range of greens, with red dirt roads outlining each holding. Mike banked over Bungoma, scanning the airstrip for goats and people. Satisfied, he took aim at the runway, lowering the airplane down until he cut the throttle and glided onto the ground. "This is it, Bungoma. That road we crossed over leads to the center of town. That'd be the best place to find a ride."

He revved the engine, and taxied over to an abandoned hanger—it's fold-up door was lying in a crumpled heap. When Mike stopped, he turned and held out his hand. "Good luck, Max. Stay away from those black Suburbans, and come see me in Isiolo when you come back."

Max stepped out in Kenya, again, and started walking. The sound of Mike's airplane was being replaced by the music from Bungoma. The instruments were trucks and cars moving people in and out of the market town. The sun was dimmed by the smokey air. It smelled like burning cane. Through the noise and dust he also caught the scent of cooking. His hunger convinced him to find a place to eat and observe Bungoma. A stranger walking around in this place would be noticed, but in a cafe he'd have the chance to look out on the scene without being seen by everyone. His nose lead him down a side street that opened up on a square ringed with small shops and two cafes, one on each side. He chose the one straight ahead so he could see if anyone was following him.

The waiter was a tall thin teenager, wearing the standard high school uniform—white short-sleeve shirt and black slacks. His English was perfect. When the food was served Max asked about buses or shuttles to Kampala.

"There is a bus, every day, but it's too late today. It leaves at five in the morning."

"How about tourist shuttles, or car rentals?"

He pointed to a shop across the square. "Tourist shop. They would know."

Max saw the safari posters on the front window. "Do many tourists come through here?"

"We're halfway between Nairobi and Kampala, everyone comes through here—not many stop."

The tourist shop's door was open, and bright guitar riffs floated out. Somali music was coastal, finding harmonies with the Arabian Peninsula. This music was made for dancing, twirling under the sky with your arms stretched out. The notes circling around and around. He looked over the rack of brochures—game parks, mountain climbing, holidays at the beach and lots of hotels.

A man sitting behind a large dark desk emerged from the dark leather chair behind it. "May I help you?"

"I'm looking for a ride to Kampala, Entebbe actually."

"Ahh, to the airport?"

"Yes. Are there any tourist shuttles? I heard the bus is gone already."

"We don't have many tourists. But, as you can see, we have many attractions." He was pointing to the brochures. "So, you need to get to your airplane? America? I was in Boston once. Do you have time for a coffee?"

Max hesitated, then agreed. He had the impression that he was being set up for a sales pitch, but it came with coffee, and the promise of conversation that might uncover a way to Entebbe. "I'm trying to reach Entebbe by dark. How long does it take from here?"

“Sit, I’ll get us coffee. I have some ideas for your journey. You won’t get there before dark though, it takes six hours to get to the international airport. Sit, I’ll work on it. You are?”

“Rod.”

“I’m Mustafa. Please, have a seat.”

Oriental carpets draped the walls in a corner and cushions surrounded and a low, round brass table with a hammered edge. He took a cushion facing the front door, and Mustafa’s inner office. He listened to the grinding of the beans. Twice Mustafa peeked out while talking on the phone. In Max’s current frame of mind paranoia still had a voice. Mustafa reappeared holding a tray with a French press, and two old oriental cups.

“So, I may have your ride to Kampala, not Entebbe, but very close, I’ll know very soon. Now coffee.” Mustafa slid forward toward the table and slowly plunged the press into the coffee. His movements were theatrical, his fingers all knew their places, and his expression was reverent. “So, I want to know what you think of this coffee. Please take the first half of the cup as it is. I have milk and sugar, but I don’t think you’ll want it. Go ahead.”

Max brought the cup to his lips, first breathing in its aroma. Any anxiety he was feeling about judging Mustafa’s coffee was relaxed when he tasted it. The figures on the cup were dancing beneath the cloud of Middle Eastern scents. “The spices. There are so many flavors.”

“These beans are from my family’s plantations in the mountains of Ethiopia. It’s the finest coffee in the world. You’ve heard that of course. What your drinking is grown from Yemeni stock.” He drank slowly, thoroughly enjoying it so much that Max hesitated to bring up his ride. Mustafa looked up from the rim of his cup, “Caramel that’s what I taste today, every time I taste something new, or something very old...Ah, your ride. My son and his bandmate are going to Kampala to see Kanda Bongo Man in concert tonight. I'm lending them my mini bus so that they can include you. They'll call when they're on their way to pick you up."

"That's great. I can pay for the ride."

"That would be good. The fuel is very expensive now."

"Would a hundred cover it?"

Mustafa thought for a bit, then went to his desk and began adding numbers on a calculator, the keys sounding like the beads of an abacus. "The minivan is registered as part of the tourist industry, so at the border I'll need to pay a little tax both ways." He pulled out a receipt book, wrote down a number, stamped it with his logo, then handed it across the desk. This was business. Max fished out two hundred. "I'll send some coffee with you too." The phone call came as they finished the coffee—the boys were on their way.

He heard a van door open, then laughter. They were the color of sunshine, reflecting the sounds of the Soukous that had been swirling around the little shop. The boys wore screaming yellows and oranges—making noise because they could.

"Hi, I'm Rod, the one you're taking to Kampala. Hope you don't mind."

The tallest musician came forward right away. "I'm Bandi, this is Willy. It's perfect, you're making it better. My father's minivan is a much better for the trip. We're sorry about not taking you all the way to Entebbe, but if we don't leave right away, we'll be late."

Max cradled the bag of coffee. Mustafa offered his goodbye, with his hand over his heart, bowing.

"Thank you, Mustafa, I will remember this last stop in Kenya."

"Don't make it your last."

Bandi drove and Willy was the deejay for the trip. He looked back at Max, sizing him up for the tunes. He was blown away when he heard Johnny Clegg's *Cruel, Crazy, Beautiful World.* Willy was watching him as the first bars played. Obviously proud of his selection. "You know this one!"

"Yeah, heard it in Nairobi last summer. Play more of the Soukous, that's new to me. Can you play guitar like that?"

"Drums." Willy had a bright smile as he considered how to educate Max in the art of Soukous. With his cassette case open in his lap his fingers tapped each one, before he selected three.

"I'll put these on for you after the border. The Kenyan police are too serious for party music."

Bandi laughed, and looking in the rear-view mirror he asked, "You've got your passport?"

"Yep."

"Cool."

They started passing lines of trucks on a siding road. It went on for several kilometers. Bandi said that the trucks were aid convoys returning from either Sudan, or Dadaab. "Uganda now requires them to be fumigated before they enter. They just started this new business. They charge up to one hundred shillings. Ugandan trucks pay much less of course. We have a pass." Bandi pointed to a bright blue T on the corner of the windscreen.

They slowed at a delta, where three lanes were separated with orange cones. A white gloved guard directed cars to the right, waving the van straight ahead to an empty booth. Bandi collected all the passports. When the guard handed all the Kenyan passports back continued to hold the Canadian one. He walked slowly to where he could compare the picture with the face. Max smiled, the guard did not. Through the window Max saw two computer monitors with solitaire cards being clicked and dragged by uniformed agents.

At the Ugandan side, the passports went out again. This time they were each stamped as the agent as Bandi talked about the concert tonight in Kampala. Max's passport only elicited a brief look through the window before it too was stamped. The road away from the border wound through another Bungoma sized town, slowing for animals and people at the central roundabout. On the other side, the highway straightened out and they were able to cruise at sixty miles an hour. Bandi said they would be in central Kampala by seven.

The towns came and went, small and smaller, each one beginning with garbage, then a central square with a roundabout or four-way standoff. Willy rolled his window down and said, "Listen to what they're playing. Do you recognize it now?" He took his role of musical tour director seriously. Mostly he would let the music speak until it said something that a novice might miss. Like a guide altering him to a pair of eyes hidden in the tall grass. He'd missed so much. He'd missed the parts that were not at war, the towns and savannas that breathed in tune with the land. The villages where children were in schools and crops were tended. The music circled endlessly.

By five in the afternoon the sun was beating in from the west. He'd wake for a few seconds when the van would change its rhythm, noting the sun's descent into the tree tops. The road was widening to welcome more traffic as they approached Kampala's sprawling eastern suburbs. When Earth finally turned away from the sun, the van came to life again.

"We're almost there. I'm looking for a good taxi stand. I can wait until you make a deal. Okay?"

"That's great, perfect."

As soon as he stepped out in Kampala, he was visible again. The first two taxis weren't interested in driving out to Entebbe—the concert would bring way more business. The third one agreed to take the fare. Max ran back to Willy's window to say goodbye. "Okay, ride's set. Thanks guys, let's do this again."

They laughed and nodded. "Oh yeah, we should. Come to Bungoma, you will be our guest, really man."

Max got in the back of the taxi, waving as they pulled out into traffic. It took half an hour to get through the city and out to the Kampala-Entebbe Road. As they got closer, he saw the red lights of the airport. Hotels and caravans lined the lakeside, but the music and light were on the right. He slowed the driver as they passed bars and open-air clubs with NGO vehicles parked along the street. When he looked back to the left, he saw a hotel with the giant, throbbing Ace of Hearts on the sign.

"Stop!"

Two Weeks Later

Hani walked into the salty breeze, listening to the music of guy-wires slapping against aluminum masts in the marina. Fiumicino's fishing fleet was idle, and the normally busy street along the quay was filled with quiet conversations around restaurant entrances and families gathering for a holiday stroll. She was asked to take a picture of a young couple with their shivering dog, and once more for a whole family—four generations, with the masts swaying in the background.

She'd spent Christmas in Larnaca, unable to get a flight to Rome for several days. She strolled through the city in Mattie's warm sweater and bright orange socks, stopping at the Alitalia office twice each day. Her hotel faced south, and at night she'd follow the few lights from passing jets heading north.

When she made it to Rome she bought a long wool coat, and a warm scarf. She also bought one of the new Nokia cell phones, which she now held in her hand, deep in the pocket of the warm coat. Max called when his train from Zurich arrived at Termini Station an hour ago. Zoe called from America again right after that. She checked her signal, leaving the short antenna extended.

She turned away from the sea and walked back towards the bistro where she'd reserved a table by the window for their rendezvous. The low ragged clouds had disappeared to the east and the sun now warmed her face. She stopped when she saw the bistro's sign. Closing her eyes, she turned into the sun's warmth until she heard the tinkling bell. When she got closer, she could see him being led to their table, watching as he spoke to the waiter. He turned and their eyes met. She held his gaze then opened the door. The bell was ringing softly as they reached each other, embracing, as the waiters and diners began to applaud.

The End

Made in the USA
Las Vegas, NV
17 January 2024

84415133R00218